PRAISE FOR
STAR TREK®: PRESERVER

"SWEEPING . . . TRAGIC . . . BREATHLESSLY
PACED . . . ENGROSSING."
—*DREAMWATCH*

"PACKED WITH ACTION. . . . SHATNER AND
THE REEVES-STEVENSES KNOW ALL THESE
CHARACTERS AND THE AFFECTION SHOWS
THROUGH."
—MICHELLE ERICA GREEN
MANIA MAGAZINE

"AN ELECTRIFYING SCIENCE FICTION
NOVEL."
—*REGISTER-PAJARONIAN*

Books by William Shatner

TekWar
TekLords
TekLab
Tek Vengeance
Tek Secret
Tek Money
Tek Kill
Man o' War
The Law of War
Believe (with Michael Tobias)
Star Trek Memories
Star Trek Movie Memories
Get a Life!

STAR TREK: ODYSSEY
(with Judith and Garfield Reeves-Stevens)
    Book 1: *The Ashes of Eden*
    Book 2: *The Return*
    Book 3: *Avenger*

STAR TREK: THE MIRROR UNIVERSE SAGA
(with Judith and Garfield Reeves-Stevens)
    Book 1: *Spectre*
    Book 2: *Dark Victory*
    Book 3: *Preserver*

WILLIAM SHATNER

STAR TREK® PRESERVER

with
Judith Reeves-Stevens &
Garfield Reeves-Stevens

POCKET BOOKS
New York   London   Toronto   Sydney   Singapore

POCKET BOOKS, a division of Simon & Schuster, Inc.
1230 Avenue of the Americas, New York, NY 10020

Copyright © 2000 by Paramount Pictures. All Rights Reserved.

STAR TREK is a Registered Trademark of Paramount Pictures.

This book is published by Pocket Books, a division of Simon & Schuster, Inc., under exclusive license from Paramount Pictures.

All rights reserved, including the right to reproduce this book or portions thereof in any form whatsoever. For information address Pocket Books, 1230 Avenue of the Americas, New York, NY 10020

ISBN: 0-671-02126-5

First Pocket Books mass market printing April 2001

10 9 8 7 6 5 4 3 2 1

POCKET and colophon are registered trademarks of Simon & Schuster, Inc.

Printed in the U.S.A.

Everything changes.
She was young and innocent.
That changed.
She loved me.
And that, too, deepened and changed.
I loved her.
And because of that, I changed.
She died.
Perhaps that, too, will change.

ACKNOWLEDGMENTS

A bow of acknowledgment to Gar and Judy Reeves-Stevens. Two of the most talented, subtle, wise people you'd ever want to meet. And boy, can they write.

PROLOGUE

All was chaos.

In the universe of James T. Kirk, his bride lay dying, their unborn child within her, both victims of an assassin's poison, beyond McCoy's ability to save.

In the seething plasma storms of the Badlands, three starships obscured by sensor masks held open an impossible portal to another reality.

And through that portal, in the realm known as the mirror universe, Captain Jean-Luc Picard and his Enterprise *waited for a legend's return.*

To save his wife and child, that legend had traveled to the nightmare of the devastated mirror Earth, to penetrate the hidden enclave of his greatest enemy. His only hope.

James T. Kirk had at last found what he searched for.

And now would have to pay the price. . . .

Kirk limped along in Tiberius's wake.

His head ached, the inside of his lip was split, and at any other time in his career he would have jumped Tiberius the instant his back was turned and strangled the pompous, self-righteous, murderous monster without a second thought.

But needed Tiberius alive. At least until he had the anti-toxin Teilani needed. Tiberius might survive another few seconds past that moment. But only seconds.

They reached the alcove outside the transporter room. Kirk watched Tiberius walk past the terrible photograph of the hangings at Starfleet Headquarters without paying it a moment's notice.

As Kirk came to it, he couldn't help himself. He paused to check the photo for another name, MCCOY. *And found it.* How is that possible? *he asked himself.* That identical people can have such different lives?

"Old friends?" Tiberius asked. He had turned back to see Kirk looking at the photograph and walked back to join him, as if they were on a tour of an art gallery.

"Do you have *any friends?" Kirk asked grimly.*

"How can I?" Tiberius replied. "I once was, and will be again, absolute master of life and death throughout known space." To Kirk, it sounded, incredibly, as if his counterpart was actually being sincere. "Everyone wants to be my friend, James, to curry favor, to bask in some slight reflection of my glory. But if I were to allow that, choosing one or two favorites or familiars here or there, how could I be fair with my subjects? How could I be honest? Come along, James. So much to do, so little time."

Tiberius started down the corridor again.

"In my analysis of your woefully inadequate career," he continued, "I believe I have identified many of your flaws. Chief among them, your foolish persistence in believing that you are like ordinary men." Tiberius glanced back over his shoulder. "You are not *like ordinary men, James. You never have been. We never have been. But only I have been able to rise above your shallow concerns about being a man of the people."*

"*Do you ever shut up?*" Kirk asked.

They had come to another large white door. Tiberius placed a hand against the scanner plate on the wall beside it, and the door silently slipped open.

"*I hope you realize,*" Tiberius said, "*at some dim level of your perception, that the only reason I have allowed you to live this long while insulting me is because I do respect you.*"

"*Why didn't you respect Teilani?*"

Tiberius paused in the open door. "*Incredible as it may seem to you, I don't care about your Klingon-Romulan hybrid concubine. Intendant Picard, on the other hand, seemed to find her remarkably attractive, but if he did anything to Teilani, it wouldn't be fatal.*"

Kirk suppressed his rage. It would not do to assault his counterpart again. Tiberius was better trained, more practiced in hand-to-hand combat. He would have to choose his time precisely. He might not be able to outfight his opponent, but Kirk was certain he could outthink him. Once the antitoxin was his.

But until then, he couldn't let this smug bastard continue to lie, unchallenged.

"*If you don't care about Teilani, why did you send one of your children to poison her?*"

"*I did no such thing.*"

For the first time, Kirk felt he had said something that Tiberius was interested in.

"*I was there. I saw it. I recognized the child in your . . . crèche.*"

Tiberius took on a serious expression. "*Which one?*"

"*I can't be sure. A boy. Eight years old. He was in pyjamas.*"

"*Where did this take place?*"

"*Don't play games with me! You know where it took place.*"

Tiberius's face flushed red, as if his temper had gained control of him. "Assume I don't know. Assume one of my eager commandants decided he'd make my day by sending an assassin after Teilani without telling me. Do you have sufficient imagination to do that?"

"Chal," Kirk said. But he'd be damned before he'd let Tiberius escape responsibility for what he had done.

"A backwater world. Of no importance in your universe. A lifeless cinder in mine. What did this child do to Teilani?"

"Poisoned her," Kirk said. "With a Klingon nerve toxin."

Again, Tiberius took on an expression of legitimate interest. "Follow me. I have something to show you on my computer."

Kirk wasn't certain what was going on, but finding out where Tiberius's computer was could definitely provide him with an edge. He followed Tiberius past the exhibition of atrocities depicted in the photographs on the wall. He couldn't help but notice one.

"Ahh," *Tiberius said as he saw what Kirk was looking at.* "One of my personal favorites." *The small name plaque on the image said* PAVEL A. CHEKOV. *But what it showed was a desiccated body in a transparent tube. Then Kirk remembered what that tube was. An agony booth.*

Tiberius preened as if proud of the photo. "I believe you share in some of the glory of that day. That week, actually. My good friend at the time, Mr. Spock, informed me that Chekov moved against me while you were conducting your laughable masquerade on my ship. When I finally returned to the real universe, I found poor Chekov in the agony booth, as punishment, but my torturers were at a loss because of the leniency you had shown him.

"So, I made leniency my showcase. I had the agony booth set to medium intensity. Think of a dull toothache throughout your body, in every part. Bearable, but most

*uncomfortable. And then I kept Pavel in it. It took thir-
teen days for him to die. It had a bracing effect on my
crew. Set a standard throughout the fleet."*

"In my universe, he became head of Starfleet."

*"Which could explain a great deal about your Starfleet,
don't you think?"*

Kirk didn't want to engage this beast in any topic of conversation other than the one that had brought him here.
"Where's the computer?"

Tiberius pointed through the door. Kirk entered.

The computer was on a console before him. It looked like
a standard Starfleet system, the kind he'd expect to see on a
starship. Past it, on either side of the long narrow room they
had entered, Kirk saw transparent display cases. At the end
of the hall, Kirk saw a pair of bright red sliding doors that
made him think of the original *Enterprise.*

Tiberius went to the computer console and input a series
of commands, angling his body so Kirk couldn't see what
his authorization codes were. When he stepped away again,
there was a visual sensor recording of the boy who had
attacked Teilani. The same one who was in the crèche on
the other side of the alcove.

"That's the boy," Kirk said.

"You're certain?" Tiberius asked. *"Perhaps it was this
boy?"* He pressed a control on the console and a new image
appeared.

"That's the same one," Kirk said.

"Or, perhaps this one?" Tiberius asked.

Another new image. But again, the same boy.

Then Kirk looked at his hands, said the word that
answered his questions. *"Clones."*

*"Exactly. Three of that young one. And what might be of
interest to you is that one of him is missing in your universe.
I sent a signal to activate a number of secret bases and*

assets over there. The group of children he was with never reported back."

Kirk tried to process that information. *"What are you saying? That someone just decided to use that boy to kill Teilani as a coincidence?!"*

"Someone who knew how *to use him, yes. That seems a reasonable assumption."*

Kirk didn't understand the choice of words Tiberius had made. *"What do you mean by* use*?"*

"You don't know?"

Kirk shook his head and stepped to the side as if avoiding confrontation, but he did so to give himself a better look at the keyboard. *"Right now, it seems I don't know anything."*

"That's a start," Tiberius agreed. *"As I said, I can't have friends. No peers. You can't imagine the disappointment you were to me. But still, I have to make preparations for the future. We both seemed to have achieved a second chance at life. Perhaps we'll get a third. Who knows? But in the meantime, I created clones."*

Tiberius grinned. *"Oh, not exact duplicates. Replication drift can be dangerous, and I was looking to the long term. So they're all half me—half us—and half various other people whom my research showed had satisfactory genes. And when I began adjusting their genetic heritage, it seemed a simple matter to enhance it here and there. Multiplied strength, vastly increased endurance. Hyperintelligence. And . . . a built-in method of self-defense."*

Kirk waited for the rest of the explanation he knew would come. And it did.

"I borrowed here and there from other successful species."

"Species?!" But then Kirk knew the answer before Tiberius could continue. *"Poisonous ones. The toxin wasn't painted on the boy's fingernail; he produced it."*

"*Mystery solved. Let's go down there.*"

"*No!*" Kirk insisted. "*It's not solved. Who set that child on Teilani?*"

"*What does it matter? You said she's dead.*"

"*She's in stasis. You must know what toxin the boy produced. You must have an antitoxin!*"

Kirk didn't like the way Tiberius remained in place, folded his arms, and began to smile, horribly.

"*You think I have the capacity to save Teilani?*"

Knowing the terrible door he was opening, Kirk gave the only answer he could. "*Yes.*"

Tiberius laughed, the sound hollow, mocking. "*Just one small detail overlooked, James. Why would I want to?*"

There was only one thing Kirk had to offer. "*You want to kill me.*"

"*I do. And here you are. Not much of a bargaining chip, I'm afraid.*" *Tiberius walked closer to Kirk, watching him closely.* "*But you are serious? You want to save Teilani. You have to save Teilani. No matter what the cost?*"

Kirk hesitated. He feared what Tiberius might be suggesting.

But more than that, he feared what might happen if he did not hear more.

"*What do you want me to do?*" *Kirk said, and with those words he knew his soul was forfeit to Tiberius.*

From his counterpart's triumphant smile, Kirk was certain Tiberius knew the same.

"*Come with me,*" *Tiberius said.*

He turned his back on Kirk again and walked halfway down the line of display cases, stopping in front of one that had a small figure in it.

Kirk joined his counterpart to look inside that case.

And was almost sick.

"*Balok?*" *he said.*

"The one and only. Brilliant scientist. Lonely starship captain. And an extremely disappointing ambassador from the First Federation. He does, however, make an excellent trophy."

Kirk was overwhelmed by the butchery before him. The figure in the case was the diminutive alien who had tested him and his crew back during his first five-year mission. The encounter had marked the beginning of a still ongoing, if unconventional, relationship with the First Federation. But here, in this universe, Balok was a stuffed *specimen* in Tiberius's chambers of horrors. His mouth permanently twisted into a smile as he perpetually contemplated the glass of tranya that had been wired to his lifeless hand.

"Before I was finished with him," Tiberius said affectionately, *"Balok gave me many secrets. I think you saw the Tantalus field at work. That was one of his. Captain Pike seemed far too eager to keep all the spoils of the Fesarius for himself, so I used the Tantalus field to rid the Enterprise of him, earning his rank for myself."*

Tiberius frowned, as if recalling a terrible defeat.

"But after a time, torture seemed to have little effect on Balok. From what my men and I could translate from his ship's computers, there was a vast base of Fesarius-class ships just outside Imperial space. I used all my skills to make him reveal what I wanted to know, and in the end, before he died, he told me where the base was located."

Kirk could guess what had happened. "He lied to you."

"Imagine my disappointment."

Kirk looked at the mummified body of the little alien. He could imagine Tiberius's rage. This was the result of it. Absolute insanity.

"So my question for you, James T. Kirk, is do you know where the First Federation base is?"

Kirk nodded. Of all the questions Tiberius might have asked of him, that was one he could answer.

"Do you have the antitoxin that can save Teilani's life?" Kirk asked.

Tiberius matched Kirk's acknowledgment. Then he held out his hand.

"I believe this could be the beginning of a most profitable relationship, James. Something to give each of us what we want most."

Kirk looked at that hand for long moments.

It couldn't just be a yes-or-no situation, to accept that hand or not. There had to be a third option. There always was a third option.

But not this time.

Because there was no more time.

Kirk took Tiberius's hand in his and shook hands with the demon who dwelled within him.

Because of what he was choosing to do at this moment, Teilani might live.

But James T. Kirk was utterly and hopelessly defeated.

ONE

☆

Admiral Leonard H. McCoy, M.D., was too stubborn to die.

He was 149 years old. The total mass of implants in his body, including ceramic-composite hips, heart-boosters, and synthetic muscles, easily outweighed his original parts, and he wasn't complaining. He hadn't submitted to these admittedly experimental procedures because he was afraid of death. He'd lost that fear in his first five-year mission on the *Enterprise*. A few landing parties with Jim Kirk and death was something you came to know on a first-name basis. You also learned how to ignore it.

But after almost a century and a half of fighting the good fight, McCoy could no longer ignore the fatigue of battle. He was just plain tired. Because no matter how many skirmishes he had won, for himself and uncounted others, there was always that knowledge that in the end the war would be decided in the adversary's favor.

Here and now, in one of the most secure medical facilities on the entire Klingon homeworld of Qo'noS, he faced defeat once again. This time, the confrontation and its likely outcome asked more than he could bear.

11

The woman in the harshly angled stasis tube before him was dying, and with her, her unborn child. And like a black hole reaching out to engulf and destroy all that it touched, her death and the child's would inevitably sweep so many others down into the ultimate darkness.

One especially.

Jim Kirk.

The woman was Teilani of Chal. A deliberate mixture of Romulan and Klingon heritage, created with the genetic capacity to save her people in the event of the unthinkable—total war between the empires and the Federation.

In time, the threat of that war had vanished, but Teilani did not squander her gift. A by-product of a war that never took place, she brought peace to her own troubled world and led it to full membership in the Federation. Then she brought peace to the Federation by risking her own life to help defeat the Vulcan Symmetrists.

But, most important, Teilani of Chal had brought peace to the tumultuous life of James T. Kirk.

She had been his equal in all that fueled Kirk's life. McCoy himself had seen them race their champion *ordovers* along the tropical beaches of Chal as if the universe existed for no other purpose than as an arena for their competition. The doctor had watched visual sensor records that showed Teilani sneakily edging past Kirk in the airlock of their shuttle to be the first to jump headlong into space in an insanely difficult orbital skydive.

And McCoy had seen fire of a different sort between the two.

Kirk and Teilani walking those same beaches they had raced across by day. But slowly, quietly, hand in hand, wordlessly sharing the moment of the ocean and the setting suns of the world that was their home.

Kirk and Teilani at one another's side in work as well. In

the forest clearing where Kirk had labored to cut and fell the trees that made the walls and roof of their house, Teilani a vibrant force beside him, quick to pull a rope, shove a timber into place, or steal a kiss, tease a laugh.

That clearing on Chal, that hand-built house, that was where McCoy had last seen Kirk and Teilani together as they were meant to be. Embraced by their friends. Embracing each other. Celebrating their marriage and their future. Anticipating the greater blessing to come, in the promise of their unborn child alive in Teilani's swollen belly.

On that day, McCoy had seen in his friend's eyes a fulfillment he had never expected to see there. A peace McCoy had glimpsed only rarely before, whenever Jim Kirk took the center chair of his starship and gave the command to move on, to explore, to discover all that the universe had to offer. Yet command of a starship is a gift given only to a few, and never for long. And when the day had finally come for Kirk to stand down, McCoy had grieved for his old friend, fearing Kirk's life without command would be without purpose, nothing more than a hazy existence of idle distraction.

But that had been before Teilani.

More than a partner, a lover, a wife, or a mother to his child, Teilani caused Kirk's rebirth.

McCoy felt the sting of tears and did not wipe them away, not questioning how after a lifetime of loss, one more death could affect him so.

In all the years McCoy had known Kirk, he had never seen him more alive than he had the night that Kirk and Teilani joined in marriage.

And only hours later, McCoy had never seen Kirk so devastated than when he learned that the reason for his bride's collapse was that she had been deliberately poisoned.

"How much longer?" M'Benga asked.

McCoy wore a small, transparent lens over his left eye. It was an offshoot of the Universal Translator, providing visual translations of the Klingon readouts on the medical equipment. Klingon anatomy McCoy had finally mastered. But the Klingon language was another matter.

"Can't be sure," McCoy said. He knew he sounded as tired as he felt. "No more than twenty hours. Maybe as few as two."

"Can we save the child?" M'Benga asked.

Dr. Andrea M'Benga, great-granddaughter of McCoy's old colleague on the first *Enterprise,* placed her hand on the faceted observation port of the stasis tube. The gesture pleased McCoy. He thought too many doctors today saw themselves as engineers. Dealt with their patients through machines and computers and manipulative forcefields. But touch was important. Feeling. Understanding. McCoy liked M'Benga. Even if she was crazy.

Now he struggled with the only answer he could give her question. He *couldn't* save Teilani. The proof of that diagnosis was twisted across her face—a virogen scar that marred her beauty, though truth be told, Jim never seemed to notice it.

In any other person, any other being, McCoy knew, that scar could be healed, made to disappear without a trace. But because of who Teilani was and the uniqueness of her genetically engineered heritage, that scar was beyond the power of current medicine to remove. That same fierce genetic resistance made her resistant to the medical stasis field, as well.

Immediate treatment had only slowed the deadly action of the toxin that had poisoned her. Even total stasis could not arrest its spread.

"Doctor?" M'Benga said. Her hand remained on the stasis tube. Through the faceted port, Teilani's image was repeated as if reflected through a broken prism. "Can the child be saved?"

McCoy licked his dry lips. They tasted like some foul combination of cinnamon, lemon, and burnt meat. It came from the scent of Klingon antiseptic, he knew. The Klingons were just as advanced as Starfleet when it came to medical isolation and sterilization fields, but their old battlefield traditions died hard. Klingon physicians, their staff, and their equipment were ritually and regularly bathed in the cloying fermented liquid that killed virtually all bacteria on contact. Just a suggestion of that scent was enough to bring back vivid memories of all of McCoy's earlier visits to this world. He hadn't enjoyed any of them.

"Maybe," he said in answer to M'Benga's question. It was the best he could do. "But we'll have to drop the stasis field and . . ." He couldn't finish. He didn't have to. M'Benga understood. She lifted her hand from the tube.

Within minutes of the field shutting down, Teilani would die.

"What would *he* want?" M'Benga asked simply.

McCoy knew precisely whom she meant. Knew what Kirk would want.

Kirk would want to return from his dangerous mission into the mirror universe with the antitoxin that would save Teilani and his child.

He would want to beam in unexpectedly at the very last second and—

"Admiral McCoy!" a Klingon voice barked. "There is an emergency Starfleet communication for you!"

McCoy turned to see Dr. Kron striding toward him, holding a small communicator, heavy boots clanking on the metal floor. Klingon medical facilities tended to be well armored, with low ceilings and thick, metal-clad walls.

Tradition again, McCoy knew. Recapturing the feel of the deep-underground military medical facilities built during the Age of Heroes, when worldwide wars had engulfed Qo'noS for generations.

Like that of most Klingon physicians, Kron's armor also spoke of centuries of tradition. Its most prominent feature was a slash of blood-pink gemstones across his heart. And into his belt was thrust a *d'ktahg* dagger of surgical steel, perfect for performing field phlebotomies. At least on Klingons, McCoy knew phlebotomies did some good—sometimes.

McCoy took the communicator from Kron's massive hand. He touched his own Starfleet combadge. "Why aren't they using this?"

"We are in a secured facility," Kron rumbled. Even his breath smelled like the antiseptic. "Regular communications channels are jammed."

McCoy nodded. Klingons were happy only when they expected the worst. He spoke into the communicator. "McCoy here."

"Admiral," a familiar voice replied from the device. *"Commander Riker here."*

McCoy's pulse quickened with new hope. The *Enterprise* had returned. Could that mean—

A transporter harmonic grew in the medical lab, drowning out whatever else Riker had to say.

McCoy turned to see a shaft of light take shape, and resolve into—

The wrong captain.

"Admiral McCoy," Jean-Luc Picard said. His eyes studied McCoy's companion as if her presence surprised him. "Dr. M'Benga."

"Where's Jim?" McCoy asked, even though Picard's frown told him the whole story.

"We waited as long as we could," Picard said somberly. He walked over to the stasis tube, stared down at Teilani. "Until the portal began to close. But he didn't make it back."

"Not even a signal?" McCoy asked.

"Nothing. I'm sorry."

"What portal?" M'Benga asked.

Picard looked up. "That's classified, Doctor."

Starfleet bureaucracy. McCoy had no patience for it. "She knows everything anyway," he told Picard. "Probably more than you do."

M'Benga folded her arms. "Teilani was poisoned by Starfleet operatives."

"That's impossible," the captain said. McCoy enjoyed the way the man almost sputtered.

"They didn't mean to kill her," M'Benga went on. "But they wanted to 'encourage' Kirk to work for them, so they needed something to hold over him."

By now Picard had his reactions under control. He remained silent.

"So Kirk would track down his mirror-universe counterpart," M'Benga continued. "Tiberius." She paused, then added, "And before you ask me what makes me think any of this is true, I should tell you I worked for them, too. For Project Sign."

McCoy could see from Picard's reaction that he understood the significance of that, but had no intention of discussing it. Instead, the captain looked back at Teilani.

"Can anything be done for her?" he asked.

McCoy's eyes held his answer. M'Benga's response spelled it out. "There's a chance we might be able to save the child."

With that, McCoy knew the moment had come. After more lifetimes than any one man could reasonably hope for, James Kirk could not defeat death for his life's partner.

There would be no last-minute beam-ins, no brilliant new
strategies to turn defeat into victory. Time, the odds, the
gods themselves would finally claim the victory that Kirk
had always denied them.

Kirk would lose.

Teilani would die.

And Kirk's friend McCoy would try his utmost to pick
up whatever pieces he could.

Ignoring Picard, McCoy addressed the Klingon physician
who had listened without comment to the grim exchange.
"Dr. Kron, prepare to shut down the stasis field."

The Klingon nodded, his heavy brows knit together in
the sadness of the moment.

McCoy directed his next words to M'Benga. "We'll have
two minutes at most. The Klingon surgical pallets aren't
programmed for Chal anatomy, so—"

"We can beam her to the *Enterprise*," Picard interjected.
"The sickbay is—"

McCoy cut him off. "I helped design that sickbay. It
can't handle Chal physiology any better than this facility
can." He turned back to M'Benga. "On Earth, it's called a
cesarean section."

"I'm familiar with it," M'Benga said. "I performed two
on Chal during the virogen crisis."

"Then get ready to perform your third."

One of Dr. Kron's nurses—two and a half meters of solid
muscle in black leather armor—slapped a surgical kit down
on the equipment tray beside the stasis tube. The metal
blades of its various cutting implements clanged.

McCoy frowned. "Can't use protoplasers on Chal flesh."

But his warning was unnecessary for M'Benga. "I know
the historical methods, too. Including physical scalpels."
She cringed as she said those last words though, as any civ-
ilized physician would.

That established, McCoy took a breath to steady his nerves, preparing himself to fight the battle again. "Dr. Kron," he said, forcing himself to keep his voice clear and steady, "shut it—"

The hum of a transporter harmonic cut off his final word.

M'Benga stared past McCoy, her mouth dropping open with amazement.

Picard's broad grin was one of recognition.

McCoy turned to the figure resolving from the light. But he already knew whom he would see. *You'd think I'd know by now,* he thought.

McCoy was not disappointed.

James T. Kirk had done it again.

TWO

☆

To those who had built it more than a century ago, Memory Alpha would be unrecognizable.

What had once been a cold and austere academic outpost designed to store and safeguard the sum total of all scientific and cultural information from each world of the Federation was now a vibrant world in its own right, home to a colorful and constantly changing population of scholars and artists from across the known quadrants.

Lifetimes could be spent sifting through the continuously growing collections of Alpha's data, discovering lost insights in ancient scientific records, bringing forgotten arts to new life, searching for unsuspected patterns in the histories of more than 150 member worlds, thousands of cultures, trillions of lives.

And sometimes, just sometimes, those patterns were found.

"A disaster," Admiral Abernath Hardin said. His tone suggested he was not convinced.

T'Serl cleared her throat, glanced at her colleague.

But across the polished bronzewood conference table from her, Lept merely scratched under his moss-green headskirt, and offered no assistance. As researchers, the young Vulcan and elderly Ferengi were a formidable pair. But Lept had already made it clear that any dealings T'Serl wished to undertake with Starfleet would be completely up to her.

"Actually, Admiral," T'Serl finally said, "disaster is not an altogether appropriate word."

Hardin steepled his fingers, tapping two together in polite impatience. "You used it."

Because another Vulcan would have understood the context, T'Serl thought impatiently. But humans, they needed everything spelled out in holographic letters a meter high and preferably projected directly onto their retinas.

"Cataclysm," T'Serl said. "Apocalyptic cataclysm."

The admiral at least stopped tapping his fingers. "The destruction of a world?"

T'Serl looked back to the center of the conference table above which was holographically projected the vivid display that was the centerpiece of her presentation. On one side of the slowly rotating model was a three-dimensional cauldron of seething fractal solids. On the other, the cauldron's chaos was abruptly converted into a flat, two-dimensional plane. Anarchy converted into absolute order. The image was chilling.

Chilling, that is, to anyone possessing the slightest understanding of psychohistory. And Admiral Hardin, it seemed, did not.

"More than a world," T'Serl said.

"The Federation?" Hardin asked, his eyebrows rising. His light tone revealed his continued lack of comprehension.

"More than the Federation," T'Serl answered. "More than the galaxy."

"The universe?" The admiral's disinterested skepticism was becoming shaded with hostility.

But T'Serl could not turn back. Just this meeting alone, with one admiral who sat on the Federation Council Technology Committee on Strategic Planning, had taken more than six months to arrange.

"The destruction of the universe. Yes, sir," she said. "That's what all our findings indicate." She glanced at her Ferengi colleague as she stressed the word "our."

Hardin stared at T'Serl's display in stern contemplation. The hologram was the small conference room's only light source, and painted the faces of its observers as if they had gathered around a primitive woodfire, hoping to divine the future.

"What timescale are we looking at?" the admiral asked.

As a scientist, T'Serl knew that the answer she was about to give should be couched in qualifications and assigned an error factor, plus or minus. But Hardin was not a person who wanted to hear estimates and best guesses. He was an admiral. He was in Starfleet. He was a human. He wanted facts, only facts, black or white, yes or no, up or down.

"Three months," T'Serl said, ignoring the small, strangled noise that issued from Lept's throat at her pronouncement.

Hardin leaned back in his chair, but whether he was subconsciously distancing himself from T'Serl or the truth she spoke, T'Serl didn't know.

"Just so I understand this," Hardin said, "you're telling me that your . . . psychohistorical research predicts that in three months the *universe* will come to an end?"

T'Serl nodded. "That is correct."

"How?"

"The research does not indicate the means by which—"

"You mean you don't *know?*"

Facts, T'Serl told herself. *No equivocation.* "Not to any acceptable degree of certainty."

"Then the word you're looking for is 'No.' "

"No." T'Serl kept herself from looking at Lept. But she could already hear the Ferengi reminding her that he had told her this would happen.

"So," the admiral said sharply, "three months from now, we might wake up and find that a subspace anomaly is about to swallow space-time, or—"

"No, sir."

Hardin's eyes flashed. "So you *do* know."

T'Serl briefly allowed herself to wonder if the admiral's obstinacy was deliberate, then plunged ahead, still determined to make him listen—and understand. "Psychohistory does not deal with natural phenomena, Admiral. It is the study of sentient beings operating en masse, in accordance with basic, predictable trends of sociology, psychology, political dynamics . . ." She stopped as the admiral raised his hand.

"You've already defined it for me," he said dismissively. "You find the patterns in human behavior, then make predictions about what groups of people will do."

T'Serl forced herself to remain silent. As published by the Vulcan Academy of Science, the definition of psychohistory ran 15,387 words. And Vulcan was an eminently concise and precise language.

"So what you're saying," the admiral continued, "is that the end of the universe will be caused not by some natural phenomenon, but by something a group of people will do on purpose."

T'Serl couldn't help herself. *He has to understand.* She drew herself up and tried again, her voice stiffer than she would have wished. "Actually, Admiral, though psychohistory most often deals with groups of people and collections of events, its true strength as a predictive technique rests in its ability to identify key decision points in the progress of history, and to suggest where individuals might arise to force those decision points along one path or another."

"An individual?" the admiral asked, frowning.

T'Serl nodded. "It is impossible to know who the individual is, or will be, although it is highly possible to know when and where that individual might appear. As it is—"

"Popping corn," the admiral said suddenly.

The inane human response succeeded in stopping T'Serl. She stared at him, uncertain even as to what language he had spoken, let alone what he meant.

The admiral ended her confusion. "It's a popular food from Cestus III. Very small hard-shelled fruits called kernels. Heat them in oil. The moisture in each kernel vaporizes, expands explosively to break the hull and cook the expanded starchy meat."

Humans will eat anything, T'Serl thought with disgust that she was careful to keep from her face. She glanced at Lept, but he had adopted a false look of fascinated interest that she knew bore no connection to whatever it was he felt. A Ferengi's facial expression could be as unforthcoming as a Vulcan's.

"The point is," the admiral said, "you throw a handful of popping corn into hot oil at a given temperature and you can say almost to the second when the first kernel will pop. You just can't say *which* kernel it will be."

T'Serl relaxed. The human was making a valid point after all. "An apt analogy," she said.

Now more at ease than at any other time in their meeting, the admiral actually winked at her. "What you mean is, Not bad for a human."

Hardin was right, but T'Serl refused to give him the satisfaction. "I am not certain what you mean, Admiral," she said coolly.

The admiral bestowed an annoying smile on her, then became serious again, lifting one hand to gesture at her display. "So if you can't say *what* is going to destroy the universe, then can you at least say from which cultural group the person responsible will arise?"

"The Federation."

Hardin shook his head, not satisfied with that answer. "You'll have to do better than that. The Federation's got one hundred and fifty—some—odd members at last count. Counting colony worlds, maybe fifteen thousand planets. Population in the tens of trillions."

"It is precisely those numbers that make psychohistory possible as a science," T'Serl said. "On a planetary scale, populations of only a few billion are too small to allow for full predictive analysis. But on a galactic scale, human behavior does become quantifiable." She would have preferred to say "sentient behavior," but the word "human" had grown beyond its originating species and today was commonly used to describe any thinking, rational being.

"Quantifiable enough to identify a threat," the admiral said with a nod. "But not quantifiable enough to say where that threat will emerge, or who will be responsible." He steepled his hands again, waiting for her next response.

T'Serl regarded him for a moment. "Given our present operating conditions, that is correct."

Hardin tilted his head, clearly intrigued by what she had not said. "Are you suggesting that under different conditions, you might be able to make more precise predictions?"

"Given adequate resources, yes."

T'Serl used years of discipline to still her sense of anticipation. The moment of truth was approaching for the admiral. She heard Lept stir beside her.

"And what resources would those be, Dr. T'Serl?" the admiral asked.

T'Serl made her outrageous request calmly. "Complete access to the entire Memory Planet Dataweb."

Hardin's thick eyebrows rose up his forehead. "When you say 'access,' I take it you mean 'control'?"

"That is correct."

The admiral sat forward, hands flat on the table before him, as if he were about to impart a secret to a friend.

"Dr. T'Serl, Manager Lept, as of 0800 hours this morning, there were 53,872 accredited researchers on Memory Alpha. Memory Beta usually has close to the same workload. Memory Gamma, Epsilon, the other specialized satellite planetoids, easily double that number again. So on the entire Memory Planet Dataweb, perhaps two hundred to two hundred and twenty thousand researchers are working at any given time, not counting tens of millions of daily subspace access requests from educational institutes, nonspecialists, and subscribers."

"The dataweb is a remarkable achievement," T'Serl agreed. It was among the most sophisticated data storage and retrieval networks ever created. But she studied the admiral, not sure if he had understood her request after all.

"And you are asking me to ask Starfleet to ask the Federation Council to kick all those researchers off the web so you can use the *entire* network to perfect your model of what might happen in three months."

T'Serl nodded with relief. Hardin had understood her perfectly.

But then the admiral said, "You can't be serious."

"Admiral Hardin, the universe is at risk. Given that situation, it is not logical to deny us exclusive use of the dataweb."

"I don't care about logic," the admiral said.

Tell me something I don't know, T'Serl thought.

"I care about results," Hardin added. "And you don't have any."

T'Serl pushed aside the sudden surge of frustration she felt. That could be dealt with later, during meditation. But the admiral must be dealt with now. She gestured to her three-dimensional display. "Those are our results. The defining moment is clearly identifiable."

"A pretty picture doesn't cut it, Doctor. Not one based on suppositions and estimates."

"But until we have access to the dataweb, that is all we will be able to provide."

For a moment, the admiral looked from T'Serl to Lept, as if asking for either researcher to offer something new. Then he stood up, obviously signaling that their meeting was over. Even the conference room's environmental controller seemed to read Hardin's intent and slowly increased the level of illumination.

T'Serl rose to her feet as well, betraying no sign of the sudden apprehension and fear that swept over her.

"Admiral, this is too critical a situation to ignore," she said.

"I'm not ignoring it, Dr. T'Serl. I'll forward a report to my committee. I will authorize additional dataweb access for you, as much as I can. But I don't have the authority to cut off access for anyone else."

"Who does have the authority?"

Hardin rubbed a hand over his chin, thoughtful. "People who will need to see a lot more than a colorful, three-dimensional graph. Unless . . ." Hardin hesitated.

"Please continue," T'Serl said.

"Without implying any disrespect for you or your work, Doctor, is there anyone else you can think of who might be able to make your case for you?"

"You mean, anyone of greater stature."

Hardin nodded. "I'll be honest. It will take me a few weeks at least to force this to the attention of anyone who can make a difference. So if there's someone you know who might be able to cut through the bureaucracy, someone who might be more familiar to the committee, even to the Council . . . well, it couldn't hurt to have that someone on your side."

T'Serl accepted the admiral's useless advice graciously. "But in the meantime, you will do what you can?"

"Of course, Doctor. But I'm just one . . ." He paused as if a new thought had come to him. He turned his gaze to the display again. In the brighter light, it appeared semitransparent, as insubstantial as smoke.

T'Serl was afraid to speak. If the human had come up with an unexpected idea, she didn't want to risk him losing it before he was able to articulate it.

"Doctor, you say whatever you think is going to happen in the next three months is going to be deliberate?"

"That is correct."

"And what's on this graph of yours, it shows the decision point where one individual is going to cause the destruction of the universe?"

"Correct again."

Hardin studied her with an intensity that T'Serl was unused to encountering in humans. "What if the decision goes another way?"

"I beg your pardon?"

"Well, if that's a psychohistory decision point, where one man—or woman—will emerge from the chaos of history to bring on the end of the universe, doesn't it also mean that there will be someone else to emerge to fight him or her? Isn't that how history works? Opposing forces?"

"Well, yes," T'Serl said warily. Human logic could be beguilingly simple, though seldom complete. "But, Admiral, we aren't talking about a planetary war being declared or a political assassination or . . . or any other event in which history will continue on past the decision point, along one path or another. Depending on what happens at that moment on the graph, history . . . history might end."

"But then again," Hardin said, "it might not. Right?"

T'Serl agreed, but made her reluctance to do so apparent.

"I'll be in touch," the admiral said. He walked for the doors, they slid open, and for a moment the quiet room filled with the outside corridor bustle of Memory Alpha's crowded academic wing. Then Hardin was gone.

The moment the doors had closed again, Lept cackled. "Told you so." His eyes were bright with all the reactions and emotions he had repressed in the meeting.

"I knew you were going to say that," T'Serl said with irritation.

The old Ferengi pushed himself up from the table, reached inside his jacket for his tin of beetle snuff. "Of course you did. Because you're a psychohistorian. And a crackling good one, too."

But T'Serl dismissed her colleague's assessment. "I couldn't predict how this meeting would end," she reminded him.

"But you knew anyway," Lept insisted. "Not by logic. But in your gut, heh?"

T'Serl had worked with Lept long enough to permit herself a small smile, imperceptible to anyone except those who knew her best.

"Oh, I see that Vulcan grin from ear to ear," Lept said gleefully. Then he sniffed a pinch of pulverized beetle shell and sneezed heartily. "That'll clear your ears, my dear."

T'Serl sighed as she gave the Ferengi a handkerchief. He always forgot to carry one. "Since my approach proved ineffective, what course of action do you suggest we take now?"

Lept used the handkerchief, folded it carefully, then tucked it back into his jacket with his snuff tin. "Let's just see."

He picked up the padd T'Serl had used in her presentation to the admiral, made some adjustments on it that altered the display in the table's center. As the room lights dimmed again, the hologram became brighter, more solid, more real.

"See where we are now?" Lept asked.

A small point of light floated among the fractal chaos that was the forward progression of the Federation. Thousands of tendrils of cause and effect spun off from key foci, so many that they kept the pattern in constant motion and change, yet overall the same. The effect was like staring at the surface of a wind-driven sea—each individual wave random and unpredictable, but overall, the texture of crest and trough presenting a unified whole against which anomalies could be easily identified.

"Now watch what happens," Lept said.

T'Serl raised an eyebrow. Around that floating point of light an island of stability formed, as if in the storm at sea a sudden patch of smooth ocean had magically appeared. No fractal disorder was evident in that region. It could mean only one thing.

"*We* are a focus?"

Lept shrugged. "Or, more probably . . ." He was a great believer in teaching through questions. The Suraktic Method, it was called on Vulcan.

T'Serl responded to the Ferengi's gentle prodding. "We will *overlap* a focus."

"In other words . . . ?"

"Events will seek us out."

T'Serl peered deep into the seething representation of future history, and against all logic wished that she had somehow succeeded with Admiral Hardin. That he had agreed to provide the computing resources required to increase her model's predictive resolution a millionfold. Because somewhere in that roiling sea of possibilities, an individual was being hidden.

"One individual," T'Serl said.

But Lept shook his head, held up two fingers. "It's a decision point, remember."

T'Serl understood. "Two," she said.

One destined to destroy the universe.

One destined to save it.

Their identities cloaked by disorder, shrouded by chaos.

"Do you know the story of Schrödinger's cat?" Lept asked.

T'Serl was very familiar with the tale—an old Earth thought experiment from the days of the human physicist Albert Einstein. In one version of the experiment, Schrödinger's cat was locked in a box with a poison-gas capsule. The capsule would either break or remain whole, depending on the random behavior of a decaying radiation source over a given period of time.

According to some views of quantum physics, Schrödinger's cat existed in superposition, neither dead nor alive, until the moment the box was opened and an observer actually saw the captive feline. Only then did the probability waves collapse and one state or the other—life or death—become real.

Then again, T'Serl knew, according to other views of quantum physics, whenever the universe reached a decision point in which two outcomes were equally possible, the universe itself split, so that both outcomes had equal existence. In one universe, the cat continued to live. In the other, it died.

"On Vulcan," T'Serl told Lept, "a similar thought experiment is known as T'Pral's *sehlat*."

Lept chuckled, then coughed. "Still the same idea, heh? Superposition of states. The *sehlat*'s dead and the *sehlat*'s alive, both at the same time."

"Until the probability waves collapse by the act of observation," T'Serl agreed.

But the graph before them was too coarse to allow precise observation of what was to come, too imperfect. Like the locked box into which T'Pral had placed her unfortunate *sehlat*, Schrödinger his cat.

"Superposition," Lept said again.

T'Serl looked over at him, wondering if he was implying something, trying to lead her to a conclusion she had missed.

"Both at the same time," the Ferengi said, smiling broadly.

T'Serl used her logic, but it revealed a nonsensical answer.

"You mean the two individuals?"

Lept said nothing, which was his way of encouraging her to continue.

"Existing in superposition," T'Serl said. "The destroyer *and* the preserver."

Lept held up two gnarled fingers, then folded one down.

"The *same* person?" T'Serl asked. She peered into the graph, looking for any indication that what Lept was suggesting was even remotely possible.

But she saw nothing.

"That is most illogical," she concluded.

"Of course it is," Lept agreed. "But wouldn't it be . . . fascinating?"

The Ferengi grinned at her, then looked back at the graph.

T'Serl followed his gaze, trying to see what her mentor saw.

Two people.

One person.

Destroyer and preserver both.

Impossible, she thought at last. *Completely illogical.*

But still, logic and possibilities aside, if there was any truth to Lept's conclusion, she couldn't help wondering who that one individual might be.

THREE

☆

The antitoxin worked.

But then, Andrea M'Benga never doubted that it would.

James T. Kirk was like that.

She had stepped aside when Kirk had beamed into the claustrophobic intensive-care unit where Teilani's stasis tube was being monitored. She had marveled at how much was communicated between Kirk and McCoy with so few words.

The medical stasis field had been shut down. McCoy had infused the antitoxin into Teilani before she had regained consciousness. And in less than five minutes, her life-sign readings had climbed back into the realm in which recovery would be possible.

Teilani would be bedridden for days, weakened for months, but she would live.

As a physician, M'Benga wondered how this was possible. McCoy had not once asked Kirk how he had obtained the antitoxin, nor what its composition was. Instead, the physician had unquestioningly accepted the dosage information Kirk had imparted, and used the antitoxin as instructed.

M'Benga wondered how long it had taken for that level of trust to grow between the two men. She wondered when she might share a similar level with her captain, Christine MacDonald.

But for now, M'Benga knew, concerns about her own career could wait.

She needed to talk with Kirk about Project Sign. About how he had been betrayed by Starfleet.

She took her moment when Teilani, still unconscious, was being scanned by Klingon sensors.

"Captain Kirk," she said as she approached him, interrupting a conversation he was having with Picard and McCoy.

Kirk smiled at her—a polite, reflexive response, she could tell. There was something darker in his eyes, some untold sorrow that colored each expression, every word. "Jim," he said.

"We need to talk."

Kirk seemed to sense her urgency and tried to excuse himself from Picard and McCoy.

But Picard apparently had no intention of excusing anyone.

"I agree," he said. "We should *all* talk."

M'Benga wasn't certain how to proceed. But McCoy gave her a look that said arguing with two starship captains was even more of a no-win scenario than the *Kobayashi Maru.*

M'Benga went for a full-out, frontal assault. "Jim, you've been deliberately manipulated by Starfleet."

Picard was the first to respond. "Doctor, I find that difficult—no, impossible—to believe."

"But you do know about Project Sign?" M'Benga asked. She was surprised by the look Kirk and Picard exchanged then. They both seemed to know Project Sign, and to share suspicions about it.

McCoy stepped into the silence. "It looks to me that you're all standing there with different pieces of the puzzle."

No one responded.

"Oh for—" the doctor muttered. He forced a smile at M'Benga. "My dear, why don't you tell *me* about Project Sign."

So M'Benga did. All of it. Drawing on every recovered memory that had been returned to her three days earlier by her knight in shining armor—a plain and simple Cardassian tailor on Deep Space 9.

When she had finished, McCoy raised his first objection.

"What I don't understand," he said, "is why Starfleet Command would feel the need to set up a secret division to handle the suspected threat of an invasion. One of Starfleet's main missions is to protect the security of the Federation. There's nothing secret about that."

"There is," Picard said quietly, "if there are those within Starfleet who believe the invasion might already have occurred."

"What?" M'Benga said. That supposition didn't fit in with anything she remembered about her role as a medical investigator for Project Sign. A role which entailed her memory being suppressed after each investigation she completed for them. "That makes no sense."

"I disagree," Kirk said. "It makes perfect sense. Starfleet Command wouldn't deliberately put Teilani in danger to make me work for them. But a smaller division, operating without oversight, convinced the fate of the Federation was in their hands and no others' . . ." He looked at Picard.

"Captain Hu-Linn Radisson," Picard said.

"Whom I remember as a small and older woman, and you remember as tall and muscular," Kirk added.

"I don't know what you're talking about," M'Benga said.

"Dr. McCoy was right," Kirk told her. "We each have a

piece of the puzzle. But the puzzlemakers have veiled whatever truths they've told us in layers of lies."

"Why?" M'Benga asked.

"Fear," Picard said. "A classic response."

"But fear of what? That Starfleet has been compromised? That the Federation Council has been taken over from within?"

"If the people of Project Sign believe that's true," Kirk said, "than what better reason to trust no one?"

M'Benga couldn't believe how calm Kirk and Picard were, as if they each had faced the imminent destruction of the Federation a dozen times before.

"Gentlemen," M'Benga said, making no effort to hide her frustration, "who is the enemy here?"

"That's a question with three possible answers," Picard answered.

Kirk agreed. "One: There is no enemy. Project Sign is an entity that feeds on its own paranoia. Wouldn't be the first. Won't be the last."

"Two," Picard continued, "there is the enemy that Project Sign *believes* is the enemy. Given the Project's capabilities and concerns, I would guess their suspicions are directed in some way to a threat arising from the mirror universe."

"Possible," Kirk said, looking thoughtful, the shadow in his eyes stronger, as if the air around him was no longer fit to breathe. "But the mirror universe isn't a secret to Starfleet Command. And I've seen no evidence of any one group within it powerful enough to threaten the entire Federation."

M'Benga thought Picard's own eyes would pop from his elegantly shaped skull. "Jim, the mirror Alliance *hijacked* the *Enterprise.* They tried to transport her back to the mirror universe. They've been replacing key personnel throughout the Federation with mirror counterparts."

"Jean-Luc," Kirk countered, "we *saved* the *Enterprise.*

Mirror counterparts can be and are detected in most cases. And Starfleet is preparing to work with the Vulcan Resistance now that the Prime Directive no longer applies to the mirror universe. I agree it's a threat to us, but no different in kind from the Romulans or the Dominion."

The two starship captains considered each other's position in silence, as if allowing for the possibility the other was right, though not necessarily accepting it.

"What's the third answer?" M'Benga finally asked.

"The real enemy," Kirk said. "An enemy so hidden that not even Project Sign knows its identity."

"That could explain the Project's intense paranoia," Picard said slowly. "If they've identified a threat to the Federation, but have yet to discover from where the threat originates."

For M'Benga, that simple conclusion was the piece of the puzzle she had been missing.

"Captain, that's it," she said excitedly. "All the work I've done for Sign has been related to identifying, or at least *trying* to identify, the genetic structure of different beings." *So many different beings,* she thought. *Far more than anyone in authority will admit.*

Once again, flashes of impossible memories played through her mind. The wonders she had seen in Station 51, Starbase 25-Alpha, the underground labs on Zeta Reticuli IV. She needed more time to understand the implications of many things she had recently remembered. But for Kirk's sake, and the Federation's, she knew she *had* to talk about her last encounter with Commodore Twining.

"The last group I examined," M'Benga continued, "were genetically modified children who had originated in the mirror universe."

Kirk instantly became grim, the darkness within him no

longer hidden. "It was one of those children who attacked Teilani."

"But I've examined dozens of other beings over the past ten years. Klingons. Ferengi. Other species I've never seen before or since."

"And they never told you who the beings were, or why it was necessary for you to identify them?" McCoy asked.

M'Benga shook her head. "I always had the sense that there was something unusual about the subjects they presented to me. Either having to do with the technology they used, or where they were discovered. But I only handled the biological side of the investigation. I'm positive that somewhere in Starfleet you'll find engineers, physicists, who knows how many other specialists, all having been recruited the way I was, used for specific investigations, then stripped of their memories."

"A threat and no enemy," Picard said. "It fits."

M'Benga studied Kirk, was surprised by what she saw. Whatever emotion he had been keeping in check, sorrow or rage she didn't know, ruled him now.

She could also see that Kirk didn't care what Picard's conclusion was. He didn't care about this conversation or anything around him. And M'Benga wasn't the only one to notice the change.

"Jim?" Picard asked. "What is it?"

"Nothing," Kirk answered. He looked past them all to Teilani and the Klingon medical team who attended her.

"She's going to be fine," McCoy said.

But M'Benga could sense that whatever unacknowledged passions raged through Kirk, at this moment they were not connected to his bride.

"I know," Kirk said. "I . . ." Whatever he had been about to say, he changed his mind. "The baby?"

"He'll be fine, too," McCoy said.

A sad smile came to Kirk then. "You weren't supposed to tell us which it was going to be."

M'Benga realized Kirk meant the baby's sex.

"I have to call the baby something," McCoy protested. "He, she, I really don't know. I'm your doctor, not hers."

"Sorry, Bones."

M'Benga stopped the laugh of recognition that almost burst from her. Bones. That's what her captain called her. A Starfleet tradition, she decided.

"And speaking of being your doctor," McCoy said, "I should give you a once-over, too. You look awful."

Kirk grimaced at M'Benga. "Aren't doctors supposed to take a course in bedside manners?"

"I did," McCoy said. "From him." He pointed to Dr. Kron. "There's an examination room back in—"

McCoy faltered, and M'Benga saw why. Dr. Kron was stomping toward them. For a moment, she wondered if pointing at a Klingon doctor was considered a deadly insult. From the expression on Dr. McCoy, he was probably thinking the same thing.

"Yes?" McCoy said. "Is something wrong?"

M'Benga was startled at Kirk's reaction to the question. She wondered what he had gone through to get the antitoxin and bring it here without the help of Picard and the *Enterprise*.

"Nothing is wrong," Kron said. "It is a time for celebration."

No one understood what he meant.

Then Kron pounded a heavy hand on Kirk's shoulder, making the human wince.

"It is time for a new warrior to join the never-ending battle for honor," Kron bellowed. *"Qapla'!"*

And for just that instant, the darkness lifted from James T. Kirk as M'Benga saw his eyes grow wide in wonder, and he whispered, "It's time . . ."

• • •

McCoy had long since lost track of how many new lives he had helped bring into this universe. Human, Vulcan, a Horta or two or three hundred. It was all part of the job, and a part that he loved.

So there was no possible way he was letting some hulking Klingon midwife deny him the chance to deliver the child of James T. Kirk.

Teilani was awake now, though she couldn't speak because of the ventilator tube in her throat. Tri-ox could do nothing to help oxygenate her Chal blood, and there had been no time to move her to a proper birthing room where other Klingon devices might have provided less intrusive support.

But Teilani grasped Kirk's hand as he stood at her side, and McCoy could see all the communication that was necessary flow between those two just through that simple touch.

It's all going to work out, McCoy told himself. Kirk and Teilani were together again. Their child would have a gifted life, basking in the love of his—or her—parents.

And whatever nonsense Project Sign was up to, well, that would be the concern of Picard and his crew.

As far as McCoy was concerned, Starfleet, the Federation, the universe itself owed so much to Kirk that it was time Kirk took something back.

"I see the head," McCoy said, beaming.

He looked up to see Kirk smile at Teilani, both hands now on hers, just the way things should be. Then again, to also see the happy couple surrounded by hulking Klingons in white leather surgical scrubs was something McCoy had never imagined and still had a hard time accepting. Leave it to Jim Kirk to do things completely differently from the way anyone else did them.

"Push," M'Benga urged at McCoy's side. "Almost there."

McCoy could sense that the young doctor's excitement was almost the same as his. And he was glad to know she was ready to back him up. His hands weren't what they used to be, synthetic nerves notwithstanding. A normal birth he could handle without question. But just in case, it was good to know one of Starfleet's best was ready to step in, along with about two tonnes of combined Klingon medical expertise.

"There," McCoy said as a final contraction delivered the child into his waiting hands.

It was smaller than he knew would be best, but it was also a month premature. At least by normal standards. Given that the child was some combination of Romulan, Klingon, and human DNA, it was difficult to say what was normal.

Certainly the caul that encased it was common enough in human births, and M'Benga stood ready with a small Klingon scalpel to free the child.

What was unusual to McCoy was that a premature fetus seldom presented itself headfirst. With no medical tricorder that could make sense of the baby's life signs, McCoy and M'Benga had been prepared for a breech birth, more typical of this timing. McCoy hoped the ease of delivery presaged a life free of trouble for the child.

He held the tiny being in his hands, safe and secure, as M'Benga swiftly pulled at the caul and slit it open, tugging it back from the baby's mouth so—

M'Benga gasped.

McCoy's shock was almost like one of electricity.

The scalpel slipped from M'Benga's hand, clattered on the metal floor.

McCoy saw Dr. Kron begin to move in. But this was Jim Kirk's child. This was McCoy's life to defend.

Cradling the child, McCoy deftly cleared its mouth and airway, ignoring what he saw, going by training, by instinct, by his need to bring life into being.

The child shuddered, coughed, then drew in its first breath and wailed.

McCoy glanced up at Kirk and Teilani. Tears in Kirk's eyes. Tears of joy.

"Bones," he said, almost laughing, "*now* you can tell us!"

He reached out for the child. Teilani strained her head up.

"Boy or girl, Bones?"

M'Benga's trembling hands removed the last of the caul.

McCoy's trembling hands lay the child on Teilani's shrunken abdomen.

Its wail became a screech.

The small pointed masses that ringed its face . . . McCoy sobbed . . . that ringed where its face should be . . . were not some type of calcium deposit, as he had thought.

Quivering nodules of raised flesh traced its limbs. The caul was not an amniotic sac, but a web of flesh that grew from its back, webbed its arms.

"Bones . . ." Kirk said in strangled shock. "What is it . . . ?"

But Leonard McCoy had no answer for his friend.

The child was alive. Without a sex. Without a species. Some nightmarish combination of genes that had never existed before, combined to give life to what some would call a monster.

Teilani moved an uncertain hand down to stroke her baby's head. But at the moment of contact, though its eyes were closed, the small being spit and twisted, writhing away from its mother's touch.

Two Klingon nurses had begun a mournful chant. Teilani's life-sign monitors began beeping with alarm.

The child slipped from Teilani and McCoy caught it, then looked at Kirk.

The tears that streaked his friend's face were no longer those of joy.

McCoy handed the child to a nurse. He felt dizzy, exhausted, suddenly felt M'Benga's sure hands helping to support him.

"Why?" Kirk whispered.

A question that could have no answer.

For now.

FOUR

─────── ☆ ───────

Jean-Luc Picard had ceased trying to comprehend the life of James Kirk years ago.

For most careers, even one in Starfleet, there was a natural ebb and flow: start young, work hard, rise through the ranks, make a difference, step aside, write memoirs, fade away.

But as far as Picard could tell, Kirk was on his third pass through the cycle without ever having hit the last stage; the less said about the nexus, the better.

Yet Picard also knew that such extraordinary achievement demanded its price. Whatever unprecedented rewards had been earned by and bestowed upon his friend and colleague, Picard knew they'd been balanced by equal punishment.

All too frequently, extraordinary success in any arena cost friendships with those left behind. Inevitably, fame resulted in a loss of privacy. As for those odd coincidences and unexpected strokes of synchronicity which Picard could only label luck, even these beneficent markers of fate commonly brought with them the seeds of self-doubt.

But however philosophical Picard was about the balance of any individual life, including his own, he could craft no reasonable rationale, no possible cosmic accounting, that could explain the tragedy that had overtaken his friend now.

No one deserved what had happened to Jim Kirk.

But until and unless Kirk reached out to him for help, Picard felt powerless to offer comfort. Even then, he was not sure what he could do.

Now, less than half an hour after the delivery of her and Kirk's malformed child, Teilani remained under intense watch in the intensive-care unit of the Klingon medical facility. Whether succumbing to shock or to the aftereffects of the antitoxin treatment, Kirk's new wife had passed into unconsciousness shortly after the child's birth.

The infant itself had lapsed into a state of unresponsiveness and now lay within its own stasis tube, as Starfleet's best medical practitioners of past, present, and future attended to it. McCoy and M'Benga and the *Enterprise*'s own Beverly Crusher and her staff were augmenting the Klingon medical equipment with whatever the *Enterprise* could provide.

As for Kirk, he sat across the room from the hurried but deliberate medical team working desperately to save Teilani. Uncharacteristically, he was a passive witness only, as if he were viewing some meaningless holographic reconstruction of an event that was of no interest to him.

Picard sat beside him, searching his mind for something—anything—he could say or do that might make the slightest difference. He began with the causes of Kirk's torment. Kirk's bride was desperately ill. Kirk's child was challenged in ways medical science could not explain or, for now, correct. These facts were obvious.

But beyond those facts, Picard knew, lay the real problem, something more difficult, if not impossible, for an outside observer to understand. Between the time of its birth and its placement in protective stasis, that child had not been touched by its father, never held in his arms. Especially given that its mother might be dying, the isolation of the child from its father seemed heartless, heartbreaking. Yet no one had forced this choice on Kirk. The decision had been his own.

The silent struggle in which Kirk was apparently now engaged confirmed once again what Picard knew from experience: Of all the enemies faced in life, the hardest to battle and overcome was one's inner self.

"The *Pauli*," Kirk suddenly said.

"I beg your pardon?" Picard was startled, both by Kirk's sudden decision to speak and by what he had chosen to say first.

"That was the name of the science vessel in the Goldin Discontinuity. After we rescued the *Enterprise*, stopped Tiberius." Kirk glanced at Picard, eyes distant, stony. "I was on the *Heisenberg*."

"Captain Radisson's ship," Picard said, glad that Kirk was finally talking. Perhaps now he would be able to help his friend.

Kirk nodded. "With Spock and Bones and Scotty. But Teilani . . . they took her to the *Pauli*. There was a Romulan physician on board, they said."

"On a Starfleet vessel?" Picard asked. As far as he knew, the only Romulan personnel to take part in exchange missions with Starfleet these days were engineers involved in cloaking or singularity-drive technologies.

Kirk plunged on, ignoring his question. "That's when Teilani had her full physical. Everything was fine. The child was healthy, they said. Developing normally."

"Jim, that was months ago." Picard spoke as gently as he could. "The child . . . the child might have been normal then. So many things could have happened."

Picard felt the chill of deep space in Kirk's eyes. Hate, Picard feared, was the only emotion that could survive in such coldness.

"They poisoned her, Jean-Luc."

Picard understood. "Project Sign," he said softly.

"Who knows what they did to my . . . my child."

Picard couldn't fault Kirk for what he was feeling. But as his friend, he became even more determined to deflect Kirk from the path he was choosing. The child's genetic structure was unfathomable for now. Beverly had said that none of the *Enterprise*'s standard medical scanning techniques could make any sense of it. So it was extremely important that Kirk not arrive at false conclusions. He leaned forward, closer to Kirk. "Jim, you don't know that anyone did anything to your child. Wait for the medical report. We have to understand what's—"

"*We* don't have to do anything," Kirk said, cutting him off. "That's my wife. My . . . child."

Picard sat back calmly in his uncomfortable Klingon chair. He wouldn't argue with Kirk. Not about this. "I'm not your enemy," he said. "I never have been."

"Then don't tell me what to think."

"Jim, all I want to do is help you and Teilani and your child."

Kirk's eyes were on a computer display above the main door to the ICU. "I know you do," he said.

Picard looked over to the display, wondering why it had drawn Kirk's interest. Everything on the dark computer screen was written in the glowing letterforms of *pIqaD,* but he could read enough of the Klingon script to see it held no information about Teilani, only general updates about the facility and a local time readout.

Then Picard saw Kirk reach within the civilian clothes he wore and withdraw a small device.

He offered the device to Picard.

"What's this?" Picard asked as he turned it over in his hand. It was half the width of a general-reference padd, but slightly longer and much thinner.

"Tell Spock it uses Tantalus technology. He'll explain." Kirk stood up like a prisoner about to face his executioner.

Picard got to his feet also. Automatically, he gave his jacket a tug to smooth it. "Are you going somewhere?" he asked.

Kirk's half-smile was colored by grief and exhaustion. He placed a hand on Picard's shoulder.

He's saying good-bye, Picard thought incredulously. *But why?*

"You never asked me how I got the antitoxin," Kirk said. "Never asked how I got back from the mirror universe after the portal had closed. What happened to T'Val and to Janeway."

Picard hadn't seen any need to waste the time Kirk needed for his family, feeling certain that Kirk would tell him everything he needed to know, when he needed to know it. It seemed that time might be now.

"Very well," Picard said. "How *did* you get back? What happened to the women?"

Kirk squeezed Picard's shoulder, hard, for just an instant. Then he took his hand away. "You already know, Jean-Luc."

The hair on the back of Picard's neck bristled.

Then Kirk took a final look at the treatment bed where Teilani lay, at the stasis tube where his child waited in limbo. "I have to go," he said.

"Jim, no. You can't leave them now." Not only could Picard not understand Kirk's action, he didn't *want* to understand.

"I have no choice," Kirk said.

Just then the massive doors to the ICU slid open and an

urgent-faced Klingon guard entered, looking for Dr. Kron. The quick conversation between the guard and the physician was in clipped Klingon, most of it unintelligible, but Picard heard one word quite clearly: *"Enterprise."*

He stepped away from Kirk, loath to leave his friend, but unable to avoid it.

"What did you say about the *Enterprise?"* Picard called out as he strode over to join the two Klingons.

Kron wheeled about sharply. "There is a second."

Picard stared at Kron, without comprehension.

"A second *Enterprise,"* Kron growled. He jabbed a thick finger toward the ceiling. "It just *decloaked* in orbit."

"Another . . . *Enterprise,"* Picard repeated. "Decloaked?"

Less than a heartbeat later, he understood *everything.*

Picard turned back to Kirk. "Jim, no! You can't! Together we can fight him!"

But Kirk shook his head. "Spock will explain," he said quietly. "And . . . if not, look after them."

Standing well away from all others in the Klingon intensive-care unit, Kirk closed his eyes, waiting for his fate to claim him.

To Picard, it was as if his friend was telling him the fight had already played out, and Kirk had lost.

"Shields!" Picard shouted to Kron. *"Full shields on this facility at once!"*

"They are already in place," Kron roared back, obviously unused to taking orders from *tera'nganpu'.*

Picard slapped his combadge, aware those shields would not be enough. "Picard to *Enterprise!* We need to ionize the atmosphere over the—"

But he was too late.

Kirk dissolved into a glowing swirl of quantum mist.

Taken by the *Enterprise.*

The wrong *Enterprise.*

Seething with anger, Picard tapped his combadge again. "Picard to Riker," he said, looking at the device Kirk had given him. "Will, wherever he is, whatever it takes, get me Spock."

Whatever nightmare Kirk faced now, Picard was determined his friend would not face it alone.

FIVE

─────── ☆ ───────

"My Spock betrayed me," Tiberius said.

Kirk wasn't interested. He had been on this debased and adulterated *Enterprise* for two weeks as it traveled at high warp, cloaked by a Tantalus mask beyond the capability of Starfleet to detect.

For two weeks now, he had served as audience, confessor, and court jester to his mirror-universe counterpart—Emperor Tiberius the First.

But Teilani is alive, Kirk told himself, repeating the thought over and over. *Teilani is alive.*

That was the bargain he had made; the reason he had sold his soul to a devil who wore his face.

The antitoxin for information.

Life for death.

Because death was how this would end.

When the moment was right, when the bodyguards looked away, when Kirk and Tiberius were alone for only a few seconds, Kirk would kill the man in the mirror, and then . . .

Kirk knew his options were finally at an end. There

would be no escape from this ship and crew. No other ending possible. No other fate for him to choose.

Just as Tiberius and he had been born together in their separate universes, they would die together in this one.

Knowing that was Kirk's only consolation.

"You're not paying attention to me," Tiberius said.

Kirk looked at his counterpart. During the past two weeks, Tiberius had changed his appearance, cut his long queue of dark hair, changed its color to match the natural gray of Kirk's, even trimmed his sideburns to Academy points. A precaution, Kirk knew. To make it easier for Tiberius to take Kirk's place, in case unanticipated events might warrant that kind of deception.

But Kirk knew that possibility would never arise.

"You're thinking about how you're going to kill me," Tiberius said.

Kirk nodded. He was finally becoming used to the fact that he and Tiberius thought so much alike. Being freed of the necessity to keep secrets made life much more simple.

"Spock betrayed you," Kirk said, bringing his counterpart back to the topic at hand.

Tiberius laughed.

They were in a private lounge on the mirror *Enterprise.* Kirk presumed that in a Starfleet Sovereign-class vessel, this would have been the ship's bar, a place for officers and enlisted crew to mingle freely in their off-duty hours.

But on this dark *Enterprise,* the lounge was a playroom for Tiberius. In addition to the bar and the food replicators along one long bulkhead, there was a large circular bed, a holographic projection system, even an agony booth surrounded by plush antigravity chairs, as if awaiting an audience.

Kirk ignored the furnishings, though. He concentrated on the tall observation windows through which he could see the stars moving at warp.

That was where he belonged. Not in here.

"Betrayal," Tiberius scoffed as he paced in front of those windows, his reflection a ghost among the stars. "The price one pays for greatness, don't you agree?"

"I wouldn't know," Kirk said. He was standing by the bar. He rarely sat in Tiberius's presence. It was psychological, he knew. He wanted to be as ready as possible to leave whenever Tiberius dismissed him.

"Ah, of course," Tiberius agreed. "You have no idea what greatness is. You squandered your gift and your talents to be a lackey of the spineless Federation."

Kirk didn't argue. There was no point. He merely pictured Tiberius dying. The image gave him the strength he needed to continue this charade.

Tiberius gulped down the last of whatever he was drinking, tossed the glass he had used aside.

A green-skinned Orion girl, wearing only a sash of bronze-colored leather, ran forward at once from her place beside the bar to collect the glass and wipe the last drops of its contents where they had spilled on the deck.

A second Orion girl immediately approached Tiberius with a tray of other drinks and food, held it ready for him. But he waved her aside and, ducking her head in obeisance, she quickly retreated backward to the bar.

For the first few days of this voyage, Tiberius had tried to make T'Val and the mirror Janeway fill the roles of the unfortunate females who attended him. Neither had shrunk from frankly expressing their displeasure at their flimsy costumes or their unwanted duties. T'Val had managed to slash Tiberius's chest with a blade hidden in her mechanized hand. Janeway had simply gone for his throat. Kirk had no answer for why Tiberius had permitted both to live, but the two women were now in what passed for this ship's sickbay, being treated by its EMH.

"But I *knew* Spock would betray me," Tiberius said.

Kirk said nothing in reply, offered no sign of encouragement or of disinterest. He had heard this story three times on this journey. If it weren't for the presence of the counterparts of Riker and La Forge behind him, both armed with disruptors, it would be the last time he would hear this story, too. But for now, all things considered, he was content to wait.

"So I *was* prepared for him," Tiberius said, clearly annoyed by Kirk's silence.

"Of course you were," Kirk answered. "That's why your own Alliance turned against you."

Tiberius laughed again. "James, James, James—no one's ever spoken to me the way you do. *Twice.*"

Kirk shrugged. "I've told you where the *Fesarius* base is. You could kill me."

But Tiberius shook his head. "After months of torture, Balok told me where the base was, too. So I killed him. Least I could do to reward him, end his suffering. I am a compassionate man to those who acknowledge my power. But then I learned he had lied to me. The coordinates were useless. And in the meantime, the First Federation had opportunity to withdraw completely from the quadrant. So never let it be said that Tiberius does not learn from his few mistakes.

"So when I see the base, James. When I step aboard a Fesarius-class, First Federation vessel, *then* I'll kill you."

Kirk said nothing. Balok, the diminutive alien starship commander, was stuffed and on display in Tiberius's base on the devastated mirror Earth. Kirk had no doubt that Tiberius planned to do the same to him.

Tiberius smiled thoughtfully. "Provided, of course, that you don't kill me first."

Kirk returned the smile. They both knew how this must end.

But for now, Tiberius ignored the future, reliving the past. "For ten years, Spock had been my intendant. If I can be said to have made a mistake in that respect, it was in thinking that his logic would be the equal of mine. It wasn't. He abandoned the order and security of the Empire I had created by moving against me. A coup. And *his* mistake was that he made it bloodless."

Kirk watched the stars as Tiberius droned on, explaining how he had easily escaped Earth, how he had personally brokered the Alliance between the Empire's greatest enemies—the Klingon Empire and the Cardassian Union.

Ten months later, the Alliance Armada had met a weakened Imperial Fleet at Wolf 359, decimated it, and advanced to Earth.

"Of course," Tiberius continued, "it was even more obvious that the Klingons and Cardassians would betray me. But that suited my plans. My goal was to have both my enemies—Spock and the Alliance—devastated by war, while I remained on the sidelines, waiting to choose my time to return and conquer the remnants of all who dared turn against me."

Kirk idly glanced to the main doors of the lounge where Commandants Riker and La Forge stood guard. Both men instantly and defiantly stared back at him, hands on their weapons.

Kirk found La Forge's gaze more disconcerting than Riker's. In the mirror universe, Tiberius had given the blind man multispectral ocular implants that appeared to be based on Borg technology—holographic lenses surrounded by dull gray metal rims, each set deeply into a weeping eye socket. Like insect legs, tendrils of nerve transducers pierced La Forge's forehead and cheeks to hold the implants in place.

"I had a hibernation ship waiting for me," Tiberius said, seemingly oblivious of the unspoken exchange between his guards and Kirk. "Left the battle unseen, joined my loyal generals, slipped into coldsleep for what was supposed to have been a year. Long enough for the Alliance to have crushed Spock's pitiful remnants of my Empire, and begin turning against themselves."

But something had gone wrong, Kirk knew. The hibernation ship had gone off course and that single year had become seventy-eight—a familiar enough number.

By then, the Terran Empire was little more than a despised memory; Spock was a dying rebel commander living on the run with his daughter, T'Val; and humans and Vulcans were slaves to the Alliance of Klingons and Cardassians first forged by Tiberius.

Finally, the hibernation ship carrying Tiberius and his generals had been discovered in deep space by a Klingon research vessel. Tiberius and the others had been awakened. When their identities had been confirmed, the Klingons altered course to bring them back to Qo'noS for war-crimes trials.

But en route, a female Klingon historian had succumbed to Tiberius's passions, become his lover, and helped him and his generals take over the ship. The gullible historian was a romantic who believed she was helping bring about a return to a time when history was made by individuals, not institutions.

The irony of that pattern of events, so similar from one universe to the next, did not escape Kirk.

"Of course, after all she had done for me, all she had made possible," Tiberius concluded, "I made sure that she died easily. Unlike her captain."

Kirk leaned against the bar, now.

"Am I boring you?" Tiberius asked.

"Always," Kirk said.

Instantly he regretted his answer. He was all too familiar

with the quick temper he saw rising in his counterpart's eyes.

Tiberius pointed to the Orion girl who had offered him a tray of food and drink. "Here," he commanded harshly. "Now."

The Orion picked up her tray and hurried toward him, her bare green feet silent on the carpeted deck.

Kirk took a step forward, knowing what was going to happen.

Tiberius's first blow knocked the tray aside, dramatically shattering and spilling its contents. His second struck the female, lifting her off her feet and dropping her to the deck.

Kirk charged without thought, and was stopped instantly by a double blast of disruptor energy against his back.

Then he was sprawled on the deck, too, beside the young Orion. For just a moment, he almost wished that Riker's and La Forge's disruptors had been set to full power, not just stun. The struggle would have been over then. He could rest.

Tiberius looked down at Kirk and the girl, both equally powerless and inconsequential to him. "You're so predictable, James. No wonder you never achieved anything in your life."

Then Tiberius reached down for the girl, keeping his eyes on Kirk the whole time. "Now watch this." His taunting smile was cruel. "Though I doubt you'll enjoy it as much as I will."

Kirk tried to shout out a challenge to Tiberius, but his throat was numb. He tried to reach out for the monster's boot, but his hand was weak, trembling, of no use.

Tiberius dragged the girl away and Kirk could do nothing except watch in frustrated helplessness.

And then Intendant Jean-Luc Picard's voice sounded from the combadge Tiberius wore on a chain around his neck.

*"Emperor, we are approaching the coordinates Kirk pro-
vided. Sensors confirm a large, carbonaceous asteroid is
present, as he described."*

"When will we arrive?" Tiberius asked.

*"With respect, Emperor, we should stand off and scan for
any sign of treachery."*

Tiberius's answer was a growl. "I have waited long enough,
Intendant."

It was clear Picard understood what was being asked of
him. *"At maximum warp, ten minutes,"* he answered.

"Prepare a shuttlecraft," Tiberius ordered. He stood over
the Orion where she lay near the agony booth, her leather
sash in his hand, its bindings ripped. Condescendingly, he
dropped it on her. "Stand up," he told her.

Eyes wide with fear, a thin trickle of green blood at the
corner of her mouth, she did, clutching the sash to her chest.

Tiberius looked back at Kirk. "Are you ready to complete your betrayal of the Federation?"

Kirk hid the sudden feeling of triumph that surged
through him. As he had anticipated, Tiberius was going to
take him to the First Federation base. It would be a fitting
place for them both to die.

Kirk struggled to his feet, sharp pains stabbing his back
where the disruptor blasts had hit.

"Good," Tiberius said. Then he turned to the Orion and
viciously struck her again.

He walked away from her as she fell to the deck, this
time unconscious. He glared at Kirk as if daring him to say
anything.

Kirk had nothing left to lose.

"Why?" he asked.

"Because I can," Tiberius answered. "And the heart-
break, James, is that you could have, too." His eyes peered
deep into Kirk's soul. "And you know it."

The only thing that kept Kirk from striking Tiberius then was the knowledge that sometime in the next hour he would be able to kill him, instead.

Holding his emotions, his dignity, his life in check, Kirk followed Tiberius to the hangar deck.

An hour more, Kirk promised himself.

What more could happen in an hour?

SIX

☆

From the command chair on the bridge of his own *Enterprise,* Jean-Luc Picard saw, but did not understand.

"Is that really a First Federation base?" he asked Spock.

The somber Vulcan sat to Picard's left, his dark, unreadable eyes fixed on the main viewer. "It is."

The viewer held a computer-enhanced image of an oblate asteroid at extreme magnification. It was slightly more than eleven hundred kilometers along its largest axis, slightly less than seven hundred along its smallest. Enhancement was necessary because Picard's *Enterprise* was more than forty light-years from the closest sun and the background glow of distant stars was not enough to illuminate the small dark body. By visible light alone, the asteroid would be noticed only as a fleeting shadow against the starry arc of the Milky Way.

Another enhanced area of the viewer showed a small dot of light representing the mirror *Enterprise,* approximately half a light-year ahead of Picard's ship and, at its current warp factor, ten minutes away from the asteroid.

In visible light, Spock had told Picard, the mirror

Enterprise would not even cast a shadow. Nor could it be detected by any known form of radiation or gravimetric distortion. Whatever technology masked the mirror ship's presence, its sophistication made the Romulan cloaking device appear to be little more than a magician's illusion of smoke and mirrors.

Tantalus technology, Spock had called it, though without offering any further explanation. And, apparently, the only reason that the *Enterprise*'s sensors had been able to pierce Tiberius's mask at all was because of the Tantalus tracking device Kirk had passed to Picard on Qo'noS.

"But why?" Picard asked Spock. "If Jim knew we were following him, why take Tiberius where he wanted to go? Why not give him false coordinates?"

"I assure you, Captain Kirk's actions are most logical," Spock said. "Since he cannot be certain that we *are* following him, he had to choose a destination where he would have an advantage on his own. Unlike the captain, Tiberius has not been to this base, otherwise he would not need directions to it."

Picard knew that Kirk had initiated first contact with the First Federation. Kirk's unorthodox response to Balok's test—a response which Starfleet historians had come to call the Corbomite Maneuver—was taught to all first-year cadets enrolled in Introductory Exopsychology. But Picard hadn't known that Kirk had continued interacting with the First Federation. Usually, any follow-up to an unanticipated first contact was handled by a team of specialists.

"Have you been to this base?" Picard asked Spock.

"I have."

Riker joined in from his chair to Picard's right. "What will we find there?"

"If luck is with us, nothing."

Picard and Riker exchanged a subtle look of surprise at

hearing a Vulcan mention luck. But then, Spock was not an ordinary Vulcan.

"And if luck isn't with us?" Picard asked.

"Starfleet's best estimates suggest the First Federation arose within the galactic halo, where stars are several orders of magnitude more distant from each other than in our own local space. The technology they developed for traveling between stars is completely different from our warp drives."

"In what way?" Riker asked.

"Unknown," Spock said simply. "After several diplomatic exchanges, two of which occurred at the base we are approaching, representatives of the First Federation decided that our Federation was insufficiently advanced to enter into full contact."

"The Prime Directive," Picard said.

"Precisely," Spock agreed. "They have their own version of it, and our diplomats were hardly in a position to disagree when the First Federation decided to invoke the principle of noninterference in their dealings with us."

"And the base?" Riker asked.

"Similar to one of our own spacedocks, Commander, but on a much vaster scale. The asteroid was ejected from its original solar system eons ago and is now forty-three light-years from the closest star. The First Federation chose it as a base of operations in this region because it is virtually impossible to detect except by happenstance, or unless its coordinates are known. Self-constructing devices hollowed out the asteroid and used the raw material they removed to fabricate living quarters, power plants, and a fleet of Fesarius-class ships."

"A fleet?" Picard sat back in his chair. Balok's *Fesarius* had been more than a kilometer and a half in diameter. It was faster and incalculably more powerful than even Starfleet's latest Sovereign-class vessels. "How many, exactly?"

"Seventeen when I was there," Spock said. "Though there were berths for up to fifty-one. The First Federation has a fondness for prime numbers."

"Captain Spock, is it at all likely, or even possible, that the First Federation would have left a *fleet* of their starships behind after all these years?"

"I calculate the probability that they did so to be ninety-two point five five percent."

Picard stared at the Vulcan, not knowing how to begin to question that number.

"Remember," Spock continued, "the First Federation employs self-constructing robotic devices to build their ships from asteroids. Thus the ships represent no economic drain to their culture and they can build and have built many more than they actually use at any one time."

"Incredible," Riker said.

"Not necessarily," Spock pointed out. "As the central worlds of the Federation have moved away from a money-based economic system, the real cost of even ships like the *Enterprise* is negligible. As installations such as Utopia Planitia become more automated, to construct a vessel such as this from the sands of Mars, using solar power, will cost nothing at all. In time, Starfleet's shipbuilding program is likely to become a self-organizing, self-supporting, and completely autonomous operation."

Picard stared at the tiny point of light on the viewer, chilled by the incalculable threat it contained. "And Tiberius is about to obtain that technology for himself."

"Unlikely," Spock said.

"You've calculated those odds as well?" Picard asked.

Spock hesitated, as if after a lifetime of Vulcan self-control, he still had to struggle with a sudden feeling of sadness. "There is an eighty-eight-point-two-percent probability that Captain Kirk will kill Tiberius at the base."

"I'll take that as good news," Riker said.

"And by doing so," Spock continued impassively, "there is a ninety-nine percent probability that Captain Kirk will die as a result."

"We will do everything in our power to prevent that from happening," Picard said.

Spock acknowledged the captain's promise with a slight nod, but no sign of relief or of optimism.

Then Data spoke up from his position at ops. "Captain Picard, the duplicate *Enterprise* is slowing."

Picard straightened up in his command chair. He had been expecting the changeover. "Match speed, Mr. Data. Continue to hold in the ship's wake."

The only good thing that could be said about the Tantalus mask was that it seemed to work both ways. While the mask was engaged on the mirror *Enterprise,* the sensors on Tiberius's ship appeared to have as much difficulty looking out as anyone else had looking in.

On Picard's *Enterprise,* Spock, La Forge, and Montgomery Scott had analyzed the tracking signal that Kirk had somehow managed to transmit from within the Tantalus mask. Their conclusion was that Tiberius would not be able to detect any pursuing vessel farther away than a quarter light-year. Especially if that vessel held a course that matched the infinitesimal zone of subspace sensor disruption that most starships generated as a result of their passage through warp space.

The instant Tiberius dropped his mask, though, Picard's *Enterprise* would set off every alarm on the emperor's ship.

Data gave a new update. "They are entering standard orbit of the asteroid," he reported.

"Battle stations," Picard ordered. He looked back at his security officer, Lieutenant Commander Zefram Sloane. The young, slightly built human, who traced his ancestry back to the first families to settle Alpha Centauri II, and from there to Africa, studied his security displays intently. "Just as in the simulations, Mr. Sloane. Punch through his shields first so the transporters can lock on to Kirk and beam him out. Then take out his warp capability."

Picard knew that being forty-three light-years from the closest solar system with nothing but impulse drive meant Tiberius's ship might as well be out in the Delta Quadrant with the real *Voyager.* Without warp capability, it would take decades for the mirror *Enterprise* to reach the nearest planet.

Riker leaned toward Picard. "Given what Spock has told us," he said, "we'll have to do something to keep Tiberius away from any First Federation ships in that base."

Picard nodded. He had already prepared plans for that contingency. "Will, you and Data will each lead an away team to respond to any beam-outs from the ship to the base." He turned to Spock. "Captain, we'll rely on you to guide the teams according to your memory of what's down there."

Spock stood. "I will accompany Commander Data's team."

Picard stood as well, smiled at the Vulcan. "You'll be able to communicate with both teams more efficiently from the bridge. We'll prepare the auxiliary science console for your use." Picard could see Spock readying a protest, and knew that argument would not be based in logic. "We'll get Jim out of there," Picard said gently. "Please remain on the bridge."

"That would be the . . . most logical course," Spock agreed.

Logical, Picard thought, *but not the best.*

Riker stood up. "Data."

The android left the ops console and was instantly replaced by Lieutenant Karo, a Bolian. Beside him, Lieutenant Ilydia Maran, the ship's only Trill on this mission, remained at navigation.

Data and Riker moved quickly toward the closer of the two turbolifts serving the bridge.

Picard saw Spock sit at the auxiliary science station.

Everything was accounted for. Everything would go as planned. Picard sat back in his command chair.

Then the mirror *Enterprise* dropped her Tantalus mask.

Only seconds later, alarms screamed on Picard's bridge as sensors detected the first quantum torpedoes being launched from that ship.

"Evasive maneuvers," Picard said calmly.

The structural-integrity field generators whined as the massive vessel suddenly changed course. The inertial dampeners lagged and Picard clutched the arms of his chair to keep from being tossed to the deck.

The first singularity explosions flared against the forward shields.

But Picard ordered his ship to continue its rush for the First Federation base.

If Tiberius gained control of what might be hidden within it, then the fate of two universes would be at risk.

And Picard knew that to prevent that from happening, even the life of James T. Kirk was expendable.

SEVEN

☆

The type-7 shuttlecraft spiraled from the hangar bay on the mirror *Enterprise* as phaser fire lit up the massive ship's shields like an exploding sun.

Inside the cramped shuttlecraft, Tiberius was at the helm. Kirk struggled uselessly against the induction ropes holding him in his passenger seat.

"Predictable," Tiberius said. His hands moved quickly, expertly over the controls. "Your word is worthless."

"I don't know what you're talking about," Kirk said. He saw the distant stars spin dizzyingly beyond the viewports as the small shuttle shot through the overlapping boundaries of the forcefields protecting the mirror *Enterprise*. The forcefields flashed off and on in an ever-changing pattern in order to allow the shuttle to safely escape.

"I don't need sensor reports to know that's the *Enterprise* firing on me," Tiberius said. "You betrayed me, just as Spock did."

"Picard was ordered to find you," Kirk told him. "With or without me. So why're you surprised that he did?"

Tiberius entered a complex series of flight commands,

as if he planned to put the shuttle on automatic pilot. But Kirk didn't understand why he'd do that in the middle of an attack when constant course adjustments would be necessary.

Multiple flares from quantum fire flickered through the viewports. Kirk braced for impact. Tiberius pressed a single control.

The fire was extinguished.

The spiraling stars dimmed, greatly reduced in numbers as if the viewports had just been heavily tinted.

The shuttlecraft's readouts showed that all evasive maneuvers had stopped. It flew straight and true for the asteroid below. The *Enterprise* no longer targeted it. The battle lay behind them.

"We're masked," Kirk said.

"James, did you ever stop to think why we didn't just beam down?"

At once, Kirk knew the answer. Transporter beams could be traced. But a shuttle protected by a Tantalus mask was undetectable.

Unless that shuttle carried a Tantalus homing beacon.

"By the way," Tiberius said as he leaned back from the shuttle's controls. "Your homing beacon is no longer operative."

But Kirk wasn't about to give Tiberius any satisfaction. "What beacon?"

Tiberius sighed as if he were dealing with a child. "The beacon I allowed you to steal from my base on Earth. The beacon I allowed you to activate when we left Qo'noS. So I could test my new *Fesarius* against a Starfleet vessel."

Kirk shook his head. "Your problem is, you think everyone's out to get you."

"James, everyone *is* out to get me."

Kirk didn't reply. He knew that there was only one way

for a shuttlecraft to enter the First Federation base below. And if Picard had come this far, then he must have Spock with him, and Spock would know what had to be done.

Kirk caught Tiberius staring at him, as if suspicious of Kirk's continued silence.

But Kirk still said nothing. There was no need to. Tiberius was in his last few minutes of life.

Like a mind reader, Tiberius said, "Be patient, James. You'll have your chance."

"I know." Kirk settled back in his chair, oblivious now of the binding induction ropes that held him captive.

He would not have to wait much longer.

"Captain Picard," Sloane said from his security station, "the shuttlecraft has disappeared!"

"It is employing the Tantalus mask," Spock confirmed.

The bridge rocked as the *Enterprise* took another phaser hit from its duplicate.

The strained voice of Geordi La Forge came over the bridge speakers. *"Engineering to bridge."*

"A moment, Mr. La Forge," Picard replied. He twisted around in his chair to look at Spock. "Is Kirk's homing beacon still on the ship, or is it on the shuttle?"

"The beacon stopped transmitting fifty-two seconds ago," Spock said. "Just before the shuttlecraft launched."

Another hit shook the bridge.

"Captain!" La Forge said insistently. *"The other ship is concentrating on the critical field boundaries above the nacelles."*

"They've had months to discover every weak point of this ship," Picard said, still not completely recovered from the shock he had felt when the Klingons identified a second *Enterprise* in orbit of Qo'noS. . . .

• • •

Montgomery Scott hadn't been surprised, though. On board Picard's *Enterprise,* he had studied the Klingons' sensor records and proudly proclaimed, "I knew it wasn't a transporter!"

Almost eight months ago, the *Enterprise* had been captured by a force of Klingon and Cardassian infiltrators from the mirror universe. They had taken the ship to a secret complex hidden in the vast plasma storms of the Goldin Discontinuity.

At the complex, a mysterious structure resembling a spacedock was being constructed. As it neared completion, the *Enterprise* was moved within it, and it became obvious to everyone present that the device was some type of transporter which would be used to send the *Enterprise* into the mirror universe to serve Tiberius.

But despite what everyone else thought about the device, Montgomery Scott was a lone voice in the star-filled wilderness, constantly proclaiming to anyone who would listen that the device could not be a transporter because no functioning transporter could ever be made that large.

When the device had been briefly activated, transporter effects had been recorded, but the *Enterprise* had not vanished.

Only portions of her had: critical computer cores, certain bridge consoles, even Picard's command chair.

Starfleet specialists had patiently listened to Scott's objections, but the official finding was that captains Kirk and Picard had successfully defeated an enemy operation to beam the *Enterprise* to the mirror universe. The device, which had been destroyed shortly after the *Enterprise* had been recovered, was identified as a Very Large Transporter Array that utilized "advanced" techniques.

That was the end of the investigation.

But Scott had not accepted that conclusion.

For good reason.

"It was a *replicator!*" Scott had proclaimed to Picard at Qo'noS. "Don't ye see, Captain? Why steal *one* starship when ye can replicate an *entire fleet!*"

Picard and La Forge had listened carefully to Scott's analysis of the procedure. How the so-called transporter device had actually been a one-to-one replicator. If Kirk and Picard had not interfered, Scott estimated that, given the plasma energy and raw-asteroid mass available in the Goldin Discontinuity, Tiberius could have replicated a Sovereign-class starship every eight and a half days.

Of course, Scott had explained, not every component aboard a starship *could* be replicated. That was why precisely focused transporter beams had removed certain critical pieces of equipment, particularly computer and control units.

Picard had interrupted Scott's report at that point. "Mr. Scott, in addition to the ship's computers, Tiberius also stole my chair."

Scott had shrugged. "From an engineering point of view, I agree that makes no sense. But maybe it meant something personal."

Having faced the concrete evidence of a duplicate *Enterprise* which had beamed Kirk from the medical facility on Qo'noS and then vanished while in orbit, Picard was inclined to accept Mr. Scott's explanation. But the missing chair still bothered him.

He could understand why Tiberius would want to steal one of Kirk's command chairs. *But why mine?* Picard had wondered.

Unless, he had thought, *the chair isn't meant for Tiberius. . . .*

Now the bridge reverberated with the explosive concussions of a sustained phaser barrage.

"Shields at sixty-three percent," Sloane warned.

Picard polled his bridge crew. "Are we making *any* headway against them?"

Spock responded first. "Their shield signatures do not correspond to Starfleet technology. I surmise that the duplicate *Enterprise* has been retrofitted with a different defensive system."

"Tantalus technology?" Picard asked.

"Unknown at this time," Spock replied.

The main viewer suddenly flared with light and a power surge blew out two life-support consoles in fountains of sparks.

"What was that?" Picard demanded.

"Some kind of energy pulse," Sloane said.

"Captain Picard!" La Forge said over the comm link to engineering. *"That power surge took out two warp-containment backup systems. We can't take much more."*

Picard's hands gripped the arms of his chair. *We're being beaten by a reflection of my own ship!* It was clear that Tiberius had outfitted his mirror *Enterprise* with new and different weaponry and shields.

"Picard to Riker. What is the status of the away teams?"

Riker's reply was instant. "Sir, both teams are suited and ready to go. But we can't beam through the asteroid's surface to the interior. Sensors indicate it's layered with degenerate matter that can block all subspace transmissions."

Picard turned to Spock again. "If we can't beam into the base, how *do* we get in?"

Spock raised an eyebrow. "I was not aware that beaming would not be possible. As I recall, there is only one main opening into the interior that is suitable for vessels." Spock answered Picard's next question before Picard could ask it. "That opening is offset three degrees from the asteroid's central axis at its nominal north pole, within a large, distinctive crater. However, the passage is curved, so beaming through it might not be possible either."

"Understood," Picard said. "Helm, withdraw from the asteroid, warp four."

A second later, the enhanced image of the asteroid shrunk swiftly on the viewer. Two final flashes of phaser fire rocked the ship, and then the engagement was over.

"No pursuit," Lieutenant Maran said from the nav console.

"Slow to impulse, continue to withdraw," Picard said. He was aware of Spock standing beside him, hands folded behind his back.

"I put it to you," Spock said, "that however difficult it is to engage the mirror *Enterprise,* it will be impossible to engage a Fesarius-class ship. If, indeed, such a ship is present within the base."

"Have no fear, Captain Spock. I'm not abandoning Jim. Just changing tactics."

"Fear is illogical," Spock said.

"In this case," Picard replied, "I strongly disagree."

Then he gave his new orders to Riker and Data.

As far as the captain of the real *Enterprise* was concerned, this battle was far from over.

EIGHT

☆

Even if there had been light to see by, the shuttlecraft would have remained imperceptible as it landed on the nameless asteroid.

Inside the small craft, Kirk heard a scraping sound as the shuttle's landing skids made contact with the asteroid's surface. There was no other sensation. Local gravity was so inconsequential that it did not make itself felt over the shuttle's artificial field.

Tiberius powered down the shuttle. The interior lighting dropped to a warm amber glow. Kirk saw him shut off even life-support. In less than two hours, the temperature inside would drop below −200°C. Whatever Tiberius's plans, Kirk realized, he didn't intend to return to this shuttle.

Tiberius left Kirk tied to his passenger chair and stepped to the rear storage compartments. The forward viewports were completely obscured and Kirk watched Tiberius's reflection as if in a dark mirror.

Tiberius was putting on an environmental suit.

The shuttlecraft had no airlock.

If Tiberius opened either hatch, Kirk would suffocate within a minute.

He twisted his arms, but the induction ropes didn't move. As long as power ran through them, they were as solid as hull metal.

Kirk heard heavy footsteps. Looked into the viewports. Saw Tiberius standing behind him in a Starfleet-issue environmental suit, the helmet under his arm.

Tiberius also looked into the viewports, watching Kirk's reflection even as Kirk watched his.

"Do you understand now?" Tiberius asked.

Kirk stared into the reflective surface, and for a disorienting moment it seemed to Kirk as if the two images were one, and he were holding this conversation with himself.

"Understand what?" Kirk asked.

"Where you are. What is about to happen. What this shuttlecraft is."

With the suddenness of a knife slash, Kirk realized what Tiberius meant. And even in the dim lighting, Tiberius obviously saw that understanding blossom within his counterpart. "That's right. You have reached the end. You *will* die. And this shuttlecraft is your tomb."

Tiberius put a hand on the back of Kirk's chair. "Think of it, James. At the temperature of interstellar space, your flesh will become harder than rock. No decay. No corruption. You will become an eternal monument to my greatest victory."

Kirk wrenched both arms against the induction rope. "Never."

"Ah, well," Tiberius said. "Predictable to the end." Then he twisted his helmet into position, locked it, and tapped the controls that switched on the suit's life-support systems.

Kirk stared in furious frustration as Tiberius turned his back on him and walked to the rear of the shuttlecraft. To the aft loading hatch.

"No!" Kirk shouted. This wasn't what Tiberius had said. He was going to take Kirk *into* the base. They were going to be together. Kirk was going to have his chance to attack his dark reflection and destroy him.

But Tiberius had lied.

In his way, the emperor was as predictable as he so often claimed Kirk to be.

Kirk's next shout carried no words. It was primitive, inarticulate, the cry of prey as the predator's fangs closed over a defenseless throat.

In the reflection, Kirk saw Tiberius reach out to a control panel on the bulkhead.

Then all the lights went out.

In the absolute darkness of the shuttle, Kirk felt the vibration of inner machinery coming to life beneath the deck.

He knew it had to be the loading-hatch motors coming to life, sealing his death.

He held his breath.

The *Enterprise* came about and raced for the asteroid at warp factor six.

"Mirror *Enterprise* is diverting all power to shields," Sloane reported.

Picard nodded. That's what he would do in the same situation, if he had the same proven forcefields protecting his ship: brace to take the first blow of an attack in order to see what his opponent's strategy was.

But Picard's strategy had nothing to do with the mirror *Enterprise*.

"And . . . *mark!*" Lieutenant Maran called out.

Instantly Picard's *Enterprise* dropped to warp one.

The sudden pop of the Heisenberg compensators rang throughout the ship.

"Hangar bay one," La Forge announced from the bridge speakers. *"The* Tombaugh *is away."*

"Hangar bay two," Montgomery Scott added. *"So is the* Lowell."

"Resume warp six," Picard ordered.

The ship smoothly accelerated beyond the boundaries of normal space.

Behind her, protected within the high walls of what had at first appeared to be an ordinary crater slightly more than two kilometers across, two shuttlecraft used maneuvering thrusters to change their orientation until they hung nose down. Moments later, the impulse vents of both small craft glowed and the shuttles dove down toward the crater's floor, until it was apparent that within the crater was the disguised opening to the installation hidden deep within the asteroid.

The crater had not been in the location Spock had remembered, though. A century earlier, when Spock had been here last, the asteroid had had a stable spin, and though it did not have a magnetic field, the Federation's mapping conventions would therefore have used the spin to identify a north and south pole at either end of its rotational axis.

But sometime in the past century, the spin had been perturbed. Now the asteroid wobbled through a convoluted rotational period with no absolute axis. Picard hoped that meant the First Federation had stripped it of all valuable equipment, including inertial dampeners to control its spin, and the undefeatable starships that were Tiberius's goal.

But since hope was not enough to guarantee the survival of the Federation, Picard listened with satisfaction as the shuttlecrafts' commanders reported in: Riker on the *Clyde Tombaugh;* Data on the *Percival Lowell.*

Though high-speed warp transport was a technique slowly being perfected in Starfleet, and becoming used more often in emergency situations, Data had not been aware of any attempt to beam two fully crewed shuttlecraft from cargo transporters at the same time, while in warp. Data had also not been aware of any reason that it couldn't be done. Since Picard rarely let the impossible stand in his way, the maneuver had been attempted and had succeeded.

Whatever else Tiberius might hope to discover within the First Federation base, now he would also find two fully-armed Starfleet away teams.

"Sir," Sloane suddenly reported. "The mirror *Enterprise* is changing orbit. She's moving toward the entry crater."

That had been Picard's main concern: Would the commander of the other ship detect the shuttlecraft as they beamed in?

Apparently, the commander had.

"All about," Picard ordered. "Stand by on phasers and quantum torpedoes." Now the only way his away teams would be able to stop Tiberius was if *he* could stop the second *Enterprise*.

Picard wondered who its commander was.

But given the ship's actions so far, he was certain he already knew the answer to that question. The same answer explained why Picard's command chair had been taken. It *was* personal.

So as Kirk battled himself somewhere on the asteroid's surface, Picard now prepared for a battle with himself in space.

Kirk's lungs strained. His body tensed. He knew the instant the loading hatch opened and the shuttlecraft explosively decompressed that he would have to exhale in order to prevent rupturing his lungs. But some oxygen would remain in his bloodstream.

That he would only, at most, be buying himself another

few seconds of consciousness and of life did not trouble him. If he had to, he would struggle for only one single extra second.

But in the same moment he had drawn what might be his final breath, he had come up with a plan.

The induction ropes holding him to the passenger chair were powered by current from the shuttlecraft's power distribution system. Tiberius had shut down the shuttle's generators, so all the power being used for the Tantalus mask, emergency lights, the hatch motors, *and* the induction ropes was coming from the fusion batteries.

And the battery controls were in the center of the flight console.

Kirk was certain he could reach them with his foot, switch them off with a kick from his boot heel.

With their power supply cut off, the induction ropes would release him, and he could close the hatch and repressurize the shuttle.

He estimated the action would require him to remain conscious in full vacuum for almost a minute, but Starfleet trained its cadets to function at least that long.

Kirk's only concern was that he would still remember that training. These days, he sometimes found it hard to believe that he had ever been a cadet at all.

The rumbling beneath the deck stopped. But just for a moment.

Kirk listened intently for the instant rush of air that would accompany the opening of the hatch. Instead, he heard a hum, and then the shuttlecraft filled with bright blue light.

The hum was followed by silence; the blue light by the slowly restored glow of the emergency lights.

His lungs threatening to burst, Kirk looked up into the viewports so he could see what Tiberius was doing at the back of the shuttlecraft.

Tiberius was gone.

Kirk exhaled.

There was only one explanation possible: a transporter pad at the back of the shuttle. And with that realization, Kirk understood Tiberius's plans at once. While Picard would be looking for Tiberius in this universe, Tiberius had just beamed into the mirror universe. There, he would make his way to the center of the First Federation base and, by beaming back to this universe, would have his pick of any Fesarius-class ship left behind.

It was the same strategy T'Val had used to avoid the Alliance on Earth's moon when she had abducted Kirk and taken him to meet with the mirror Spock.

But Kirk would see to it that this time the strategy wouldn't work.

He shifted in his chair, swung his foot up, then brought it down on the battery-power controls. On his second try, he was successful.

At once, the emergency lights faded out again, gravity disappeared, and the induction ropes became limp strands of soft carbon fiber.

Kirk began floating out of his chair, held down only by his arms. He braced his knees under the flight console, then yanked one arm free of the ropes, then the other. A moment later, he was spinning through the shuttlecraft, slowly floating to the deck in almost absolute darkness. He estimated the asteroid's natural gravity was about one-twenty-fifth of Earth-normal. It was not going to be helpful.

Moving cautiously, Kirk gave a small push with his hands and floated from the deck to the pilot's chair. He could see the arc of the Milky Way through the viewports, so he at least knew where the flight console was beneath them. But the light of those distant stars was not enough for him to see anything else in the shuttle.

He used one hand to grasp the pilot's chair and keep himself in position, then lightly ran his other hand over the console, searching for the master generator controls. They were mechanical, designed to be used when the computer had shut down.

He found them: three small rocker switches, almost antique in design.

And an instant before he switched them on, he asked himself what he would do if he were Tiberius.

Slowly, he moved his hand from the master controls, certain the generators had been rigged to explode the moment they were restarted.

Instead, he found the center of the flight console and began pressing the control surface until he hit the battery switches again.

The emergency lights returned. Gravity slowly increased. The stars outside the viewport vanished as the Tantalus mask was reestablished.

Kirk moved quickly to the back of the shuttle and discovered a transporter pad recessed into the deck. He recognized it as a nonstandard design. Two detached deck panels were beside it. One had been removed to reveal the hidden pad. The other seemed to have hidden only an empty storage area of about the same size.

Kirk opened a storage locker and found the shuttle's remaining environmental suits. Before putting one of the suits on, he searched for and located a tricorder. He scanned the suit with it, looking for any sign of sabotage. He found none.

A minute later he was in the suit, locking the helmet in place. He activated the suit's life-support systems, then used the tricorder again to determine if there were any slow leaks. Again, he found nothing.

Kirk studied the transporter controls on the bulkhead, set them to duplicate the last beam-out, used the tricorder one final time to be sure the transporter wasn't rigged to self-destruct, then energized the system.

The shuttlecraft dissolved into light around him. He prepared himself for the change in gravity he would feel when he rematerialized on the asteroid in the mirror universe. He knew there wouldn't be a shuttlecraft there, so he expected to appear on its barren surface.

The light of the transporter effect faded as did the artificial gravity field of the shuttle.

Once again, Kirk was in near-total darkness, except for the river of stars that formed the Milky Way.

He waited for his feet to connect with the asteroid's surface.

They didn't.

He looked down—an awkward movement in his suit—and saw stars. Only stars. They continued their sweep through space beneath him.

In the same shocked instant, Kirk's inner ear informed him he was beginning to spiral in zero gravity.

Kirk consulted the tricorder.

From the quantum signature of an errant gas molecule, the device confirmed that Kirk *was* in the mirror universe.

But the asteroid was gone.

Kirk spun slowly in empty interstellar space, forty-three light-years from the nearest star.

Completely alone. Completely without hope.

He could almost hear Tiberius laughing.

The mirror *Enterprise* changed course. Instead of continuing her heading for the asteroid's entry crater, she swung about to face her attacker, bow to bow. The first spread of quantum torpedoes followed an instant later.

"Mr. Maran, maintain heading," Picard commanded. "Phaser batteries, target torpedoes and fire at will."

Picard knew his ship. The *Enterprise* could withstand at least another dozen torpedo strikes without compromising her shields. Under normal circumstances, even the first few phaser hits—or whatever kind of energy the other ship was firing—would not be of immediate concern.

The problem was that the commander of the mirror *Enterprise* knew every weak spot in Picard's ship's design. If the enemy's phasers continued to hit at the shield boundary overlaps by the warp nacelles, the *Enterprise*'s shields would become inadequate to protect the ship, even while at fifty percent of their optimal strength. And there was little that Picard could do about that under present conditions. Starfleet knew about the subtle design flaw and had scheduled the installation of reconfigured shield generators for *next* month.

Picard felt his bridge rock with the first impacts of quantum torpedoes against forward shields. At the same moment, energy beams played over the nacelles.

"He's going for those weak points again, Captain," La Forge warned from engineering. *"Another minute and he'll punch right through."*

Picard knew the game his opponent was playing. But he was convinced that the commander of the mirror *Enterprise* had orders that made fighting Picard's *Enterprise* a lesser priority. That commander's overriding concern had to be the two shuttles already heading deep into the base to intercept Tiberius, assuming that Tiberius had followed the same route in his masked shuttle.

Picard intended to let him get back to his primary mission.

"A second spread of torpedoes has been fired," Sloane reported.

"I want half of them to hit," Picard ordered. "Mr. La Forge, stand by to initiate venting."

"Standing by," La Forge confirmed.

Picard smiled tightly at the resignation in his engineer's voice. La Forge was not convinced that Picard's plan would work. He probably wasn't convinced it was sane.

"Torpedo impacts in five seconds," Sloane said. He began counting down, and at "Zero," Picard said, "Mr. La Forge—now!"

Just as before, the instant the first quantum torpedoes detonated against the *Enterprise*'s forward shields, the mirror *Enterprise* laid in a devastating phaser barrage concentrating on the nacelles.

But this time, something else happened at the same time.

From each nacelle, Geordi La Forge vented ten percent of the *Enterprise*'s antimatter supply. The antiproton gas clouds expanded rapidly in the vacuum of space, trailing from the nacelles and collecting against the aft shields like wind caught in a billowing sail.

Three seconds later, every transporter pad in the *Enterprise* beamed gas cannisters into those clouds; medical oxygen, biolab nitrogen, the type of gas didn't matter.

The near-instantaneous reaction of the normal matter of the cannisters and their pressurized contents with the antimatter was like igniting a cloud of vaporized hydrazine in an unbreakable bottle.

Instantly the full interior volume of space surrounding the *Enterprise* and contained within her shields lit up with an explosive plasma. For a handful of seconds, what had once been a starship now appeared to be an ovoid nova.

On the bridge, Picard and the others clapped their hands to their ears as the sound of that explosive concussion thundered through the hull. But Picard did not have to give his next orders over that deafening roar. La Forge and his engineering team, along with Sloane and the bridge crew, knew exactly what they were to do and the sequence they must follow. Picard's plan had been that precise.

As the matter-antimatter explosion began to fade, La Forge performed an emergency shutdown of the ship's warp engines and matter-antimatter reactor. He then explosively released the warp-core hatch and began a three-minute warp-core ejection countdown.

At the same time on the bridge, Lieutenant Commander Sloane took a deep breath and shut down the ship's shields, including the low-power navigational forcefields that swept interstellar dust from the bow. At the helm console, Lieutenant Maran switched off the autostabilizing thruster systems as well, then reluctantly removed her hands from all other controls.

The end result was that the *Enterprise* burst out from a gaseous fireball, trailing wisps of glowing plasma, slowly pitching stern over bow while spiraling to port.

Her hull was blackened. Her running lights flickered and went out. Her warp-core hatch spun away like a leaf in a storm.

Picard's ship was powerless, out of control, and three minutes away from completely losing her warp capability, if she hadn't already lost it.

Exactly as Picard had intended.

In the darkened bridge, Picard tapped his finger against the side of his chair, waiting for his opponent's next move.

If this had simply been a contest between two starship captains, each master of his own fate, Picard knew that the mirror *Enterprise* would approach from behind and either pick away at its victim with pinpoint phaser strikes until Picard signaled for surrender, or unleash all its firepower against the unshielded *Enterprise* and turn the ship into a cloud of ionized gas.

But Picard suspected that the commander of the mirror *Enterprise* was not his own master. No one who served Tiberius could be.

Long seconds passed. "We're being scanned," Sloane said.

Picard had anticipated that. His opponent's sensors would show that the *Enterprise* was running on emergency power, her warp engines offline, and her warp core now two minutes, thirty seconds from ejection.

On the ship's internal communications systems, recordings from multiple disaster-training holodeck scenarios ran, filling the radio and subspace spectrums with emergency calls detailing casualties, system failures, and desperate pleas to abandon ship.

The main viewer showed the stars rushing by as the *Enterprise* spun, just in case the mirror *Enterprise* was able to pick up that visual-information channel as well.

"Yes!" Sloane suddenly shouted from his station. "She's resuming course for the entry crater!"

The bridge crew cheered.

"An admirable bluff," Spock said to Picard.

"Thank you," Picard replied.

But he knew the game was far from over.

NINE

─────────── ☆ ───────────

Kirk did not need Spock to tell him that panic was illogical.

Or that rapid, unchecked breathing would also use up his suit's air supply much too quickly.

So, instead, he concentrated on fighting every instinct in his body, relaxing every muscle, breathing slowly, in full acceptance of his situation.

And then, alone, floating forty-three light-years from the nearest planet and nearest hope for survival, Kirk examined his options.

First, he put aside the problem of why the First Federation asteroid did not exist in this location in the mirror universe. Every other astronomical body existed in both universes. Whatever made this one different was a question he could only answer later.

What he needed to focus on now was how Tiberius had planned to escape this same dilemma.

Once again Kirk consulted his tricorder. It confirmed that the mirror-universe coordinates into which he had just beamed were the same as those Tiberius had used only a few minutes before him. Since Tiberius was no longer here, that meant that Tiberius had already made use of some means to return to Kirk's universe, with the obvious intention of reappearing within the First Federation asteroid base.

And that implied that Tiberius had had access to *another* transporter. But how? And where?

Kirk's mind raced. Since it was highly unlikely that Tiberius had arranged for another ship to be present at these coordinates in this universe—especially considering he had not known where Kirk would lead him—Tiberius must have had some sort of transporter device *with* him.

Kirk immediately pictured the empty storage area he had seen hidden below the deck of the shuttlecraft.

"A portable transporter?" Kirk said aloud.

He wasn't certain if it was possible to build a transporter small enough to be carried by one person. But the Borg had developed miniaturized, personal transporter technology. And if the transporter Tiberius used was in any way based on Balok's Tantalus technology, then Kirk was willing to accept that such a device was not only possible, but probably inevitable.

And that meant . . .

Kirk activated his tricorder, had it sweep for life signs.

It found one.

Human, two point three kilometers distant, moving away at a relative twenty-two kilometers per hour.

Tiberius.

Kirk's pulse rate quickened. He had another chance.

He quickly directed his suit's maneuvering system to upload his counterpart's position, heading, and velocity from the tricorder, then lay in an intercept trajectory.

"Intercept trajectory calculated," the suit's computer stated.

"Engage," Kirk said.

At once he felt his backpack thrusters swing him around with a series of short microbursts, then hold him in position. A second later, he gasped as his backpack suddenly kicked him forward. For a few moments, he felt sharp pressure on his back, and then the thrusters cut out and all sensation of movement ceased.

But the readouts on the small display inside his helmet showed that he was now moving at forty-four kilometers per hour relative to his target.

"Target intercept in six minutes, fifty-five seconds," the computer announced.

Tiberius was still too far away for Kirk to be able to see him, and there was so little light that, without the tricorder, Kirk knew the odds were good that he might pass within meters of his enemy, unseen.

But Kirk couldn't allow that to happen. He had known orbital skydivers who had dropped from their shuttles without atmospheric parachutes, counting on their ability to rendezvous with a second skydiver only a few thousand meters above the ground so both could land in tandem on a single chute. A missed linkup meant an abrupt stop a few seconds later.

Kirk, though, knew he was in the opposite position. If he failed to reach Tiberius before Tiberius energized his portable transporter, then Kirk would continue to fall through space at forty-four kilometers per hour for more than a billion years before he had the slightest chance of coming near another world.

And the only way Kirk would accept that fate would be if he knew Tiberius fell with him.

Controlled only by its stationkeeping thrusters, the mirror *Enterprise* headed toward the asteroid, as if it intended to crash bow-first.

But its target was the entry crater. The ship slowly passed alongside its ragged walls, then slipped down and into the curved, kilometer-wide passageway that led to the asteroid's hollow interior.

The mirror ship itself was 680 meters long, more than half the width of the passage. A Starfleet crew would have found piloting the huge vessel within the narrow passage very similar to maneuvering within the tight confines of a spacedock. But the mirror *Enterprise* was not controlled by an experienced Starfleet crew.

It veered too close to one wall of the passage, overcorrected, veered uncertainly toward another, then came to a hesitant, relative stop as if to back up.

But backing up was not an option.

Several more kilometers along the passage lay the vessel's targets.

Two tiny shuttlecraft.

When the mirror *Enterprise* caught them, they would not have a chance.

"And it's . . . gone," Sloane reported.

Instantly, Picard issued his orders. "Cancel warp-core ejection. Mr. Maran, bring this ship into trim and set course for the entry crater."

In space, the *Enterprise* slowed her wild tumbling to come about.

Once more, she set course for the asteroid.

Minutes after the mirror *Enterprise* entered the passageway to hunt Picard's two shuttlecraft, Picard's ship entered to hunt the hunter.

"Intercept in thirty seconds," the computer announced.

Kirk looked up from his helmet display to the starfield directly ahead.

There!

He saw a shadow blot out a handful of stars. A rapidly growing silhouette of—

The shadow changed shape. Tiberius was turning—he'd set a proximity alarm.

Kirk slapped his tricorder to a magnetic holder on his belt, then used his forearm controls to override his suit's computer.

"Intercept in fifteen seconds."

His quarry began sliding sideways against the stars, using his own suit thrusters to change course and evade pursuit.

Kirk adjusted his own vector to stay on target, moving close enough to see that Tiberius carried a large rectangular object, the size of the nonstandard transporter pad Kirk had seen recessed into the shuttlecraft's deck.

"Five seconds," the computer warned.

A series of yellow lights began to glow on the object as Kirk's counterpart changed direction again, slowly spiraling as he focused on operating the object's controls instead of controlling his thrusters.

Kirk forced himself to slow his own approach but not as smoothly as the computer might have. He began to wobble, saw he was about to miss Tiberius.

A large, circular lens on the object began to pulse with blue light. The color was unmistakable: a transporter being energized.

If Tiberius managed to beam out in time, Kirk knew the transporter pad would remain behind. But given its size, he doubted it would have enough power for a second transport. He *had* to reach Tiberius before the full transporter effect could begin.

Tiberius looked away from the portable pad and in the blue

glow from the dematerializer lens, Kirk saw his own face looking back at him. Then Tiberius activated his thrusters and began to slide in another direction.

The transporter pad's inertia made it lag a moment, until Tiberius pulled it closer to him.

Kirk saw his opportunity. He threw out one hand as he passed by and managed to snag the edge of the pad.

Now both he and Tiberius started to spin slowly around the pad's center of gravity. The spinning movement was disorienting. Kirk's arm felt increasingly heavy.

Tiberius pulled himself closer to the pad. He stretched out his other hand, trying to touch the pad's glowing lens.

Kirk reached out for the lens as well. He had to block Tiberius. If the transporter effect locked on to Tiberius's hand, it would propagate along his body and send him back to Kirk's universe.

Two meters separated Kirk from his counterpart. The lens was less than a meter from each of them. The two men could see each other in the light it gave off.

Kirk's fingers began to lose their hold on the pad.

Balance shifted again. A wild oscillation was added to the spin.

Tiberius grinned.

Kirk tightened his grip, then brought his hand back from reaching for the lens and slapped at all his thruster controls at once.

With a violent kick, the unbalanced combination of transporter pad and two spacesuited figures began a high-speed rotation in a third direction. Tiberius's hand fell away from the lens as he scrabbled to maintain his own hold on the pad.

Then Kirk's hand slipped free and he fell away from the pad and his enemy as if falling into a bottomless pit.

But as he stared back at the pad, he saw that the sudden change in mass had altered the spin rate again, forcing Tiberius to lose his grip as well.

Kirk saw the portable transporter pad—the only way back to his universe—spiral away, the light from its lens flashing as it spun. In seconds, it was only a twinkling blue dot of light.

Kirk reached for his tricorder so he could instruct his suit computer to lock on to the pad and thrust him toward it.

But his belt was empty, the tricorder knocked loose.

In his surprise, Kirk looked toward his belt, then realized that by doing so, he had lost his visual fix on the receding pad.

He looked back at it, couldn't see it.

But he did see a speeding shadow against the stars.

Tiberius was thrusting toward the pad.

Kirk thrusted toward Tiberius.

On the main viewer, the rough, stone walls of the passage curved slowly by, its pockmarked surface thrown into high relief by the *Enterprise*'s powerful navigation searchlights.

Picard sat forward in his command chair, alert to every background sound on his bridge.

Somehow, the First Federation had introduced degenerate matter into the asteroid's crust, making it completely impenetrable to sensors. Only line-of-sight scans could tell him what was directly ahead of his ship.

Thus, there was no way to know how far ahead the mirror *Enterprise* was. It might appear at any moment around the next curve in the passage, dead ahead, or even nestled to the side in one of the passageway's random widenings. And if that ship had activated its Tantalus mask, Picard would have no warning of its presence until the mask dropped and a torpedo was launched.

While a single torpedo might not do much damage to the *Enterprise* herself, it could cause the stone passage to collapse, locking Picard's ship in position, unable to defend herself from a subsequent barrage.

Picard looked up as Lieutenant Karo issued a report from ops. "Sir, sensors continue to pick up significant traces of hydrazine."

"That means they're still maneuvering through this on their reaction-control thrusters," Sloane added quickly.

Though Picard generally did not like his officers stating the obvious, he allowed himself a smile at Sloane's enthusiasm. Lieutenant Maran was skillfully taking this *Enterprise* through the passage on impulse propulsion alone. So far, she had used reaction-control thrusters only twice.

On the other hand, if the mirror *Enterprise* was staffed with an inexperienced crew, then it was even more galling that the vessel had twice fought the *Enterprise* herself to a standstill.

"Coming up on fifty-kilometer mark," Maran announced from the helm. "Mark."

Picard turned in his chair, looked back at Spock. "Captain Spock, do you recall how far this passage extends?"

"At the time I visited this base," Spock said, "we entered in the *Fesarius*. That vessel traversed the passage in less than a minute."

Once more Picard marvelled at First Federation technology. Here he had been impressed that one of his officers was able to safely guide the *Enterprise* through what was little more than a rabbit hole, achieving a speed of almost 100 kph. Careering through its abrupt twists and turns at more than ten times that rate would be beyond even Data's capabilities.

Picard turned back to his mission. "Any sign of an impulse wake from either the *Tombaugh* or the *Lowell?*" he asked his bridge crew.

"Not yet, sir," Sloane answered.

The answer didn't trouble Picard. Any wake that Riker's and Data's two shuttles might have left would have undoubtedly been dispersed by the passing of the duplicate *Enterprise.* But still he sighed, impatient. Surely, the passage had to come to an end soon.

When that occurred, Picard fervently hoped his *Enterprise* would be facing her counterpart again, and not a fleet of First Federation dreadnaughts.

"Coming up on fifty-five-kilometer mark," Maran called out.

"Sir," Lieutenant Karo suddenly said. The Bolian's medial face ridge tightened in concern. "The hydrazine traces have just dropped out of our sensitivity range."

Picard leaned forward. "Perhaps they finally went to impulse," he said. Perhaps they were about to find the wreckage of the mirror *Enterprise* up ahead, spread along the passage walls.

"And I now have acquired impulse wakes from the shuttles," Sloane added. "No sign of damage or . . ." His voice trailed off.

Picard put the two reports together, understood their implications. If the hydrazine had stopped, that meant the mirror *Enterprise* had stopped as well. And if the shuttle impulse wakes were now evident, then that meant that the ship that hunted the two shuttles was still to pass through this section of the passage.

Which could only mean—

The bridge jumped forward as the *Enterprise* bucked in response to a powerful explosion.

"Sir!" Sloane shouted, stating the obvious once more. "The other ship—it's behind us!"

The hunter was the hunted once again.

TEN

☆

In the last few seconds, there was no time for clear, rational thought.

It was all or nothing.

Once again, Kirk clearly saw the transporter pad. Slowly spinning, it was only a few dozen meters from him, its blue light still flashing with each revolution.

Once again, he clearly saw the silhouette of Tiberius pass before the stars, less than half the distance to the pad than Kirk.

There was only one way he could reach the pad before Tiberius.

Kirk tapped the controls that would fire all his thrusters at full power.

A muffled clicking noise sounded in his helmet.

"Thruster reaction mass is exhausted." The computer's polite explanation was a death knell telling Kirk he could do nothing more.

Kirk saw his victorious nemesis reach the spinning pad and grab it. Saw the transporter pad continue to spin in the grasp of its captor, though the added mass of Tiberius slowed down the rate at which it did so.

Almost clinically at this moment of his greatest failure, Kirk noted how Tiberius's momentum had also altered the pad's trajectory. Now Kirk was going to miss it by meters. And without sufficient thruster reaction mass, he lacked any way of altering his own course.

He was reduced to mere witness as Tiberius attempted to slow his rotation with the pad even more.

Five seconds, Kirk thought. In five seconds, Tiberius would reach around to the operational side of the pad and begin the transport process.

Five seconds. In that eternity of time, Kirk's attention began to drift. Then stopped. Abruptly.

Reaction mass.

He was breathing it.

Swiftly working by instinct, without considering what his next action might cost him in his very near future, Kirk found the emergency oxygen inlet valve on his chestpiece, twisted it open, then pressed his thumb firmly against the release tab.

Instantly his helmet rang with a pressure alarm as an explosive puff of fine ice crystals shot out to his side.

Kirk had just leaked his suit's air supply into space, but in reaction to the air's escape, his body had begun to spin again, his heading once again toward the pad held by Tiberius.

Kirk twisted the valve shut and tried to breathe, but his life-support pack hadn't yet refilled his suit. The stars streaked past his newly fogged helmet visor. The pressure alarm still rang in his ears, but in the low pressure, it sounded far away.

He saw the glow of the transporter effect blossom before him. Like the dawn of a blue sun.

Tiberius became a creature of light.

Kirk reached out for him.

He couldn't breathe. Couldn't think. Could only spin into endless, star-filled night.

And then consciousness left him before he could know if his hand had grasped anything at all.

Deflected by the explosion, the *Enterprise* was thrown off her axis, driven toward the nearest wall of stone.

"Raise all shields!" Picard ordered over the shrill collision alarms.

If Riker had been present, Picard knew his first officer would have questioned that order. To raise shields in the constricted passage would effectively double the volume of the shape that Lieutenant Maran had to maneuver. The shields extended far enough away from the ship that they would inevitably drag along the passage walls, making the *Enterprise* bounce like a waterborne craft caught in a river canyon, slammed from rockface to rockface, scraping bottom with each run through the rapids.

But Sloane wasn't Riker. He activated the shields without protest. A second explosion shook the bridge, though not as violently as the first.

Then only a moment later, the main hull shields made contact with the passage wall beneath the ship.

The *Enterprise* nosed sharply down, then rebounded upward until her topside shields struck the opposite wall.

"Sir! All aft batteries ready to fire!" Sloane called out.

But Picard didn't intend to engage in all-out battle in the passage. If it collapsed, he wouldn't even be able to transmit a call for help through the asteroid's crust.

"All batteries stand by," Picard ordered. "Helm, take us through. Maximum speed."

"Aye, aye, sir," Maran acknowledged.

The Trill was the third host of her symbiont, Picard knew, but even though she had the experiences of two previous lives to draw upon, she was unable to prevent tension from sharpening her voice.

"Mr. Sloane," Picard continued. "Drop all shields except aft."

Again the young lieutenant carried out the order without comment.

Picard studied the changing image on the main viewer, tracking Maran's prompt increase in speed.

"Well done, Lieutenant," Picard said approvingly. "We know we can outrun them in here."

The ship rumbled as a new attack struck them.

Tracking torpedoes! Picard had wondered when the other commander would think of that. Different models of quantum torpedoes could travel at warp velocities, at almost any range of impulse speed, or even lie in wait with stationkeeping thrusters. Though warp would be impractical in this passage, even a minimal impulse speed of a few hundred kilometers per hour would be enough to catch the *Enterprise.*

Sloane's confirming report came only seconds later. "Captain, they're firing tracking torpedoes," he announced.

Picard issued his next order. "Watch those aft shields, Mr. Sloane. It's going to be a rough ride for the next few minutes."

"Aye, aye, sir."

Now the *Enterprise* banked and swerved as Ilydia Maran used all the concentration of her joined minds to anticipate the random curves of the passage ahead.

Slowly Picard's ship increased her speed, though each incremental burst made it more difficult to negotiate turns in an optimal flight path.

Again and again, the ship's elongated saucer hull came within meters of scraping stone. Her leading nacelle domes faced the same risk.

And every few seconds, a new torpedo joined the chase to add another energy load to the already-compromised aft shield.

But the ship that launched those torpedoes—a vessel now powered by impulse thrust, as Picard had guessed—began to fall farther and farther behind. The skill of its helmsman was no match for that of Lieutenant Maran.

Unfortunately, Picard knew, speed was no longer what would determine the outcome of this hunt.

Even if the mirror *Enterprise* carried only Starfleet's standard loadout of quantum torpedoes, that firepower would be more than enough to finally overcome the single aft shield protecting Picard's *Enterprise*.

Like Theseus pursuing the minotaur through the maze, the mirror *Enterprise* pursued the *Enterprise* through the passage.

Picard hoped the fate of his ship was not that of the beast.

If it was, his *Enterprise* would not escape.

Kirk awoke as a wall of blue fire slowly dissipated and darkness returned.

For a time-stopping moment, he knew he had failed. Tiberius had transported back to Kirk's universe, leaving Kirk to . . .

His suit was filled with air again. His lungs worked easily.

The stars were gone.

Kirk could feel his body spinning, so he knew he was still in space. He could see the status lights on his helmet display, so he knew his eyes still functioned. And since all the stars could not disappear at once, he knew that something was blocking them from his vision in every direction.

There was only one possible answer.

He had caught Tiberius in time. They had both transported back to Kirk's own universe. And they were now in the hollowed-out center of the asteroid, in the First Federation base.

Kirk remembered that the base was a vast installation,

kilometers across. But when he had seen it last, it had been brightly illuminated by strings of fusion lights that traced an equatorial band around the artificial central docking cavern.

But Kirk could see no interior lights at all, which gave him hope that the base had been abandoned, the ships removed.

Then again, in this absolute darkness, he knew he and his counterpart could be spinning through space only a few dozen meters from a Fesarius-class ship and not be able to see it.

At least Tiberius is in the same situation, Kirk thought. And then he wondered if Tiberius had even made it through the transport. Kirk tried to recall the strength of their collision. Was there any chance at all that he had dislodged Tiberius from the transporter effect, to drift forever among the mirror-universe stars? Did Tiberius face the death he had wished for Kirk?

Knowing Tiberius's fate, Kirk thought, would make his own dying here easier.

A flash of dim, multicolored light caught his attention, the flicker so quick that Kirk almost ignored it, thinking it the result of a stray particle of cosmic radiation hitting his retina—an illusion all space travelers had experienced since the first lunar voyages.

But a moment later, he saw the light again. Brighter now. Closer.

The third time he saw the light, he realized that it was something approaching him, and that it was the rapid spinning of his own body that made the light appear to be flashing.

The fourth time he saw it, he knew it for what it was: reflections from the interior helmet display of another environmental suit, speeding toward him.

Kirk's question had an answer.

He braced for impact.

Picard's crew quickly adapted to the battle within the passageway.

To extend the life of the aft shield, two teams of engineers directed tractor beams behind the *Enterprise*. The beams deflected or at least slowed down the quantum torpedoes as they raced up from behind.

La Forge vented more antimatter from the nacelles, then momentarily dropped the aft shield. The cloud of antiprotons began to fill the passage in the ship's wake.

Seconds later, the cloud began to glow. The leading edge of the rapidly thinning antimatter gas was reacting with the normal matter of the passage walls. The result was the creation of billions of small though spectacular explosions.

The casings of the first quantum torpedoes to reach the cloud dissolved into energy and threw the torpedoes off course, damaging their mechanisms so badly they failed to trigger detonation when the torpedoes collided with the passage walls.

Moments later, the mirror *Enterprise* reached the cloud. Its leading shields rammed the antimatter gas forward, compressing the cloud to denser and more dangerous levels which reacted even more violently with the surrounding stone. The explosive hail of debris released by the stone walls hit the ship immediately after its shields rushed by.

The duplicate ship slowed, as if its helmsman believed the ship was striking the walls themselves.

Ahead, Picard's *Enterprise* raced on, nearing the passage's end.

"Still no torpedoes," Sloane reported.

Picard nodded, gratified with the success of the maneuver he had ordered. Centuries ago, releasing clouds of anti-matter had been tried in space battles, but was quickly abandoned. The gas dispersed too quickly in vacuum to do more than singe an enemy craft's hull, or slightly degrade its sensors.

But in the tight confines of this passage, the old technique had taken on new life. The only drawback was that La Forge was now insisting the *Enterprise* could not afford to dump more antimatter and still expect to make it back to the nearest starbase.

"Captain Spock," Picard said. "Are you any closer to an estimate?"

The Vulcan was beside the helm console, speaking with Lieutenant Maran, even as she flew the ship through the twisting passage. Picard had approved the consultation. Trills were exceptionally well equipped to deal with the challenge of attending to two different tasks at the same time.

"At this speed," Spock reported, "and based on additional reflection upon my first visit to this facility, I estimate we will reach the interior of the asteroid no sooner than three minutes fifteen seconds, no later than four minutes ten seconds. I regret I cannot be more precise."

Picard suppressed his smile. "And Mr. Maran knows what to expect?"

"I have been briefed, sir," she replied.

Picard settled back in his chair. There hadn't been a torpedo impact for more than a minute. There was a chance that the mirror *Enterprise* was no longer even in pursuit.

"Captain," Spock suddenly said, "we are now in the final stretch of the entry passage."

Picard studied the image on the main viewer. Nothing seemed different. The rough, curved walls continued to stream past at more than 300 kph, still lit by the *Enterprise*'s rarely used searchlights.

"How can you tell?" Picard asked.

"The passage is now straight. We are no more than twenty kilometers from the base."

"It's straight all the way?"

"Correct," Spock said.

"Then we can go faster, can't we, helmsman?"

"Aye, aye, sir." Maran's hands moved over her controls and the passing walls blurred.

Then Lieutenant Karo reported from the ops console. "Sir, I can detect the end of the passageway. Sixteen point four kilometers."

Picard shook off the sense of unreality he felt. He was used to dealing in velocities faster than light, in distances measured in light-years. Yet for now, his *Enterprise* was constrained to limits no different from those of antique, atmospheric flying craft.

And then he realized that if *his* ship could travel faster through the straight part of the passage, then—

The collision alarm sounded.

Picard's stomach tightened. The mirror *Enterprise* had entered the last stretch as well.

And it was gaining.

ELEVEN

☆

Kirk used his arms to shield his helmet visor. He bent forward, drew his knees up to change his center of gravity, to speed his rate of spinning. Then—

Impact!

Tiberius hit him sideways, clasped him, not letting go.

They tumbled together in darkness.

Kirk's inner ear registered the disorienting motion. He felt the rise of nausea.

Then a hand—groping for his forearm suit controls.

One of Kirk's hands closed on Tiberius's. His other hand grabbed for any part of his counterpart's suit.

There was a sudden jerking movement and suddenly he and Tiberius were face-to-face. The maglocks on their equipment belts had engaged: They were inextricably joined, unable to fall apart now, free to use both hands to attempt to damage each other's suit.

Kirk saw his own face in Tiberius's helmet, lit by the display screen lights. He knew Tiberius saw the same face—flushed, beaded in sweat, its helmet visor fogged with its wearer's exertions.

Tiberius tried to force his arms together to reach the emergency oxygen inlet on Kirk's chestpiece.

Kirk brought his hands up between Tiberius's arms and forced them apart. Then he went straight for Tiberius's helmet lock.

The flash of apprehension in Tiberius's eyes told Kirk his enemy knew death was mere centimeters, mere seconds away.

Then Kirk's padded fingers found the first lock-release on Tiberius's helmet collar.

Just as Tiberius found the first lock-release on Kirk's.

"Four hundred meters and closing," Sloane counted out. "Three hundred ninety."

"Why aren't they firing?" Picard asked.

Two engineering consoles suddenly flared with a power surge. Picard heard and felt his ship rumble and pitch.

"Their shields have impinged on ours!" Sloane reported. "Shields have failed!"

Picard had his answer: Any explosion at this distance would have damaged both ships. Especially since even incompatible shields operating on the same frequencies could neutralize each other, as had just happened.

"Distance to base!" Picard said.

"Nine kilometers!" Maran answered.

"Distance to the other ship!"

"Two hundred meters and closing!" Sloane answered.

Picard jabbed the intraship control on the arm of his chair. "All hands brace for impact!" He twisted around to the security station. "Mr. Sloane, full power to the structural integrity field!"

The bridge filled with the whine of the ship's generators as her network of internal microforcefields grew stronger.

"Ninety meters!" Sloane shouted. "Eighty . . . seventy . . . they're going to ram us!"

Picard gripped the arms of his chair. He wasn't going to lose this one. "Bridge to engineering!" he called out.

The mirror *Enterprise* shuddered, buffeted by the ionized gas expelled from its prey's impulse engines. But still she pushed on, the forward edge of her saucer now only twenty meters from making physical contact with the nacelles of Picard's ship.

Suddenly, tractor beams shot out from the *Enterprise* and the rapid exchange of gravitons stole momentum from her duplicate and pushed Picard's ship ahead.

But seconds later, additional tractor beams from the mirror *Enterprise* met and canceled the first set.

The inertial links between the two vessels set up an inevitable instability in their balance. Like counterweights on a long beam, the two massive craft began oscillating side to side.

Ten kilometers from the end of the passage, the *Enterprise* ended the impasse and shut off her tractor beams.

Her pursuer lurched forward, saucer dipping down to collide with the fantail deck outside the *Enterprise*'s main hangar.

Sparks flew in vacuum as duranium hit duranium.

Debris rained back to crash over the mirror *Enterprise*'s bridge.

Flames and smoke fed by pressurized hydraulic lines and leaking atmosphere erupted from the *Enterprise*'s stern.

The mirror *Enterprise* pulled up, losing speed as she scraped the bottom of her engineering hull against the passage wall.

But the *Enterprise* put on a final burst of speed and rushed on, only seconds from disappearing into the cavernous darkness at the passage end.

The mirror *Enterprise* recovered quickly, resumed its trajectory, and increased its speed as well, rushing to join its prey in the darkness for the final encounter.

Kirk pushed back, keeping his hands on the locking ring of Tiberius's helmet. He shifted as best he could to keep Tiberius from working the lock on his own.

He still had the advantage of a few seconds' lead over Tiberius. Those few seconds were all he needed.

He flipped his thumb and the left helmet lock released.

Tiberius's eyes widened.

Kirk knew his counterpart would be hearing the hiss of escaping air now. Would be hearing his suit's computer calmly announcing precisely how many seconds of life-support he had left.

Then Kirk heard his own helmet lock release, heard his own air escaping, his own suit's computer inform him he had ninety seconds of life remaining.

Teilani, Kirk thought. *Our child . . .*

He moved his right thumb to the second lock.

And then light exploded over them both and reflexively, they both strained to find its source and saw—

The *Enterprise* erupted from a circular passage, bringing light with her as her stern flared with explosions—shuttle-craft warp cores going critical on the main hangar deck.

And then, as if Picard's ship were instead some enormous alien acrobat, it nosed up, then inverted, and came to a relative stop. Trailing streamers of smoke, the ship hung directly above the opening from which it had emerged.

For long moments, the starship was a dying candle. The flames on her stern slowly diminished as the vessel's automated damage-control systems beamed away unstable warp cores from damaged shuttles, cut off the flow of gases and hydraulic fluids, and fire at last surrendered to vacuum.

The light the *Enterprise* had brought to the vast internal cavern dimmed until darkness was restored.

Until a moment later when a second *Enterprise* burst through the opening, its navigational lights ablaze—

—and was instantly engulfed by a devastating barrage of phaser fire from the motionless *Enterprise,* all of the surprise attack concentrated on a point midway between the duplicate ship's two warp nacelles.

The instant the mirror *Enterprise* had cleared the passage, it had raised its shields. But Picard's phaser blasts struck before those shields could reach full strength.

The second ship's shields were overcome within seconds.

Immediately, the target coordinates of Picard's phasers moved to the nacelles themselves. Surgically fusing the intermix bypass matrices. Abruptly releasing the warp engines' coiled and pent-up energy.

Like a Jovian thunderstorm, rippling sheets of discharged energy leapt from the mirror *Enterprise*'s nacelles.

Flickering bolts of purple-blue fire arced across the gap between the nacelles, freeing even more warp energy, which then sprayed out across the closest grounding target—the rest of the ship.

The entire surface of the mirror *Enterprise* crawled with balls of strobing, lightning-like discharges that swiftly overloaded all internal power systems.

The stricken ship's navigation lights winked out. Then the lights that defined her viewports flickered and failed, deck by deck.

Thirty seconds after reaching the First Federation base cavern, the duplicate *Enterprise* was reduced to a slowly spiraling, powerless hulk encircled by a random storm of fading, fifty-meter-long sparks.

The hunt was over.

• • •

In his command chair, Picard released the breath he had held unconsciously. "It seems they didn't discover *all* the *Enterprise*'s weak spots," he told his stunned bridge crew. "Well done."

Spock's hands were clasped behind his back as he studied the slowly tumbling starship caught in the *Enterprise*'s searchlights. "Am I to understand that *every* power distribution system on the vessel has been deactivated?"

"Starfleet corrected the intermix design flaw in this ship three months ago," Picard told the Vulcan. "Mr. Sloane, beam a communications link to the bridge of that vessel, and take her under tow."

Sloane acknowledged the commands, then Picard requested a full sensor sweep of the cavern.

And as if a switch had been thrown, the instant the ship's sensors reached out, the First Federation base came to life.

As the ships battled, so did Kirk and Tiberius.

The vessels' dramatic entrances had slowed the struggle between the two spacesuited figures, but did not stop it.

As phaser fire defeated underpowered shields, Kirk opened the second lock on Tiberius's helmet.

Kirk knew he had only to twist the helmet a few centimeters to the side and it would come free.

As purple-blue fire flashed through his visor, Kirk saw Tiberius's hate-filled face painted with the imperial colors of death.

Kirk placed a hand on both sides of his counterpart's helmet.

Saw the emperor's mouth distort in a last, defiant soundless cry of protest.

Felt Tiberius unfasten the second lock on his own helmet.

Felt Tiberius's hands on the sides of his own helmet.

But Kirk did not protest his fate. He knew why he was about to die. And that Tiberius never would know.

Then an even more intense light burned through Kirk's visor.

Beyond Tiberius, he saw bands of fusion lights igniting. Ringing the base cavern. Filling it with illumination. Showing all that was within it, with absolute clarity.

And as Kirk saw what was there, despite the alarms blaring in his ears and the computer's countdown to extinction, he began to laugh.

Picard stared at the image that brightened on the bridge's main viewer.

There were Fesarius-class ships in the base. But how many, he couldn't be sure.

Because not one of them was intact.

It was as if the cavern were filled with shattered eggshells.

The broken, spherical hulls of the kilometer-and-a-half-wide ships were floating in chaotic disarray, not one hull section larger than a third of a full ship.

"Fascinating," Spock said.

Kirk stopped laughing. He looked at Tiberius, wondering if in these final few seconds, his adversary would understand. That the ships he had counted on to win him back his empire no longer existed. That his quest had been a failure before it had even begun.

Kirk saw an unfamiliar expression shadow that familiar face.

Fear.

It's about time, Kirk thought.

And then he snapped Tiberius closer to him as if in an embrace and wrenched his helmet to the side and in a puff of frozen vapor, that helmet tumbled away from his enemy—

Just as his enemy twisted off Kirk's own helmet.

Locked together in certain death, they tumbled through the ruins of the First Federation, bleeding air as they spun.

The last thing Kirk saw was light.

The light was blue.

It was there and then it was gone.

Kirk looked up into a pale-gold face.

"How do you feel?" Data asked.

Kirk looked beyond the android. Saw other Starfleet personnel in environmental suits.

He sat up on the deck of the shuttlecraft. Felt an emergency transporter pad beneath him. Felt the heat in his face—vacuum burn.

"Where's Tiberius?" he asked, the words instantly provoking a ragged cough in his raw throat.

Data stepped back, checked the tricorder he held. "Your counterpart was beamed to Commander Riker's shuttle. You might be interested to know that those were also his first words when he regained consciousness."

"My counterpart?" Kirk repeated. Tiberius had made a point of changing the details of his appearance to more closely match Kirk. Could he actually get away with that deception? "But you know who I am?"

"Please do not be concerned, Captain Kirk. Your quantum signature confirms your identity, just as Tiberius's quantum signature confirmed his."

Kirk got slowly to his feet, using the moment to come to grips with the fact that he wasn't dead. And that neither was Tiberius.

"I saw the ships engage," Kirk said. He fumbled with his bulky gloves. His eyes felt dry.

"Captain Picard prevailed over his counterpart," Data explained.

Kirk began trembling. His fingers weren't working properly. He couldn't take off his gloves. "Have you . . ." He coughed again, felt light-headed for a moment.

"Let us help you," Data said. The android nodded to two other members of his away team and they began to disconnect and remove Kirk's environmental suit.

Ordinarily, Kirk hated that kind of attention, refused that kind of help. But he couldn't deny to himself that he was beginning to feel weak. He shook his head to clear it, trying to understand what was wrong with him.

"Teilani. Have you heard anything about Teilani?" he asked.

"We have been traveling under a communications blackout," Data said. "We have no news."

Kirk stepped out of the final pieces of his suit. Now he began shivering. He felt someone put a blanket over his shoulders. He saw a crewman aiming a medical tricorder at him.

"Well?" Kirk asked irritably. He thought of Teilani being poisoned at the wedding. What if Tiberius had exposed him to something similar? Something intended to take effect while he was held prisoner in the shuttlecraft on the asteroid's surface.

The young crewman frowned apologetically. "Uh, according to this, sir, you're . . . well, you're going into shock."

"What?" Kirk grabbed for the crewman's tricorder. He had battled a Gorn with his bare hands. Taken on a murderous Klingon as an entire planet tore itself to pieces around him. Destroyed half the Borg homeworld. And now a simple, zero-gee tussle was putting him into shock? Impossible.

The crewman held the tricorder out of reach, looked at Data.

"Give me that," Kirk demanded.

Data nodded at the young crewman, who handed Kirk the instrument. Kirk flushed with annoyance as he realized he would have to hold it at arm's length to read its display. Why did those Starfleet geniuses have to keep making their devices smaller?

He gave up trying to make sense of the readings, handed the tricorder back. "I'm f-feeling fine," he said, shivering even more.

"Commander Data," the shuttlecraft's pilot called back. "Captain Picard has requested our immediate presence."

Data took firm hold of Kirk's arm as he steered him to a passenger chair in the forward cabin. "Does he require us to beam back?" the android asked. "Or may we return in the shuttle?"

Kirk was disgusted with himself as he almost fell into the chair. His legs felt so weak, he might not even be able to stand up again unaided.

"No, sir," the pilot told Data. "He wants us for a retrieval mission."

"Retrieval of what?" Data asked.

Kirk looked straight ahead, out through the forward viewports. The shuttle was weaving through the scattered remnants of the First Federation ships, heading toward the *Enterprise* which held position a few hundred meters away from the cavern wall. Everything was brightly lit now. Everything was clear.

"Apparently, they've found something, sir. Up ahead."

Kirk's heart fluttered in his chest. His temples ached from the pounding of his pulse. *How could this be shock?* he asked himself. *I've never—*

A second shuttlecraft swept past the viewports, also heading straight for the *Enterprise.*

Kirk's eyes fixed on the craft, knowing Tiberius was aboard.

Then Kirk twitched as a spray hypo hissed against his neck. He tried to bat it away but he couldn't even raise an arm.

Damn technology, Kirk thought, staring down at his replacement hands. The fine scars showing where the clonal buds had attached to his wrists were almost impossible to see. But he knew they were there. Even now, almost eight months after his original hands had been burned beyond any chance of repair, their replacements did not possess full sensitivity.

"What did you give me?" he asked faintly. He already knew the answer, though. His heart was slowing. It was easier to breathe.

"A mild sedative, sir," the young crewman said. "And some tri-ox."

"Sedative," Kirk mumbled. "I don't . . ." It was suddenly unimportant to bother finishing his statement. Involuntarily, he took a deep breath. Felt his eyelids flutter. Sleep. He wanted to sleep. The blanket was warm.

"Commander Data," the pilot said, and the distant sound of that voice made it seem to Kirk that the man was much farther away than just the next row of seats. "Is that . . . is that what it looks like it is?"

Kirk tried to concentrate on that puzzling question and on the questions and answers that followed.

"Data to Captain Picard."

"Go ahead, Mr. Data."

"Is that the object you wish us to retrieve, sir?"

"Absolutely. Starfleet protocol requires that we do not attempt to beam the artifact. It is to be physically moved to the ship."

"Understood, sir."

Artifact? Kirk thought fuzzily. *Physically moved?*

Something about that protocol sounded familiar. Made him remember . . . but he wasn't sure what.

Somehow, he forced his eyes open again, looked out the viewports blearily. *Just for a few seconds,* he thought. Then he could sleep.

The engineering hull of the *Enterprise* rushed by like a ghostly whale disappearing in a cloudy ocean. The pilot had moved the shuttlecraft into the shadow cast by an enormous section of a ruined Fesarius-class hull.

Kirk's rapidly degrading attention fixed on a stream of fine debris defining a bright beam of light that blazed down from the *Enterprise,* as if pointing the way.

The shuttlecraft banked, its forward motion stopped, and Kirk sensed it was landing on the cavern wall. Then, as the shuttle settled, Kirk saw what it was the *Enterprise* had found.

Everything left him then.

The effects of the sedative were nonexistent.

The aftermath of facing death with his counterpart meant nothing.

Kirk pushed himself unsteadily to his feet, leaned forward beside the pilot, staring ahead in a harrowing combination of shock and recognition.

"Do you recognize it, Captain?" Data asked curiously.

Kirk did. A lifetime ago, he had found the first one, opening the door to a mystery that Starfleet still hadn't solved.

Now, Tiberius had brought him to a second.

And Kirk couldn't shake the feeling that somehow, this one had been waiting for him.

TWELVE

☆

"It is a Preserver obelisk," T'Serl said.

"Correct," Picard agreed. Then he waited patiently as the young Vulcan and her elderly Ferengi colleague began to walk around the one-to-one holographic reconstruction of the artifact Picard and his crew had recovered from the ruins of the First Federation base four weeks earlier.

Picard used the moment to more fully examine the interface chamber of the Memory Planet Dataweb in which he was meeting with the psychohistorians.

In one sense, standing here on the chamber's precariously elevated observation platform, the Memory Alpha facility reminded him of the stellar cartography projection room on the *Enterprise*—a towering space almost completely wrapped by holographic screens. But where stellar cartography presented star maps and navigational data, there appeared to be no limit to the information the interface chamber could display.

Picard looked up rather than down, still finding the lack of railings on the elevated platform unsettling. Even restricting his gaze to this one direction, he was unable to count the number of data windows that filled the curved walls above the platform. Overwhelmed by the wealth of two- and three-dimensional arrays, he glimpsed visual records, schematics, public-information streams, the flowing abstract color patches of Medusan navigation charts, and even entertainment re-creations. The sensation of almost floating in the middle of an all-enveloping context of flickering graphs and strings of words and numbers in scores of different languages and representational systems was stunning, even disorienting.

But whatever he was able to see, Picard knew T'Serl and Lept saw and sensed more. Both psychohistorians wore full interface suits—snug, black, one-piece garments criss-crossed with the multicolored webs of a sensory-feedback network. The two scholars had bronze-colored audio inducers attached to their jaws, as well as chest-mounted, Benzite-like respiration wands that arced up to within a few centimeters of their mouths, trailing white clouds of scented vapor. In addition, each wore silver retinal-projection visors capable of feeding separate channels of visual information to different portions of individual eyes.

Taken together, the sensory-augmentation devices in their suits enabled the two researchers to perceive and manipulate *all* the information manifested in the interface chamber—by sight, sound, smell, physical texture, relative size, and spatial location.

Picard knew that minds capable of processing the complex presentation of such information were exceedingly rare, even within the Federation's population of trillions. The fact that two such rarities—T'Serl and Lept—had agreed so readily to meet with him made him more confident than ever that he had come to the right place. He felt sure that back on Qo'noS, Jim Kirk would also be pleased. And relieved.

Picard looked over to see Lept hobble back into view, then stop to run one gloved hand over the smooth, silver-green surface of the obelisk, as if tracing the random veins of the pale rust color that marbled it. The aged Ferengi—considered one of the most brilliant marketing geniuses in the history of his world, always the first to anticipate a trend—gazed thoughtfully at the holographic reconstruction. He seemed absolutely captivated by it.

Picard shared Lept's reaction to the obelisk. Each newly discovered Preserver artifact was a possible key to understanding the greatest archaeological mystery in the Federation. So far, no two had been found to be exactly alike. Common belief was that once some kind of underlying similarity was recognized, the puzzle would be solved.

The original of this Preserver artifact—officially catalogued as PA-119—was constructed of the same impossible phase-transition compound as were all the others, and had the same general shape: an elongated pentahedron whose four triangular sides were deeply indented by a concave arrangement of four triangular planes, creating the overall impression of the structure as a spearpoint with four vanes.

But the size and proportions of this obelisk were subtly different from all the others, as all the others were slightly different, each from the other.

As measured on site by Data and Riker, PA-119 was 4.783 meters tall. Near its base, at its widest point, it was 2.201 meters across, tapering to an apex width of 18.323 centimeters. The finial, which was again completely different on each of the other known obelisks, extended another 24.971 centimeters. The lower half of the finial was a cube of phase-transition compound seamlessly fused to the main structure. Its upper half was a raised disk of the same material, with a vertically grooved edge.

So far, Starfleet researchers were according great importance to the fact that the raised disk was not a perfect circle. Nor was it a perfect representation of any other geometric shape. Rather, it was distorted, as if it had been sculpted in freehand by an untrained artist. The debate over just that one irregularity would undoubtedly consume archaeologists for years.

Because, as yet, none of Starfleet's myriad Preserver study groups had been able to discover a pattern to any of the obelisks' proportions. None had been able to offer any reason for the differing sizes, shapes, and finials. None had been able even to speculate how a solid phase-transition compound could retain its physical characteristics outside its only known context: the extreme heat and pressures found at the core of a white dwarf star.

When Picard looked at the obelisk, he didn't just see an artifact of a highly advanced technology. He had the unsettling sensation of looking at something that had been made by beings with a completely different definition of physics; perhaps even a different definition of reality.

Lept finally stepped back from the holographically reconstructed artifact.

"When did you say this sensor record was made?" The diminutive historian moved his surprisingly large, gloved hand through the air as if operating an unseen control surface. A holographic data window opened in midair directly in front of him and to one side of the obelisk.

"The obelisk was discovered and retrieved one month ago," Picard said. The data window displayed the visual sensor log he had brought for the historians. It showed an overhead view of the retrieval site as seen from the *Enterprise:* two shuttlecraft anchored to a cavern wall; Data and Riker and two full away teams, all in environmental suits, attaching precision tractor bands to the obelisk.

Lept's black-gloved hand idly scratched behind one

tufted, deeply wrinkled ear. "And where did you say you found it?"

Picard smiled at the Ferengi's apparently innocent request. *A Ferengi is a Ferengi is a Ferengi,* he reminded himself. "I didn't, Manager. The location is classified."

T'Serl walked out from behind the obelisk to stand beside Lept. The tall Vulcan addressed Picard abruptly. "Does Starfleet know you're on Memory Alpha?"

Picard took no offense at her tone. Most Vulcans believed that wasting time and words was illogical.

"I'm on leave, Doctor. My ship—"

"The *Enterprise,*" Lept said with a half-cough.

"That's right. The *Enterprise* is in spacedock for minor repairs and upgrades, and—"

"So Starfleet doesn't know you're here," T'Serl interrupted.

"No, not specifically," Picard answered. "Though they can reach me at any time."

T'Serl and Lept exchanged a quick glance, but Picard wasn't able to judge the significance of it. The young Vulcan and old Ferengi made such odd partners that Picard hadn't yet been able to judge any part of their unlikely relationship.

T'Serl looked away from him again, up at the obelisk. She removed her silver retinal-projection visor and attached it to a contact plate on her black-clad upper arm. "What is your estimate of Starfleet's reaction if your superiors found you were discussing this matter with us?"

Picard shrugged. "I don't know if they would have one." Reflexively, he began to tug down on his jacket, then remembered he wasn't wearing his uniform. Since his civilian jacket hung open, it didn't ride up and required no adjustment, however habitual the gesture had become.

"Starfleet's discovery of the new artifact," he continued, "was widely reported in archaeological circles. And since

Starfleet has an ongoing study program which engages many civilian consultants and which works in conjunction with the Federation Archaeology Council, I assure you that I am not revealing classified information or breaking any regulations by being here or showing you this."

Behind Lept's transparent silver visor, Picard could see the Ferengi historian's sunken dark eyes narrow. "So," Lept said, "would you say you have come to us on official Starfleet business?"

Picard didn't understand why the two historians were so concerned about Starfleet's involvement in his presence here today. "No, Manager. I am not here as a Starfleet captain. I have come to you as an archaeologist. An amateur, to be sure. But this is simply one of my own—"

Again, T'Serl interrupted. "Given your other 'amateur' accomplishments, may we conclude that you believe there is some connection between the Preservers and Dr. Richard Galen's ancestral species?"

Coming from anyone other than a Vulcan, Picard would consider T'Serl's constant interruptions a sign of rudeness. But he acknowledged that she did have a point.

Six years ago, Picard had played a pivotal role in completing Dr. Galen's most astounding discovery—that the genetic structure of humans, Vulcans, Klingons, and Cardassians carried a remarkable message originally encoded four billion years earlier by the first humanoid species to evolve in the galaxy and begin interstellar exploration.

That species had found themselves to be alone, and so had seeded life throughout the galaxy, with the result that, in a very real sense, most life-forms in the Alpha and Beta quadrants were distant members of the same family.

But though the discovery at last suggested a solution for the puzzling mystery of why it was possible for alien species, such as humans and Vulcans for example, to have offspring together, in the end Galen's ancestral species had raised more questions than it had answered.

The most important question being: Was the Galen ancestral species one and the same as the Preservers?

Picard didn't know the answer to that, but he had his suspicions.

"I don't know if there is a connection," he answered. "Personally, I doubt it."

In the subtle quiver of a single eyebrow, Picard sensed T'Serl's intense interest in his answer.

"I would be intrigued to hear you detail your doubts," the Vulcan said, "but our available time is restricted today. You have shown us the retrieval of a historically important artifact from an undisclosed location. Yet you suggest that you are meeting with us merely to pursue an amateur interest in your avocation."

"Jean-Luc Picard an amateur," Lept snorted. "Starfleet's gain is archaeology's loss, eh?"

Picard said nothing. He could sense that T'Serl was building toward a conclusion.

She was. "An amateur interest which could be more efficiently served by directly accessing the Memory Planet Dataweb from any remote location. In short, your presence on Memory Alpha is unnecessary. And your desire to confer with two psychohistorians is illogical." She stared intently into his eyes. "Unless you have neglected to share all of your reasons with us."

With that, Picard abandoned his plan to extract maximum information from the historians while revealing as little of his own information as possible. At the same time, he experienced the odd sensation of suspecting that T'Serl and Lept had somehow anticipated his arrival on Memory Alpha, and that they already knew what he wanted. But he quickly put the idea from his mind. Not even psychohistorians were able to anticipate the actions of a single person with such precision.

Remembering the burgeoning Vulcan fondness for the human game of poker, Picard laid all his cards on the table.

"I have come to you because the two of you are the most expert psychohistorians in the Federation."

Lept snorted, then attempted to cover his intemperate reaction with a series of coughs.

T'Serl ignored the Ferengi and began reciting a list of names familiar to Picard. "Garen of Odessa Prime. R'Ma'Hatrel of the Cygnate Cooperative. Savrin and T'Pon of the Seldon Institute. These are the giants of today who have stood on the shoulders of Asimov and defined contemporary psychohistory."

Picard nodded. "I agree, they are the most *prominent* specialists. But I maintain that you two are the most expert."

"Keep it up, young man," Lept snickered, "and we'll have to adopt you." Still laughing to himself, the Ferengi unfastened the shoulder seam of his close-fit black interface suit and reached inside as if searching for something.

T'Serl continued as if she had not heard her colleague's irreverent comments. "Very well, why does the discovery of another Preserver artifact lead you to require a consultation with psychohistorians? I remind you that so little is known of the Preservers, psychohistorical analytics cannot be applied to them."

"If they ever existed at all," Lept added, reaching deeper within his suit, giving the impression he had begun wrestling with himself.

Picard was aware of the argument to which the Ferengi referred. It held that the concept of a single, ancient species called the Preservers arose from the inborn human need to see a pattern in the archaeological record, even when no such pattern existed. Critics maintained that every space-going culture behaved in certain ways like the purported Preservers: by founding colony worlds dedicated to keeping alive endangered cultural groups and modes of living; and by distributing plants and animals across dozens of worlds so that in the event of a planetary extinction event on one planet, life would continue elsewhere.

Thus, opponents of the Preserver hypothesis argued it was ludicrous to interpret *all* preservation efforts over eons of time as the result of *one* omnipotent species operating consistently over billions of years. The only reasonable explanation was that what pro-Preserver researchers saw as archaeological evidence of a single Preserver species was no more than a misinterpretation of multiple independent preservation activities undertaken by dozens of extinct and unrelated cultures over millennia.

But Picard was not a supporter of that interpretation. "I don't deny that some archaeological findings interpreted as evidence of the Preservers have been classified in error. However, I feel the preponderance of evidence permits no other conclusion than that the Preservers are real."

"And that evidence would be?" T'Serl asked.

Picard gestured to the holographic re-creation. "The obelisks. This is the one hundred and nineteenth to be found in the Alpha and Beta quadrants since the first was discovered one hundred and eight years ago."

T'Serl was not impressed. "One hundred and nineteen artifacts are still not a large enough sample on which to employ psychohistorical techniques. Especially when the species allegedly responsible for manufacturing those artifacts is thought by some researchers to have sustained a coherent, unbroken chain of civilization from two billion years ago, continuing to one thousand years ago.

"Instead," T'Serl continued stiffly, still unconvinced by Picard's explanation for his presence, "there is considerable justification for concluding that over time, unrelated cultures have *purposely* created near-duplicate obelisks in conjunction with their own preservation efforts. The symbol of the obelisk thus can be seen as a cultural talisman. In much the same way that some non-Vulcan societies have adopted the image of the Vulcan IDIC to declare their solidarity with the ideals of logic."

Picard played his last card. "Dr. T'Serl, Manager Lept, unlike PA-28, discovered by Hikaru Sulu, this obelisk is not two billion years old. And unlike PA-1, discovered by James Kirk, it is not one thousand years old." He could sense another sudden though subtle increase in T'Serl's attentiveness. Lept, on the other hand, grinned as he pulled out from his interface suit what Picard recognized as a beetle-snuff tin. It appeared the Ferengi had lost interest in the conversation.

Picard answered T'Serl's next question before she could ask it.

"This obelisk is only *six* years old," he said.

Lept paused, two fingers pinched in his snuff tin. He squinted at Picard. T'Serl switched off her respiration wand and folded it back into the chestpiece of her interface suit. "I presume you have ruled out forgery."

"Forgery, replication, misidentification, deliberate interference in the site . . . every possible explanation for that creation date has been examined, and discarded," Picard said.

Lept made a grunting sound in the back of his throat, as if he was trying to clear phlegm. "And once you've eliminated the impossible, whatever remains, no matter how improbable, must be the truth, eh?" He winked at T'Serl. "She says one of her ancestors said that. I think it's a Vulcan joke."

T'Serl's stony manner did not soften. "I would prefer

to examine Starfleet's findings for myself. But for the sake of argument, if I accept that you have discovered a Preserver artifact manufactured within the past decade, then logic suggests that the Preservers still exist, and are still active."

Picard nodded. He didn't bother to add that once Starfleet researchers had reached those same conclusions, all further work on the obelisk had been classified beyond even his clearance. But since he had no access to any work conducted past that point, he had been truthful in stating that nothing he knew could be considered secret.

"If you will not reveal the location at which the obelisk was discovered," T'Serl said, "will you reveal to us the context in which it was found?"

This is it, Picard thought.

"What do you know about the mirror universe?" he began, hesitating as he caught the momentary look of alarm that swept across T'Serl's face, before being quickly erased by her impressive self-control. But the powerful—for a Vulcan—emotional response absolutely confirmed for Picard his suspicion that T'Serl did know more than she had chosen to reveal to him.

Lept made a show of examining a pinch of iridescent snuff, as if debating whether or not to use it after all.

T'Serl busied herself disconnecting her interface gloves. "Was this artifact discovered in the mirror universe?"

"No."

T'Serl began taking off her gloves. "No, it was not discovered there? Or no, you are not at liberty to divulge where it was discovered?"

"It was not discovered in the mirror universe."

T'Serl clipped her gloves to the belt of her suit, then opened and closed her hands, flexing her long fingers as if the gloves had been too tight. "Then what *is* the connection between the artifact and the mirror universe?"

Lept let the snuff fall from his fingers. It glittered as it floated down to the tin. "Starfleet has classified most information about the mirror universe," he said. "From official presentations, we know it is remarkably similar to our own universe, even to the extent that many individuals have duplicates. For that to be true, it follows that up until very recently, our universe and the mirror universe shared a common history."

Picard agreed. This was all public knowledge for those who cared to seek it out. He frowned as T'Serl began pacing, hands folded behind her back, her long strides taking her precipitously close to the edge of the observation platform.

"Also from public records," she said, "we know that the Vulcan and human populations of the mirror universe have experienced a devastating war in which the Federation has been conquered."

"The Empire," Picard corrected, staying well away from the platform edge himself. "Instead of a United Federation of Planets, there was—"

"The Terran Empire," T'Serl said, turning on her heel just before another step would have sent her plunging off the platform. "I am quite familiar with the politics of the war, Captain. I was merely describing what was publicly known. Now you have brought up details which Starfleet has tried to restrict."

Lept suddenly sneezed, startling Picard, who hadn't seen him inhale his snuff. The sound echoed in the hollow, cylindrical chamber.

T'Serl walked over to the Ferengi and from a small pouch on her belt, handed him a handkerchief which he used to enthusiastically blow his nose. "Thank you, my dear." He looked over at Picard. "I can see where this is going, young man."

"Perhaps you would be so good as to enlighten me," Picard said dryly.

"What is it historians do?"

"Study the past," Picard answered.

"And psychohistorians?"

"Study the past to predict the future."

Lept cackled with amusement. "You've read the abstracts, at least. But sometimes historians do more than predict the future—they predict the past!"

"In what sense?" Picard asked as T'Serl turned her back on her Ferengi colleague to once again contemplate the obelisk. If these two were playing out some elaborately choreographed interrogation of him to confuse him, they were succeeding.

"Why, we study the great 'what ifs' of history! What if the Cardassians had discovered the Bajoran wormhole before the Bajorans? What if the Pakleds had outbid the Ferengi in the Great Auction of Oh-Five? What if my colleague's esteemed Surak had drowned when his ship capsized while escaping from General Solon's pursuing army?" Lept paused to study Picard, and the captain had the sudden suspicion that the old Ferengi's flighty ways might be little more than an act.

"Imagine, if you can, young man, alternative outcomes to those historic turning points. How would the past eight years have unfolded if the Cardassians had made first contact with the Dominion? Would Ferenginar still exist if the Pakleds had turned around to sell Iconian quantum-decoupler technology to the Breen? And what would be the fate of the Federation today if the Vulcan Time of Awakening had not taken place two thousand years ago?

"Historians ask those questions incessantly. How could things be different? Why are things the way they are? And every historian I know is fascinated by the mirror universe. How can our universe and that one be so similar, yet so unlike?"

T'Serl was no longer studying the obelisk. Instead, Picard became aware, her intent gaze was now upon him.

"I can understand why you haven't applied psychohistory to the Preservers," Picard said slowly to the Ferengi. "But I am surprised that you haven't done so with the mirror universe."

"What makes you think we haven't?"

"Is that right?" Picard asked T'Serl.

The Vulcan's response was to stride toward him briskly. "Computer, display fractal cohesion grid T'Serl, 777,534."

Picard stepped back as a holographic display suddenly formed directly in front of him: a three-dimensional mass of fractal solids, shifting through colors and shapes like a storm-tossed ocean of paint, all contained within a two-meter cube.

T'Serl walked around the display to stand at his side. "Are you familiar with psychohistorical representational techniques?"

"Unfortunately, no," Picard said. He recognized the display for what it was, but had no way of understanding what information it conveyed.

"This is the sociopolitical state of the Federation as it existed approximately one year ago, expressed in standard Seldon notation. The display shows it progressing at a rate of two hundred hours each second. I regret that we do not qualify for more intensive data-processing capabilities which would allow us to increase the temporal and causative resolution."

Picard understood the theory of psychohistory as well as any layperson might be expected to, though he had not studied it sufficiently to understand its application. "I can't pretend to comprehend what this display depicts," he said. "But I can sense the profound beauty that underlies it."

T'Serl nodded. "Though the human-perceived connection between beauty and mathematics is illogical, I understand what you are trying to say."

Picard recognized Vulcan condescension when he heard it and knew the best course of action was to ignore it. "Dr. T'Serl, what does this display tell you about the state of the Federation?"

"Computer, accelerate to time code zero minus fifty-nine days and hold."

The fractal mass pulsed more rapidly, colors flashed through it, and then it abruptly halted, half of it frozen like a still image of towering storm clouds, the other half a flat and featureless plain.

"Is that where your data end?" Picard asked, gesturing to the section without change.

T'Serl glanced at Lept. "In a sense," she said. "The dividing line from fractal chaos to absolute order is time code zero. But more to the point, do you see that small region within the fractal grid at zero minus fifty-nine days?"

A few centimeters from her pointing finger, Picard saw a small island of stability: an anomalous domain of perfect order embedded within perfect chaos. He took a guess. "Is that a psychohistorical decision point?"

"Well, *I* am impressed," Lept said.

"Even more impressive," T'Serl said, with a meaningful look at Picard, "its location maps to us."

The explanation meant nothing to Picard. He waited a moment, expecting her to continue, but she didn't. "I'm sorry, I don't understand."

"In causative space-time, that psychohistorical decision

point overlaps Memory Alpha, specifically Manager Lept and myself. *He* and *I* have become a focus of history."

Picard puzzled through the ramifications of that statement. He knew psychohistorians claimed to be able to predict the development of key moments in ongoing events when a single decision could affect the course of history. But what did it mean when psychohistorians themselves appeared to control the future?

"How is that possible?" Picard asked.

Now Lept approached him, from the other side of the fractal display. "It means, young man, that instead of us going out to study events, events will come to us."

"And since psychohistorical predictive events are decided by people," T'Serl added as she took a step closer to Picard, "thus *people* will come to us."

Picard instinctively stepped back as Lept held up a crooked, black-nailed finger too close to his face. "Or one person."

In the instant it took for Picard to look from Lept to T'Serl, understanding flowed through him. "You mean to say that this graph predicts *my* arrival here today?"

Lept shook his head and stepped closer to Picard. His beetle-snuff-scented breath was warm and oddly spicy. "Actually, what this graph predicts is the end of the universe. See where the flat section starts? No change. No history. End of everything. Very bad for business, I might add."

"And because of this display's limited resolution," T'Serl said, her voice also disconcertingly closer to Picard, "we are aware that a key decision point leading to that state will occur at our current temporal coordinates."

"In other words," Lept breathed into Picard's ear, "psychohistory told us that today we would be visited by the person *responsible* for the coming destruction of the universe."

"But what it couldn't tell us," T'Serl concluded as she brought her hand to Picard's shoulder in a surprisingly intimate gesture, "was that that person would be you."

Before Picard could even open his mouth to begin to protest, he felt T'Serl's fingers expertly find the *katra* points at the base of his neck, then squeeze.

His visit to Memory Alpha had ended.

THIRTEEN

The cold air of Qo'noS smelled like blood and Kirk was sick of it.

He hated the memories it brought of all the Klingons he had known. He hated the buried past that metallic scent uncovered. Most of all, he hated what the air of this world had done to his bride.

She walked beside him on this narrow, leaf-strewn path through a thick grove of wirebraid trees. Though he had set a slow pace and the slope was gentle, he could hear each labored breath she took, see each warm exhalation mist the cool, damp air.

A few meters ahead, a fallen tree trunk lay beside the path. The polished bark of its russet trunk suggested that others had rested there over the years.

Kirk squeezed Teilani's hand and nodded at the fallen trunk. Without protest, she allowed him to guide her toward it, too weary even to acknowledge her exhaustion. They sat in silence.

Kirk looked up and down the path, checking on their Klingon bodyguards. They waited discreetly, almost out of sight, but with weapons held loosely, always at the ready.

Kirk still wasn't certain who owned this estate, with its grand lodges and streams, hunting forests and private guards. All he knew was that as the *Enterprise* had limped home from the First Federation base, Picard had contacted Worf on Deep Space 9, who had contacted someone else on the High Council, who had . . . Kirk hadn't followed the process past that. The imponderable complexities of Klingon politics and familial connections were far removed from anything he needed or wanted to know about at present. It was enough that his friend Picard had made the arrangements, and that he and Teilani now had a place to stay that kept them close to their child.

With that thought of their child, Kirk sighed deeply, still not free of his own exhaustion, which had overwhelmed him a month ago at the base.

"I know," Teilani said, her first words on this walk.

Kirk saw the same heaviness in her eyes, shadowed in darkness against skin far too pale. Her pallor made the twisted slash of her virogen scar seem red in comparison, as if the wound were still fresh, her body still battling the disease he thought she had long vanquished.

She shouldn't be this way, Kirk knew. According to McCoy, the effects of the neurotoxin were almost at an end. But also according to McCoy, the injuries Kirk had sustained in his battle with Tiberius at the First Federation base were healed.

The truth, Kirk feared, was that his and Teilani's hearts still labored under stress and strain that McCoy couldn't measure. No one could. Except for Kirk and his bride.

What dwelt within them both was no longer an exhaustion of the flesh, but of the spirit.

The spirit of our child, Kirk thought. Here on Qo'noS, he seldom thought of anything but their child. And he knew without asking that Teilani did the same.

"Bones says they'll know more when the next set of tests is finished." The useless words sounded hollow to Kirk even as he said them. But he couldn't bear the silence of this sad forest. In this region of the world, at this time of the Klingon year, the wirebraid trees had lost their leaves. A soundless breeze barely stirred the gray, spiked branches against the faded yellow sky.

The barren branches reminded Kirk of hands frozen in the act of reaching up in supplication, never to receive whatever it was they sought.

Just as his hands had never touched his baby. Their baby.

At six weeks, the child was still in a baffling state of unconsciousness, sealed within a medical stasis tube, beyond anyone's touch. Dr. McCoy had assembled a team of experts from Starfleet and the Klingon Empire, and had even used his personal connections to prevail upon two respected Romulan physicians to confer unofficially by subspace. But the mystery was no closer to solution. And no treatment was possible until that mystery was solved.

McCoy had even told Kirk that it could very well be that no treatment would be necessary. But until he and his colleagues could be sure, they needed to conduct more tests.

Yet, now, after a full six weeks of urgent, intensive study, McCoy and his illustrious team still could not say if the baby's condition was the result of some congenital syndrome, of exposure to disruptive environmental agents, or was simply the natural outcome of the blending of Kirk's and Teilani's DNA. It was the last possibility that haunted Kirk: He was the first human to have had a child with a native of Chal.

"I didn't think there were any more tests left," Teilani said tonelessly. "We have to accept what has happened."

Words rushed out of Kirk as if someone else were speaking. "Teilani, what *has* happened? When you can tell me that, then maybe we can talk about accepting it." He regretted what he said and his tone of voice at once. But he had said what he felt, and he couldn't apologize for that.

"We have a child, James. Our Joseph."

The mention of that name was like a cold hand around Kirk's heart. It was a family name, passed down through the generations, now to be passed to his son. So many dreams, so much hope, all contained in one simple name that might never be spoken.

Kirk had to stand, to walk off his frustration before it came out in more words he would rather not say.

"Teilani, I want to know what's happened to our child. I want to know *why* this has happened. Is it genetics? Is it some defect in my cells left over from who knows what I've been exposed to over my career?" He paused, knew he shouldn't, not now.

"Or is it something wrong with me," Teilani said, voicing what Kirk never wanted to say.

He didn't reply. His great fear was that what had happened was in some way his fault. But his greatest fear was that it was Teilani's. He knew he wasn't perfect. Yet for all his faults, he was confident in his ability to learn and to change, however reluctantly.

But if it was Teilani's fault, something she had done or hadn't done during her pregnancy, if that's what McCoy discovered, Kirk had looked deep inside himself and did not know if he could forgive her.

Yet even as he made that hard, dark confession to himself, he was overcome by his love for her.

He dropped to his knees beside her, pulled her close in an embrace that could never be released, his emotions in turmoil, telling him to walk away and to never leave, both at the same time.

So he clung to the one straw fate allowed him, the one possibility that even McCoy couldn't rule out.

"It was Radisson," he whispered to her, feeling the soft-
ness of her hair against his face. "It was Project Sign that
did something to you and the baby, when you were examined on their ship." He breathed in the scent of her, feeling
anchored by her presence in his arms, knowing without
doubt he could forgive her of anything.

Kirk wanted his life to be only this moment. To hold
Teilani close with no sorrow for the past, no fear for the
future. Just this perfect moment.

But not even James T. Kirk could stop time.

He heard the dry leaves crackling on the path a heartbeat
before Teilani tensed.

As if feeling a cloud slip from his grasp, Kirk leaned
back, releasing the woman he loved.

Then he rose to his feet to face the man on the path;
the man whose footsteps he knew as well as he knew his
own.

"I have some news," Tiberius said, "direct from our mutual
friend."

"What do you mean there's no Captain Hu-Linn
Radisson?" McCoy sputtered.

In the entrance hall of the river lodge, Spock took off the
heavy, dark-blue cloak he had worn against the chill of
Klingon autumn. Their Klingon hosts did not permit anyone
to beam into or out of the estate, so a walk to and from the
perimeter gate was always required. "I believe I have
expressed myself clearly, Doctor."

"I know you're doing that on purpose," McCoy said
accusingly.

"Hanging up my cloak?"

"No! Pretending not to understand me!"

Spock arranged his cloak on one of twelve gold-tipped
kreffin horns that angled out from the dark wood-paneled

wall. "Dr. McCoy, I assure you that I do not have to *pretend* I do not understand you."

McCoy looked up at the massive wooden beams that supported the high-arched ceiling blackened with centuries of woodfire. He chose his strategy. "Look, Spock, any other time I'd be as happy as a catfish at a rodeo to take you on in a war of words. And I'd win, just like I always do."

"Why would a catfish be happy at a rodeo?"

McCoy waved a finger at his old friend. "See? I won again. You just don't have the mastery of idiom you think you have."

"Doctor, I fail to understand how a catfish could be happy at all."

"Exactly my point," McCoy said with sweeping finality, using self-control of almost Vulcan proportions himself to avoid revealing that he didn't have any idea what he was talking about, either. It was just so damned enjoyable to see that predictable blink of confusion come over Spock. Someday he'd take a picture of it. Hang it on the wall. Throw darts at it. "Now, getting back to Jim."

Spock blinked an unprecedented three times. "We were not discussing the captain."

"Spock, forget about the catfish. We were talking about Hu-Linn Radisson."

"We were not talking about her, either. I merely stated that Starfleet has no record of any personnel by that name."

"And you don't think that has anything to do with Jim?" McCoy threw his hands up in the air. "Spock, we all met with the blasted woman. Radisson told—no, she *threatened* us. We were not to discuss anything at all to do with Project Sign. Not her. Not her fancy starships with holographic crew that can open up some kind of entrance portal to the mirror universe. Not anything."

"I recall the meeting."

Spock began walking toward the main hall. His boots were loud against the wooden floor. McCoy suspected the acoustics were deliberately designed to make footsteps echo noticeably—the trick made guests sound impressively massive, and also made it extremely difficult to sneak up behind anyone. Trust the Klingons.

He hurried to fall into step at Spock's side, his own footsteps equally as loud. "And you're not troubled that the woman who threatened us, who intimidated Jim, who arranged for Teilani to be medically examined on a ship none of us were allowed to board, has just *vanished?*"

McCoy's voice rose as he gave his recitation of events. He saw and did not appreciate the subtle frown such emotionalism always provoked in his Vulcan companion.

"As I have stated, Doctor, according to Starfleet records, Hu-Linn Radisson could not have vanished, because she never existed."

They had reached the main hall of the lodge, where the lodge staff kept food and drink laid out for their visitors.

McCoy followed after Spock, past the long wooden-plank tables with their vats of steaming brain stew and shifting bowls of writhing *gagh.* The Vulcan's destination was the small stand set up to one side, half-hidden by an iron cage of firewood, where a meager supply of Vulcan vegetables was kept in blocks of storage gel, as if it were an afterthought, or an embarrassment.

"For heaven's sake, Spock, we already knew *one* version of her didn't exist," McCoy said heatedly.

Spock studied a self-warming container of *plomeek* soup. "Dr. McCoy, I share your frustration," he said mildly. "But I do not take out that frustration on those who are not responsible for causing it."

McCoy sighed. He hated it when Spock was being reasonable. It took all the fun out of baiting him. "I'm sorry, Spock. It's just that . . . six weeks!"

"More tests?" Spock asked.

McCoy nodded. "We've run out of all the standard ones. *And* all the experimental ones. Now we're making them up as we go along." McCoy tried, but he couldn't keep the sound of total defeat from his voice.

Spock peeled back the cover of the soup container and instantly the orange-colored broth began to simmer. "Upon reflection," Spock said, "I should have been more forth-coming when you greeted me at the door. It is clear that a Captain Hu-Linn Radisson does exist, and that her involve-ment with Starfleet is classified at the highest levels, beyond even the reach of Vulcan diplomatic intelligence."

An apology from Spock was rare, and many times in the past had been the occasion for well-deserved gloating. But not now. McCoy knew the stakes were too high this time.

"What else did you find out?" McCoy asked with a shiver. He was glad Spock had carried his soup to a small table near the raging fire. Their Klingon hosts had provided individual power converters for heating the visitors' bed-rooms, but for the rest of the lodge, fireplaces were the sole source of warmth.

Spock took his seat at the small table and McCoy sat down across from him. They had no other company in the huge room to overhear their conversation.

"Starfleet would not even admit the existence of Project Sign," Spock began.

"That's a surprise."

Spock contemplated his steaming container of orange broth. "Therefore, while I was on Vulcan, I conducted fur-ther inquiries through diplomatic channels. They permitted me access to . . . a broader range of information sources."

McCoy made no comment about the logic of Spock having to break the rules. He understood the unusual relationship that the world of Vulcan had with Starfleet. The Fleet had been established upon the formation of the United Federation of Planets, just about a century after first contact between Vulcan and Earth. Yet it had been almost another ninety years before Spock had become the first Vulcan to enroll in Starfleet Academy. And even that could be attributed to an individual act of youthful rebellion by the half-human Spock against his Vulcan father, rather than a sign of his world's acceptance of the Fleet.

Prior to their first encounter with humans, Vulcans had prided themselves on their policy of peaceful exploration. Then the Romulan Wars had come and it was Earth Forces who had stopped the Romulan expansion in under four years. By comparison, the Romulans' earlier war with the Vulcans had lasted for one hundred years.

Given Earth's relatively quick victory over the Romulans, Vulcan leaders had reluctantly seen the benefit, if not the logic, of humanity's apparently contradictory policy of peaceful exploration conducted by heavily armed starships. Less than a year after the establishment of the Romulan Neutral Zone, the Federation came into existence, with Vulcan as one of its founding members.

But still, McCoy knew, even after two centuries of successful partnership, some Vulcan leaders maintained a sense of detachment from the Federation which all too often seemed to them to be unduly dominated by humans. It was common knowledge that the Vulcan diplomatic corps, especially, wasted no opportunity to seek out treaties under its own, unofficial initiatives. In fact, just such a clandestine mission to Romulus had taken up almost a century of Spock's own life while the Federation had officially looked the other way.

So it was not at all surprising to McCoy that Spock's contacts in the diplomatic corps might now have provided him with information that Starfleet might not have willingly volunteered unless attention-getting pressure had been applied.

"I take it you found something useful through those sources," McCoy said.

Spock scooped a slow, deliberate spoonful of his soup, prompting the thought in McCoy that sensual pleasures were wasted on Vulcans. "As we expected, Project Sign is an official Starfleet operation, though one that is not officially acknowledged."

Spock finally placed the spoon in his mouth. But McCoy could not detect any expression on the Vulcan's face as to whether the orange soup was delicious or disgusting.

"As a currently organized operational division," Spock said, placing his spoon in the container again, "Project Sign was created in 2275, under the authority of Starfleet's Technical Intelligence Division." He lifted the spoonful of soup to his mouth.

Almost mesmerized by the relentless rhythm of the spoon's rise and fall, and the stupefyingly fierce but welcome heat of the open fireplace, McCoy had to force himself not to nod off as Spock's calm voice continued.

"Sign's key personnel, however, were drawn exclusively from an earlier study group formed in 2268. The study group was designated Project Magnet. Its operational authority came from Commodore Wilbert B. Smith."

McCoy shook his head, clearing it as much as indicating his disagreement. "Spock, I can remember a few Commodore Smiths from back then, but not a Wilbert. Never heard of anything like Project Magnet, either."

"I am not surprised," Spock replied as he sipped another

spoonful of soup. McCoy braced himself for some feeble Vulcan attempt at humor directed at the frailty of human memory in general, and McCoy's in particular.

But Spock was obviously treating this matter as seriously as was the doctor. "Upon its inception, Doctor, Project Magnet was classified at the highest levels of Starfleet. Even now, after more than a century has passed, little is known about it."

"Little," McCoy said, "which means something *is* known."

"Records suggest it was hastily formed in response to a hitherto unsuspected threat facing the Federation."

"A threat? In 2268?" McCoy searched his memory. The events of that year were unusually vivid for him. He had been given a death sentence—a diagnosis of xenopolycythemia, a blood disease for which there was no cure. He had actually resigned his commission to make the most of the days remaining, until he had discovered a cure.

But what else happened about that time? he asked himself.

"The cloaking device?" McCoy said. "That was when Jim nearly started a new Romulan war, wasn't it?" He leaned forward, elbows on the table. "And there was something else involving the Romulans . . . some kind of superweapon?"

"The polaric ion reaction device," Spock confirmed. "Subsequently outlawed by treaty."

"That's not much of a threat then." McCoy sat back in his chair. "You've got me, Spock. If there was some new threat to the Federation that year, I certainly didn't know about it."

"You are wrong, Doctor." Spock dipped his spoon into the seemingly bottomless soup container. "We all knew about it. Everyone on the *Enterprise*. But we didn't know the importance of what we knew."

For just one brief and admittedly irrational moment,

McCoy wondered how Spock might look wearing a container of *plomeek* soup on his head. Someday the loquacious Vulcan would get to the point.

Then he did.

"The Preserver obelisk," Spock said.

McCoy sat upright. "Of course. The first one. Jim found it." Then confusion struck him. "And Starfleet considered it to be a *threat?*"

"In hindsight, it was a logical response." Spock efficiently spooned up the last drops of his soup. He then settled back in his chair as if he had just finished a feast and began to set forth the reasons for Starfleet's extreme reaction to the existence of the obelisk.

And McCoy was surprised to realize that he agreed with Starfleet's position. *Almost* in its entirety.

The first obelisk had been discovered by Kirk on a Class-M planet, home to the descendants of a tribal community of humans abducted from the central plains of Earth's North America almost a thousand years earlier. Even at the time, McCoy recalled, he and Kirk and Spock had understood the significance of those people's original abduction. It had occurred just prior to the arrival of the most recent wave of Europeans to colonize North America in the sixteenth century—subsequently decimating the indigenous North American population. The colonial invasion of Earth's North American continent had cost entire cultures, traditions, and languages, all lost forever.

That was where the name "Preservers" had come from. For on the Class-M world, it had been the obelisk that had protected and maintained the original culture of the transplanted humans. At the time, the abduction event itself had seemed to McCoy to have been a benign intervention in the history of a troubled and warlike world—Earth.

But Starfleet, apparently, had quite a different view of

the obelisk and whoever had created it. First, Kirk's initial discovery was seen as confirmation that, as recently as one thousand years ago, Earth was under detailed observation by a technologically superior species. Second, since the tribal group had been abducted from the plains a century *before* their way of life was to be destroyed, the makers of the obelisk were viewed as capable of making reasonably accurate predictions about the likely development of human history. Third, and most unsettling to the Project Magnet scientists, researchers, and Starfleet commanders, was the fact that they could find no evidence the Preservers had made *any* attempt to make contact with humans.

"All right," McCoy said when Spock had finished. "I admit it's unnerving to think that we've been under some alien magnifying glass. But I don't see what's so upsetting about the Preservers not contacting us. What if they have their own version of our Prime Directive, like the First Federation does? Maybe they're waiting till we perfect transwarp drive, or grow two heads . . . or who knows what else?"

"If there had been only one obelisk, Doctor, I would agree with you."

Spock's manner was gravely serious as he went on to the question of the Preservers' motivations, pointing out how similar artifacts had continued to be discovered since Kirk had found the first. And that those newly discovered obelisks had always been found in conjunction with transplanted groups of plants, animals, or sentient beings.

McCoy thought it through. He could see the reasons for Starfleet's concern. The evidence suggested that whoever or whatever the Preservers were, they had existed as a coherent society for more than two billion years—a time span longer than any known, extant, corporeal, sentient life-form that existed in the Alpha and Beta quadrants.

The proof was illustrated by the likely fate the tribal

group on the Class-M planet would have suffered on Earth if they had not been abducted. The histories of a hundred different worlds contained examples of what happened during the initial stage of global exploration and expansion—when two cultures meet, the culture that is least technologically advanced seldom survives.

For all that Starfleet pressed for the ongoing exploration of the galaxy, it wasn't just McCoy who understood the unspoken question that accompanied each unexpected first contact: What would happen to the Federation when it finally met a more advanced culture that had no Prime Directive?

"All right, Spock, I understand Starfleet's being nervous. But isn't it *logical* to assume that since the Preservers haven't initiated contact with us after all this time, it's because they don't intend to?"

McCoy was positive he saw the faintest flicker of a smile pass over the Vulcan's face. "Very well, Doctor, since you have brought up the point, let us examine the logic of the situation."

McCoy groaned, but Spock still hadn't told him what it was he had discovered through his diplomatic sources. He would have to let Spock tell him his way.

"What motive could the Preservers have for not contacting us?" Spock asked.

"I already told you," McCoy said impatiently. "They've got their own Prime Directive."

But Spock shook his head. "If that were truly the case, then surely they would have hidden their artifacts, instead of leaving them standing prominently out in the open. Our own First Contact office goes to great lengths to hide our presence from precontact worlds under our observation."

McCoy reluctantly saw the point Spock was making. "In other words, the fact that they've left the obelisks where we can find them is already a limited form of communication. They're letting us know that they're there. And that they're watching us."

Spock nodded. "And that logically suggests that no form of a Preserver Prime Directive applies."

McCoy stared past Spock into the billowing fire that filled the enormous fireplace. Ten singing Klingons could easily stand side by side in the vast opening. McCoy half-suspected they did just that for some chest-thumping ritual that would make sense only to Klingons. He put the thought aside and turned his attention back to Spock and the Preservers and their artifacts. "So if they're communicating with us, Spock, even one-sidedly, the question is what are they trying to say?"

"Precisely," Spock agreed.

"A warning?" McCoy suggested. "You know, you people aren't looking after things, so we've saved these dinosaurs on Sawyer IV, these aboriginal humans on Miram III. And there was that transplanted colony of pre-logic Vulcans we found on the second five-year mission. Didn't an obelisk turn up on that world?"

"Correct," Spock said.

"So what about it, Spock? Does it make sense that they're teaching us by example?"

"No."

McCoy took a deep breath, knowing Spock wouldn't be rushed. "I hope you're going to explain why not."

"I'm puzzled that I have to," Spock said. "Ask yourself this question, Doctor: What were the Preservers preserving at the First Federation base?"

McCoy had no answer.

"I remind you," Spock continued, "that the First Federation base was an airless asteroid, incapable of supporting any form of life. Even prior to its being hit by the smaller asteroid that penetrated its crust six years ago and destroyed the fleet of starships within."

McCoy didn't like where this was leading. "That first obelisk Jim found, it had an advanced tractor beam unit of some kind, to deflect an asteroid from a collision trajectory that would have killed the humans on that world."

"And as humans have known since the Third World War, Doctor, anyone who possesses the ability to alter the orbit of an asteroid so that it will *not* collide with a world, by definition also possesses the ability to *deliberately* cause an asteroid to impact a world."

"You're saying the obelisk at the base was placed there to *cause* the collision that destroyed the ships?"

"Logic permits no other answer."

"Why?"

Spock looked at McCoy with an expression of Vulcan apology. "To prevent Tiberius from obtaining a fleet of Fesarius-class starships."

McCoy slumped back in his chair, appalled by the ramifications of Spock's conclusion. "So what you're saying is, the Preservers aren't really preserving anything. They're *manipulating* us."

Spock nodded, and McCoy knew that the Vulcan shared his own deep unease.

"What's the opposite of the Prime Directive?" McCoy said. " 'Thou *shalt* interfere in the development of primitive cultures'?"

"Whatever the answer to that question, Doctor, I believe we now know why Project Sign was established, and from what threat they are attempting to shield us."

McCoy pushed back his chair noisily and stood up. There was only one thing to do now. "We have to tell Jim."

But Spock remained seated. "By now," he said, "the captain has already been told."

FOURTEEN

☆

"It's just as I explained," Tiberius said. "Everyone *is* out to get me."

"Even the Preservers?" Kirk didn't bother to hide his disdain. Unsurprisingly, Tiberius had come to a typically self-centered conclusion about everything Spock had uncovered.

Kirk pushed his hands deeper into the pockets of his thick Klingon jacket. His own body heat was like a wall of warmth protecting him from both this alien world and his counterpart.

In contrast, Tiberius stood before him on the forest path, jacket open, hands exposed. It was as if he were proclaiming Nature itself incapable of subduing him. "I understand, James. You're just jealous they didn't come after *you*."

Kirk didn't reply. He was still struggling to make sense of the machinations that had brought Tiberius here, not as an enemy, but as an ally.

Supposed ally.

Four weeks ago, when the *Enterprise* had returned from the First Federation base, Spock and Picard had become the architects of an unprecedented agreement with Starfleet

Intelligence. T'Val and Kate Janeway would be allowed to return to Vulcan and rejoin Intendant Spock. But the mirror Picard and the rest of the crew of the duplicate *Enterprise* would remain in custody along with their ship. Kirk could understand the reasoning. For more than a century Starfleet had held that the mirror universe was off limits, protected by a special application of the Prime Directive.

But then agents of the mirror-universe Alliance had mounted a guerrilla invasion, hijacking Picard's *Enterprise* and replacing Starfleet personnel with mirror counterparts. In the face of these provocations, Starfleet had lifted its Prime Directive restriction. Thus, the crew of the duplicate *Enterprise* could be considered prisoners of an undeclared war. Though Kirk knew they would be treated fairly and humanely, they would also be thoroughly questioned while in custody at a secure starbase.

Except for Tiberius. He had been allowed to return to Qo'noS with Kirk.

Kirk had not protested Spock's and Picard's decision. His battle with Tiberius was over. His counterpart was no longer in a position to take command of a fleet of invincible starships. All Kirk desired now was to return to his wife and his child. He wouldn't even care if Spock were to somehow find logic in proposing Tiberius as the new commander-in-chief of Starfleet. All Kirk wanted was to go home.

But Kirk *had* questioned Spock and Picard about their intentions. Both had cited two chief reasons for their decision and for Starfleet's eventual, if reluctant, acquiescence.

First, Spock and Picard maintained, in Tiberius's long career he had escaped from facilities with far more stringent security arrangements than most Federation starbases could provide. It was therefore necessary to locate another, uniquely suitable, and impregnable prison for Tiberius. Such a facility existed on Qo'noS—an isolated military estate, sealed off with forcefields, staffed by armed guards, and ringed by webs of high-resolution sensors designed to locate prey for Klingon ritual hunts.

Spock's and Picard's second reason was that Starfleet's knowledge of the mirror universe could be increased immeasurably by having Kirk and Tiberius together recount their individual histories, in order to determine which pattern of events remained the same, and which patterns were different. And since Kirk could not be expected to remain apart from Teilani and their stricken child, logic also dictated that Tiberius travel to Qo'noS with Kirk.

Starfleet Intelligence, for whatever reason or combination of reasons, had agreed.

But Kirk knew there was a third reason behind Spock's and Picard's request to keep Tiberius in custody—a reason they had not chosen to share with Starfleet or Kirk, though Kirk suspected it had something to do with the Preserver obelisk at the First Federation base. As a scientist and an archaeologist respectively, Spock and Picard were both unusually concerned by the obelisk's presence at the base.

But Kirk's concerns were those of a husband and a father. Nothing else mattered more to him now.

"Admit it, James," Tiberius said. "The real reason you've holed up here and withdrawn from the rest of the universe is because you finally understand how you've squandered your life, accomplished nothing."

Kirk looked down the path to where Teilani remained sitting on the fallen tree trunk. He saw her bodyguards like living shadows among the trees, was certain she didn't even know they were there.

Instead, she was staring at the sky as it darkened with an approaching storm. She was so small in this forest. So alone and full of pain. All he could think was that he loved her more than he had words to express, and he knew that in her way, despite the pain that consumed them, the pain that threatened to push them apart, she loved him with equal passion.

"In my life," Kirk told Tiberius, "I've accomplished more than you could ever imagine."

Tiberius sneered at him. "You started out as what? One starship captain among twelve? Then among fifty? And now? You're a captain in name only. You don't even have a ship."

"I have love."

"From one woman? James, you could have been the emperor of this ghost universe of yours. You could have had a thousand women."

"I only want—only need—one."

Tiberius pulled his jacket tight as if chilled. Leaves swirled around his boots, caught up in a sudden wind. "You're serious? One lone woman with gray in her hair, a scar that mars whatever beauty time hasn't already obscured, and a womb that bore you a monster?"

Kirk clenched his fists in his jacket pockets. He wanted to crush Tiberius like the dead leaves of this barren forest, to bury him here with everything else that was decaying. But he would not fight against someone who was, in the end, so unworthy.

"That one woman," Kirk said, "means more to me than this universe or yours." He turned his back on his counterpart, on his past, whose outcome had already been written. He began to walk along the path taking him to Teilani, and their future, in which his role was still his to define.

"No wonder the Preservers didn't choose you."

Kirk halted, his boots grinding the path's gravel to fine powder. "What makes you think they chose *you?*" he asked his counterpart.

Tiberius told him.

• • •

McCoy didn't like the way Kirk looked.

In the blazing light of the hearthfire and torches of the Klingon lodge's great hall, Kirk's pale face was splotched with red. In reaction to the cold wind outdoors or to anger, McCoy didn't know which. But either way, the mottled skin was a sign to the physician that Kirk still was not himself.

Kirk, being Kirk, though, had concerns other than his personal health.

"Didn't Jean-Luc stop to think that maybe this had something to do with *me?*" Kirk's indignant voice echoed beneath the smoke-blackened beams of the lodge's high, pitched ceiling. It cut through the growing howl of the storm-driven wind outside.

Spock, as usual, was unperturbed by his captain's emotional outburst. Tiberius appeared to be encouraging it. Refraining from useless judgment, McCoy restricted himself to following the scene closely. He wished only that he had a medical tricorder to monitor Kirk's pulse, respiration, and blood pressure.

"We concluded that your first priority was Teilani and your child," Spock said quietly.

"Of course it is," Kirk agreed hotly. "But that doesn't mean I can't have other priorities."

"We thought it might be best if you were free to focus on your family, without distractions."

Kirk glared at Spock, and gestured toward Tiberius, who lounged in a chair near the lodge's massive fireplace. "You don't call *him* a distraction?"

"The recordings you both are making, comparing your careers, are an ongoing process, with no critical time limits. You are free to do as little or as—"

"Spock, stop there. Right now. *You* do not make decisions for me."

McCoy felt he had remained silent long enough. "C'mon, Jim, don't hold it against Spock. We were all doing what we thought was best for you."

"Bones, do I look like I'm in a life-support chair like Chris Pike? Do you all think I've lost the ability to look after myself?"

"Are you asking me as a friend? Or as your physician?"

Kirk stared at him and then at Spock. "You're all in this together, aren't you?"

Tiberius smiled. The expression was unpleasant to McCoy, both familiar and unfamiliar at the same time.

"Ah, the memories this brings back," Tiberius said almost wistfully. "My own Spock and McCoy always at each other's throats—until Spock had McCoy executed for the good of the Empire. But please, please, James, go on. Being a victim of conspiracy *is* the price one pays for power. All true leaders are betrayed at some point."

"This isn't a conspiracy," Kirk snapped. "It's two friends who've stepped over the line. And not for the first time."

Spock spoke as if he hadn't even noticed Tiberius's interruption. "Very well, what would you have us do?"

Kirk's answer was to the point. "First, I want to talk to Jean-Luc."

"Captain Picard is on leave," Spock said firmly. "He cannot be reached."

The red patches on Kirk's cheeks darkened. He shifted restlessly from one foot to another, the motion suggesting he was ready to storm from the hall. "A starship captain out of Starfleet's reach? Don't give me that, Spock. I know what's going on."

He probably does at that, McCoy thought. *Why do we even bother to try to keep anything from him. . . .*

"Tiberius just finished telling me your theory about the Preserver obelisk at the base."

"Then you know that at present we are engaged in determining the accuracy of our theory," Spock calmly replied. "And there is nothing you can add to that investigation."

Kirk took a deep breath, his self-control clearly beginning to fray. "Spock, if you want to talk theory, you're four weeks too late. Tiberius is convinced that the Preservers are after him *personally.*"

Kirk waved one hand in the direction of his counterpart. *"He* believes that the Preservers' actions show they want to control the galaxy. *He* believes they see him as a direct threat because that's what he wants to do, too—*and* has proved he can do it. Believe me, the only thing on *his* mind is getting off Qo'noS and going hunting for them himself. That's action, not theory."

Kirk pressed on. "And I know Jean-Luc's taking action, too. He's not on leave. He's probably off talking to Starfleet Intelligence or some other group of experts about the mirror universe and the Preservers—trying to build a consensus before committing himself to the next step."

Close enough, McCoy thought. Picard was on Memory Alpha, talking to the two psychohistorians he'd identified as the most likely non-Starfleet source of the background information he felt he needed.

Spock paused, a telltale sign McCoy recognized as signaling the Vulcan's capitulation to Kirk. "Captain Picard has not approached Starfleet Intelligence."

McCoy saw a real smile touch Kirk's lips, but just briefly, but it was the first in weeks. "That's because of Project Sign, isn't it?" Kirk asked. "If Radisson's operation has gone rogue, Starfleet Intelligence might be compromised. Maybe even all of Starfleet Command." He shot a glance at Tiberius. "How's that for a conspiracy?"

"There is another possibility," Spock said. "The Preserver threat may already have been identified. I have learned that

Project Sign has its origins in Project Magnet, and Project Magnet was formed in the same year you discovered the first obelisk. A telling coincidence, I believe."

McCoy didn't understand Kirk's sudden look of surprise. "Magnet? That's where Sign came from?"

It seemed Spock was puzzled by Kirk's response, as well. "According to the best sources," the Vulcan said, "Magnet was merely a preliminary study group. Sign was authorized to take action."

Kirk shook his head emphatically. "Spock, Project Magnet was formed *before* I found the obelisk."

Spock regarded Kirk gravely. "You are aware of Project Magnet?"

Kirk chewed his lip, looked off into the fire. "It was, uh . . . Stone? Commodore Bob Stone?"

The name sounded familiar to McCoy, but he couldn't place it.

But Spock's Vulcan mind could. "Are you referring to Commodore Robert Stone of Starbase 11?"

"That's it," Kirk said. "I remember speaking to him about it. I'm not sure when. But he was commander of a starbase at the time, only a year or two away from making admiral, and he accepted a transfer back to Earth to head up Project Magnet. He didn't say what it was, but . . . I don't know, years later, when I was an admiral, I ran into him at a spacedock on Earth. He was still a commodore. We had a drink. He told me to watch out for Starfleet study groups. Never give up the center chair the way he had. That's why I remember what he said."

Spock looked over at McCoy as if asking for confirmation of Kirk's story, but even with the details Kirk had provided, McCoy couldn't remember a Commodore Stone from Starbase 11.

"Captain," Spock said, almost sounding apologetic, "it

was many years ago. Your memory of the timing of events may not be as precise as you believe."

"Spock, I'll be the first to admit that I can't keep all our old missions straight. I'm sure I've forgotten some of them completely, and I've mixed up other ones. But let me explain why I'm so sure about this one."

Kirk had begun to pace back and forth before the fireplace, and now he stopped to face Spock. McCoy saw a thoughtful look come over Kirk's counterpart and didn't trust it or him.

"Do you remember where you were when the Federation declared war on the Klingon Empire?" Kirk asked Spock.

Even McCoy could answer that question. Just as could any adult who was alive at the time. When Starfleet had broadcast the first Code 1 alert in its history, it was one of those pivotal, defining moments for an entire generation.

"We were one day out from Janus VI," Spock said. "I was meditating in my quarters when the alert tone sounded on my viewer."

"*Everyone* remembers where they were that day," Kirk said, "and what they were doing. For me, our first five-year mission is divided more or less in half by that event. And I *know* that Bob Stone told me about Project Magnet *before* the declaration of war, and that I found the Preserver obelisk *after*."

"If your recollection is correct," Spock said, "then it suggests there *is* no correlation between the Preservers and Project Sign."

"That worries you," Kirk said. "Why?"

"If Project Sign was not created in response to the Preservers, then what other threat are we facing? Presumably one which was identified in 2267."

"Or else," McCoy suggested, "Starfleet has known about the Preservers for longer than anyone knows."

"That's possible," Kirk said. But then he hesitated and McCoy could see him working on something, trying to capture another memory. "When I met with Captain Radisson on the *Heisenberg,* she told me about Project Sign. She said . . . she said that in my first five-year mission, I had made a discovery that led to Starfleet undertaking an ultrasecret research project, to determine the ramifications of . . . of what I found. At the time, I thought she was referring to when we first crossed over to the mirror universe, but she didn't . . . didn't confirm or deny it."

"An interesting supposition," Spock said reflectively. "We did cross over to the mirror universe prior to your discovery of the obelisk."

McCoy was troubled. "So what does that mean, Spock? Was Project Sign created to study the mirror universe or the Preservers?"

"Or, indeed," the Vulcan mused, "in response to some other discovery."

But before McCoy could say anything more, he saw that Kirk's impatience was bringing the discussion to an end.

"Gentlemen, this is fascinating, I'm sure, but we're spending too much time on the past. What does it matter *what* Project Sign was originally supposed to study? What does it matter *when* Starfleet found out about the Preservers? But what *does* matter is that Sign is somehow connected to the Preservers today. And if it does turn out the Preservers are interfering in the development of the Federation, what we have to ask ourselves is, *Why?"*

"Unfortunately, we do not possess enough data to answer that question," Spock said.

"Then let's stop all this talking and go get it," Kirk said. "Action, Spock. Not theory."

To McCoy, it was like watching Scotty restore the flow of power to a balky warp engine. Outwardly, there was no apparent difference in Kirk. But something had just changed. The air of the lodge was charged with a new hum of energy. There was a force in Kirk that had been repressed too long, that was building to an explosion, just like the wind that roared outside, the beginning of a full-scale Klingon storm. The wildness of the blazing Klingon fire was captured in Kirk's eyes.

McCoy sighed in resignation, accepting the inevitable. *It's probably just what Jim needs to shake him out of the morass he's in,* he thought. But he was troubled by his diagnosis. Why did it always have to be all or nothing with the man? Why did he only seem to come alive when there was some personal, physical challenge in his way?

McCoy didn't know what Kirk would do next, nor what that meant for his wife and his child. But it was clear that Kirk's sojourn on Qo'noS was coming to an end.

"Get me Jean-Luc," Kirk said, and McCoy recognized a command from the center chair when he heard it. So did Spock.

Kirk was back.

And he had a new mission.

If the Preservers *were* out there, McCoy thought, then with Jim Kirk on their trail, he almost felt sorry for them.

Almost.

FIFTEEN

☆

"It doesn't trouble ye, lad?" Montgomery Scott asked.

Commander Will Riker looked away from the double-height viewports that opened onto the vast interior of the spacedock facilities of Starbase 25-Alpha. "I'm sorry, Mr. Scott. What doesn't trouble me?"

The engineer frowned, gestured to indicate the entire installation that surrounded them. "This starbase. I mean, it's not listed in any of the fleet installation guides. There's a Starbase 25, sure. But an *alpha* designator? They use those for shuttlepods, not gargantuan spacedocks floatin' out in orbit of a neutron star where no one in their right mind would even *think* of stoppin' for a visit."

Riker knew what Scott meant, but he was equally sure this wasn't the place to discuss it. The events of the past few weeks had led him to assume that every word he spoke here, every action he took, was being monitored, recorded, and analyzed.

He hated to do it, but he had to talk Scott out of his well-placed paranoia.

"Scotty," Riker said with a winning smile, "you know as

well as I do that Starfleet has secret installations all over the quadrant. They're necessary for advanced technology development, munitions manufacture, communications interception . . . there is a war on, you know."

The truculent set of Scott's jaw telegraphed the engineer's disapproval of Riker's light, joking manner.

"It's unseemly of ye to humor an old man," Scott said.

"You're not an old man," Riker said. "You're the best engineer Starfleet's ever had." *Sure hope* that *doesn't get back to Geordi,* Riker thought. "And you were the only one in the *entire* Fleet who knew that structure in the Goldin Discontinuity wasn't a transporter."

Scott folded his arms and gave Riker a skeptical stare.

Riker sighed. "All right, you want the truth, here's the truth. If I were a commander of a secret starbase, I'd put hidden sensors through the whole thing. I'd have computers listen to every conversation in the base, and alert Starfleet Intelligence agents to any that even remotely suggested unhappiness with the secret base."

Scott's gaze turned frosty.

"And then," Riker continued, "just to be sure the secret starbase remained secret, I'd lock up anyone—and I mean anyone—who was a potential security risk and I'd throw away the keycode."

Scott scowled, the grimace twisting his thick moustache downward. If there was one thing the veteran engineer liked more than engineering, Riker knew, it was complaining about Starfleet bureaucracy. And Riker was letting him know that this wasn't the place to do it.

"Message received," Scott said stiffly.

"What message?" Riker asked. "I'm sure this starbase is run according to the Uniform Code of Starfleet Justice. Surely you don't think that anyone would be illegally monitoring our conversations here?"

"Heavens, no," Scott grumbled. He looked back out the viewports. "That would be as likely as seein' two *Enterprises* floatin' out there."

Riker took in the view, too. And, of course, there *were* two *Enterprises* in the spacedock: the original, NCC-1701-E; and her mirror-universe duplicate, newly emblazoned with the registry code NX-1701, though there was still no name on her to replace the one that had been removed.

Both ships now showed no sign of their epic chase and battle at the First Federation asteroid base. Damaged hull plates had been replaced. Scorch marks scoured. The new main-hangar-deck module installed on Picard's *Enterprise* was indistinguishable from the original. Even the nacelles of the duplicate had been completely restored.

However, those were just the exterior repairs. Internally, the original *Enterprise* required at least another week of component replacement and testing. The duplicate, Riker had been told, would remain here for at least an additional six months. Riker presumed that meant the ship would be studied for clues to the advanced replicator technology that had created it, and not because repairs would take that long.

"Have you had a chance to examine the upgrades Tiberius put on his ship?" Riker asked. That seemed to be an innocuous change of subject.

Scott snorted in scorn. "I wouldna exactly call them 'upgrades,' Commander. Workarounds is more like it. They couldn't handle our phaser components, so they slapped together some plumber's nightmare that uses twice the power for half the effect."

Suspecting he was being recorded, Riker restricted his reply to a noncommittal *hmmph*. The almost-certain probability of surveillance certainly put a damper on any real conversation he would like to have with Scott.

First and foremost, Riker thought, he wanted to ask the

engineer about Intendant Spock and his daughter, T'Val. And about Kate Janeway, the mirror counterpart of Captain Janeway of the *Voyager*.

Riker had seen the three of them escorted off the *Enterprise* at the same time the staff of Starbase 25-Alpha had placed Commandant Picard and the 137 crew members of the duplicate *Enterprise* in detention. But the sighting had just been a glimpse. The orders direct from Starfleet Command had been unequivocal: Under no circumstances were any members of the *Enterprise*'s crew to engage in any direct conversation with the mirror crew. The only exception was Data. Apparently, the mirror universe contained no counterpart for the android; thus only Data was safe from replacement by a mirror duplicate. *Good thing,* Riker thought. *One Lore was bad enough.*

"Och," Scott said suddenly, "will ye look at that!"

Riker stared in fascination as the mirror *Enterprise* began to flicker, then disappeared completely, leaving the first *Enterprise* floating on her own in a web of airlock tunnels and construction braces.

"Looks like they repaired the Tantalus mask," Riker said.

Scott laughed derisively. "I'll agree with ye when I see the ship come back. Knowing how to turn the mask on isn't the same as knowing how to turn it off. I already told them that."

"You mean there's a chance they *can't* turn it off?"

"Commander, if the mask generator is in the same condition it was in yesterday, I'll bet ye a month's pay—if we were bein' paid, that is—that right now, not only is every component of that ship invisible to everyone on board her, so are her exalted Starfleet work crews." He shook his head mournfully. "Amateurs. They have no idea what they're dealing with."

"And you do?" Commodore Nathan Twining asked.

Riker turned around quickly. He hadn't heard the doors to the corridor open. Neither had he heard a transporter. How long had the commodore been present?

But if Scott shared Riker's surprise or apprehension, his prompt response to the commodore revealed neither.

"Sir, I have no idea how that mask works, either. But I have no problem admitting it. The team leader you have over there—"

"Captain Keyhoe?"

"Aye, he's the one. He's as baffled as I am, only he's refusing to admit it."

Commodore Twining smiled blindingly as if Scott had made a particularly amusing joke, and once again Riker was struck by the man's impossibly perfect appearance. Every silver-flecked hair on his head was cut in precise alignment. His large, even teeth were almost shockingly white. The immaculate condition of his uniform suggested that the completely crease-free garment had resolved out of the replicator less than a minute ago. And the same exacting standard extended to every member of Twining's staff, from ensign to captain, who all looked to Riker as if they were constantly turned out in their parade best. Riker found himself wondering what that standard said about the commodore's priorities.

But the mystery of Commodore Twining extended beneath surface appearances. Even after four weeks at this base, overseeing the repair work on the *Enterprise*, Riker didn't yet know to what division of Starfleet the commodore reported.

What he did know was that the man wasn't the commander of the starbase. That was the job of Captain Kev Randle, whom Riker had seen only twice. Neither was Twining's rank even officially part of Starfleet's chain of command. "Commodore" had been a flag-officer rank a century ago, but in Riker's experience, today it was simply an informal title given to the senior captain within a group of ships' captains.

However, after the first meeting between Commodore Twining and the command staff of the *Enterprise*, Data had confirmed for Riker that though the honorary rank was no longer in common use, it did still remain in Starfleet's files, and several personnel currently held it. Unfortunately, the files that Data was able to access had not revealed who those personnel were, or which divisions they worked for.

"Don Keyhoe can be a bit single-minded," the commodore said with an easy smile. "I take it you'd like to be a member of his team?"

"The captain doesn't seem interested in my help," Scott replied gruffly.

"I'll talk to Don again. See if he could use an extra pair of hands."

"Is the captain on the replicated ship right now?"

"I believe so."

Scott raised his eyebrows. "Might be a wee bit of a while before anyone's talking to him again, seems to me."

Twining smiled once more. "I'm sure they'll determine how to switch the mask off, even if they are invisible."

Twining's statement confirmed Riker's suspicions about surveillance. *I'll bet he's heard* every *word,* Riker thought. *Probably for the past four weeks.* "Is there something *I* can do for you, Commodore?" he asked.

The commodore's response took a new direction. "Captain Radisson has asked to meet with you."

Riker did his best to conceal the sudden interest that flared in him. Hu-Linn Radisson—the mysterious commander of the Project Sign ships that had opened a portal into the mirror universe. He had heard Picard and Kirk talk about meeting her, though Kirk said Radisson was of short stature while Picard described her as large and imposing. Captain Spock had theorized that the discrepancy could be explained if one considered the possibility that nothing experienced by any of the visitors to Radisson's ship had been real—only holographic illusions.

Whatever Radisson really looked like, Riker could only conclude that the layers of deception that clouded her real identity proved that she herself was as highly classified as the project she worked for.

"I'm at the captain's disposal," Riker said.

Twining nodded as if that was the only answer he had expected. "Very good." He tapped his combadge. "Twining to the *Heisenberg*. I'm with Commander Riker and he is ready to meet with Captain Radisson at her convenience."

"Thank you, Commodore." The voice that replied sounded like a standard Starfleet computer.

Then the same voice came from Riker's combadge. *"Commander Riker, please prepare for transport."*

Riker was puzzled. "Excuse me, Commodore, but where exactly will I be meeting with the captain?"

But the question came too late.

Twining and Scott and Starbase 25-Alpha dissolved into quantum mist, as Riker was beamed away—

—and reappeared on Mars.

For a moment, Riker's mouth dropped open as his first breath revealed the hot, dry metallic scent of a terraformed Martian desert. The gentle pressure of his boots in the red sand reflected the light pull of gravity, just over a third that of Earth's.

There was no mistaking where he was, however unlikely the transition had been.

A moment ago, he had been on Starbase 25-Alpha, orbit-

ing a neutron star three hundred light-years distant from the
Earth and Mars at the center of Sector 001.

No transporter technology was that powerful.

Unsettled and needing an explanation, Riker looked up
and saw the distant sun of his home system in the red
planet's salmon sky, then realized he was seeing it filtered
through a faint grid pattern of . . .

He looked into the distance, saw cliffs rise up, supporting the overhead grid, then knew where he was—in a
Zubrin crater. At least that's what the term used to be for a
few thousand hectares of Mars made habitable under a cov-
ering of transparent, nanoplastic membrane. The Martian
pioneers had called it "poor man's terraforming," changing
the planet's biosphere one crater at a time.

But that's impossible, Riker thought. Nanoplastic membranes hadn't been used on Mars for centuries. All the terraformed regions today were protected by multiply redun-
dant interplexed forcefields. This had to be—

"Commander Riker!"

Riker turned to see a long trail of red dust hanging in the
still air, churned up by the magnificent sorrel horse that gal-
loped toward him in the eerie stuttering gait Earth horses
instinctively adopted in low-gravity worlds.

Astride the horse, riding bareback, was a young woman,
no more than twenty, Riker guessed, with long red hair
secured in a ponytail that streamed out behind her. She
waved at him.

But as the horse drew nearer and slowed, Riker revised
his estimate of the woman's age.

She was in Starfleet uniform, and her rank was captain—
unlikely for someone younger than twenty-eight, unattain-
able for someone only twenty. Despite appearances, she
had to be much older than she looked.

Riker covered his nose and mouth as the horse came to a

full stop in a low-gravity billow of red dust. The equine was clearly Martian bred-and-born. A genetically engineered breed of pony grown to horselike stature in Martian gravity, whose delicate legs could never withstand the greater gravity of Earth.

The rider kicked up a leg and gracefully dismounted, appearing to almost float to the ground. Her freckled face shone with sweat and her uniform boots and jacket were streaked with Martian red.

The woman held out her hand. "I'm Captain Radisson. A pleasure to meet you at last."

Riker smiled, shook her hand, admiring this third incarnation of the enigmatic captain.

The Radisson Kirk had met was, he said, about a meter and a half tall, perhaps sixty years old. The Radisson Picard had met was over two meters tall, with imposing shoulders and a physique like a plus-grav powerlifter. But this Radisson stood only a few centimeters shorter than Riker, with a slim build, and was impossibly young for her rank.

"The pleasure is mine," Riker said. "Are we on a holodeck?"

Radisson laughed. "It's my ready room, actually. You're on the *Heisenberg*. We're docked thirty-six kilometers outside the base." She gestured behind him. "Pull up a rock, Commander."

Riker looked over his shoulder and saw a cluster of black boulders a few meters away. To one side of them, a vividly green plant rose up out of the red desert, its slender stalk wreathed in broad leaves veined with pale-green spirals that reminded Riker of the arms of an opening wormhole. The lone plant in the desert, combined with the overhead membrane, led Riker to guess that Radisson's program re-created one of the great homestead ranches of the Martian frontier days.

Riker chose a rock next to the green plant. "So," he asked Radisson, "do you study history, or is this just a good place to ride?"

Radisson's pleased smile was infectious, mischievous. "Do you recognize where we are?" she asked.

She reached down behind another tumble of rocks and brought out a copper watering can. Water sloshed inside it.

Riker surveyed his surroundings. The haze in the atmosphere trapped and heated beneath the nanoplastic membrane prevented him from seeing the opposite crater walls to the west. But he could still make out a geodesic dome a few kilometers away, in the center of a collection of low buildings that were little more than boxes constructed of traditional, microwave-fused Martian sandblocks. There were no structures or landmarks that he could specifically identify, though.

"Early Mars" was the best he could do. "Pre-Revolution."

Radisson nodded. "Did you know that people from Earth always call it 'The Martian Revolution,' but that Martians call it 'The War of Independence'?"

"Either way, we all live by the Fundamental Declarations," Riker said. He had sensed a touch of pride in her reference to the Revolution. "Are you from Mars?"

Radisson carefully poured a thin stream of water around the base of the plant. "No," she said, but didn't offer anything more until the copper can was empty. "This is Fort Lincoln."

Riker sat up with renewed interest. "Really?" He looked again at the distant buildings. "Then that dome is . . ."

"Gundersdotter's Dome," Radisson said. She put the watering can down and pushed aside a few fluttering, escaping strands of hair, leaving red streaks on her unlined forehead. "Where the Declarations were written."

"And where Rayla Gundersdotter was assassinated when the Consortium's militia blew out the membrane supports."

"You know your history," Radisson said approvingly.

"The granting of independence to the Martian Colonies—"

"Which the Martians call the *winning* of their freedom."

"—was a turning point in the development of Earth's own world government."

"The recognition that all worlds are created equal."

Riker eyed Radisson thoughtfully. "Are we having a debate, Captain?"

Again, she sidestepped his question. "This is the day, you know."

"What day?"

She pointed to the unseen walls of the crater. "Right now, the Consortium's militiamen are on the western peaks, finishing the programming of their charges. In a few minutes, they'll go off along a thirty-kilometer wedge. Less than sixty seconds after that, the atmospheric pressure in this crater will drop from eight hundred millibars to only ten. The temperature will fall from twenty-six Celsius to minus eighty. Fifty-three people will die instantly outside Gundersdotter's Dome, and twelve more will die inside when the militiamen arrive and blow out its airlock."

"And fifty days later, Earth will revoke the Consortium's development licenses and Mars . . . 'wins' her freedom."

Radisson stood, squinting off into the distance, as if she could see the militiamen kilometers away, in their battlesuits camouflaged with random splotches of red and black and pink. "Was there another way?" she mused, as if lost in thought.

Riker shifted on the boulder in an effort to find a more comfortable position, rubbed at his beard and drew his hand away in surprise. There were fine particles of Martian sand on his fingers. He had rarely experienced a holosimulation with such attention to detail.

"Well?" Radisson asked, turning back to him. "Do you

think there was another way for Mars to be free? Another direction history might have taken?"

"I'm sorry," Riker said. He had thought she was being rhetorical. "Eventually, I suppose. But Earth had so many other issues to contend with at the time that . . . it took violence to bring the plight of the Martian Colonies to their attention."

Now Radisson studied him intently. "So you approve of violence in the furtherance of political goals?"

Riker wished he knew what Radisson really wanted of him. "Is there some point to this conversation I'm not aware of?" When Radisson did not immediately answer him, he prompted, "You asked to see me." The simulation was impressive. Radisson, intriguing. But he was running out of patience.

"You're very direct," Radisson said. "That's good." She sat down on a boulder opposite Riker, drew up her knees and wrapped her arms around them as if she were on a camping trip. Then she finally got to the point.

"Back at the beginning of Starfleet and the Federation, in the heroic era of the Daedalus-class starships, captains and their crews would receive their orders, then set off on voyages that would last years, almost all of them spent beyond the reach of command. A single starship captain could commit the Federation to a peace treaty or start an interstellar war, all on his own judgment."

"That's still true today," Riker said.

Radisson shook her head. "Not to the same extent. With booster relays, the entire Federation is less than twenty subspace-days across. Five hundred years ago on Earth, it took longer than that to carry a letter from London to New York."

Riker took a guess. "Are you considering sending me on a mission that will involve being out of contact with command?"

Radisson's face was transformed by a wide, delighted smile. "You're making this so easy, Commander. That's exactly what I'm considering."

Riker waited.

"No questions?" Radisson asked.

Why not? Riker thought. "Are you the same Captain Radisson who met with Captain Kirk at the Goldin Discontinuity?"

Radisson seemed puzzled by the question. "Yes."

"And you're the same Captain Radisson who met with Captain Picard?"

"Of course. Why would you think otherwise?"

Riker began to feel uneasy. "It's just that . . . you don't resemble either of their descriptions of you."

Radisson cocked her head at Riker as if he had just spoken in Vulcan. "Really?"

Riker had expected at least some kind of explanation, even if untruthful, but not outright denial. "I . . . with all your holographic simulation capabilities, I thought perhaps you appeared in holographic disguise."

"You did?"

Now Riker was flat-out uncomfortable. He stood up. "You must admit your ship has the ability to do so."

Radisson looked up at him. Her open face was still friendly. "But why would I appear to Kirk and Picard, and to you, in anything other than my true appearance?"

Riker fumbled for words, but all he could manage was "Project Sign."

Radisson's voice cooled. "I see. Someone's been talking." She stretched out her legs and stood up, brushing sand off the back of her trousers. "I must say I am disappointed, Commander."

At once Riker saw the point of her denials. She'd hoped to put him off guard. To provoke him into revealing something he ordinarily wouldn't. If it had been a test, he had failed.

That meant to Riker that under the circumstances he had nothing to lose by going on the offensive. "Captain Kirk and Captain Picard were concerned by your deception."

"Are you?"

"Yes."

Radisson frowned. "I find that difficult to believe." She tapped her combadge three times, then Riker heard his own voice play back.

"Scotty, you know as well as I do that Starfleet has secret installations all over the quadrant. They're necessary for advanced technology development, munitions manufacture, communications interception... there is a war on, you know."

"Commander Riker, I would think that you, especially, would understand the need for caution in certain critical missions."

Riker judged it time to surrender. He didn't enjoy playing games when he didn't know what the stakes were. "Captain, I think it's time you told me why you brought me here."

Before Radisson could reply, Riker heard a long and far-off rumble, like something enormous being torn, thunderously loud, but muffled by distance.

Radisson looked up, expectant. "There it is!" she said excitedly, and pointed to the west.

The ground beneath Riker's boots began to tremble as the pressure waves from the explosions ringing the crater finally reached his position. Radisson's mount whinnied nervously.

Despite his knowledge that this was only a simulation, Riker felt a momentary twinge of alarm. The re-creation was that good.

The fading echoes of the explosions vanished, supplanted by a rushing roaring sound, like that of some approaching giant wind.

"There!" Radisson said.

She pointed to the western horizon and from the haze Riker saw a wall of mist rise, blood-red at the bottom, shading upward through pink to pure white at the top.

Riker at once knew what he was witnessing: Mere kilometers away, the atmosphere-trapping membrane was no longer intact.

The pure-white upper edge of the advancing wall was the moisture of the escaping atmosphere crystallizing into white snow in instant response to falling pressure and temperature. The blood-red lower edge was red Martian sand stirred up by the remaining atmosphere rushing upward and away from the rest of the crater. The pink between the white and the red was the red sand mixing with the clouds of frozen vapor.

Then long white streaks shot by overhead like the contrails of high-speed atmospheric craft.

A wall of wind slammed into Riker's back, knocking him forward, facedown in smothering clouds of red dust and dirt.

The sorrel horse reared, snorting in panic.

Choking and coughing, Riker turned his head, raised himself up to see Radisson beside him. She held her arms out wide as if to embrace the inevitable coming of the vacuum and death.

Riker struggled to his feet, even as his eardrums popped in the dropping pressure.

Incredulous, he thought he heard Radisson begin to laugh wildly, triumphantly . . .

Just as she called out—

"End program!"

Riker almost lost his footing as the Zubrin crater vanished along with the pressure of the howling wind and he was in . . .

He looked around.

He wasn't sure what he was in.

Elegantly curved, white-paneled walls flowed smoothly from the floor and into the ceiling, making Riker feel as if he were in a giant sculpture. But Radisson was beside him, still laughing with exhilaration, brushing red sand from her uniform. Riker looked down and saw a thin coating of the sand on the floor around his boots. His heels made the sand crunch.

"Relax, Commander, you're still in my ready room," Radisson said.

She walked over to what Riker assumed was a desk, whose white base appeared to have grown seamlessly from the floor, or from the deck if this was indeed Radisson's ship, the *Heisenberg*.

To one side of the desk, Riker recognized the green plant from the Martian simulation. The copper watering can was still beside it.

"*Has* this been a test of some kind?" Riker demanded.

"A conversation," Radisson said crisply. She touched the surface of her desk and a small, holographic viewscreen formed in front of her. The heavyset figure of a bearded Klingon, also in Starfleet uniform, appeared on it. "Stanton," she ordered, "you may bring in the data records now."

"At once, Captain," the Klingon growled. Then the viewscreen vanished.

"A conversation about what?" Riker asked, wondering if Picard and Kirk had felt as manipulated and confused as he did right now.

Radisson sat down on the corner of her white desk, reaching out one freckled hand to stroke the green plant's leaves.

"What do you think, Commander? We talked about freedom. About revolution. About people like Rayla Gundersdotter willing to die for what they believe in."

"Are you asking me if I'm willing to die for what I believe in?"

Radisson shook her head. "Not what. Who."

Riker stared at her, uncomprehendingly.

"Captain Jean-Luc Picard has been taken prisoner," Radisson said.

"What?! When? Who's responsible?"

A hidden set of doors opened in the far bulkhead and the Klingon officer stepped into the room, with something held in one hand.

Before the doors closed behind the Klingon, Riker caught a glimpse of the *Heisenberg*'s huge bridge. It appeared to be at least three times the size of that of the *Enterprise,* and Riker was able to see perhaps twenty crew members staffing consoles above which floated holographic displays.

"Thank you, Commander," Radisson said as she stood up to accept what appeared to be a silver padd from the Klingon officer.

"May I ask why Commander Stanton is wearing a Starfleet uniform?" Riker asked, still reeling from Radisson's disclosure about Picard. The last he had heard, Worf was still the only Klingon in Starfleet.

"It's not important," Radisson said dismissively. To the Klingon she said, "You may go offline now."

The Klingon nodded, glared at Riker, then dissolved into holographic static.

Before Riker could formulate another question, Radisson had walked toward him and placed the silver padd in his hand.

Riker stared down at it, completely confused. "What is going on here, Captain?"

Radisson nodded at the padd. "That's all we know. That's what you'll need to get your captain back. If he's still alive."

Riker's grip on the padd tightened. He felt the hot rush of anger. His voice rose as he challenged Radisson to explain herself and her actions. "Why this charade? Why not transmit this information to every ship in the Fleet?"

Radisson's grim expression aged her by several decades. "Commander Riker, Project Sign has been preparing for war for almost one hundred and fifty years."

"What war?" Riker had had it with Radisson's enigmatic pronouncements.

"A war that . . . will destroy us. It will rob us of our identity. It will erase what we believe in. Everything will be taken from us."

"By what enemy?" Riker persisted.

Radisson walked back to her desk and sat down behind it. "That's the question we asked for decades. *Where* is the enemy? From what direction will the first sign of attack come?

"But what we didn't know," Radisson said as she met Riker's eyes directly, "was that the attack began long ago. The enemy is already among us. We spent so much time and effort looking out to the frontier, we neglected to look back at ourselves."

"What does this have to do with me?" Riker asked.

"We are unable to transmit the information in that padd to the fleet, Commander, because we don't know who we can trust anymore."

"You're saying you can trust me?"

"We believe so, yes."

Riker finally saw where this was going. "Because I'm willing to die for the Federation," he said flatly.

Radisson shook her head. "In the end, Commander, soldiers don't die for their worlds or their politicians. They die for the soldier beside them.

"I met with Captain Kirk in this room—we experienced the San Andreas quake of 2005 together. *He* was willing to die for his wife. And so, by fighting for her, he fought for us."

Riker's grip tightened on the silver padd until it felt he would crush it. "You manipulated him, too."

"We prefer to think we inspired him. Revolution, or war of independence, take your pick."

Riker drew the only conclusion that made sense to him. "If I find that you've deliberately put Captain Picard at risk so that I—"

But Radisson wouldn't let him finish. "We did nothing of the kind, Commander. I just finished telling you. We didn't know who the enemy was."

Radisson sat back, then turned to stroke the green plant again. "We sent Kirk off against the wrong person. And now it's just a matter of time before he comes back after us."

"Captain Picard was right," Riker said contemptuously. "You are out of control."

Radisson reluctantly turned away from the plant with a sigh.

"Not out of control. We're losing."

"Against *whom?* The Dominion? The Romulans?"

"Commander Riker, if you use the information in that padd, and you're willing to die for your captain, then maybe you'll save him. And if you do, then maybe the Federation will be saved, too."

"Maybe?" Riker was outraged.

"We can't see the future, Commander. But maybe you can save it for us. Before . . ."

"Before what?" Riker demanded.

"Before James T. Kirk destroys us all."

SIXTEEN

☆

At least my kidnappers arranged for a good ship, Picard thought.

In his low-ceilinged stateroom, he had a mini-replicator with decent food fit for humans. The sonic shower in the compact head was new. The color of the bulkhead panels could be changed by means of a simple decor interface. And the stateroom's general-purpose reading padd could access a library of over ten thousand volumes from many different worlds, even though the works were without exception noncontroversial classics. The library had obviously been designed for a civilian passenger liner.

However, judging from the vibrations he felt through the deck, and the subsystems he could hear when he listened at the bulkheads, this ship was equipped with a fifteen-meter Vulcan-made oblate warp core powered by a Centauran, Type III matter-antimatter reactor. That was a tricky configuration to maintain at high efficiency, and so was usually found in custom-built yachts, warp racers, or smugglers' ships.

Since T'Serl and Lept hadn't struck him as either criminal types or sports fliers, Picard concluded that the two psychohistorians were simply exceedingly well funded.

But by whom, and for what purpose?

Answering either of these questions was not proving simple for Picard, especially since the reality of his situation was that his stateroom, no matter how well equipped, had no viewports and no door. It was a cell by any other name.

But, Picard reasoned, if his captors had wanted him dead, they wouldn't have allowed him to wake up from T'Serl's nerve pinch. Instead, as Spock might say, logic suggested that T'Serl and Lept had some further use for Picard. Which also suggested to Picard that he would eventually be released from this cell.

Which meant he would eventually have a chance to launch a counterattack.

The opportunity presented itself on his third day of captivity.

The library padd on the writing desk chimed and Picard saw T'Serl's face appear in a communications window on the device's small screen.

"We will talk with you now," the Vulcan said without preamble.

"You've had three days to talk with me," Picard replied. He hit the padd's Off switch.

A moment later, the padd chimed again, indicating to Picard that his captors could override its controls.

But they can't override me, he thought.

Picard picked up the padd by one end and slammed it against the edge of the desk. The padd's case splintered with a brief cascade of sparks.

He dropped the damaged device to the deck and ground his heel into it.

Then he waited.

Within three minutes, he heard a faint transporter tone and saw a portable communications interface materialize in the center of his stateroom cell. The interface was about the size of an emergency medical kit and had a heavy-duty housing, suitable for use on rugged away missions.

Picard studied the device. He wouldn't be able to smash this one.

A moment later, T'Serl reappeared on the portable interface screen.

"We understand your emotional need to express frustration at your captivity," she began.

But Picard was already in the head where he had carried the interface. He placed it on the floor of the sonic shower, set the acoustic inverter to maximum, then turned the shower on to full power.

He watched in satisfaction the screen image of T'Serl smear into a rainbow of random colors as the device's isolinears began vibrating in response to the sonic assault. T'Serl's voice over the internal speakers was quickly reduced to a mere warbling squeal of static.

The back-and-forth competition between Picard and his captors continued for another fifteen minutes.

Just prior to the third attempt to beam in yet another communications device, all power to Picard's stateroom was cut off. The sonic shower no longer worked, and the only source of light was the latest interface's screen.

Picard, who had to admit he was enjoying the contest, covered the newest interface with the sheets and cover from his bed. Then, in absolute darkness, he swung it repeatedly against the bulkheads until the muffled, distorted sound of T'Serl's voice broke off with an electronic hiss.

Moments later, in the next escalation, he was struck by a wave of dizziness as the gravity shut down and a fourth communications device was beamed in.

The light of the transporter effect caught the furniture and small effects in Picard's stateroom floating as if under water.

That quick glimpse of the room was all Picard required to plot a course to the desk, where he shoved the fourth interface into a large, lower drawer. Then, in pitch blackness, he made his way to the head, floated inside, and shut the door behind him.

Picard knew the stateroom's head was so small, there would be a definite risk that anything beamed into it would materialize in the same volume of space he occupied. He doubted his captors would be willing to take the risk of either killing him, or blowing out a hole in the hull of their cruiser.

He was right. The darkness quickly dissolved in transporter sparkles.

Picard smiled. He'd won the battle. Now all he had to do was win the war.

When the transporter effect faded, Picard found himself in a small theater. Before him, banked tiers of seats, enough for forty people at least, faced the small raised stage on which he now stood. The stage itself was framed by a vertical ring of holoemitters—the kind used to create sets and backdrops for plays and other entertainments, again common on passenger liners.

Picard blinked as the theater was plunged into darkness and bright spotlights blazed down upon him. He held up a hand to shield his eyes.

"Is this what you desired?"

T'Serl's composed Vulcan voice originated from the tiers of seats, but the lights were too bright for Picard to see anything beyond the stage.

"I 'desire' to be released," Picard said.

"That will be determined at a later time. First, we will talk."

"I don't wish to talk under these conditions."

"Then you will never be released."

Picard stepped forward, testing his limits.

And was thrown back at once, barely managing to remain on his feet.

The security forcefield was a meter in front of him.

"Captain Picard," T'Serl said from the darkness, "it is illogical for you to continue to resist. You are completely enclosed by forcefields. Your only chance for freedom is cooperation."

Picard began to look for the forcefield nodes that he guessed were hidden in among the holoemitters. But the spotlights made his search impossible.

"Let me see you," he said.

A moment later, the spotlights winked out and the houselights intensified. Now the stage and audience areas were equally lit.

T'Serl sat in an aisle-side seat of the third row. She had donned simple Vulcan meditation robes. In the middle of the back row, Picard saw the short figure of Lept, resplendent in a brightly checkered Ferengi banker's suit gleaming with gold threads.

"We will talk with you now," T'Serl said.

Picard tabled further resistance for the moment. "It appears I have no choice but to listen."

The Vulcan psychohistorian was direct. "Our research indicates an unknown alien presence is involved in an ongoing effort to influence the development of the Federation."

When Picard said nothing, T'Serl added, "Our research indicates that you are an agent of that alien influence."

Picard's reply was equally to the point. "Then your research is wrong."

"Young man," Lept spoke up loudly from the rear of the theater, "none of us has anything to gain by wasting time. So answer this: Why did you come to us on Memory Alpha?"

"For exactly the reason I stated," Picard said simply. "I wanted to know if your research had uncovered any connection between the Preservers and the mirror universe."

T'Serl got to her feet and began to walk down to the front of the audience seats. "You are a respected Starfleet officer. Why come to two civilian researchers when you have all the resources of Starfleet to draw upon?"

Picard watched her approach, then stop before the stage, looking up at him. It was time he decided how much he should reveal. And that decision depended on whether he believed they were innocent, or the enemy.

He made his choice.

"There is a possibility that Starfleet . . . might be compromised. Also by an unknown alien influence."

Lept jumped to his feet and clapped his hands loudly. "Ha!" the old Ferengi exclaimed.

T'Serl's reaction was merely to slip her hands into the folds of her robes. "Do you suspect the Preservers?" she asked.

"I don't know," Picard answered truthfully. "There is also the chance that certain Starfleet personnel have been replaced by their mirror duplicates. I do not know the source of the threat. Nor do I know for a fact that the threat is real."

"So," T'Serl said, "by claiming to look for the same threat we have identified, you wish to convince us that we should work together."

Picard made a point of looking straight into her eyes. "That would be logical."

"Not quite! Not quite!" Lept hobbled down from the back row to stand with T'Serl. "If you *are* an agent of the alien influence, why, you'd tell us the exact same thing, to convince us that you're not. That's circular logic which my colleague can tell you is not logic at all."

Picard held his ground. "How do I know that you two aren't agents of the 'alien influence'?"

T'Serl and Lept exchanged a quick glance, then T'Serl addressed Picard again. "This is how you will know: Computer, reconfigure Theater Four for astronomical observation."

"Please step away from the seats," a computer voice responded.

Unseen mechanisms thrummed as the elevated stage on which Picard stood descended until it was flush with the main deck. Then the holoemitter frame split in two and slid into opposite walls. The lighting in the theater dimmed as, at the same time, a new source of illumination appeared from behind Picard.

He turned, not making a move to leave the stage, judging it still likely enclosed by forcefields.

The back wall of the theater was opening like a hangar door to reveal a large viewport at least five meters high and fifteen meters wide.

Beyond the viewport, seen from the height of a standard orbit, was the last planet Picard expected to see.

Earth.

Picard was exultant. *I've won,* he thought. *This sector is filled with Starfleet resources. An emergency broadcast of only a few seconds and I'll have more than a dozen ships and a thousand security officers racing to my aid.*

"If you plan to surrender," he said evenly, "you've certainly come to the right place."

"Then you recognize this world?" T'Serl asked. She and Lept walked past Picard, toward the viewport, skirting the section of the deck that had been the stage. Their action confirmed for Picard his assumption about the forcefields.

"Of course," he said. "It's Earth." But there was something about T'Serl's question that made him uneasy. For just an instant, Picard wondered if somehow T'Serl and Lept had brought him to the mirror universe.

He looked more closely at the planet before him, traced the shoreline of South America, making note of every fractal fold. He brought his eyes farther north, traced the Yucatán Peninsula, the Florida panhandle, the islands of Nuevo Cuba, Jamaica, and Hispaniola. All were exactly where they were supposed to be.

Nothing Picard saw resembled Jim Kirk's description of the mirror Earth: a dying planet, its atmosphere and oceans dark, its landmasses pitted and scarred by a savage Alliance bombardment. This planet was vibrantly blue and richly green. It could only be—

"Look beyond the terminator," T'Serl said.

The planet's demarcation line between night and day lay far to the west, almost reaching the North American Rocky Mountains. Picard looked past it, to the planet's nightside.

He caught his breath in surprise.

There were no cities. No transportation corridors. No sign of artificial lights of any kind.

"This world is *not* Earth," T'Serl said. "It has no name, only a registry number. In Starfleet maps, it is Site 2713."

Picard stared again at the landmasses and oceans. "That's not a Starfleet map designation. There should be a star name or number, then a planet number. . . ." *How is this possible?* Picard thought. Except for the absence of lights beyond the terminator, the planet was an *exact* duplicate of Earth. "Have we traveled in time?" he asked.

T'Serl walked into Picard's line of sight before the planet. "Unfortunately, Captain Picard, your reaction to this world would be the same, whether you are telling the truth, or lying."

Picard didn't want to play any more games. "What world is this?"

"Exactly what it appears to be," T'Serl said. "A duplicate Earth. Precisely. Exactly. As recently as two centuries ago, the nightside would have been lit up by major cities, just as they were on your Earth."

Picard stared at T'Serl. "Are you saying someone *built* this?"

"This and two others," Lept said.

Picard shook his head, completely overwhelmed. *"Three Earths?"*

"To date," T'Serl said, "Starfleet has located four duplicates of Qo'noS. Two duplicate Vulcans. One duplicate Andor."

Picard found it difficult to believe what he was hearing. "I've never even heard of *any* duplicate worlds."

The Vulcan nodded. "If you're telling the truth, Captain Picard, then that's understandable. There are many things Starfleet knows which it does not share."

"But why?"

Lept waved a hand at the viewport. "Why? Look at what's out there, young man. An exact duplicate of one of the most important worlds in the history of the Federation. And it's just one of *ten* duplicate worlds. The technology behind this is . . . incomprehensible."

"To say nothing of the motive," Picard added.

"And that is precisely why we are here," T'Serl said.

"So you can tell us what the motive is," Lept concluded. He watched Picard expectantly.

Picard frowned. "I assure you . . . I know nothing about this phenomenon."

T'Serl drew a small, handheld communicator from her robes.

Lept waved a crooked finger at Picard. "You've made a mistake, young man."

"What mistake?"

"You didn't ask what happened to the cities down there, did you? You didn't ask what happened to the people, either. Why? Because you already knew the answers."

T'Serl held up her communicator. "There was an accident on that planet, Captain Picard. Wishing to prolong their lives, the humans who lived there created a self-replicating biological catalyst to alter their genetic structure accordingly, only to discover that they had manufactured a deadly virus.

"The adults died within days. But the children's aging process was lengthened by a factor of six. Until they reached puberty. And then they descended into madness and died as well."

Picard felt the shock of recognition. "Then I *do* know this world. Kirk found it. I've read the reports." He stared out the viewport again. "But . . . the reports said it was a Class-M world with humanoid life-forms. They didn't say anything about . . . it being a duplicate of Earth."

Picard's mind reeled as he tried to comprehend the enormous conspiracy that would be required for Starfleet to keep such a secret from the public, not to mention its own officers, for so many decades.

"If you are telling the truth, Captain, how can you be surprised by that?"

T'Serl regarded Picard sternly. "Imagine what the reaction of ordinary citizens of the Federation would be if they were told that there exists an alien presence so powerful, so unfathomable, that duplicate *worlds* can be created? Such knowledge could very well undermine the social order, the religious beliefs of a hundred worlds, the very foundation of our galactic civilization."

"Come now, young man, *think* for a moment," Lept urged. "Consider the implications of these duplicate worlds.

If this version of Earth has been artificially created, is it not possible that *your* version of Earth is also a construction, based on some other *original* Earth halfway across the galaxy?"

"But why?" Picard said. Unbelievably, the two psychohistorians had just raised an even more troubling notion that threatened the very concept of accepted reality.

"Logic suggests only one answer," T'Serl said. "My colleague and I have come to the conclusion that these duplicates exist for the same reason that scientists establish identical initial conditions and then change only certain variables."

Picard was finding it difficult to draw sufficient breath. "Your theory is that Earth—*my* Earth—is just . . . an *experiment?*"

"Your Earth," T'Serl said, "this Earth, my Vulcan, who can say how many more duplicates exist in regions unexplored? The most likely conclusion is obvious and inescapable."

Lept stated that conclusion with authority. "We are property."

"And now, Captain Picard," T'Serl said, "you have evaded all our efforts to question you gently, so we must resort to a more direct method of interrogation."

"I tell you both I know nothing of any of this," Picard said. "Nothing."

"We are no longer the ones you must convince," the Vulcan replied. Then she said the single word, "Energize," and Picard once more was taken by the light.

SEVENTEEN

Dr. Andrea M'Benga didn't know where to look or what to think.

She was in the pediatric center of First City's largest hospital, in Admiral McCoy's temporary office space. And she was watching the admiral and Kirk argue as if at any moment one was going to throw a punch at the other.

She had been on Qo'noS for a month now, as part of McCoy's ad hoc medical team, trying to understand and, if possible, treat the mysteriously afflicted child of Kirk and Teilani of Chal.

Officially, M'Benga had requested and been granted accumulated leave since her rapid departure from Deep Space 9. But she still considered that all the work she had done over the past four weeks was for the benefit of Starfleet and the Federation.

Unfortunately, Starfleet and the Federation didn't seem to show any concern for her in return.

Almost immediately after Tiberius had beamed Kirk out of the Klingon intensive-care unit where Teilani and the child were first treated, M'Benga had had sudden second thoughts about what she had revealed to Kirk about Project Sign.

It wasn't that she didn't think Sign was a legitimate Starfleet operation. Or that she now thought of herself as an unknowing victim of the operation's policy of memory suppression for those working for it. She was certain no one had forced her to do anything. She'd been a willing participant.

But she had begun to rethink something else. What if she had drawn the wrong conclusion? What if it *was* agents of Tiberius who poisoned Teilani to get to Kirk, and not agents of Sign? Especially since it was Tiberius who then kidnapped Kirk.

M'Benga had had no difficulty accepting what Garak had uncovered about Project Sign on DS9. But she'd been unable to believe that Starfleet could be involved in such an insidious undertaking. At least, not without further evidence.

So, while Picard had immediately left Qo'noS to track down Kirk, M'Benga had attempted to contact her commanding officer for Sign-related matters: Commodore Nathan Twining.

Yet, even as she had made her request over a secure Starfleet communications interface at the Federation embassy in First City, M'Benga had experienced the first stirrings of misgiving. When *was* the last time she had ever seen a commodore in Starfleet? The rank was as old and musty as a laser pistol.

In any event, Starfleet Command had bounced back her request within a day. There was no record that a Nathan Twining of any rank had ever served in Starfleet.

M'Benga had spent the next day at the embassy, accessing the personnel roster for the last Starfleet facility at which she had met Twining—Agricultural Research Station 51 in orbit of Alpha Centauri IV.

She had called up and viewed the image of each staff member.

But she did not find the man she knew as Nate Twining.

M'Benga had then asked three trusted advisors what her next step should be.

From Earth, Captain Christine MacDonald told her to enjoy her leave, because she'd be recalling her in about six months. MacDonald had a new ship—the Sabre-class *Endurance*—and was looking forward to reassembling her command staff from the *Tobias*.

From Deep Space 9, Dr. Julian Bashir had strongly suggested that she not attempt to make contact with any section of Starfleet that seemed to be operating outside authorized command channels. The message from the usually easygoing young physician had been so adamant that M'Benga wondered if Bashir had been speaking from experience.

But it had been Admiral McCoy, here on Qo'noS, who had given her the best advice. He had told her to be patient, to wait for the commodore to reappear, then sock him in the nose and contact Jim Kirk. Because, the admiral had assured her, if Nate Twining *did* have anything to do with what had happened to Teilani, there wasn't a force in the universe that could keep him safe from Kirk, or keep Kirk from discovering the whole truth.

What had impressed M'Benga so much about that advice was that McCoy had given it to her while Kirk was still missing in space. Yet the admiral talked as if he had no doubt that Kirk would be back—another example of the absolute faith the two men inspired in each other. It was fascinating to watch. Even moving.

But that just made the present heated confrontation between Kirk and McCoy in the admiral's temporary office in First Hospital's pediatric center all the more surprising and confusing to M'Benga.

"I absolutely forbid it!" McCoy yelled at Kirk. "I'm an admiral! I outrank you! I *order* you not to leave Qo'noS!"

Kirk stabbed the admiral's massive, metallic desk with a rigid finger. The desk looked almost to have been carved out of a single block of irregularly melted nickel-iron meteorite. "I'm not in the medical corps, Bones. You don't have command authority over me."

"Then I'll find an admiral in Operations who *does* have authority!"

"Fine," Kirk said. "Try it. By the time you try to explain why you're attempting to interfere in my life, we'll be long gone."

McCoy flopped back in his oversized Klingon chair, his bluster evaporating momentarily. "Jim, maybe you are pigheaded enough to go off on some wild space hunt for the Preservers. But how can you put Teilani through that? After what she's already been through?"

Kirk's response was also stepped back. To M'Benga, it was as if he only desired to match McCoy's fire, not overwhelm it. "I'm not the one telling her to go. I explained to her what I planned to do. She said she was coming with me. End of discussion."

McCoy folded his hands. "And have the two of you given any thought to what happens to your baby in the meantime?"

M'Benga saw the warning flash in Kirk's eyes. He moved forward. M'Benga tensed, sure Kirk was about to pound his fist on McCoy's desk, but at the last moment he pulled back. "Bones . . . you said yourself, the child will remain in stasis until the Romulans get here."

M'Benga could see the argument Kirk was going to make. McCoy had prevailed upon his Romulan colleagues to actually join him on Qo'noS. Given the current state of affairs in the Alpha and Beta quadrants, the Romulan involvement was strictly unofficial. In fact, M'Benga knew, without Captain Spock's diplomatic contacts, she doubted it would have been possible for any Romulan to travel within a dozen parsecs of the Klingon homeworld.

But doctors Preln and Troltan were two of the Romulan Empire's leading geneticists and were eager to examine a child who was a unique blend of Romulan, Klingon, and human genes. Science often had a way of standing apart from politics.

"Three more weeks," Kirk told McCoy, his frustration evident. "That's how long Spock says it will take the Romulans to get here. That's time that Teilani and I can use to do something to help. Maybe even find an explanation." Kirk's tone dropped back to that of an old friend. "We'll come back, Bones. Both of us. When it's *time* for us to be here. And when there's something we can offer."

"What can you do in three weeks?" McCoy asked, reluctant, but already relenting. "Where can you go?"

Kirk shook his head as if the details weren't important, as if the only thing that mattered was that he would be *doing* something.

"Tiberius has some ideas. He—"

"I can't believe you said that," McCoy exclaimed, half-rising from his chair. "Can you tell me how that psychopathic mass-murderer ended up being on your side? Or should I ask how you ended up on his?"

"Relax, Bones. Tiberius isn't on anyone's side but his own. But right now, the Preservers are our common enemy."

"What happens when they're not?" McCoy asked, placing his hands flat on his desk as he leaned forward to challenge Kirk. "Or when you've discovered all you *can* discover and it's not enough?"

Kirk shrugged. "Then we're back to where we started. He'll try to kill me. I'll try to kill him."

"Listen to yourself. 'Try to kill him.' Don't you think that's wrong?"

To M'Benga, Kirk's face became a mask. "I've seen the mirror Earth, Doctor. Trust me, I'm using Tiberius as much as he's using me."

"I don't see why you have to use him at all."

"He's bait. If the Preservers came after him once, maybe they'll come after him again."

Shaking his head, McCoy straightened up, sat back. "Someone probably should come after you," he grumbled. *"Force* you to retire."

"I will when you will."

McCoy frowned, suddenly finding something of interest to study among the stacks of Klingon printouts and reading padds on his desk. "Half my replacement parts are on loan from Starfleet Medical. If I try to retire, they'll repossess my legs, my lungs, and a few other parts I'd rather hold on to."

McCoy tidied a few stacks on his desk.

Kirk broke the silence. "I believe that this is what our mutual friend would call an impasse."

McCoy sighed heavily. "It's not an impasse. You're doing what you want to do, as usual. No matter what anyone else thinks. When has anything been different?"

"It's what I *have* to do, Bones. There's a difference."

"I know, damn you."

And with those last words, it was as if the argument had never taken place.

M'Benga prepared to ask a question of her own, but just then her combadge spoke to her.

"Starfleet communications to Dr. Andrea M'Benga."

Kirk and McCoy both turned to her, surprised. She'd been so quiet an observer of their exchange, it was clear to M'Benga they had forgotten she was still here.

"Pardon me," she said, embarrassed, then tapped her combadge. "M'Benga here."

"Doctor, revised orders have just been forwarded from Starfleet Command. Please access them at once from a secure Starfleet communications node."

"Acknowledged." M'Benga stood up. "Dr. McCoy, perhaps we can discuss the lab protocols after lunch?"

M'Benga was relieved when McCoy shifted into his medical persona without hesitation. "I'd rather have them in place before Jim goes galavanting off to Finagle knows where." He picked up a padd from his desk. Its case was Starfleet gold. McCoy held it out to her. "You can use this to access your orders if it'll save you time."

M'Benga took the padd, thanked him, then self-consciously input her identification codes.

A Starfleet Command text message appeared at once.

M'Benga stared in disbelief.

"Good news?" Kirk asked.

"Well . . . yes, definitely," M'Benga said. She looked at Kirk, then at McCoy. "Christine's assignment has been changed. They've given her the *Pathfinder.* Effective immediately."

Kirk and McCoy at once offered her their congratulations and their good wishes to pass on to her captain. M'Benga nodded, but her attention had been diverted. The *Pathfinder* was an Intrepid-class ship, just like Janeway's legendary *Voyager.* It was also twice the size of the *Endurance,* with quadruple the capabilities, at least. So why—

"Is something wrong?" Kirk asked, interrupting her thoughts.

"No, sir. It's just that, well, Christine was scheduled to receive a new science-vessel command, but not for another six months."

"In Starfleet, Dr. M'Benga, they're all science vessels," McCoy said.

"Not like this one, sir. It's . . . a huge career move for the captain. And for all her command staff." M'Benga's mind momentarily filled up with everything she would have to do now: arrange shipment of her personal effects from DS9; figure out the fastest way to get passage off Qo'noS and—

"I'd appreciate it if we could go over those lab protocols before you start getting packed," McCoy said.

The admiral's words caused a pang of real regret to strike M'Benga.

"I . . . I hate to run out on you in the middle of this," she said to both Kirk and McCoy. "I could ask for another few weeks of leave. I've got it coming."

But Kirk dismissed her impulsive offer immediately. "Your captain's asked for you. You have to go. We'll get by."

"But what about Project Sign?"

Kirk reached out to shake her hand.

"You opened that door for us, Doctor. Your help has been invaluable. You've made it possible for us to move on. How much more could we ask for?"

Kirk's warm smile of thanks was genuine and gracious, especially considering he was in the midst of his own misfortune. M'Benga took his hand and almost felt her knees grow weak at the smile, the touch, the voice. No wonder Kirk could convince his crew to follow him anywhere. She would.

"I just wish I could have done more, sir."

"I understand," Kirk said, and she was convinced that he did. "And I know our paths will cross again."

"I'm counting on it."

Kirk dropped her hand and turned back to McCoy. "Bones, you two finish up your business. I'm going to make arrangements for a ship." He smiled again at M'Benga. "Doctor, again my thanks. And Teilani's, as well."

M'Benga nodded, still somehow under the man's influence.

She watched Kirk start toward the metal door leading to the corridor, reach it, then abruptly step back as the door swung open.

Spock entered the room, wearing his uniform, holding a padd. And though he was Vulcan, his usually impassive face showed alarm.

"Spock, what is it?" Kirk asked.

"I have attempted to contact Captain Picard, to inform him of your plans."

M'Benga saw Kirk take the padd Spock offered and quickly scan whatever report it displayed. "And . . . ?"

"The captain is missing."

Kirk looked up at Spock, then over at McCoy, who had already jumped to his feet.

"Let's not waste time with Federation Security," Kirk said, speaking quickly. "We have to contact Riker right away."

"I have already attempted to do that, as well," Spock said.

"Attempted?" McCoy repeated.

"Captain Picard is not the only one missing," Spock said. "So is Commander Riker. And the *Enterprise.*"

M'Benga stared at Kirk, having expected concern or outrage. But instead he seemed elated. He was smiling.

"Gentlemen," Kirk announced, "it appears our opponents have made the first move. The next one's up to us."

Admiral McCoy had promised M'Benga that if anyone could find out the truth, it would be Kirk.

Now it seemed Kirk thought so, too.

M'Benga was sorry she wouldn't be around to see how this would end.

EIGHTEEN

☆

When Picard had resolved from the transporter beams into the ruins of a city, he knew at once that T'Serl's duplicate Earth was an abandoned world.

Fully half the buildings surrounding him had fallen in or over. Even those still standing were buttressed by slopes of crumbled façades and shattered windows, well on their way to becoming rubble like the rest.

Architecturally, to Picard's trained eye, the city, when intact, had been reminiscent of Earth's twentieth-century Europe: a hodgepodge of brick and concrete-slab designs, punctuated by an occasional tower of steel and glass. All bore the stamp of dull rigidity and oppressiveness that characterized construction in the era before widespread use of carbon-composite supports and structural-integrity fields.

The roadways between the decaying edifices were nearing the end of their existence as well. Jagged outcroppings of buckled asphalt and concrete slabs were all that remained of paved surfaces now almost completely covered by rampant vegetation. Small mounds here and there suggested that ancient ground vehicles had been buried, first by debris, then by soil, and now by wild grasses and bushes.

Another few centuries, Picard had thought, and explorers would require sensor sweeps and core samples to establish that civilization had ever arisen here.

But now, some fifty hours after his arrival, he was reserving his energy and attention for his own near future. By his most optimistic reckoning, he had less than one more day to live.

The virus that had killed all the adults of this world, and that had threatened its children, had just claimed a new victim. Picard's first symptom—a small skin discoloration—had appeared within ten hours of his arrival. Twenty hours after that, painful blue blisters had spread over his hands and the side of his face.

Now, it was near sunset of his third day, and Picard was resting in the shadow of a low, decomposing wall of brick. The wall edged what he assumed was once a park. The clearing behind it was an overgrown jungle devoid of noticeable structural ruins. But he was beginning not to trust his judgment. He had had no food or water for fifty hours, and was feeling ill and weak and angry.

"Is it really worth all this?"

Picard looked around to see where T'Serl was this time. He found her a few meters to the right. As twilight deepened, the Vulcan psychohistorian's three-dimensional image took on a slight internal glow, making her holographic ghost easier to see.

"You tell me," Picard said wearily. "I'm dying because of you."

A transporter hum blended with the faint rustle of leaves as a second small holographic projector, no larger than a wine bottle, took shape in the dirt a few meters in front of him. A moment later, after the projector had resolved into solidity, a holographic image of Lept formed between the device and Picard.

Picard sighed. Both projectors had continuously tracked his rambling exploration of this city, beaming into and out of the various sites in which he found himself. And each materialization had included the hectoring images of T'Serl and Lept.

"Young man," the old Ferengi said crossly, "you're dying because of your own stubbornness."

Picard made an effort to will his anger away. "Manager, I will say it again. I have *nothing* to tell you. I am *not* an agent of the alien influence. I am a starship captain, guilty of nothing more than attempting to do my duty, attempting to help a friend, attempting to . . . to solve a mystery."

T'Serl's holographic image adjusted her robes as the Vulcan severely stared at him. Picard knew there must be visual sensors on the two projectors because the images of T'Serl and Lept were able to make direct eye contact with him. That suggested that his own image was being generated and displayed up on the orbiting vessel from which the two psychohistorians were safely monitoring him.

"You are aware there is a cure for the virus you have contracted," T'Serl said.

Picard's smile was wry. "Oh, is that why there're so many other people about?"

The Vulcan continued as if she had not heard him. "A limited form of terraforming is in progress which is unsuitable for sustained habitation. When the Federation sent sociological and disaster-relief teams to this world, the population consisted of a few hundred thousand children. Some of them centuries old. When treated with the cure, they began aging at a human-normal rate and it became obvious that they were not equipped to reestablish their lost culture. So they were evacuated to education and resettlement centers, with this world held in trust for them and their descendants by the Federation."

Through the lengthening shadows, Picard looked past the glowing holograms of T'Serl and Lept to a steep-walled canyon formed by the heavily vine-draped skeletons of tall buildings. The buildings' ragged outlines were streaked by blood-red fingers of light from this ravaged Earth's setting sun. "And no one ever returned to claim this world?"

"That's not in Starfleet's best interest," Lept said matter-of-factly. "Not until they determine how this world was constructed in the first place. And whether the same was done on Earth."

"Hence the terraforming project," T'Serl added. "Many of the plants around you have been genetically modified to cleanse the biosphere of the artificial virus. Starfleet agricultural specialists estimate it will take approximately an additional three hundred years before this planet is safe again for humanoid habitation."

Picard wiped his hand over his forehead, felt sweat run down into his eyes, and it had nothing to do with the temperature. He had developed a fever. "Why not . . . why not just inoculate everyone with the cure?"

"The virus can be carried on particles of dust and remain viable for centuries. All newborn children and visitors would be at risk. All it would take is one person to have resistance to the vaccine, or one carrier to bypass transporter biofilters and return to a transportation hub to infect half the Federation."

The glowing hologram of Lept turned and spoke to the glowing hologram of T'Serl. "Good answer, Doctor. But maybe the captain was really thinking about something more personal."

"Go to hell," Picard said. He knew precisely what Lept was insinuating: that he had wanted to know why they didn't inoculate *him*.

Picard struggled to his feet. What was the point of suppressing his anger any longer? Its release was all he had left.

"My dear," Lept murmured to T'Serl, "would you agree that the disease is progressing more rapidly than the clinical models suggest?"

As Picard stood up, out of the protective shadow of the low wall, he saw the sun on the far horizon, a swollen red ball blurring atop the canopy of the encroaching jungle.

"Captain, what are you attempting to do?" T'Serl asked, puzzled.

Picard took a deep breath, trying to maintain his balance, determined to find the strength he would need to pick up one projector and smash it against the other.

"Doctor, I propose we go to the next stage," Lept said. "While he can still respond."

"Oh, I can respond," Picard said. He stepped forward unsteadily.

"Very well," T'Serl said to Lept as Picard moved through her glowing image.

Then, before Picard's hand could grasp T'Serl's projector, it vanished in a sparkle of transporter energy. At the same time, he heard the harmonic of the second projector being beamed out, as well.

"*Bastards!*" Picard staggered as he shook a fist at the rapidly darkening sky over the empty city and silent jungle. "If you want to kill me, at least have the decency to fight me in *person!*"

But he received no response.

The sun sank from view. Above the horizon, the deep-red sky shaded upward to indigo and then, finally, to black.

Picard sought out the stars, but found no constellations that he recognized. At least, he thought, whoever or whatever had brought this duplicate Earth into being lacked the power to duplicate the stars.

And with that thought, fear swept through him.

"The mirror universe," he said to himself. *Could that have been* created, *too? Just like these duplicate worlds?*

Picard stumbled and fell to his knees as the world began to spin around him. His increasing loss of balance was the disease, he knew. But beyond the physical shock, there was the mental one. *Somehow, somewhere, could there be alien beings powerful enough to bring entire* universes *into being?* By any definition, such beings would be *gods*.

Picard fought the desire to sob with despair, to roll up into a fetal curl and will himself into unconsciousness. *"Merde,"* he cursed, defiant to the end. How could he die when there were such mysteries to be solved?

"Answers," he whispered, determined to remain in control until the end. "I need to find the answers. . . ."

And he did.

The chime of a transporter was followed by another and another, until Picard's kneeling form was surrounded by six incandescent ghosts.

T'Serl and Lept had returned with four others. All of them holograms.

Picard couldn't stand. He had difficulty breathing. But he studied each of the new images to see if he recognized any of them.

There was a round-shouldered Tellarite, muzzle fur white with age. A Tiburon female with extravagant, finlike ears. And two elderly Vulcans, a man and woman, both in scholar's robes.

"Who the hell are you?" Picard muttered.

And as soon as the first one answered, Picard instantly knew who the rest were.

"I am Garen of Odessa Prime," the Tellarite grunted.

"R'Ma'Hatrel of the Cygnate Cooperative," the Tiburon female said.

"We are Savrin and T'Pon," the female Vulcan said.

Picard knew of them. From the Seldon Institute. The four scientists were the giants of psychohistory.

Then Picard became aware of T'Serl's glowing form advancing toward him, her holographic feet illuminating the blades of grass she walked through, yet did not disturb.

"Captain," she said, speaking loudly as if to be sure she commanded his drifting attention. "Watch carefully." She pointed to the ground before Picard.

Groggily, Picard stared ahead, seeing nothing.

A small equipment pallet resolved in front of him. In its center, a spray hypo.

"That is the cure. I suggest you—"

But the hypo was already in Picard's shaking hand and he pressed it to his neck.

The pallet also held emergency-ration packets of food and water. Picard ignored the food, went for the water first. For the next few minutes, he took only measured sips of the life-restoring liquid, refusing to let his captor see the hope that surged through him, that threatened to have him weeping with relief, and screaming out his thanks.

Such emotion, such untrammeled feelings were foreign to him. *They're a symptom of the disease,* he kept repeating to himself. *The disease can be controlled.*

Within ten minutes, he even began to believe it.

Picard stood up without difficulty.

Then looked down at his hands. In the glow of the circle of six holographic ghosts, Picard saw the virus blisters already fading. He touched his face and felt their absence there, as well.

T'Serl had told him the truth. There was a cure. He would live.

"Now are you prepared to talk?" T'Serl asked.

"I've been prepared to talk since I came to see you on

Memory Alpha," Picard said. A wave of hunger hit him. His stomach growled.

"At the time, we didn't know who you really represented," Lept pointed out.

"And now you do?" Picard reached down and picked up one of the food packets, tore it open, sniffed it tentatively. A seaweed wafer. He frowned.

"Only that it seems unlikely that you are an agent of the alien influence."

Picard bit into the wafer carefully. Salty, but with too little flavor to be objectionable. Definitely a Ferengi product. Designed to be the least objectionable for the broadest possible market.

Picard spoke around a mouthful of seaweed. For a moment, his intention to control his emotions was forgotten. He didn't try to hide the anger that he felt. "How did your attempt to kill me convince you I am who I said I was?"

"We ask you not to be bitter," T'Serl said.

Picard laughed. The sound was harsh. "Bitter does not begin to describe what I'm feeling right now. Disappointed, yes," Picard said. "Astonished, most definitely. But your behavior here is so unprofessional and despicable that 'bitterness' fails by many orders of magnitude to describe my revulsion."

The hologram of Savrin stepped closer. The bald Vulcan was shockingly frail and his eyebrows were white. Yet when he spoke, his voice was strong and assured.

"We would not have harmed you, Captain."

"Unfortunately, your intentions and their results might not have matched. I heard Manager Lept say the disease progressed more rapidly in me than you had predicted it would."

T'Pon moved up beside her mate. Where her shoulder touched Savrin's, Picard saw the shimmer of a holographic interference pattern.

"The terminal phase of the disease is preceded by coma, Captain Picard. Had you fallen into a coma, we would have treated you at once. You were never in any danger."

"Tell me, Savrin," Picard asked, "is it logical to have expended all this effort to discover what you could have easily confirmed through a mind-meld?"

"If you *had* been under the control of the alien influence," Savrin corrected him, "no Vulcan would risk a mind-meld. No, this tactic was logical."

"But if you wanted to threaten me, why didn't you just hold a phaser to my head? Why bring me here?"

"This is not the appropriate venue for a debate concerning interrogation techniques," R'Ma'Hatrel interrupted. The Tiburon's voice was deep and oddly melodic. "Time is at a premium."

"Oh, of course. Because of the end of the universe," Picard said, not regretting for an instant his mocking tone.

"You doubt our findings, young man?" Lept asked.

"What do you think?" Picard said. "Those same findings said that *I* was responsible!"

"Our colleagues may have made an error in interpretation," Savrin offered as an explanation.

"I'd certainly agree with that," Picard said.

"But *not* in their collection of data," Savrin finished.

"Pie-carrrd," Garen suddenly growled. "*Who* sent you to Memory Alpha, hey?"

Picard turned to the Tellarite. "No one sent me. It was my decision."

Garen snorted. "Impossible. You don't wake up one morning and out of the mud say, I go see psychohistorians today. Ha, no!"

"The Preserver obelisk, then," Picard said irritatedly. They were still questioning him, testing him, as if he had not spent the last two days on a deserted planet without food or water and infected by a lethal virus. "That's what made me think of conferring with Dr. T'Serl and Manager—"

Lept broke in. "Not so fast, young man. Y'see, psychohistoric analytics apply to people, not things. *No* amount of data we could ever accumulate could lead us to predict that on such and such a day an *artifact* will be found. Not possible. So whatever brought you to us, we *know* that there is a person behind that decision. Perhaps that person is connected to the discovery of the obelisk. Perhaps he or she is not. But that doesn't change the mathematical certainty that whoever that person is—which is to say, the person who is responsible for your visit—*he,* or *she,* is the person who will be responsible for ending the universe. Yes, that's quite clear now."

Picard's hand stopped with the remaining portion of the seaweed biscuit halfway to his mouth. He was suddenly aware of nothing else but Lept's glowing, holographic face.

It can't be possible, Picard thought. *Can it?*

Even in holographic form, he saw the grin that split Lept's face as the old Ferengi waved a finger at him, his short form almost hopping with delight. "Aha! It's making sense to you! I can see it on your face." He turned to the two Vulcans. "Can you see it there? Oh, of course you can't! You have no idea what to look for." Lept looked back at Garen and R'Ma'Hatrel. "Professor Garen, Hattie my sweet, you can see it, though, can't you?"

Garen grunted. R'Ma'Hatrel confined her response to a nod that caused the finlike flanges of her ears to undulate.

Lept turned back to Picard again. "Out with it, young man! Who sent you to us? Even if it *seemed* to be your own idea."

Picard was silent. He didn't know where that answer might lead.

Surprisingly, it was T'Serl who seemed to understand his

dilemma. "Captain, we have not forgotten that you told us that the location from which the artifact was recovered is classified. However, you also told us you were able to say the obelisk was not from a location within the mirror universe."

Picard nodded. He folded shut the seaweed biscuit wrapper. His hunger had vanished.

"But may we assume," T'Serl went on, "that the recovery location was in some way *linked* with the mirror universe?"

"Yes," Picard said. He knew he was telling her nothing new. Why else would he have asked if she and Lept had ever made a connection between the Preservers and the mirror universe?

"And was it linked through a person?" T'Serl asked.

"It was," Picard said. Then he was startled because Lept clapped his hands.

"Now you've got it!" the old Ferengi cackled.

"A person who exists in both this universe and the other?" T'Serl persisted.

"Yes," Picard said again. He grasped the conclusion they'd reached, but not the reasoning that had led to it. "Doctor, could you explain the significance of these questions?"

Garen growled. "It so obvious, human! As plain as snout on your . . . well, as snout on *my* face!"

Picard looked to T'Serl. Her point was not clear to him.

She understood his confusion. "Psychohistory is a tool which allows us to identify decision points before they happen," she explained. "We have identified a decision point which can result in the destruction of our universe."

"Ahh," Picard said. "And since psychohistory deals with people, not things, you believe that one person will be responsible for that decision."

"Not *one* person, young man," Lept said. "It *is* a decision point, after all."

Picard drew in a quick breath as understanding flooded through him. "You mean, one individual who is . . ."

"Two individuals," T'Serl confirmed. "One destined to destroy the universe. One, perhaps, destined to save it."

Picard nodded, at last knowing exactly what the Vulcan meant, wondering why it had taken them so long to ask, and so long for him to understand.

"So what d'you say, young man?" Lept cried out. "Is it time to talk at last? Do you have an answer for us? A name for the destroyer *and* the preserver?"

"I do," Picard said. "James Tiberius Kirk. Both of them."

NINETEEN

"Logic has nothing to do with it," Spock said.

That statement brought absolute silence to the conference room aboard the *U.S.S. Sovereign.*

Less than five minutes ago, Spock's mirror duplicate had been beamed up from Vulcan to meet face-to-face with Tiberius for the first time in more than a century. The intendant's health had suffered badly during the century he had lived as a fugitive in the mirror universe. He had spent the past few months on Vulcan, being treated for early-onset Bendii syndrome brought on by stress and poor nutrition. Though the disease was at least under control, the side effects of the syndrome and of various drug interactions included occasional intervals in which traditional Vulcan self-control was lost. This, unfortunately, was one of those intervals. The intendant's face was still twisted by undisguised hatred as he stared at Tiberius.

Kirk knew the two adversaries' mutual antipathy was so strong that at any moment the silence could give way to violence. He had to keep everyone speaking, so he went first. He cleared his throat. "I can't believe you said that, Spock."

The Spock of Kirk's universe placidly folded his hands on the conference table before him. "It is true, nonetheless."

"I will not help you," Spock's counterpart shouted angrily. "I will not help *him*. Absolutely not!"

Tiberius leaned forward from his chair. "Spock," he said to the intendant, drawing out the name. "Haven't you been listening? We're these people's only hope." Tiberius grinned. "It's the chance you've been waiting for. To do good. How can you refuse when even I can't?"

"I do not know what hold you have over these people," Intendant Spock bitterly replied, "but I will not support any course of action which will, in the end, provide *you* with an advantage."

"He will have no advantage," Kirk said firmly. "I guarantee it."

"How can I trust you?" the duplicate Vulcan asked.

"You don't have to," Kirk answered. He pointed at Spock. "Trust *him*. Intendant, the reason you're on Vulcan now, being treated for Bendii, is because of Spock. The reason why your daughter is not being held prisoner with the rest of Tiberius's crew is because of Spock. The reason why the Federation is finally sitting down to discuss providing aid to the Vulcan Resistance in your universe is because of Spock. How can you not trust him? He's you."

The intendant rubbed at his pure white goatee, his haunted eyes looking past those gathered at the conference table. Where he turned his attention, beyond the viewports of the conference room, the rich red lands and copper-green seas of Vulcan passed by majestically.

Kirk knew what the Earth of the mirror universe looked like—a dying world, scorched, scarred, poisoned. Under the Alliance, the mirror Vulcan had fared little better. *Its bio-*

sphere was left intact, the mirror Spock's daughter had told Kirk. But nothing else was. And it had been Intendant Spock himself who had negotiated the terms of mirror Vulcan's surrender.

Kirk knew firsthand the internal conflict now attacking Intendant Spock. Even the existence of a flourishing version of his world would torment him. It would remind him of all that had been lost because of his own actions.

The intendant wrested his attention away from the viewports and back to the conference room and to his duplicate. "Captain Spock, indulge me by bringing logic *back* to the equation. If *I* help you, then why do you also need Tiberius?"

Tiberius answered quickly, before Spock could. "You heard what James said. You and I are wild cards, Spock. We don't belong in this universe. Whatever patterns are in place, whatever processes the Preservers have set in motion, you and I—our entire universe—threatens their plans. And the two of us are a much more formidable threat to them than just one."

"It is not an exact analogy," Spock said, "but it is close."

Tiberius shrugged. "You just haven't thought it through as logically as I have."

Kirk was amazed anew by his own duplicate's arrogance. And again he wondered if the seeds of that overbearing ego were hidden within himself, as well. Self-assurance and unshakable confidence were necessary requirements for any starship captain. Yet where was that fine line between what those qualities had become in Tiberius, and what they had become in him? Or was the difference he saw only in his imagination? Was he in truth Tiberius?

Kirk became aware of Tiberius studying him thoughtfully. "You agree with me, don't you?" his counterpart said.

Kirk refused to expose any of his own self-questioning. "Let Spock finish."

"Very well," Spock said. "Our planned course of action inescapably arises from our initial postulates. Postulate One: The Preservers have, for reasons unknown, interfered in the natural development of certain worlds of the Federation. Judging by the locations in which the first one hundred and eighteen Preserver obelisks have been discovered, we can say with certainty that one of their goals has been to preserve specific life-forms, and specific cultural groups of sentient species, from extinction.

"Postulate Two: Six years ago, the newest Preserver obelisk to be discovered was put into position at the First Federation asteroid base. Its function was to create a collision between the base and a smaller asteroid, with the result being the destruction of the fleet of starships stored there.

"It is logical to assume that the reason the ships were destroyed was to keep them from Tiberius's control. Thus, we can conclude that the Preservers have a vested interest, again for reasons unknown, to prevent Tiberius from acquiring the means by which to carry out his plans for conquest."

"You see, Spock?" Tiberius said to the intendant. "The greatest, most powerful aliens in the galaxy, and they're afraid of *me*. You really did choose the wrong side."

Kirk knew he shouldn't, but he couldn't resist. "Tiberius, if you recall, our hosts at the Klingon lodge did not provide us with *glob* fly swatters because *glob* flies were a threat to us. They were only an annoyance. But we swatted them anyway."

Tiberius fixed his gaze on Kirk. "You're forgetting something, James. The smallest insect can carry a disease to bring down the largest animal. The Preservers wanted me off the playing field. I guarantee you that means I am more than an annoyance to them."

"In any event," Spock said forcefully, to head off any further conversation not on topic, "there is no evidence that the Preservers have ever tried to interfere in *your* activities, Intendant. Thus, you are *not* a useful substitute for Tiberius. However, the fact that the Preservers moved against Tiberius once, suggests that they will do so again."

"And that," Spock's duplicate said forcefully as well, "is where your logic becomes uncertain."

"Only because the Preservers' desire to constrain Tiberius has, as I have already stated, nothing to do with logic," Spock countered.

"I cannot accept that," Intendant Spock said with finality. "I will not accept that."

Kirk contemplated the two Spocks for a moment. They had argued each other to a standstill, and if the mirror Spock was as stubborn as his counterpart, Kirk knew the stars would burn out before either gave in. Which left him only one option.

"Gentlemen," Kirk said, "let *me* try to explain the logic of the situation—*and* the emotion."

Kirk restrained a smile as both Vulcans, simultaneously, regarded him with the same skeptical look he knew so well.

"Logically," Kirk began, ignoring their dual vote of nonconfidence, "if the Preservers wanted Tiberius 'off the playing field,' the simplest way would be to kill him."

"Precisely," Intendant Spock said. "The fact that they did not, indicates—"

"*Indicates,*" Kirk interrupted, "that they want *more* than his removal. They want to make a point. Teach a lesson. Make him remove himself from the game."

"That makes no sense," the intendant protested.

Spock merely raised one eyebrow, waiting for the rest of Kirk's argument.

"As a logical decision, no," Kirk agreed. "But as an emotional one, it makes perfect sense."

Now both Spocks began to argue with Kirk at the same time, but he waved his hands and shook his head, asking that they just let him finish.

"You're missing the most important point here," Kirk said. "When did the Preservers put the latest obelisk in place?"

"Six years ago," Spock said.

Kirk looked at Tiberius. "And when did you begin work on your base in the Goldin Discontinuity?"

Tiberius narrowed his eyes in suspicion, but answered. "Three years ago."

"Was that your first crossover into this universe since the incident in which we exchanged places?"

Tiberius nodded, clearly having no idea what point Kirk was trying to make.

"So," Kirk said to the Spocks, "the Preservers took action against Tiberius three years *before* he even set foot in this universe. That implies that they *knew* he was coming. That they *knew* his attempt to create a fleet of duplicate *Enterprise*s would fail. And that he would then come after the Fesarius-class ships at the First Federation base in our universe, because the First Federation had *removed* that base in his universe."

"But how could anyone know all that?" Intendant Spock asked.

Before Kirk could give the only possible answer, Spock saw it, too.

"Six years ago," the Vulcan said. "Of course."

"Of course, what?" Tiberius demanded.

"Six years ago is when Captain Kirk returned to us," Spock answered. "Before that time, history recorded him dead."

Tiberius nodded, giving Kirk a meaningful look. "History does have a way of being rewritten."

"Then you're suggesting that it was inevitable," Intendant

Spock said to his counterpart. "This meeting between the two Kirks."

"History follows patterns," Spock said. "In complex weather systems, individual clouds form chaotically, yet when they accumulate in large enough numbers, storms can be predicted. That is the reason Captain Picard went to Memory Alpha. To talk with two respected psychohistorians. To identify any patterns we may have overlooked. I suggest it is likely that the Preservers' grasp of psychohistory is as advanced as their technology."

"And the fact that Jean-Luc is missing," Kirk said, "is all the evidence I need to know that we're on the right track."

Intendant Spock massaged the bridge of his nose. Though he and Spock were duplicates, the intendant appeared much older. After his medical treatment on Vulcan, his skin had regained its color, and spiderwebs of broken green capillaries no longer stained his face. But his cheeks were still sunken, his hair still white, and though the strong tremors of advanced Bendii no longer afflicted his arm, there was still a frailty to him, an uncertainty of movement.

"Then what you are telling me," Intendant Spock finally said, "is that the Preservers are not just after Tiberius, but after the Kirk of your universe, as well."

"History has drawn them together," Spock said. "Logic returns to our analysis to suggest that where one Kirk is found, so may be the other."

Intendant Spock sighed. "And so you want me to help Tiberius plan what his next step should be, to acquire the means by which he can return to my universe and reconquer his empire."

"Precisely," Spock said. "Because, when Tiberius has decided upon a course of action, then the Preservers will move against him. And this time, we will be prepared for them."

"And then what?" the intendant asked.

"Then," Kirk answered, "we talk with them. You heard what Spock kept saying: For reasons unknown. Well, I want to know those reasons. I want to know why the Preservers are interfering in our development."

"You might not like the answer," Intendant Spock warned.

"That is a risk," Spock agreed.

"No," Kirk said. He saw his emphatic disagreement had surprised his audience, all three of them. "I don't think so. Because the truth is, the most logical action to take in order to keep Tiberius from interfering in their plans, *would* be to kill him. The fact that they haven't killed him, only destroyed some abandoned starships, tells me that the Preservers might have their own sense of ethics."

Spock and his duplicate exchanged a thoughtful glance, as if both of them were giving Kirk's words careful consideration.

But Tiberius was not. "James, I can't tell whether you're truly that innocent, or just ignorant. The herdsman doesn't kill his cattle when they stray from the herd. He simply builds a stronger fence, so none will escape until it's time to be marched lovingly into the slaughterhouse."

"My point is," Kirk said, "our first goal should be to *find* the Preservers. *Then* we can decide what to do about them."

"And my point," Tiberius countered, "is that I didn't become absolute ruler of the Terran Empire by thinking my enemies were guided by indefinable ethics. The Preservers have acted against me; they have acted against you. The only reasonable, *logical* response, is to insure that they can never take action again." Tiberius clenched and raised his fist. "It is not enough to *find* the Preservers. We must *crush* them. Otherwise, once we reveal ourselves as an even more pernicious threat, I guarantee you, James, they will crush *us*."

"You can guarantee what an unknowable alien race will do?" Kirk asked, unimpressed by his counterpart's theatrics.

"It's what I'd do," Tiberius said. "And I'm the one they want to stop."

"Then I will help you," Spock's duplicate said.

The intendant's sudden agreement was so unexpected that for a moment no one else spoke.

"So I will be present when the Preservers crush you," the intendant added.

Tiberius saluted him in mock challenge. "I've missed you, Spock. The two of us working together again, and all the treachery that implies. Just like old times." He nodded his head toward Kirk and Spock. "Just like those two."

Kirk chose that moment to pass over a padd to the intendant. "In that case, Intendant, this is where we should start. For the past month, Tiberius and I have been comparing our missions. We've been looking for points of convergence—such as our missions to Halkan, which took place at the same time in each universe—as well as any points of divergence."

"Spock," Tiberius said to the intendant, "remember that civilization we scanned on Organia? Well, it was an illusion. The humanoids were actually some type of highly evolved energy beings. Well—I suppose they weren't that highly evolved, considering what happened to them, were they?"

Tiberius began to laugh as Intendant Spock flinched at the mirthless sound.

Kirk didn't much like it either. When war had been declared between the Federation and the Klingon Empire, he and Spock had gone undercover to Organia, an apparently primitive planet occupied by a division of Klingon warriors. But the Organians were more advanced than either the Federation or the Klingons had anticipated, and had forced an uneasy truce between the two rival powers. That was how the event had played out in Kirk's universe.

However, in the mirror universe, once Starfleet had learned that a Klingon occupation force was on Organia, no attempt had been made to liberate the innocent Organian people. Instead, three starships, including Tiberius's *I.S.S. Enterprise,* had disrupted the surface of the Organian sun to induce a huge increase in solar flares. The ensuing megastorm had been so violent that it had penetrated the planet's magnetic field, sterilizing the entire world in hours. Flesh-and-blood Klingons and the energy-based Organians alike had perished. The Terran Empire considered the brutal obliteration of an innocent planet an appropriate lesson for the Klingons: No matter how savage the sons and daughters of Qo'noS believed themselves to be, the Terran Empire was prepared to be more savage.

In the end, however, outright war had been averted in both universes, although by two completely different means. But even if the details had been different, as Jean-Luc Picard had pointed out to Kirk, the patterns had been the same. The similar results of the Organian mission, among others, had prompted Picard to seek out the Federation's psychohistorians.

Intendant Spock picked up the padd, then pushed himself up to his feet. "I presume you wish me to identify missed opportunities from the past, which might logically lead to the discovery of advanced technology today, in order to help Tiberius."

Kirk, Spock, and Tiberius agreed.

Tiberius added, "Pay particular attention to the encounter with something this Spock calls a 'doomsday machine.' I don't believe the Empire ever charted one, which means it could still exist in our universe."

"I shall give the entire record my full attention," the

intendant said stiffly. "But I must return to Vulcan for a scheduled treatment."

Kirk rose to his feet, as did Spock and Tiberius. "Thank you, Intendant. We look forward to meeting with you as soon as you're able."

Intendant Spock nodded wearily and gathered his robes around him. "Later this evening. I—"

"Bridge to Captain Kirk."

The voice of Fleet Admiral Alynna Nechayev interrupted the intendant. She was the current commander of the *Sovereign,* and had taken a personal interest in Starfleet's developing position on the mirror universe.

As well she might, Kirk knew. Admiral Nechayev had been one of the highest-ranking Starfleet officers to be replaced by a mirror duplicate.

"Go ahead, Admiral," Kirk said.

Nechayev appeared on the conference room viewer. She was communicating from the *Sovereign*'s bridge. She made no apologies for her interruption. "We've just received an urgent hail from a ship approaching the Vulcan system. Someone is in a hurry to speak with you."

"Who?" Kirk asked.

"Captain Picard," the taciturn admiral said. "Or should I say, someone who *claims* to be him."

TWENTY

☆

Dr. Beverly Crusher flipped her medical tricorder shut with a practiced snap of her wrist, then read the results of her scans on the main diagnostic board in her sickbay. "No trace of the virus," she said. "Leonard H. McCoy knew what he was doing."

Picard sat up on the diagnostic bed. "I told you I was fully recovered." Riker was not convinced, even though to the eye, there were no noticeable lesions on Picard's skin, and Crusher's sensors reported no permanent damage to the captain's internal organs. As far as the commander was concerned, his captain continued to suffer the effects of his experience at Site 2713. Five days later, Jean-Luc Picard still seemed atypically listless.

Which made Riker wonder if the cause of Picard's exhaustion was something other than physical. Could it be the burden of what he had learned from the psychohistorians?

Crusher glanced at Riker and he could see that despite her medical findings, she apparently shared his suspicions about Picard's condition. "Jean-Luc," she said solicitously, "after everything you've been through, a few more days' rest still couldn't hurt."

Picard was already on his feet, ready to leave. "Admiral Nechayev appears to have taken care of that already."

At least with that, Riker had to agree. Three hours ago, when the captain had broken subspace silence to make contact with the *Sovereign,* Nechayev's first act had been to relieve Picard—*and* Riker—from command of the *Enterprise.* At the admiral's direction, Data now had the center chair.

After their initial shock at the abruptness of the order, neither Riker nor the captain had objected. Nechayev understandably was taking no chances. Picard, then Riker and the *Enterprise,* had all disappeared under mysterious circumstances. Since the admiral had once been replaced by a mirror duplicate herself, she knew from experience just how easily a substitution could take place. Her caution had even extended to denying entry of the *Enterprise* into the Vulcan system.

For that reason, the great ship now kept station in the ice halo of the system's Oort cloud. Her shields were set at minimum. Her warp core was offline. And a squadron of Starfleet fighters was positioned nearby with orders to disable the ship if she made any attempt to depart.

At any other time, Riker might have thought the admiral was overreacting. But she had Kirk and Tiberius on board. Given that combination, no doubt her paranoia was well founded.

Once Nechayev had been certain the *Enterprise* was not about to disappear again, she had stated her willingness to talk to Picard about where he had been. And what, if anything, he had learned. But at that point, it was Riker who had raised objections.

Captain Hu-Linn Radisson—whoever she was, whatever

division of Starfleet she answered to—had told Riker where to find Picard. Her information had been accurate, but fortunately the situation had not been as dire as she had feared.

When the *Enterprise* had arrived at Site 2713, it had only taken minutes for the ship's sensors to locate Picard on the planet's surface and for tractor beams to disable the small passenger liner which had abducted him.

Only when Riker had been sure of Picard's safety had he allowed the shock of seeing an exact replica of Earth to sink in.

But whatever additional mysteries there were to be solved, Radisson had said that the information she had personally given Riker could not be transmitted over subspace because Project Sign didn't know who within Starfleet could be trusted.

For the moment, Riker was prepared to accept Radisson's assessment. He and Picard had not been able to establish any connection between the civilian psychohistorians and Project Sign. Both groups, however, had independently concluded that James T. Kirk was somehow connected to whatever soon-to-occur event had the potential to destroy the universe.

And, if that supposition were true, Riker didn't want it broadcast to the galaxy any more than Radisson did.

So it had been Riker who suggested that, in the interests of security, and in the interests of sharing what they had all discovered, a physical meeting was in order.

Nechayev had agreed.

Where the truth could not be certain, paranoia, it seemed, was contagious.

The conference table was actually three engineering workbenches set up lengthwise and covered with a blue cloth. It was set up on the *Sovereign*'s main hangar deck.

Rows of shuttlecraft and shuttlepods were parked well off to either side. The still air smelled of tetralubisol and ozone. The thrum of the ship's generators echoed in the cavernous space.

To Riker, it was like meeting in a spaceport hangar. Orion freighters might be coming in to land at any moment.

At one end of the makeshift table, Picard sat in a chair borrowed from a legitimate conference room. No matching chair was at the table's other end. Instead, there was a portable viewer. Admiral Nechayev would be participating in the discussion from the security of the *Sovereign*'s bridge.

Along one side of the table, the six psychohistorians had taken their places: T'Serl and Lept of Memory Alpha; Savrin and T'Pon from the Seldon Institute; the Tiburon female, R'Ma'Hatrel; and the bombastic Tellarite scholar, Garen. Each had padds before them.

Facing them on the other side were captains Kirk and Spock, Tiberius and Intendant Spock, and at Picard's right hand, Riker.

Admiral Nechayev began by informing the assembled group that all the shuttlecraft were powered down, all airlocks sealed, and that no one would be leaving the hangar deck except by transporter under her direct command. Then she told Picard he could begin.

He wasted no time getting to the point. "In my judgment, we have *all* been manipulated."

"Define 'all,' " Nechayev asked from the viewer.

"The Federation. Starfleet. Every one of us."

"To what extent?"

Picard looked to his left. "Dr. Savrin, would you please tell these people the results of your research, exactly as you described them to me."

The thin Vulcan scholar responded with a question. "In the past three hundred years, what is the most profound historical event to have influenced the creation of the United Federation of Planets?"

"First contact," Riker said, "between Earth and Vulcan." When the *Enterprise* had traveled through time to fight the Borg, he'd been there. He'd seen it.

"Agreed," Savrin said. "A remarkable event which directly led to the creation of the Federation, ninety-eight years later."

"What makes it more remarkable," T'Pon added, "is its extraordinary juxtaposition with another, equally momentous occurrence."

Riker allowed himself a small smile. "Cochrane's first warp flight." He and Geordi had actually taken that flight with Cochrane. Not that they could share that adventure—or anything else they had experienced on their journey into the past—with anyone other than the Federation Department of Temporal Investigations. The excruciatingly humorless Agents Dulmer and Lucsly of the FDTI had made that very clear.

"Precisely," Savrin agreed. "And according to modern historical theory, the odds of that coincidence are to all intents incalculable."

Riker was surprised. He'd thought all odds were calculable for a Vulcan.

"On my world," Savrin continued, "no event in the past three centuries has been studied more closely than the decision to send that probe to Earth's system at that time. Consider this: On the previous probe of Earth, twenty years earlier, Vulcan explorers detected the unmistakable signs of impending global war. Subsequent estimations of humanity's chances for causing its own extinction within the next ten years were judged to be one in three.

"After that previous mission to Earth," Savrin concluded, "the Vulcan Academy of Science had no plans to return to Earth's system for another century."

Riker saw the problem at once. "Then what was the probe ship doing there eighty years ahead of schedule when the *Phoenix* launched?"

He heard Picard sigh, saw him lean forward to command the table's attention. "Will, everyone . . . they showed me the documentation records from the Vulcan Academy. That probe ship was initially scheduled to map gravity anomalies in the Alpha Centauri system. Three months before arriving there, the ship received new orders from the Academy of Science's communications division, to chart potential wormhole eddies created by Jupiter's interaction with the sun. Those orders are what brought the Vulcan ship to our system in time for the flight of the *Phoenix*. But no traceable authorization codes were appended."

"Are you implying," Spock asked, "that an outside agency knew that Cochrane was preparing to test a functional warp drive? And that it covertly diverted the probe ship to be in range when the test occurred?"

"Correct," T'Serl said. "An outside agency we believe to consist of either the Preservers themselves, or Vulcans working in their employ."

"What else?" Nechayev prompted. "Savrin has raised one coincidence. A compelling one, to be sure. But ship's orders change. Authorizations are misfiled. And everything in life is a coincidence. What I need to be convinced of is a *pattern* of coincidence."

"Admiral Nechayev," Savrin said, "that pattern of coincidence is exactly what psychohistory has been developed to find." He nodded to T'Pon, who then efficiently described what she and Savrin termed were the most notable and inexplicable coincidences of Federation history.

Riker listened in equal parts amazement and apprehension, and some twenty minutes and two dozen examples later from the other psychohistorians at the table, he found he was nearly convinced the entire Federation was under the control of beings little better than the old gods of Olympus.

But the admiral still had her doubts. "I don't deny that history is made up of remarkable events. For want of a nail and all that. But it seems to me that when you detail all the singular coincidences that make up Federation history, you're undermining your own theory. If *everything* is unexpected, then doesn't that mean the unexpected *must* be expected?"

"Admiral," Picard said, "you are raising all the same objections I raised in my initial discussions. But as I was informed, these remarkable coincidences must not be judged in isolation. Rather, they must be seen in the context of the duplicate worlds."

"Duplicate worlds?" Nechayev asked, frowning.

Picard first warned all at the table that any post-meeting discussion of the following topic would be considered a violation of Starfleet's secrecy regulations, then described the true nature of Site 2713 and the other known duplicate worlds.

At one point, Kirk stopped Picard to say, "We were there. My crew and I, we were on that world. McCoy came up with the cure for the disease they had created."

When Picard had finished, Nechayev immediately asked what was obviously to her the most critical question. "Captain Picard, has a Preserver artifact ever been discovered in conjunction with one of these duplicate worlds?"

"No. Not to anyone's knowledge."

"So, however interesting this theory is, its underlying connections are still just a matter of guesswork. The same question about the Preservers remains: Are we looking at the activities of one species of superaliens? Or are we misinterpreting an accumulation of data created by a multitude of different species over eons of time?"

"There is more," Picard said grimly. Then, surprisingly, he turned to Kirk. "Jim, how did you get command of your *Enterprise?*"

Kirk looked surprised by the question. "I *earned* it, Jean-Luc."

"I have no doubt you did," Picard agreed. "But you were the youngest starship captain ever commissioned at that time, were you not?"

Kirk's eyes narrowed. "I also led my class, was decorated at Axanar, and received the highest rating in tactics ever given by the Grankite Totality. Is there a point you're trying to make?"

"I'm not trying to disparage your accomplishments, or your fitness to command a starship. But according to Starfleet's rules and regulations of the day, when you first assumed command of the *Enterprise,* you were too young to be given a Constitution-class vessel, especially considering you had no previous experience as a ship's commander."

Kirk frowned. "Rules and regulations are meant to be broken, Jean-Luc. I don't have to tell you that."

"But in all of Starfleet's vast archives, there are no traceable authorization codes attached to the orders giving you the *Enterprise.* Exactly as in the case of the orders diverting the Vulcan probe to Earth's system."

Just when it seemed to Riker that Kirk would rise from the table in protest, Spock intervened. "Captain Picard, are we to understand that the Preservers' influence on the Federation's development extends to details of selecting which *individual* personnel shall be assigned to which vessels?"

Savrin answered for Picard. "The evidence speaks for itself, Spock."

Kirk angrily disagreed. "The assignment of command is not an equation. Then as now, personality is as important as the quantifiables."

"The admiral also asked to see a pattern," Picard said quietly. "And there *is* a pattern. Jim, you're not the only one."

Riker saw that that statement stopped Kirk's escalating sense of outrage.

"How many?" Kirk demanded.

"Focusing only on Starfleet command appointments made in the past twenty years," Savrin answered, "we have identified thirty-seven orders generated with a lack of traceable authorization codes."

"Are you familiar with Captain Tryla Scott?" Picard asked Kirk.

Kirk wasn't.

"She broke your record for youngest starship captain. Her orders can't be traced."

Savrin looked at Kirk. "Are you familiar with Captain Kathryn Janeway?"

"The Preservers gave her the *Voyager?*" Kirk's disbelief was unconcealed.

"No. There is no evidence of that," Savrin replied. "But the orders assigning her as science officer to the *U.S.S. Al-Batani* carry no traceable authorization. And it was her brilliance as a science officer during the Coal Sack expedition that saved that ship, ensured peace with the Marklar Associative, and helped place her on the fast track to a command of her own."

"Among my crew," Picard added, "there is a similar discrepancy in the background files of Dr. Beverly Crusher; specifically, the orders returning her to active duty following . . . a leave of absence for personal reasons. In addition, the captain of the *Tripoli*, the starship whose crew discovered Commander Data, also shares the same discrepancies in the orders that gave him that command."

Other names followed, only two more of which Riker

recognized: Captain John Scott Lewinski of the *U.S.S. Monitor,* the Defiant-class ship which had been outfitted with a recovered Borg transwarp drive and which had recently vanished in an attempt to set a new warp-speed record; and Admiral Xiaoling Sun, the commander of Starbase 541 who had helped negotiate a peace treaty with the Norlak Resurgency, one of the Federation's newest members.

But for every Starfleet officer cited such as Kirk and Janeway—who had participated in some event of critical importance to the Federation's continued security and survival—there were other individuals like Sun and Crusher whose high performance of duty so far seemed to be without immediate historical significance. Then there were others like Captain Tryla Scott, who were cut down before the promise of their greatness could be fulfilled.

"Compelling," Admiral Nechayev said. "But in the end, still circumstantial."

Then Riker realized he might hold the key to elevating the psychohistorians' theory from supposition to fact.

He rose from his place at the table, directing his words to the portable viewer. "Admiral, I believe that Starfleet, at some level, already accepts this theory as fact. Understandably, they just don't advertise it."

Nechayev's frown was not encouraging. "This had better be good, Commander."

"Project Sign," Riker said quickly. "Captain Hu-Linn Radisson met me at Starbase . . . at the facility where the *Enterprise* was undergoing repair. She gave me a complete report on the duplicate worlds. She told me where to find Captain Picard."

Spock interrupted. "Commander Riker, I point out that Starfleet will not confirm the existence of a Hu-Linn Radisson."

"But you and I, Spock, and captains Kirk and Picard, we've all been on her ship and met with her. Holographic disguises notwithstanding."

On the portable viewer, Admiral Nechayev spoke crisply. "It is hardly surprising that Starfleet has personnel whose identity Command would prefer to keep confidential. The fact that someone in Starfleet, whatever her name really is, provided you with Picard's whereabouts tells me that Starfleet Intelligence tracked down the captain's kidnappers and, to protect their sources, gave *you* the assignment to retrieve him. You're his exec, Commander. Clearly the right person for the job. I fail to see the mystery. And I certainly don't see the hand of the Preservers."

With a silent apology to Captain Kirk, Riker supplied the final details. "Admiral, there's more to it than that. T'Serl and Lept predicted that fifty-nine days before the end of the universe, they would be visited by the person responsible for it."

"I understood that they subsequently changed that prediction," Nechayev said. "Unless you now believe Captain Picard is that person?"

"No," Riker said. "But there was a limit to the . . . the temporal resolution of their psychohistorical model. They correctly identified the *reason* for the visit, though they misidentified the actual *person* who came to them."

"Commander, if you have a point, I'd suggest you make it."

Riker spoke bluntly. "Captain Picard visited Memory Alpha on behalf of Captain Kirk. And Radisson told me that Project Sign had also identified Captain Kirk as the person responsible for the universe's impending destruction. I submit that because the fact that T'Serl's and Lept's prediction identified the motivating personality behind Captain Picard's visit—"

"That's enough," Kirk said.

"—and the fact that Project Sign has independently confirmed Kirk as the person responsible, the evidence is overwhelming—" Riker stepped back as Kirk stood up menacingly.

"I won't listen to this stupidity," Kirk warned.

Spock stood as well, reaching out a hand to hold his captain in place.

"—overwhelming," Riker continued doggedly, "that James T. Kirk, whose career was given to him by the Preservers, is in fact the agent of the Preservers we have all been looking for."

TWENTY-ONE

☆

Kirk heard his own voice echo—*thunder*—in the hangar deck.

"Don't you people *see* how we've been manipulated?" Kirk said. "Don't you understand what's going on here?"

"Am I to assume that you do?" Nechayev asked from the viewer.

Kirk took a deep breath and willed his body to relax enough that Spock would release him. The Vulcan did.

"Yes," Kirk said. "Precisely because we've just exchanged information that I'm convinced the Preservers never wanted us to have." Then Kirk turned to Picard, knowing that if ever he was to lead, it had to be now. "Jean-Luc, do you remember back on Qo'noS, when Teilani was dying, and I returned with the antitoxin Tiberius had given me?"

"I do," Picard said.

Kirk needed to move to think. He began to pace along his side of the table, behind Tiberius, Spock and Intendant Spock, and Riker.

"You and I," he said to Picard, "we spoke with Bones and Andrea—" Kirk turned to Nechayev on the screen.

"—Admiral McCoy and Dr. M'Benga from Deep Space 9."
He reached the end of the table, turned back to see all
except Tiberius watching him closely. "And Bones said that
it seemed we all had one piece of the puzzle. All we knew
then was that there might be some connection between the
mirror universe and Project Sign. But then we found the
Preserver obelisk. Right where it would do Tiberius the
most harm."

Kirk stood behind his counterpart now, rested his hands
on the back of his chair. Tiberius shifted uncomfortably.

"That's because Tiberius is right. The Preservers *are*
after him. The Preservers want to stop him. Because *he's*
the random factor in their experiment."

Nechayev was puzzled. "By experiment, you mean the
Federation?"

Kirk resumed his pacing. "At the very least. Maybe the
entire galaxy, strange new worlds and civilizations we have
yet to seek out and explore. But you heard the psychohistorians: Beneath the chaos of our history, there is an
unexpected order. Subtle evidence of an unseen hand,
moving a piece here, another piece there. Putting *me* on the
Enterprise a few years earlier than I might otherwise have
earned her. Making *sure* that Vulcans and humans made
their first contact at the *instant* Earth was capable of interstellar exploration."

Kirk turned from the viewer to face the others at the
table. "That pattern exists. We can't ignore it. And the fact
that Project Sign exists means Starfleet *hasn't* ignored it."

"Hu-Linn Radisson," Nechayev said, filling in details to
show she understood his line of reasoning. "The equally mysterious Commodore Twining, who met with Commander
Riker. The advanced starships with holographic crew. You're
saying that all that is Starfleet's response to the Preservers?"

"Not a response to the Preservers themselves," Kirk said,

"but to the smoke screen the Preservers set up, to divert our attention. At some classified level, Starfleet knows we face an enemy, suspects we might face a war, yet has no idea who that enemy is, or where the first attack might come from. Therefore, *I* submit that the Preservers knew we'd eventually see evidence of their hand in our affairs, and so they deliberately created a false layer of evidence."

It was Spock who made the connection at once. "The duplicate worlds."

Kirk nodded his agreement. "That's it, Spock. Here we've been assuming that Project Sign was created in response to the obelisk I found on the world with the transplanted culture from the North American plains. But Sign came from Project Magnet. And," Kirk slapped his hand on the table for emphasis, "Magnet was formed *before* I found the obelisk. In fact, Magnet was formed when I found the first duplicate Earth—the same world the psychohistorians took Jean-Luc to.

"The duplicate worlds." Kirk swept a hand in the air. "It's a staggering concept. Think of the technology that must be required. We pride ourselves on being able to change mere *portions* of a world's surface, to hold our zoos or to save endangered species. But suddenly . . . we were faced with *artificial* habitats on a planetary scale that made our efforts look like those of children playing in a sand-pile."

Kirk could hear his voice rise with the wonder he himself felt as he contemplated the significance of what they might have discovered.

"*Of course* Starfleet classified the existence of those worlds. *Of course* Starfleet became consumed by the need to identify the builders. And while we put all our efforts, all our top scientists, into programs designed to study *that* great mystery, when we found a handful of unusual obelisks that seemed to have no current purpose, we pushed them to the side as a lesser problem."

"Jim, if we accept what you've said so far," Picard said, "then you've given us the connection between Sign and the Preservers. And, essentially, you're telling us that Project Sign is just another . . ." Picard made a wry smile. ". . . *sign* that the Preservers have manipulated us."

"In this case," Kirk suggested, "it was more like misdirection."

"Either way," Picard said, "you have yet to explain the connection to the mirror universe."

Kirk nodded encouragingly. *Almost there,* he thought. *All Picard needs is a final push to reach the same conclusion I have.*

"Jean-Luc, put yourself in the position of the founders of Project Sign a century ago. They're in a panic, dealing with duplicate planets. Then, I file my logs from the mission at Halkan when Tiberius and I traded places, and suddenly Starfleet is faced with the existence of a duplicate *universe.* Who *wouldn't* think there was a connection?"

"So," Picard reasoned out loud, "the Preservers knew we might find evidence of their existence. Therefore, they created the duplicate planets—which serve no real purpose—in order to distract our attention from what they're really doing—which we still don't know. And now, our attention has been further distracted by the existence of the mirror universe, which we believe is somehow connected to those duplicate planets."

"Yes," Kirk said.

"So what is the Preservers' *real* connection to the mirror universe and Tiberius?" Nechayev asked.

Kirk remained beside Picard's side as he looked down toward the viewer at the far end of the table.

"That's just it, Admiral. There *is* no connection. The creation of the mirror universe was the ultimate random act. The ultimate expression of chaos."

Kirk placed a hand on Picard's shoulder. "In our universe, the Federation's history has been peaceful, more or less. We pride ourselves on negotiation, understanding, noninterference. We make enemies, but eventually, we make them our allies. And those policies and philosophies which have worked for us in the past have created a momentum which carries us into a hopeful future.

"But in the mirror universe, the Preservers have *not* interfered with history. Whatever moment of . . . quantum indecision made our two universes diverge, our universe remained of interest to the Preservers. *Tiberius's* didn't."

Kirk began walking down the other side of the table, behind the six psychohistorians. *"That's* why the psychohistorians think of the mirror universe as a control group. Though for the wrong reasons. Because the mirror universe is *anything* but controlled. It is the quintessential expression of the chaos of human nature." Kirk paused as he suddenly became aware of the deep currents that ran through the pattern of his own life. "The mirror universe shows us what happens when the desires of the few supersede the good of the many."

Kirk looked across the table at Spock and Spock's duplicate, and at Tiberius, who sat between them, scowling.

"But if there was no connection to begin with, then *what* is the connection now?" Nechayev asked.

Kirk knew the admiral's patience was flagging. But it was important that she—that they *all* understood what he did. "Spock tells me," he said, "that science considers that an infinite number of parallel universes exist, constantly budding off from each other as quantum decision points are reached. But usually, those universes don't stay connected."

He looked over at Picard. "I remember talking with

Captain Picard about Commander Worf being caught in an anomaly that spread across several of those parallel realities."

"That's right," Picard said. "That was when we learned how to measure quantum signatures, so we could identify people and objects who had originated in other universes."

"But the point is," Kirk stressed for the admiral's benefit, "that there is only *one* other universe that has remained *consistently* linked to ours. And that's the universe my counterpart is from. A universe that was absolutely identical to ours until . . . Spock?"

"Until approximately three hundred and twelve years ago," Spock supplied.

"Again, First Contact," Kirk said. "What happened then that made our universes diverge, I don't know. Spock and his counterpart have their theories. Perhaps someday we'll know for certain. Perhaps we won't. But I submit that *whatever* event led to the two universes separating—a roll of the dice, a flip of a coin—that event was *random*. An event that the Preservers *did* not—*could* not—anticipate.

"Then, for two hundred years, that event didn't matter. The mirror universe was like any other of the infinite parallel quantum states. Except it *wasn't* separate. For some reason, it remained connected, there was new contact, and suddenly the Preservers were faced with a completely unanticipated problem."

Then Kirk pointed at that problem, where he sat between the two Spocks.

"Tiberius," Kirk said. "He created an empire in that other universe. Lost it. Then came to ours for a second chance to create one here. And the Preservers cannot allow him to interfere with us, because *his* plans for us will disrupt *their* plan."

"All right, that's enough," Nechayev said with a sigh. "You've woven it all together. But you still haven't told us what the picture is. What *is* the Preservers' plan? To destroy our universe?"

"No," Kirk said. "I think the events leading up to the destruction which the psychohistorians have predicted have nothing to do with the Preservers, but everything to do with my counterpart. I think Tiberius is in a position to find some source of power, some lost alien technology, *something* that probably springs from our earliest missions, and then unleash it, destroying everything. Clearly that's reason enough for the Preservers to want to stop him."

"So all we're missing," Nechayev said, and Kirk couldn't tell if she was agreeing with him or attempting to show him a flaw in his argument, "is that source of power or alien technology."

"Exactly," Kirk said.

"Then, if you're right, how do we find it?"

"We don't have to." Kirk looked at the psychohistorians, challenging them. "All we need is for these scholars to use their expertise to analyze Starfleet's most recent senior personnel postings. Given the Preservers' penchant for selecting specific people to be at particular places at particular times, then I suggest that we will find an anomaly—a junior captain or a starbase commander given an assignment apparently not in line with their experience.

"And if we find that person, and track that person, then we'll know where to find what Tiberius is destined to find. Because the Preservers will have already predicted it, just as they predicted he'd go to the First Federation base."

Kirk looked around the silent table for support.

Riker seemed troubled. Kirk hoped that meant he had successfully raised some doubts about his guilt in the commander's mind.

Picard was looking over at the rows of shuttlecraft, deep in thought.

Among the six psychohistorians, T'Serl and Lept were looking at each other so intently, they seemed to be carrying on a telepathic conversation—a possibility for the Vulcan, but not for the Ferengi, Kirk knew.

Savrin and T'Pon, the two Vulcans from the Seldon Institute, were using their padds to review text material.

The Tellarite, Garen, was vigorously scratching his white-furred snout as he stared up at the deck's distant ceiling, while the Tiburon, R'Ma'Hatrel, stared down at the floor, her ears slowly pulsing.

And while he sought no support from either Tiberius or Intendant Spock, Kirk was pleased to see his Spock nod once, as if in total agreement.

"Any questions, Admiral?" Kirk asked.

On the viewer, Nechayev's expression was completely unreadable.

"You're saying that our failure—*Starfleet's* failure—in identifying the true nature of our enemy rests in the very secrecy we erected to help protect ourselves."

Kirk nodded. "If every division of Starfleet investigating the duplicate worlds and the obelisks and the mirror universe had worked together—instead of carving up their little kingdoms and refusing to share their information—then yes, I believe the Preserver threat would have become apparent decades ago. Starfleet has been its own worst enemy—a condition which the Preservers not only understood, but exploited."

"Even if you're correct," Nechayev said—and with those words, Kirk knew he was on the verge of convincing her—"I don't think you understand the complexity of today's Starfleet. The tens of thousands of ships, the hundreds of thousands of personnel, the datastreams necessary to keep its bureaucracy functioning on a day-to-day basis. Especially given the additional strain of fighting the Dominion war. To do what you suggest, Captain—sift through gigaquads of personnel disposition reports and orders, looking for a single anomaly . . . well, it can be done, but I believe the effort will take several more years than we apparently have left."

All eyes were on Kirk now. The admiral was willing to be convinced, if he could offer one more piece of evidence. But what? Kirk didn't know.

"Captain," Spock said. "Without delving into Starfleet's datastream, it appears that there is one overriding pattern that arises solely from the facts as you have presented them."

Spock turned toward the viewer image of Admiral Nechayev. "Captain Kirk's orders to take command of the *Enterprise* may have been partially . . . inspired by the Preservers or their agents. Aboard that ship, on the captain's first five-year mission, he was on the first landing party to explore the duplicate planet known as Site 2713. He discovered the first Preserver obelisk. He was also in the first group to cross over into the mirror universe. And then, at the moment he reentered our timeline six years ago, a new Preserver obelisk was installed in the First Federation base."

Spock paused and next addressed Kirk. "I suggest that though Tiberius may be the focus of the Preservers' *current* activities, when viewed over time, it is *you* who have been a focus of their *ongoing* activities."

Kirk smiled. Spock had never let him down. "So we don't have to sift through Starfleet's *entire* datastream," he said in growing excitement. "Just those parts of it that involve *me.*"

"Correct," Spock said. "And those parts should include the records of Captain Picard and the current crew of the *Enterprise* as well as those of Admiral Nechayev and the current crew of the *Sovereign.* I would also expand it to include the personnel of the starbase at which the *Enterprise* was repaired, and the crew of the commercial liner the psychohistorians hired to take Captain Picard to Site 2713."

Spock turned back to the viewer. "Admiral Nechayev, I propose that if we use Captain Kirk as the center of a causative web, I believe we will not have far to search for a staffing anomaly such as the one you described. If, indeed, such an anomaly exists."

Kirk felt the surge of elation. The end was in sight. He looked at Nechayev on the screen. "Well, Admiral? Your decision?"

"Captain, I don't know if you're right, if you're insane, or if Commander Riker called it and you're an agent of the Preservers adding to the confusion, but it seems to me that Captain Spock's approach doesn't appear to be unreasonable."

Nechayev's voice took on added authority. "I will permit the psychohistorians to access Starfleet Command's personnel database to search for the type of anomalies they've described finding in the past. And with such a limited search, I expect we will have our results in no more than a few hours. After all," the admiral added, "how many captains do you know who've received new orders in the past few weeks?"

Then, almost shockingly, Nechayev smiled. Kirk could not recall ever having seen the austere admiral do so before.

"As far as I can remember," Kirk said in relief, "I don't know of any captain who's—"

He broke off as the solution hit him like a phaser bolt.

The search wouldn't take hours.

There was only one name to check.

TWENTY-TWO

☆

"Christine MacDonald?" Teilani asked from her side of the bed in Kirk's quarters on the *Enterprise*.

"The same," Kirk said. He sat on the edge of his side of the bed, still in his uniform. The meeting on the hangar deck had ended an hour ago. The results already confirmed. "She was the captain of the science vessel *Tobias*."

Teilani gazed out the viewport, at the stars moving by at warp speed. It was ship's night and the cabin lights were dim so the stars were bright. "She was very young."

"Yes, she was," Kirk agreed. Somewhere past those stars was the only destination that made sense to him now. A destination ordained more than a century earlier, yet only discovered in the past thirty minutes—by the psychohistorians—in Starfleet's database.

"She was very pretty."

Kirk reached out to find Teilani's hand beneath the blankets that blurred her exquisite form, put his hand over hers. "That, too," he said.

Teilani didn't return the squeeze he gave her hand, as if

her blankets were a wall between them. "She asked you to go with her."

Kirk smiled quizzically, unsure of the reason for Teilani's comment. He had had this conversation with her before. But this was new.

"I didn't tell you that," he said.

"You didn't have to. But she asked you, didn't she? They always ask you."

Kirk remembered his last voyage on the *Tobias*. "She did. But she brought me back to Chal. And to you."

"You never wanted to come back."

Kirk's puzzlement deepened. He knew she didn't believe that. "Teilani, coming back to you was all I ever wanted. It's all I want now."

Teilani closed her eyes briefly. "I'm sorry. I'm . . . I'm just so worried about Joseph."

Anger and sorrow mixed in Kirk. The name a knife in his heart, every time he heard it.

"I got through to McCoy," Kirk said uncomfortably. "Two more weeks and the Romulans will arrive to join his team on Qo'noS. We'll be back by then, too." For Teilani's sake, he forced himself to add, "Joseph . . . will be fine."

"But you don't believe that," Teilani said sadly.

She was right. Kirk found himself hating everything—everyone—that had brought them to this. Putting the wrong words in each other's mouths. Keeping secrets from each other. After all they had been through. After all the battles they had fought—and won—to be together.

"I want to believe it," Kirk said. "I . . . have to."

Teilani drew her hand from his, eased away from him, sat up, resting her back against the molded headboard. "I shouldn't have left Joseph."

They had had this conversation before, as well. "There was nothing more we could do on Qo'noS. We have to take our chance to—"

"Go looking for Christine MacDonald?"

"I didn't choose her," Kirk reminded Teilani. "According to some of the psychohistorians, the Preservers did. The same way they chose me. It's the Preservers we're looking for, remember? Not Christine."

Teilani stared out at the passing stars. "The coincidence seems rather convenient. You and Christine again."

Kirk sighed. So much for telling Teilani everything that had happened at the hangar-deck meeting, in direct contravention of Picard's warning. He'd told her how Picard had determined the Federation had been manipulated. How Riker had accused him of being an agent of the Preservers. And how with Spock's insights, he'd come up with a single source for all the mysteries they faced.

"Teilani, you *know* Captain MacDonald means nothing to me. She's a . . . a pawn of history."

"Like you?"

It was the same question Kirk had been asking himself ever since Picard and the psychohistorians had revealed the anomalies in the orders that had given him the *Enterprise*.

And it was one for which he still had no answer. "I don't know," Kirk said, troubled. The questions roiled in his gut. How much freedom did any of them actually have? Given the place and time of his birth, could he have been anything other than a starship captain? Could Tiberius, in his harsher reality, have become anything other than an emperor? Did the Preservers make everyone's fate? Or did they just see who was best suited for one role or another and help people along—the way he'd make up duty rosters to match the best-qualified crewmen with the jobs requiring their talents and training?

Or were the Preservers themselves just another layer of deception, another smoke screen hiding an even bigger mystery—one of humanity's own making?

Kirk sighed heavily, longing for the peace that action—not questions—brought him.

Teilani took pity on him then, reached out to him, took his hand in hers. "James, most people look at history, at the universe, and see chaos. You looked deeper, and you saw an order hidden there. But is it real? Or is it your *need* to see order? To believe that there's reason behind everything. That there's meaning."

Kirk held Teilani's hand tightly, wishing it were as simple to merge her being with his.

She was speaking of the universe. But he knew she meant their lives, their marriage. Their child.

Kirk couldn't say what had brought Teilani and him together, any more than he could know if the Preservers really existed, and if they did, what their plans were.

Nor did he know what the future would bring for any of them. The universe. The Federation. Their marriage. Their child. Didn't all meaning of existence ultimately spring from individual hearts and minds?

And of the two extremes of scale, which was the greatest mystery? The force that bound the galaxies in space? Or the force that bound two lovers?

Kirk found it difficult to separate one mystery from the other. What meaning did the stars have for him without Teilani? And what meaning would his love for her have, if those stars were not part of his life?

In this moment, there was only one way to distill all his questions to their essence.

"I love you," Kirk said.

"That's not what I asked you."

He kissed her. "Yes, you did. Because that's all that matters."

Teilani pulled back to look at him. "We could be home now, James. With our child, on Chal, in the home you made for us in our clearing. Why are we here?"

Kirk traced the scar on her face. Felt its undiminished ridge. Saw its angry color, eclipsed by her beauty. Knew she'd been testing him.

"Why do you think?" he asked gently. "The real answer."

Teilani smiled ruefully. He'd caught her and she knew it. Her hand touched his cheek. "You're here because you can't stand the thought of anyone having control over you. Tiberius. Nechayev. The Preservers. You won't put up with that."

Playfully, he captured her finger as it found his lips, kissed it. "You have control over me."

"Only because you let me."

He drew her close. The nerves of his hands had almost grown back completely and it was as if he touched her for the first time. "And why are you here?" he murmured, breathing in the fragrant scent of her hair.

For a heartbeat, the lightness of the moment left her. "Because I don't want to lose you."

Kirk closed his eyes, his mouth against hers. "You never will."

Teilani's blankets fell aside then, and beneath them she wore only starlight.

Kirk held his breath at her beauty.

"Yes, I will," she whispered. "But not tonight."

Their final destination still lay before them—the only

place the battle could end. But for one night, James T. Kirk and Teilani together held back time.

Safe in the *Enterprise,* safe in each other's arms, they flew toward the only destination where the mystery could be solved, because it was where the mystery had begun.

Planet Halkan.

TWENTY-THREE

☆

The hull of the *Nautilus* groaned as the deck suddenly pitched ten degrees downward.

"Alert," an artificial male voice announced. *"Hull deficiency on deck three, segment A. Watertight doors will close in ten seconds."*

Picard gazed around the cramped operations chamber of the ancient vessel as the crew strapped themselves into their seats and began flipping through procedure manuals. All around them, the computer screens at their bulky metal consoles flashed with warning readouts. The exposed pipes on the low ceiling creaked ominously.

"This was the beginning of the end," Picard explained to his command staff. "The first hull breach occurs in three minutes. Two minutes after that, they're so deep the whole thing implodes. It was fifty years before another crewed vessel returned to the oceans of Europa."

At Picard's side in the navigation alcove, crowded in beside Data, Crusher, La Forge, and Troi, Riker shook his head. "Captain Radisson has a real thing for disasters."

Picard steadied himself on a handrail as the submersible

shuddered and the angle of the deck became even more extreme. "And she has a much better holodeck system. I tell you, Will, at this point in my meeting with her, my uniform was stained with leaking coolant. My ears were popping with the pressure changes. The humidity. The smell of the trapped air when everyone retreated into this chamber." Picard grimaced. "I've never experienced such realistic detail."

Counselor Troi put a calming hand on his arm. "Sir, I can sense that just the memory of it is provoking an extreme stress response. Perhaps we don't need to experience the rest of the program."

But Picard wanted to see it through. Kirk had put together a convincing big picture at the meeting in the hangar deck, but there were still discoveries to be made by analyzing the details. He was convinced of it. "It's all right, Counselor. Unlike Radisson, I have engaged all the holodeck safety protocols."

Even so, Troi looped an arm around the railing of a tightly wound circular staircase to hold herself in position. The entire chamber thumped and vibrated as it rose and fell now.

Picard kept his attention on the holographic simulation of Heidi Rasmussen, commander of the dying vessel. He wondered if at this time she had known she was losing her ship. What that would feel like.

"Deanna," Dr. Crusher suddenly said. "Do you think *that* might be why Radisson exposed her guests to reconstructed disaster scenarios—to study their response to stress?"

"It's possible. Though I'm not sure what sort of information she'd expect to gain."

"Perhaps she wanted to see if her guest possessed emotions," Data suggested.

"But why would that be important, Data?" Troi waved a

hand to fan her face. "Standard tricorders can tell the difference between biological and synthetic life."

"Maybe," La Forge offered, "there's some difference in how people from our universe and the mirror universe react to disaster?"

Picard didn't think that was the explanation. "Again, there are simpler ways to determine which universe someone is from. Simply scan for quantum signatures."

By now the submersible's ventilation and heat-exchange systems had shut down and the temperature was soaring. Picard could see Troi looking pleadingly at him, several strands of dark hair plastered to her forehead by sweat.

"Computer," he said, "delete temperature effects from the simulation."

At once a cool flow of air commenced.

"Then maybe she's . . . just gone crazy," La Forge suggested. "Captain Radisson, I mean. There she is, cooped up on her ship, not allowed to tell anyone what it is she does, or even what she looks like, so . . ." He pointed to the operations chamber of the doomed *Nautilus*. ". . . she's become addicted to things like this for variety. To add excitement to her life."

But Picard shook his head. "No, Geordi, there was more to what she was doing than that. I think Beverly was on the right track. I believe Captain Radisson wasn't so much interested in reliving the deaths of these people, as in studying my reaction to it."

Then he and everyone except Data suddenly clapped their hands over their ears as an enormous explosion shook the small chamber and the air filled with blaring alarms and distant screams.

"Computer," Picard said, "delete audio."

Silence immediately followed. Now the doomed holograms worked and shouted unheard as the entire chamber vibrated and pitched without a sound.

Riker returned to the topic of their gathering. "I agree, Captain. When Radisson had me in the Mars simulation, my feeling definitely was that she wanted to see how *I* reacted to stress and death. Possibly also to learn how I felt about the use of violence for political ends."

"But you were shown a *deliberate* act of political terrorism on Mars, Will. What I was shown—the wreck of the *Nautilus*—was a re-creation of an *accident.* No one on the *Nautilus* knew that Europan squid existed, let alone could crack the hull of a submersible. And the catastrophic event she showed Kirk was a *natural* disaster on twenty-first-century Earth."

"Whoa," Troi suddenly exclaimed as the chamber began a violent spiral to port and she swung away from the staircase. Data caught the counselor by the back of her jacket before she could tumble over the railing and onto the main deck.

"Computer," Picard said without prompting, "delete motion simulation."

With a stomach-twisting jump, the operations chamber suddenly leveled out. Disconcertingly, however, the holographic crew members continued to sway and lean to the stern as if the *Nautilus* was still strongly angled, still descending.

"Sir, where was the plant in your simulation?"

For a moment, Picard wasn't certain what his first officer meant. Then he remembered. "The tall one with the spirals on its leaves?"

"That's it," Riker said. "I thought it was part of the terraformed Martian biosphere, but when Radisson ended the program, it was growing out of a pot in her ready room."

"In her re-creation of the *Nautilus,* it was over in that corner." Picard pointed to a section of the operations chamber now wreathed in smoke.

"What about her watering can?" Riker asked.

"I remember it. Copper." Picard looked thoughtful. "We should ask Jim if the plant was part of his re-creation, too."

All the lights except for a handful of self-contained emergency lamps winked out as a bank of consoles soundlessly exploded.

"Computer, go to visual only." Picard knew what was coming. He didn't need to be in the middle of it again.

The holographic re-creation suddenly compressed until it was as if a large, two-dimensional display screen were suspended in the center of the holodeck.

Picard and his crew watched in silence as the last few moments of the *Nautilus* played out before them. The images were reconstructed from those recorded by the ship's operations monitors, which had been restored a century later when the wreckage was recovered.

Captain Rasmussen was still at the controls when the deck split and a sheet of pressurized water sprayed up like an axe blade, halving the torsos of the two crew members caught by it.

In less than five seconds, the entire compartment was flooded and all that could be seen were a half-dozen pale cones of fading light from the emergency lamps as they slowly rolled away in clouded water.

For a few disturbing seconds, Picard could just make out the sleek silhouettes of the school of fifty-meter-long squid, outlined by their flickering phosphorescent communications nodes. Then the squid broke off their attack, returning to the depths. All that remained was the unbroken darkness of the sunless Europan sea.

Riker cleared his throat. "Radisson ended my program just before the end."

Picard nodded. "She did the same for me, and for Jim. Computer, end program."

The virtual screen was gone. In its place, the familiar,

yellow-gridded floor, walls, and ceiling of an idle holodeck returned.

"Well," Picard said, "I thank you for your attention, but I'm not sure we learned anything."

"Other than it seems likely there is a purpose to Captain Radisson's use of disaster simulations," Troi suggested.

"Maybe it was just to keep you off guard," La Forge said. "You know, to keep you so distracted you'd forget to ask her questions. Or you'd answer one of hers with too much information."

"That's a possibility," Riker agreed. "I did feel that she had the advantage over me, and she was in complete control of the conversation."

Picard shrugged. "Admiral Nechayev can do that without resorting to holograms." He tugged down on his jacket, smoothing it as best he could. "Well, then, perhaps misdirection is the answer. And Captain Radisson uses her simulations to keep us looking at the wrong details, wondering about the wrong things."

He turned to Data. "So, let us look forward, instead. Data, what do we know about Halkan?"

"A great deal about nothing, sir," the android replied. "Computer, display the Halkan homeworld."

In the center of the holodeck, a standard holographic globe materialized, then filled in with Starfleet's latest mapping data—thirty years old, Picard noted with curiosity, as if it hadn't been surveyed any more recently. When the mapping was complete, the model began rotating. A small text-display window opened in the air beside the globe to provide size, gravity, and average climate parameters.

The most notable aspect of Halkan that Picard could see was its striking color. The planet's landmasses were the color of bloodstone. The seas a deep lavender. Yet, somehow, the overall effect was that of a red planet, even more saturated than Mars.

"Halkan is a world that has enjoyed total peace for most of its recorded history," Data stated. "It exists as a non-aligned planetary government within Federation space. Relations are cordial, though the Halkans' strict ethical beliefs prevent them from establishing formal ties with political organizations employing weaponry—which includes the Federation. Occasionally, the Halkan Council does permit informal cultural, scientific, and educational exchange programs, which they see as an opportunity to promote their system of nonviolence.

"The only other significant characteristic of the planet is its geological structure. Computer, show the reconstructed formation of the Halkan system."

Picard looked up past the rotating red globe to see a second holographic model take form. At first glance, it appeared to be a simplified starfield. Then, one of the stars to the far right side flashed in a nova detonation. A moment later, a second star to the far left underwent a similar explosion.

"What we have just seen," Data explained, "are two supernovas twenty-seven light-years apart, which detonated within months of each other approximately five and a half billion years ago. Considering that our galaxy averages only one supernova event every thirty years, it was a remarkable coincidence."

Now rings of gaseous debris expanded from both exploded stars and Data continued his annotation of the holographic simulation. "The matter propelled by the supernova shock waves collided in the center of that map . . ."

The rings hit and Picard saw what was clearly the formation of a protostar.

". . . and from that matter, the Halkan primary condensed and the planets of the Halkan system formed."

"That's where all their dilithium comes from, isn't it?" La Forge asked.

"That is correct, Geordi. Dilithium is a rare, transuranic element that in nature is formed only in the violent explosion of supernova. The planet Halkan's unique astronomical history—forming in the direct collision of two supernova shock waves—has resulted in Halkan's bearing the largest known planetary concentration of dilithium in the Alpha and Beta quadrants. Given the unlikely odds of another two proximate supernova occurring virtually simultaneously, it is most likely the largest concentration in the galaxy."

"That might have been worth something, once," Riker said.

Picard understood the commander's comment. A century ago, the dilithium reserves on Halkan could have bought half the known worlds of the Federation. Today, they were virtually worthless.

Dilithium crystals were what had made high-speed warp flight possible, and in the early days of interstellar exploration they had been among the most precious natural resources on any world. Especially since their operational lifetime was so limited.

But then, methods of recrystallizing fractured dilithium had been discovered, and since crystals effectively no longer wore out, their value had plummeted.

"Those dilithium reserves are what drove Kirk to Halkan a century ago," Picard said. "And Tiberius to Halkan's mirror counterpart at the same time."

"I wonder if the presence of so much dilithium had something to do with the crossover," La Forge said.

Data looked to the side with an expression that told Picard he was accessing the *Enterprise*'s main computer banks. Less than two seconds later, the android said, "I do not think so, Geordi. According to the logs of the original *Enterprise,* the crossover event occurred during a particularly severe ion storm, when identical away teams, or 'landing parties' as they were called at the time, beamed up at the same time."

Riker grinned at Picard. "I wonder if any Vulcan would care to calculate the odds of that happening? What do you think, Captain? Another random act of chaos?"

But Picard didn't find the coincidence all that unlikely. Transporters had been around for at least sixty years, then. There would have been thousands in constant operation throughout the quadrant. And millions of mirror duplicates using them. It was just a matter of time before it happened that the same people used them at the same time in both places.

Picard smiled. "Our friend Jim does seem to excel at them."

Troi did not share the lighthearted moment between the captain and the commander. "Gentlemen, if I may interrupt this moment of masculine bonding, could someone tell me why we're even bothering to go to Halkan? Given the psychohistorians' prediction, it seems to me that we should be taking Tiberius *and* James Kirk as quickly as possible in the opposite direction."

"If this was a perfect universe," Picard said, "that's exactly what we'd do. But the truth is, I've made a few inquiries among old friends, and I can't find anyone at Starfleet who takes T'Serl's and Lept's prediction seriously.

"It was reported by an Admiral Hardin almost two months ago, and was relegated to a committee for further study. It seems there's no shortage of experts claiming that the universe is going to end on any given day. And with the new push to take the Dominion war to Cardassia, Starfleet's resources are stretched too thin as it is. There's no one to take over this mission from us."

Crusher looked confused. "Stretched too thin, Jean-Luc? That's why Command lets two Sovereign-class ships stay behind the lines as a personal transportation service? For a group of scholars no one's taking seriously?"

Picard was taken aback by Crusher's vehement protest. But then, he knew, she was always surprising him. Which was, he supposed, one of the reasons he . . . He coughed abruptly, ending a train of thought that was entirely inappropriate to entertain during duty hours.

"I had no idea you were so eager to face combat, Doctor," he said.

Something mischievous flashed in Crusher's eyes, as if his suddenly serious expression wasn't fooling her.

Picard gave a quick glance to the rest of his command staff. Judging from the half-concealed smirks worn by all except Data, the only person he was fooling about Crusher was himself.

"The *Sovereign* is a prototype vessel and a technology testbed," Picard said brusquely. "The day she sees combat is the day enemy forces have surrounded Earth and she's the last ship left in the Fleet. Until then, Admiral Nechayev will keep her quite busy flying back and forth from Earth to Vulcan on official business."

"What about the *Enterprise?*" Crusher asked. "Really, Jean-Luc, don't we have better things to do?"

"Not according to Command," Picard said. "We're a high-profile ship, and as long as we remain well behind the lines involved in ordinary duty, it's easier for other Fleet movements to escape the notice of Dominion spies. But rest assured, when the final assault on Cardassia begins, we will be called up."

"So, in the meantime," Crusher said, unimpressed, "we're baby-sitters?"

Picard shook his head. "In the meantime, I believe the

psychohistorians' prediction. And I believe we're going to Halkan to save the universe." He frowned. "I just don't know exactly how, or from what."

"Captain, if you believe the prediction," La Forge said, "doesn't that mean we're saving the universe from something Captain Kirk might do?"

Picard understood why La Forge had asked the question. He had already asked it himself. "The psychohistorians told us their field deals in patterns, Geordi. But those patterns break down when it comes to individual details. Is the universe somehow at risk? I don't know. But I am willing to accept the historians' conclusion. Is it Captain Kirk we should be concerned about? That I also don't know. But I hope to find out."

"What about Captain MacDonald?" Riker asked.

"I remember Christine MacDonald very well from our action against the Symmetrists," Picard said. "At the time, she seemed to me a very capable young officer. But, just as Kirk does, I find unlikely her one-jump promotion from command of an Oberth-class science vessel to an Intrepid-class starship like the *Pathfinder.*"

"You did say Starfleet's resources are stretched thin," Crusher reminded him.

"All the more reason to put an experienced commander in the chair of the *Pathfinder.*"

"That raises another good point," Troi said. "If the Fleet's resources *are* so thin, why assign MacDonald to the *Pathfinder,* and why send the *Pathfinder* to Halkan and not the front lines?"

Riker answered. "New commanders generally get a few noncritical missions as a shakedown cruise. Halkan hasn't had an official visit from a Starfleet vessel for about six years. So—"

"Six years?" Picard interrupted. "Are you certain about that, Will?"

From the sudden look of concentration that appeared on Riker's face, it was clear to Picard that the commander hadn't forgotten the significance of that number.

"I checked the background and it's been a comedy of errors," Riker said. "Starfleet's planned eight visits to Halkan, but something's always gone wrong."

"Let me guess," Picard said. "Orders lost. Ships diverted. Unexplained, random incidents that can't be traced."

Riker nodded, then voiced the same realization that Picard had just reached. "Ever since Kirk returned to the timeline, ever since that obelisk was placed in the First Federation base, someone has been preventing Starfleet vessels from visiting Halkan."

The pattern in the chaos, Picard thought. *The hand of the Preservers.* "Well, people," he said, "I believe we're traveling to the right place at the right time."

"The question is," Riker said, "who else will we find there?"

Picard knew Riker would have his answer soon.

Halkan was now only ten hours away.

TWENTY-FOUR

☆

Kirk stepped onto the bridge of Picard's *Enterprise*, looked around, and for the first time felt not a single twinge of nostalgia for his old ship. Nor the slightest hint of envy for those who worked here on the new one.

He knew why. His life was different now. Everything he wanted, needed, was elsewhere. With Teilani.

When this mission was over, he knew, he and his bride would return to Qo'noS. McCoy would have found the answer for what beset their child. There'd be no more barriers to their life together.

Chal waited for the three of them. Their hand-built home in the clearing. That one last stubborn stump he had promised to phaser away.

When this mission was over, his new life would begin in full.

Our new life, he thought. *Teilani, and me, and our . . . Joseph.*

He couldn't wait for the future to begin.

All it would take was one last mission.

"Jim, good to see you." Picard jumped up the wide step

265

from the bridge's main deck to the turbolift level. "How'd you sleep?"

"She's a wonderful ship, Jean-Luc. You're a lucky man." And Kirk meant it.

Picard seemed to realize his question about sleep had been deflected. He gestured to the command chairs. "Please. We're only a few minutes away."

Kirk took the chair to the left, leaving Riker's chair free to the right. Picard took his place in the center. For just a moment, to Kirk it was an odd sensation to sit on the sideline of a bridge, but still it was a sensation of placement, not of emotion.

This was Picard's ship. Kirk had different paths to explore.

Ahead on the main viewer, Kirk saw only moving stars. Data was at ops. A young Trill was beside him at the navigation console. "Have you made contact with the *Pathfinder?*" he asked Picard.

"According to the nearest starbase, the *Pathfinder* was due to arrive at Halkan yesterday."

Kirk didn't understand. "You're not in direct communication?"

"Ion storms," Picard said.

That explained it for Kirk. He had long known it hadn't been a coincidence that Halkan had been crawling with magnetic disturbances when he had last visited it. They were a constant phenomenon on the planet.

"As I recall," Kirk said, "the auroras are spectacular. They make the sky . . . lavender."

"And right now they're disrupting subspace transmissions for a good five light-years." Picard leaned closer, dropped his voice. "I thought you should know—we've learned something new in the past few hours."

Kirk listened attentively as Picard told him about the six-year gap in visits to Halkan from Starfleet.

"It all fits," Kirk said when Picard had finished. "We know the Preservers prepared something for Tiberius at the asteroid base. Sounds like they took the last six years to prepare something for him here."

"I thought you'd be interested."

Kirk was puzzled. "Just me? Haven't you told the historians?"

Picard shook his head. "Only my command staff. And you."

"Any particular reason?"

"I keep thinking of what Captain Radisson told Will. She couldn't transmit the information she had because she didn't know who in Starfleet she could trust."

Kirk sat back in mock surprise. "*You* don't trust Starfleet? Jean-Luc, I'm shocked."

Picard smiled at Kirk's exaggerated reaction. "Let's just say that given Captain Radisson's unique position—"

"*And* unique lack of identity."

"—I would tend to trust her caution, if not her intent."

Now Kirk leaned closer, spoke softly. "Who is it you don't trust here, on your own ship?"

Picard hesitated, then stood up. "Let's continue this in my ready room." He called out across the bridge. "Mr. Data, join us, please. Mr. Maran, let me know when we're on our final approach."

As the Trill acknowledged Picard's order, Data was on his feet at once. A Bolian officer instantly replaced him.

A few seconds later, the doors to Picard's ready room slid shut and Kirk, Picard, and Data were able to speak freely.

"Mr. Data," Picard began, "we were just discussing the need for secrecy in this matter."

"I believe it to be a wise precaution," Data agreed.

"Exactly who is it you don't trust?" Kirk asked.

Picard sat on the edge of his desktop. "Take your pick, Jim. How is it that Radisson knew where the psychohistorians had taken me? How is it that she knew they had identified you as the person most likely to destroy the universe?"

"Project Sign and the historians?" Kirk said. "Working together?"

"Could there be another explanation for the two groups sharing the same information?" Picard asked.

Kirk considered the question. "Well, first of all, you're a valuable senior officer, Jean-Luc. There's a war on with an enemy that includes shapeshifters, and Starfleet's already been compromised by having personnel replaced by mirror counterparts. If I ran Starfleet Intelligence and I heard you were taking leave, you can be damn sure I'd have you under surveillance, just in case."

Picard puffed out his cheeks. He apparently hadn't considered that possibility. "So Starfleet Intelligence knew I had been kidnapped by T'Serl and Lept because they saw it happen."

"You said as much to Riker on the hangar deck," Kirk reminded him.

"No," Picard protested. "What I meant was that Intelligence had *discovered* who was responsible, not that they watched it happen and took no action. That is not a comforting thought."

Kirk didn't like where the conversation was leading them, either. "We have to focus on the Preservers, Jean-Luc. We can't let ourselves be distracted by . . . suppositions and suspicions."

Picard nodded. "Misdirection again."

"Not that I disagree with the idea of holding back some information from the historians," Kirk added.

"So you don't trust them either?" Picard asked.

"Frankly, no." Kirk braced himself for a sudden dismissal. But Picard remained silent.

"I have to say," Kirk continued, "given what they accused me of, I'm rather surprised you've kept me informed at all."

"To the historians, Jim, you're an accumulation of statistics. A cork on water. A mouse in a maze. But I know you, and I just can't believe that you would ever cause harm—manipulated or not."

After so much early conflict, Kirk felt pleased that he and Picard were reaching a level of personal understanding in keeping with the instant friendship they had felt for each other. "I appreciate the vote of confidence. Now here's one for you. What if the historians and/or Project Sign are in fact agents of the Preservers?"

Picard nodded at Data. "I assigned that question to Data days ago."

"And I believe," the android said, "there is no evidence to suggest that situation is likely, or indeed possible."

"Why not?" Kirk asked.

"The actions we ascribe to the Preservers have all been subtle, behind-the-scenes machinations. Point to any one of their suspected manipulations and it is possible to explain it away as a simple random event or accident. Only when hundreds of similar actions are considered is the weight of evidence—and the Preservers' influence—apparent.

"However," Data continued, "it does appear that the actions of the psychohistorians are in strong contrast to other suspected Preserver activities. They have taken direct action by kidnapping the captain. They have allowed themselves to be captured and identified by us. And they have shared their predictions with Admiral Hardin of Memory Alpha, as well as with us. In short, they are too noticeable."

Kirk couldn't resist being the devil's advocate. "What if that's just more misdirection?"

"But why use misdirection to distract us from something we are not aware of?" Data countered. "If the historians did represent the Preservers, then when Captain Picard went to Memory Alpha, their response was faulty. It should have been to say they saw no connection between the Preservers and the mirror universe, and then to send him on his way. Instead, their actions alerted us to a possible catastrophe, and then attracted the involvement of Project Sign."

Kirk changed tactics. Arguing with Data was too much like arguing with Spock when logic was the most important element. Fun, but ultimately pointless. "All right, so we can rule out the historians. But what about Radisson and Project Sign? Maybe the reason she won't let us see what she really looks like is because she's an alien. An actual Preserver!"

Picard disagreed this time. "Jim, why would Preservers need to travel around the galaxy in Starfleet vessels?"

Kirk kept his smile to himself. He seemed to recall asking a similar question on a different mission long ago.

"No," Picard mused, "we've yet to find the Preservers. So for right now, I think it best that we protect ourselves from Sign *and* the historians, if only because we know so little about both groups. I certainly trust my people. And Spock. But not the intendant. Not Tiberius. And not even Nechayev."

Kirk read between the lines. "You're still worried about Tiberius, aren't you?"

Picard seemed surprised by the question. "Aren't you?"

"Not as long as you've got him locked up."

"But what about his organization?" Picard asked.

"What do you mean, his organization?"

"Well," Picard said, "to begin with, those 'enhanced' children Dr. M'Benga examined."

"She said they were being held by Project Sign."

"Most likely they are," Picard agreed. "But remember

what happened when Tiberius escaped from the *Enterprise* to the prison asteroid."

Whatever sense of well-being Kirk had begun the day with evaporated. He walked over to the ready room's viewport to stare at the stars. "The subspace signal."

"Starfleet is still unable to decrypt it," Data said, "but it does seem to fit with what Tiberius told you it was."

"A wake-up call," Kirk said. "A signal to alert his bases and operatives in our universe."

"That is my chief concern," Picard said. "Tiberius's operatives might be anywhere. So it is certainly wise not to advertise his whereabouts over subspace."

Kirk paced back to Picard and Data. "You're right. I keep thinking of his power resting in the mirror universe, not here."

"If the Preservers consider him a formidable enemy, then so must we," Picard said. "That is why—" He stopped.

"Is something wrong?" Kirk asked.

Picard shook his head. "No. I just felt a drop in our warp factor." As he raised his hand to his combadge, Lieutenant Commander Sloane beat him to it.

"Security to the captain."

"Good call," Kirk said.

"Picard here."

"Sir, we're about to enter the region of disrupted subspace. This will be our last chance to contact Command until the ion storms clear."

"Understood, Mr. Sloane. Transmit our log updates, then resume speed for Halkan."

"Aye, aye, sir."

A few moments later, Kirk listened carefully and thought he detected a very slight change to an almost subliminal background hum.

"There," Picard said. "Back to warp seven." He turned to Kirk. "Had we finished?"

"I believe the decision was 'trust no one,' " Kirk said.

"I know," Picard said. "I don't like it either. That attitude goes against everything Starfleet stands for. Everything the Federation is sworn to uphold. But what else can we do? We seem to be in a wholly unique situation."

Kirk was about to agree when Data interrupted.

"Actually, sir, that is not correct. There is a historical equivalent to the situation we are facing."

Both Kirk and Picard regarded the android with interest.

"Please, Mr. Data," Picard said, "any insights you can offer will be greatly appreciated."

"In the last half of the twentieth century on Earth, there was a subculture of belief which held that the planet was being visited by extraterrestrials."

Kirk didn't see the point. "But we were, weren't we?"

"Well, yes, sir. But at the time, there was no official recognition of that fact. Earth was subject to regular observation by Vulcan probe ships, and sporadic visits by other spacefarers, all adhering to a version of the doctrine of noninterference. Except for the Reticulans, of course."

"Of course," Kirk and Picard said in unison.

"On a number of occasions," Data went on, "visible-light images of those visiting probes were captured by the primitive optical sensors of the day. However, it was also a time of intense sociopolitical competition on Earth. In many countries, the military authorities that controlled the most advanced optical sensors feared their adversaries had developed the alien craft, and thus they represented a technological threat.

"As a consequence, virtually all evidence of extraterrestrial visitation collected around the planet was kept secret in multiple classified databanks, in order to keep the existence of those images from any suspected enemies.

"Additionally, nonmilitary individuals who observed

the craft, and on occasion the occupants, could not obtain official support for their experiences. Thus, on Earth, in contrast to what happened on many other worlds, there was no concerted effort to record and understand an unusual, though real, phenomenon. Instead, the official public consensus developed that not only did those events not occur—a reasonable conclusion considering the absence of evidence—it was impossible for them to ever occur."

Picard and Kirk exchanged a look of understanding.

"So your point," Picard said, "is that incontrovertible evidence existed of alien probes observing Earth. But because of a pattern of military paranoia, that evidence was kept secret, never shared or correlated, and, as a result, the truth was obscured."

"For all intents and purposes," Data said, "the truth did not exist at all."

"Do you think that might be the case now?" Kirk asked. "It's not that secrecy has prevented us from *looking* for the evidence. If we stopped being so secretive, opened all the files, we'd find the evidence is *already* there to prove beyond doubt the existence of the Preservers. As well as what they're doing to us."

"I suggest only that it is a possibility," Data said.

Picard sighed. "It keeps coming back to what Admiral McCoy told us, doesn't it?"

Kirk understood. "We all have a different piece of the puzzle."

"And if we just pulled back the veil of deception, shared what we know openly and honestly . . ."

"We'd have all the answers," Kirk concluded. "We'd have the truth."

"There's only one difficulty with that scenario," Picard said.

Kirk understood that, too. "Whoever is the last to reveal his secrets is the one with the advantage over everyone else."

Picard rubbed his temples. "As attractive as the prospect of a completely open exchange of ideas is, the stakes are too high. I can't take the responsibility of being the first to reveal all that we know, or think we know."

"Secrets," Kirk said. He thought of Teilani. The strength of their relationship was that they had none from each other. What weakened that relationship was when they suspected they did.

It seemed the Federation was no different.

"Jim, you look like you've thought of something," Picard said.

But Kirk shook his head. "Philosophy is not my strong point, Jean-Luc. Sometimes, I think the only thing that I know is that I know nothing. But I couldn't help wondering . . . what if we're all having the same conversation? Radisson and the rest of Project Sign. Starfleet Command. The Vulcan Diplomatic Corps. The psychohistorians. Even Tiberius and his people.

"What if we really do have all the answers between us, and the only thing holding us back is that we're all waiting for someone else to go first?"

"That would be a regrettable, and wasteful, state of affairs," Data said.

"Unfortunately," Picard said, "I think it might also be what's happening. Rumors of alien visitors in the past. Rumors of the Preservers in the present. The pattern hasn't changed."

"Then maybe that's our job," Kirk said. "To make that change."

Picard stood up, put a hand on Kirk's shoulder. "We can certainly try."

"Bridge to captain."

Reflexively, both Kirk and Picard went to touch their combadges. Kirk stopped with a smile. Picard touched his own.

"Go ahead, Mr. Maran."

"Sir, we are on our final approach to Halkan."

Kirk felt the vibrations that indicated the *Enterprise* had dropped from warp.

"This could be the place to start," Picard said.

Kirk hoped his friend was right.

But given what he knew of the patterns of history, he doubted it.

TWENTY-FIVE

☆

As he stepped from his ready room with Kirk and Data, Picard stared in open disbelief at the image on the main viewer.

Planet Halkan, the isolated backwater world of no particular importance, which had squandered its one chance for wealth and influence a century ago, filled the lower half of the display, a deep red ellipse sporadically highlighted by flickering webs of lightning.

But above the planet, dead ahead, where Picard had expected to see only a single starship at most, there was an enormous orbital structure.

The structure's hull was dark orange in color, broken only by the steady pulse of navigation lights and the glowing openings to its vast interior.

Unlike a Starfleet installation, the structure's shape was organic, like that of two bottom-dwelling crustaceans joined ventral surface to ventral surface, forming a large hemispherical module at top, and a long pointed tower trailing below like a tail.

Picard exploded. That shape alone was evidence enough

of what the structure was and who had built it. And the bold designators on the hull, written in the angular strokes of tallyscript, confirmed it.

"Will someone please tell me what the hell a *Ferengi* spacedock is doing in orbit of Halkan!"

"Trying to get through to the Halkan Council now, sir," Sloane reported from his station.

"Mr. Sloane, any sign of the *Pathfinder?*" Kirk asked.

"She's apparently docked inside, sir," Sloan replied.

Picard stalked to his chair, sat down. "Captain MacDonald, onscreen, now."

Kirk leaned down beside him. "Do you want me to talk to her?" His solicitous tone told Picard he had overreacted to the unexpected Ferengi presence, at least in Kirk's opinion.

"I'll be fine," Picard said stiffly. "I just—the Ferengi are known for clouding the issues where profit is at stake. We don't need any additional complications."

Kirk slipped into the chair at Picard's left without another word.

"Mr. Sloane," Picard said, "I want Commander Riker and Counselor Troi on the bridge. Mr. Data, run a full sensor sweep on the spacedock. I want to know its capabilities, and what ships are inside."

Data's acknowledgment was promptly followed by Sloane's announcement that he had located Captain Christine MacDonald.

Then the image on the main viewer changed to show the interior of the *Pathfinder*'s bridge. Picard saw MacDonald in the center chair. Though her curly blond hair was shorter than he remembered, her frank open features and quick intelligent eyes were the same. And, Picard had to admit, for someone her age who had just been given her first major command, she looked at home in the chair.

"Captain Picard, this is a delightful surprise!" Mac-Donald's smile was friendly.

Picard mustered up the most jovial attitude he could. "The feeling is mutual, I assure you, Captain MacDonald."

He tapped the arm control that would widen his visual sensor's field of vision. "I'm here with an old friend of ours."

Onscreen, MacDonald's eyes widened, then flickered with concern. "Jim! Uh, Captain Kirk! I'm . . . I'm doubly honored. I had no . . . Captain Picard, is there something going on Starfleet hasn't told me about?"

Troi should have been here by now, Picard thought. He'd have to give MacDonald some explanation for the unannounced appearance of two senior officers, to reassure her that they weren't there to second-guess her. He recalled how he'd felt in his first months of command whenever an admiral or senior captain had paid him a surprise visit to his *Stargazer.*

"Nothing at all," Picard said heartily. He leaned back in his chair, tugged down on his jacket, tried to look relaxed. "Jim is helping me with some archaeological research and . . . well, we had no idea another Starfleet vessel had arrived at Halkan."

MacDonald glanced to the side, but the field of view transmitted from her bridge remained tight on her chair and Picard could not see who was beside her. He knew M'Benga was MacDonald's medical chief, and he recalled a surly Tellarite engineer, but he was unfamiliar with the rest of her command staff. In her previous assignment as captain of a small science vessel, Picard knew, she hadn't had many.

"Well," MacDonald replied when she turned back to Picard, "for what it's worth, we had no idea the *Enterprise* was due to arrive, either. Typical Starfleet bureaucracy, I suppose."

Something changed, Picard thought. *She's just made a decision to hide something from me.* He glanced quickly at Kirk. But Kirk's neutral expression offered no clues to his reaction. He simply asked MacDonald if Dr. M'Benga had arrived.

"She made it back to Earth with three minutes to spare," MacDonald said. Her young face turned somber. "I was so sorry to hear about Teilani . . . and your child. Is there any news?"

"We expect to know more in a few weeks." Kirk's tone made it clear he would not welcome any further discussion of his family.

MacDonald shifted at once to less-sensitive topics. The usual—useless to Picard—small talk followed. He straightened up in relief when he heard the turbolift doors puff open.

Picard addressed the main viewer. "Captain MacDonald, if I could ask you to stand by for just a moment, I believe we're checking arrangements at the spacedock."

"I'm not going anywhere," MacDonald said, again with a smile, though this time it seemed slightly forced to Picard. *"Pathfinder* standing by."

Picard hit another arm control and the viewer switched back to an orbital view of the Ferengi spacedock.

He put his hand on Kirk's arm. Kirk saw Troi. "Ah, certainly." He got up and Troi took his place.

"MacDonald's hiding something," Picard told her.

Troi gave him an admonishing look. "That's *my* job. You're supposed to delegate, remember?"

"I saw that change in her, too," Kirk said helpfully. He was standing behind Troi's chair. "It was right after Jean-Luc said we were here on archaeological research. I don't think she believed you."

"Wonderful," Picard sighed. *More secrets. Just what the*

galaxy needs. "Mr. Sloane, any information on where that spacedock came from?"

"I'm uploading a database from a branch of the Ferengi Commerce Authority on Halkan."

Picard frowned. "The FCA built it?"

"Something wrong with that?" Kirk asked.

"The FCA is a branch of the Ferengi government. It generally builds dock facilities where it can establish a monopoly over a planet's import/export commerce. By Ferengi standards, there certainly isn't enough trade with Halkan to justify the construction of a facility of that size."

"Let me see what I can do," Troi said.

Picard nodded, pleased. That was precisely why he had wanted his counselor at his side. As a half-Betazoid, her empathic abilities enabled her to sense the emotional state of others, and could often distinguish truth from lies.

He set his own visual sensor to tight focus so that MacDonald would not know that a Betazoid was observing their conversation. "Mr. Sloane, put Captain MacDonald back onscreen, please."

The viewer image changed again.

Captain MacDonald had also altered her bridge sensor's field of view. Now hers was wider.

She still occupied her center chair, but now, to MacDonald's right, Picard saw a Vulcan female, also young, although she wore commander's pips. *Obviously her exec,* Picard thought. *And to her left—* He felt his stomach tense.

MacDonald had her *own* Betazoid officer. A young lieutenant with long, tied-back black hair, and the haunting, solid black pupils and irises of his species.

Picard realized at once that when he had told MacDonald about his archaeological research, about having no idea the *Pathfinder* would be here, the Betazoid would have instantly sensed the lie. That's why she had looked to the side. That's why her mood had changed.

Why keep more secrets? Picard thought. He tapped the control to widen his own sensor's field of view, so that MacDonald could see that the *Enterprise* also had a Betazoid, just in case she had forgotten.

MacDonald's face took on an expression Picard had seen many times before, usually across a poker table.

Bluff. Raise. And call.

"Captain MacDonald," Picard said, "I think it would be best if we met in person."

"I was thinking the same thing."

"One hour?"

"My ship?"

"It would be my pleasure."

"And mine."

MacDonald held his eyes a moment, then with a quick tap of her finger, she ended her visual feed.

Picard stood, looked back at Kirk. "That is *not* the same young commander I remember from the *Tobias.*"

Kirk shrugged. "That was three years ago, Jean-Luc. Last year she sacrificed her own ship to outbluff the Jem'Hadar, but managed to save every member of her crew. I don't think we should underestimate her."

"I have no intention of doing so." Picard paused a moment to consider his options, realized he had only one. "Mr. Sloane, ask Manager Lept to join us in the conference room."

Kirk nodded in understanding. " 'When on Ferenginar . . .'?"

"Either that," Picard said, "or, 'It takes a thief . . .' "

"Captain Picard," Lept said plaintively. "What, I ask you, is so wrong about a group of Ferengi with a song in their hearts and latinum in their eyes looking to the future?"

Kirk was glad this was Picard's ship. It gave him the perfect excuse to sit back and observe. And so far, that seemed to be what Picard's command staff had decided to do.

Riker, Troi, Data, Crusher, and La Forge were lost in wordless contemplation of the glowing blue surface of the conference table. Beside Kirk, Spock also remained silent. And at the head of the table, next to Picard, T'Serl made no comment as her Ferengi colleague underwent the captain's interrogation. The other four psychohistorians had not been invited to the meeting. Neither had Tiberius or Intendant Spock.

"What's wrong, Manager, is that these financial forecasts make no sense." Picard brandished the padd with the spacedock report obtained by Sloane.

Lept squinted down at a small padd displaying the same report as Picard's, then looked up impishly. "Nonsense, nonsense, and more nonsense. Look at the geological analyses, Captain. Halkan is a world rich in resources. Dilithium isn't the only transuranic element, you should know."

Picard sat back in his chair, dismissively pushed his padd halfway across the table. "Manager, listen carefully. It wouldn't matter if the entire planet were made of *solid latinum.*"

"Oh ho!" Lept cackled. "Want to bet?!"

Picard continued sternly in the face of the Ferengi's impudent facetiousness. "The Halkan Council *refuses* to enter into trade with any entity that employs military force, which *includes* the Ferengi Alliance. The planet's only trading partners today are a handful of protected colony worlds which have declined Federation membership on religious grounds. The Halkan position has not changed in two thousand years. It is not likely to change anytime soon."

"Then the Ferengi mining consortium that financed this

spacedock under license from the FCA will have made a poor investment," Lept said with an almost comical flourish. "They'll declare bankruptcy. And a new consortium will tow the spacedock to a more promising planet."

Lept's smile bared a remarkably fine example of Ferengi teeth: decidedly crooked, pointed, and yellowing. "That is the way of business, Captain. As clearly described, I might add, by the 62nd Rule of Acquisition. 'The riskier the road, the greater the profit.' So what is the problem with that?"

"The problem, Manager, is that if the only reason the spacedock was built is for the one stated in the report, then it doesn't belong here. So I remind you of the 239th Rule: 'Never be afraid to mislabel a product.' That spacedock is not what it appears to be, and I want to know the *real* reason why it's here!"

Kirk had never heard such anger in Picard, but couldn't tell if it was an act designed to put pressure on the old Ferengi, or if it was a true reflection of his frustration.

Lept pouted like a petulant child. "Well, if that's your attitude, Captain, I suggest you direct your further inquiries to the consortium responsible. I will not speak for my people to those who will not listen. 217th Rule. 'You can't free a fish from water.' " He smiled condescendingly.

But Picard wasn't finished. "I sense the 48th Rule at work here," he countered. " 'The bigger the smile, the sharper the knife.' You're excused, Manager."

The Ferengi stood up in an addled huff. "And what are you going to do about the spacedock?"

"If you have no information to share with me, I certainly have none to share with you. Good day, Manager."

Lept began to protest his dismissal, but T'Serl cut him off by simply touching his arm. She addressed herself to Picard.

"Captain, I do not need logic to know that you worry some link exists between the Preservers and the Ferengi spacedock. I assure you, no such link exists."

"Have you read the so-called report justifying its construction, Doctor?"

"I have."

"Is it logical?"

T'Serl's answer was without hesitation. "Strictly speaking, no, since it does represent a financial risk. But, as I'm sure you know, risk in business is a Ferengi tradition as much as recreational armed combat and all the risks that entails, is a tradition in the Klingon warrior culture.

"More to the point, Captain, since you are from Earth, a planet which no longer employs a monetary system, I would argue that you are not qualified to render an opinion as to the suitability of *any* kind of business risk."

Picard sat up even straighter in his chair. "Dr. T'Serl, at Starfleet Academy, written in five languages above the main entrance of the Christa McAuliffe Annex, which I walked through almost every day for four years, is a quote: 'Risk is our business.' So please do not presume to tell me my job. If you have nothing to contribute, you are excused, as well."

Kirk glanced at Spock, doubting that anyone else at the table could as accurately interpret the subtle change of color in T'Serl's face. But Spock merely raised an eyebrow at him. On his own, Kirk decided the most probable emotion T'Serl was repressing was outrage.

The Vulcan historian stood up, the movement majestic and slow. "I shall be in my quarters." She touched Lept's arm again, and he jerked around with a start, as if he suddenly had forgotten where he was. Recovering quickly, the old Ferengi dutifully followed his colleague through the doors, all the while muttering to himself quite incomprehensibly.

The moment the doors had closed, Picard looked at his officers. "How did I do?"

"Very convincing, sir," Riker said. "I thought you were going to make them walk the plank any second."

But Troi looked apologetic. "Unfortunately, Lept is a Ferengi. His emotional response was completely unreadable."

"What about T'Serl?"

"Extreme Vulcan reserve. She harbors some impatience toward Manager Lept, but there is also a great deal of respect. For a Vulcan, though, she was quite frustrated, angry almost, at being dismissed. I could sense an intense desire to know what it is we know. Or what she thinks we know."

"Any sense of falsehood?" Picard asked. "Either in anything she said, or in response to what Lept said?"

Troi shook her head. "Not in terms of outright lying. If Lept was trying to mislead us by anything he said, then I believe that Dr. T'Serl is unaware of it."

Picard reached across the conference table for the padd he had tossed away. "Mr. Data, did you discover anything unusual about the spacedock from your scans?"

"No, sir. It is a standard Ferengi design. Though approximately eighty percent of the expected cargo-handling infrastructure is still to be installed."

Kirk found that interesting. "So, it's only a shell?"

"Essentially," Data agreed. "Though from a business perspective, it does make sense not to install equipment before it is needed. And since there is so little cargo-handling trade in—"

"Excuse me," Kirk said, interrupting. "How many ships are docked inside right now?"

"The *Pathfinder*," Data said. "One Ferengi Marauder-class starship: specifically, the *Leveraged Buyout*, commanded by Daimon Baryon under a private contract to the spacedock consortium. Four Privateer-class transport shuttles. Six orbital shuttlepods of Bolian design, apparently leased under a spacedock maintenance agreement."

Kirk did a rapid, rough calculation of the sizes of those ships compared with the apparent volume of the spacedock's upper module. "It seems to me that the spacedock is virtually empty."

"That is correct," Data confirmed.

Kirk looked at Picard. "You're an archaeologist, Jean-Luc. What do you call a large, empty gift from the Ferengi?"

Picard understood the analogy. "A Trojan horse."

Data disagreed. "But, sirs, my scans indicate that other than the ships I described, the spacedock *is* empty. There are no soldiers hidden within, Trojan or otherwise."

"You mean, there's nothing hidden in the spacedock you scanned," Kirk said. "But I wonder what's in its counterpart?"

"Merde!" Picard exclaimed. "We've been looking for the Preservers in the wrong *universe!"*

Dr. Crusher spoke up, confused. "I'm sorry, how do we look for them in the *right* universe?"

"Mr. La Forge," Kirk said urgently, "do you have Intendant Spock's schematics for the dimensional transport device?"

"Of course," La Forge said.

"Can you replicate a version of it that will work with a cargo transporter?"

"I don't see why not."

Picard stood. "Jim, I take it you plan on stepping through the looking glass again."

Kirk got to his feet as well. The time for meetings was over. "You keep Captain MacDonald distracted. I'll see what's waiting on the other side."

Spock stood up beside Kirk. "I will accompany you."

"Actually, Spock, I was thinking of someone with a little more experience."

Kirk had no intention of wasting the opportunity that had just presented itself to him. If the Preservers wanted Tiberius, Kirk was more than willing to deliver him.

TWENTY-SIX

─────────── ☆ ───────────

"You forgot to tie me up," Tiberius said.

Kirk placed his hands on the *Percival Lowell*'s controls, familiarizing himself with the layout.

"It's not necessary," he told his counterpart.

Tiberius stretched out in the copilot seat beside Kirk, placed his hands behind his head. The civilian clothes he had chosen today were Vulcan in design, all in black; almost, but not quite, a Starfleet uniform of his own. "It can't be because you trust me."

"You're right," Kirk agreed. "It's because you need me."

"Dream on, James."

Kirk checked outside the viewport. On the main hangar deck of the *Enterprise,* a crewman was waving two guide lights at him, directing him toward his target.

"Oh, that's not the word I'd use for you," Kirk said. He punched on the shuttle's antigrav propulsers and the *Lowell* rose a meter, then rocked gently in place.

Tiberius yawned as he looked ahead. "Shouldn't you wait until the hangar doors open?"

"We're not going through the doors."

Kirk banked the shuttle. Then, precisely working the onboard antigravs against the hangar deck's variable gravity fields, he guided the shuttle toward the crewman with the lights, well to the side of the main doors.

Tiberius sat up, saw what was ahead. "A cargo transporter?"

"So La Forge tells me."

"You're taking me home?"

Tiberius was off-balance. *Fair trade,* Kirk thought.

"Just for a visit," he said.

"When we get there, I could rip out your lungs, steal this ship, disappear forever," Tiberius said amiably.

"You could," Kirk agreed with disinterest. He slowed the shuttle, taking it in slowly to settle on the wide dematerializer pad of the cargo transporter that had been hurriedly installed here. "But two things to keep in mind," he added. "This shuttle has no warp capability. And its controls, including the callback signal that will beam us back to the *Enterprise,* are all keyed to *my* quantum signature."

"In other words," Tiberius said appreciatively, "*you* can return without me. But *I* can't return without you."

"Oh, and did I mention I have to be alive?" Kirk said. "Brain functioning, heart beating, *and* give the proper code sequence?"

Tiberius seemed delighted at all the precautions. "I'll make an emperor of you yet."

La Forge's voice came over the comm link. *"Captain Kirk, you're locked into place, ready for transport."*

"Will you give us a countdown?" Kirk asked.

"Won't be necessary," La Forge replied. *"But we are going to have to wait for Captain Picard's party to beam over to the* Pathfinder. *Won't be more than five minutes."*

"What's the *Pathfinder?*" Tiberius asked.

"A starship."

"Starfleet?"

"Do you care?"

Tiberius shifted in his chair so he could look directly at Kirk. "What's going on?"

"I want to take a tour of Halkan on your side of the mirror."

Tiberius shook his head. "One of the great truths in both our universes is that a man can't lie to himself. You're looking for answers. I'm interested in what your questions are."

"James, are you there?"

Kirk looked up at the sound of that voice on the comm link. "Teilani—yes, yes, I am."

"We both are, *James*," Tiberius simpered.

"Is . . . something wrong?" Kirk hated having Tiberius hear his exchange with Teilani, but the shuttle offered him no opportunity for privacy.

Teilani tried to laugh, but failed miserably. *"Of course there's something wrong. Spock just told me what you're doing."*

"It's only a reconnaissance flight," Kirk said.

"You don't do 'reconnaissance,' James. I'm worried."

From the corner of his eye, Kirk saw Tiberius's face quicken with interest. "Teilani, this isn't the time to have this conversation."

"If you're crossing over just to look, then why not send a probe? And why take . . . him?"

"That's what I asked," Tiberius said in mock outrage. "Teilani, he's hiding the truth from both of us."

"James, get a phaser and stun Tiberius so we can talk."

Tiberius clutched at his chest as if mortally wounded.

Kirk sincerely wished he could use Teilani's particularly straightforward method of dealing with obstacles right now. *Sometimes,* he thought, *it is the best method to use.*

"Spock knows what I'm looking for," he said cryptically. "Shouldn't take more than an hour."

Teilani's response wasn't what she really wanted to say, Kirk knew. Knowing that, he appreciated what she did say all the more.

"Be careful, James."

"I'll be fine."

"I love you . . ."

Kirk waited, but there was nothing more.

"How does that work?" Tiberius asked.

"How does what work?" Kirk asked.

"You and . . . one woman. What keeps you with her?"

Kirk thought back to another life, to the first time he had met Teilani, when she had enticed him to Chal with the promise of eternal youth.

The promise had been a lie, of course. Chal could offer nothing of the kind to those who were not born there. Jean-Luc had faced a similar situation when the same thing had happened to him on the world of the Ba'ku.

But in the end, Teilani had kept Kirk's heart young. The promise had been kept. Just not in a way either of them had ever imagined on that first day.

"Everything," Kirk said.

He saw the frown that crossed his counterpart's face. Knew Tiberius could never understand.

"How long have you known her?"

"Forever," Kirk said. That was how he felt about the strength of their connection. And having revealed that, he waited for Tiberius's inevitable insulting reply.

But instead, Tiberius stared at him with a thoughtful expression. "The people I've known the longest . . . they've all been my enemies."

Kirk was surprised to find himself interested in the surreal conversation with . . . himself. How many times had he wondered what his life might have been like if he had made different decisions? What if he had remained in hiding on

Tarsus IV? Or married Carol? Or proposed to Antonia? Or . . . let McCoy rush out and save Edith Keeler?

Here, perhaps, he had a way to find out.

"Tiberius, in your universe, did you ever know a Carol Marcus?"

"A brief encounter. We . . . didn't get along."

"So you never had a child with anyone?"

Tiberius looked at him strangely. "Dozens, James. You met them."

But the sad lot of "children" Kirk had met on mirror Earth were not the kind he meant. They were clones with enhanced, perverse attributes, a genetically engineered mix of Tiberius's genes with those of other "suitable" species, not all of which were humanoid. Their purpose was not to become supersoldiers or assassins the way Project Sign had attempted to use them. Instead, they were the pathetic product of Tiberius's paranoia to create beings who could give him the one thing not even the emperor of the galaxy could command. The one gift that could only be given, never taken.

"Do they love you?" Kirk asked.

"I'm their father," Tiberius answered.

Kirk thought of the son he'd had with Carol Marcus, the son he'd never known, and who had never known him. Until it was too late.

And then he thought of his child with Teilani. Still asleep in timeless stasis on Qo'noS. Still untouched by his father.

"That's not enough," Kirk said. "Just being their father."

"What else is there?" Tiberius asked.

"The reason *why* the child exists."

Tiberius grimaced. "You're going to say 'love,' aren't you?"

And in his counterpart's expression of distaste, Kirk saw what lay down those long paths he had not taken in his life. All those decisions that did not lead him to Teilani, and peace.

"If you had ever felt love," Kirk said, "if you had ever been loved, you'd know that was the only answer that mattered."

Tiberius turned again to face out the viewport. "Have you been loved, James?"

"Yes," Kirk said.

"And look where that's got you." Tiberius stretched back in his chair again, hands once more behind his head, as if the conversation had never happened, never mattered. "I'd rather be feared."

We are *reflections of each other,* Kirk thought. *The same, but opposite.* Yet each of them in his own way had obtained what they most desired from others.

"The captain's party is away," La Forge announced over the comm link. *"Stand by for transport."*

"Shuttlecraft *Lowell* standing by," Kirk said. He looked over at Tiberius, fought hard not to feel pity for the man. "What's Halkan like on your side?"

Tiberius seemed surprised by the question. "My Spock didn't tell you?"

"Energizing," La Forge said.

Outside the viewports, the hangar deck shimmered into light, then faded into stars and space.

Kirk watched the sensor screens adjust to their new location in the mirror universe. "Intendant Spock told me that after we had each returned to our own universe, he had worked out a way for you to save the Halkans. So you didn't have to follow Starfleet's orders to destroy them."

Kirk tapped the maneuvering thrusters to rotate the *Lowell* and bring Halkan into sight through the viewports.

"He's right," Tiberius said as he leaned forward in his seat. "I did spare Halkan. I convinced Starfleet that the dilithium reserves did not exist. They were bait laid by the Klingon Confederacy, which had a secret treaty with the

Halkan Council. If the Empire had moved against the planet, the Klingons would have had the excuse they needed to launch all-out war."

Halkan came into view. Kirk stared in dismay at the ugly dark scars that wrapped around the planet's landmasses. It was a brown-streaked world here, not vibrant red. "You call that sparing the planet?" he asked.

"James, you forget, I'm not responsible for the Alliance. The dilithium reserves *did* exist, after all. And after the Battle of Wolf 359, the Alliance helped itself to all the Empire's treasures. The blame for this rests with Spock."

Kirk was appalled at the destruction below him. The life sensors on the *Lowell* were no match for those of the *Enterprise,* but the readings indicated that the population of this Halkan was less than ten percent the size of the population in Kirk's universe.

"But you didn't come here looking for dilithium," Tiberius stated flatly.

"No," Kirk confirmed. He reset the sensors for their new search. If there was a matching Ferengi spacedock in the mirror universe, its orbit must have carried it to the other side of the planet, because he could detect no sign of it from the shuttle's position.

"Then let me guess," Tiberius said. "The Preservers?"

"Maybe," Kirk answered. Now he set the sensors to search for the phase-transition compound unique to Preserver obelisks.

"So you can . . . offer me to them as a sacrifice?" Tiberius asked. "So they won't destroy your universe?"

"I hadn't thought of that," Kirk said. "But thanks for the idea." He input the final program commands.

Kirk heard the arrogance in his counterpart's voice. Tiberius was incapable of thinking both universes did not revolve around him.

"Here's another idea. If I'm the only person who represents a threat to the Preservers, then I'm your universe's only hope for resisting them."

"You're jumping to conclusions. Maybe the Preservers aren't interested in sacrifices. Which is why *I* want to find them and—"

An alarm squealed and all three sensor screens flashed red, indicating a signal return that was off the scale.

"Let me guess again," Tiberius said. "We've found something."

Kirk read the numbers on the displays, swiftly realized what they meant, then looked out through the forward viewports, just to starboard.

It was *there,* right where the sensors had found it.

"Actually," Kirk said, "I think something's found us."

The proximity collision alarm began to chime.

Whoever or whatever shared this orbit of Halkan, it was closing fast.

TWENTY-SEVEN

☆

The *Pathfinder*'s transporter room took shape around Picard and Troi.

As they stepped off the pad, Picard knew for a certainty that MacDonald had indeed been thinking the same thing he had.

There was no transporter technician present. Instead, Captain MacDonald herself was at the controls, and her Betazoid lieutenant was at her side.

After much-too-hearty greetings had been made, and Lieutenant Lon Darno had been introduced to Counselor Deanna Troi and they had discovered that they were both from adjoining provinces on Betazed, MacDonald took the advantage from Picard with swift action.

"Let me be blunt, Captain Picard. Since we both have our living lie detectors present, we can't play games, we can't equivocate, we can only get right to the point."

Picard found her forthrightness refreshing. "I quite agree."

MacDonald looked at Lieutenant Darno.

"He does agree," the Betazoid said. He gave Troi an apologetic smile. "But the counselor didn't appreciate being referred to as a living lie detector."

Troi returned Darno's smile with a brittle one of her own, then said to Picard, "I sense that Captain MacDonald is concerned by our presence. She already resents any authority you might invoke to take over her mission. And Lieutenant Darno is extremely nervous. He is employing a rather elementary telepathic block, and it would be rude of me to penetrate it and determine exactly what he is holding back. Unless, of course, you give me an order."

Cheeks visibly flushing, Darno addressed himself to his own captain. "Captain, Counselor Troi is not a full telepath, and has some doubt as to her ability to defeat my block. She has also employed a rather confused block of her own to prevent me from seeing what she's holding back. And . . ." He looked at Picard with some confusion. ". . . and Captain Picard . . . finds this situation amusing."

MacDonald didn't. She stared at Picard, frowning. "We're not going to be able to get much past each other, are we?"

"Why would we want to?" Picard said simply. "We're all Starfleet officers."

Darno interjected softly, "He has some doubt about that, sir."

Quietly, Troi countered with, "Captain MacDonald feels doubt as well."

Picard sighed. He made an appeal to MacDonald's common sense. "Captain MacDonald, I don't have to be a telepath to know what's troubling you. So why don't you just use a tricorder to check my quantum signature to verify to your satisfaction that I *am* the Jean-Luc Picard of this universe."

"I did that when you beamed in," MacDonald replied. "But I'm sure you're aware that anyone spending more than a year eating the food of this universe, breathing its air, would, of course, significantly alter his quantum signature."

"No," Darno said suddenly. "This *is* the real Captain Picard."

"All right. Good enough for me," MacDonald said. She gestured to the doors. "Why don't you join me in my ready room?"

Picard walked at MacDonald's side. The junior officers followed.

"Which one of us goes first?" MacDonald asked.

Picard knew she didn't mean who would lead the way to the ready room. "Let me ask the first question," he suggested. "Perhaps it will save time."

"Go ahead," MacDonald said. "I'll do my best to answer."

The corridors of the *Pathfinder* seemed longer than the ones on the *Enterprise,* but to Picard they were very familiar. When Starfleet found a design that worked, the engineers and designers efficiently applied it to as many vessels as they could.

"Were you aware there have been no official Starfleet visits to Halkan in the past six years?"

"Trust me," MacDonald answered. "I'm very much aware that this is a low-priority mission. But this is my shakedown cruise, so . . . what I mean to say is, I understand Command's decision to send the *Pathfinder* here, and not to Cardassia. At least for now."

"May I ask exactly what your mission here entails?" Picard asked.

MacDonald stopped in front of turbolift doors. "After you've answered one of my questions."

"But of course."

"Is Tiberius on the *Enterprise?*"

Picard's first reaction was to deny it, but he knew it would do no good with Lieutenant Darno standing less than a meter behind him.

"Yes," Picard said. Obviously, MacDonald had been talking to Dr. M'Benga.

As the lift doors slid open, MacDonald looked over her

shoulder and Picard caught Darno giving her a quick nod of confirmation.

"Very good," MacDonald said.

She stepped into the lift, and the rest of her party followed. "Bridge," MacDonald instructed the lift. She turned to Picard. "Now your question, Captain."

Picard matched her directness. "What is your mission here?"

MacDonald pursed her lips and looked away briefly. As if, Picard thought—recalling another captain whose ego was remarkably similar—she was frustrated by an assignment she considered far beneath her capabilities. "Show the flag, mostly."

Troi tapped Picard on the shoulder. "That's not all, sir."

"I hadn't finished," MacDonald said testily. "We're also going to provide logistical support to the Ferengi experiment."

That startled Picard. "What experiment?"

MacDonald wagged a finger at him. "My turn."

But Picard had no time for useless, competitive contests. "You said no games, Captain. It is vitally important that you tell me the nature of the Ferengi experiment!"

MacDonald looked at Darno.

Darno kept his eyes on Picard. "Anger. Impatience. I even sense fear."

MacDonald studied Picard as if he were a bomb about to detonate. "There's something to be afraid of in a simple mapping experiment?"

"There is if it can lead to the destruction of the universe!"

"Destruction of the universe?" Now it was MacDonald's turn to look amused. She glanced at Darno. But the telepath wasn't smiling. "Uh, he's . . . he's telling you the truth, Captain."

The lift doors opened. MacDonald led them across the

back of the bridge of the *Pathfinder*. Picard noted only three
crew members present. He recognized Pini, the petite,
blond communications specialist from the *Tobias*. And the
young Vulcan commander he'd seen at MacDonald's side,
now working at an open console, apparently repairing iso-
linear circuits.

MacDonald called out to the Vulcan at the console.
"Commander T'Rell, would you join us please?"

MacDonald paused, turned to Picard. "As long as you feel
she won't put you at a numerical disadvantage, of course.
She's my science officer. I suspect I'll need her insights."

Picard nodded, and the Vulcan joined them.

Once in the *Pathfinder*'s ready room, MacDonald
walked past her desk to a small armchair beneath a viewport, then pointed to the couch and other chairs arranged
around a low, round table. She waited until Picard, the two
Betazoids, and the Vulcan were settled before she herself
sat down.

Picard took a quick look around the room, wondering
how much it could be considered a reflection of Christine
MacDonald's personality. Most furnishings were standard
Starfleet-issue neutral, though with many blue accents,
apparently a favorite color.

He recognized the large holo-landscape of the Earth city
of Vancouver on the bulkhead behind her desk. He had been
there once, and with all the canals that had been built since
the Great Victoria Earthquake had submerged half the city,
he had found it as romantic a place as the simulations he
had seen of the lost city of Venice.

To one side of MacDonald's desk was an oversized ter-
rarium. Within it, Picard glimpsed several tiny lizard-like
creatures basking on rocks and branches beneath green
foliage that stretched up toward a heat lamp.

But the most intriguing item in the room, Picard decided,

was the ship's model given pride of place in the center of the low table directly in front of him. He leaned forward to take a closer look at it—an antique Constitution-class starship, one of the earliest configurations, with the old, inefficient cylindrical nacelles almost identical to Cochrane's first designs. Picard didn't have to examine the model's small plaque to know what would be written on it: *Enterprise,* NCC-1701.

Picard wondered why MacDonald had not chosen to display the *Tobias.* Most starship captains he knew kept models of their first commands. He himself had a model of the *Stargazer.* The fact that MacDonald had chosen to display a model of Kirk's was unusual, and telling.

Picard sat back in his chair. It wasn't really necessary that he understand Christine MacDonald. But he did hope he could trust her.

"Getting back to the end of the universe," MacDonald said.

Picard saw Commander T'Rell's eyebrow arch as the Vulcan heard the phrase for the first time.

"Let's do this quickly," Picard said firmly. "Lieutenant Darno can confirm what I say so I don't have to waste time with details." He cleared his throat and then gave them the summary statement. Cold. "The most prominent psychohistorians in the Federation have predicted that the universe will be destroyed within a time frame encompassing the next two weeks. The precise date can't be known with any more certainty than that."

MacDonald and T'Rell immediately looked toward Darno.

The Betazoid nodded, swallowed hard. "He is telling the truth."

"As he believes it," T'Rell cautioned.

Picard forged on. "They don't know where this event

will occur, but they believe it will occur because of actions taken by Captain Kirk and/or his mirror-universe counterpart, Tiberius. They also believe that Tiberius has been singled out for attack by the Preservers, and that this attack might be related to the coming disaster."

MacDonald sat up with a scornful explanation. "The *billion-year-old Preservers?* Sorry, Captain, you just took a left turn into dreamland."

"Uh, Captain, that's not what *he* thinks," Darno said.

MacDonald slumped back in her chair, motioning for Picard to continue, but her face still registered her disbelief.

For his part, Picard approved of his own counselor's diplomatic silence. Troi knew enough not to tell him the obvious, except if doing so served some other purpose for him.

"Those same psychohistorians," Picard continued, "have assembled a most convincing collection of data which indicates to me that the Preservers, or some other alien presence who we might as well call the Preservers, have been manipulating certain people and events throughout Federation history."

MacDonald frowned, restlessly tapping the arm of her chair.

Picard decided to refocus her attention.

"Their data also indicate that *you,* Captain MacDonald, are one of those people and that the reason you were given this command was because of the direct intervention of that alien influence."

MacDonald jumped to her feet, her eyes were ablaze with—

"Strong feelings of outrage," Troi observed blandly.

"You're sure?" Picard asked as he watched MacDonald's face turn the color of Halkan. Quite deliberately, he did not stand up, nor did Troi, although MacDonald's staff stood up as their captain did.

"Uh, Captain," Darno said urgently, "as crazy as it sounds, he believes every word he's telling you."

"I only have to believe one word," MacDonald said in icy fury. *"Crazy."*

Still seated, Picard spoke quickly to deflect and diffuse her anger. "Captain, I'm caught in the middle of this as much as you are. This is what the psychohistorians have told me. What can you tell me to convince me otherwise?"

MacDonald glared at him. "Where do I even *begin* to tell you how unacceptable that story is?"

"At the beginning," Picard suggested, wondering what else he could say that would change MacDonald's mind. "Tell me about the Ferengi experiment. To put my mind at ease."

MacDonald still glared at him.

"She's wondering if you're worth helping," Troi said. The counselor's voice strongly implied that MacDonald's decision would be negative.

Picard's eyes fell on the model in the center of the table. Inspiration struck.

"Captain MacDonald," he said, "the question you should be asking yourself is: Is Jim Kirk worth helping?"

He felt sure he knew what her answer to that question would be.

TWENTY-EIGHT

☆

"It's an obelisk?" Tiberius said. "Here?"

Caught in the glare of the Halkan primary, the orbital object moving toward the *Lowell* could have been any one of the 119 Preserver artifacts already discovered in Federation space. The shape was the same—an elongated pentahedron, each triangular side deeply indented with triangular planes so that it flew like a four-vaned spearpoint. The color, as always, a weathered silver-green, marbled by random streaks of pale rust.

But as Kirk checked the readouts on his control console, he knew without question that this obelisk was unlike any of the others in one major aspect.

Outside the viewports, it grew larger and larger.

Much larger.

Until Tiberius began to suspect the truth.

"James . . . how big is that?"

"Just over three kilometers long. Just under a kilometer and a half across at its widest."

"The power . . ." Tiberius marvelled—then exclaimed, a moment later, "It's a weapon!"

304

Kirk shut off the proximity alarm, modified the sensitivity of his multiple scans. "I'm detecting no energy output."

"Three kilometers long? In standard orbit? And it doesn't have engines of *any* kind?" Tiberius scowled in disbelief. "The gravitational imbalance from one end to another is enough to make it start tumbling in a day."

Kirk was impressed by his counterpart's familiarity with orbital mechanics.

But he was even more impressed with the obelisk.

It filled the viewports now, eclipsing the stars and Halkan.

And still it kept coming toward them.

"Activate the callback signal," Tiberius ordered.

"We're not going anywhere. This is what we've been looking for."

"What *you've* been looking for."

Kirk brought the impulse generators up to full power and said the cruelest thing he could think to say. "Are you afraid?"

"You're not?"

Kirk watched the enormous mass of the obelisk hurtling toward them, and had a realization just as momentous. "That's right. I'm not."

"At least now we know which one of us is insane," Tiberius muttered.

Then Kirk kicked in the impulse engines and the shuttle flew toward the obelisk.

He saw Tiberius's fingers dig into the fabric on the arms of his chair.

He didn't care.

He had set out to find the Preservers. It was time to take the final step.

Seen from space, the *Percival Lowell* was an insignificant white blur bracketed by two lines of glowing blue. No more than a raindrop rolling down a rockface, the small craft slipped across the surface of the obelisk, less than fifty meters away.

For the next thirty minutes, almost half the length of a single orbit of Halkan, the shuttle probed the obelisk with subspace sensors, neutron beams, force membranes, and coherent radiation at multispectral frequencies.

But the obelisk remained a mystery, unwilling to surrender any secrets.

The shuttle shifted in its matching orbit, as if sliding sideways across the obelisk's width, until it came to the angle between two sides whose edge had been polished to the impossible thickness of a single atom.

The shuttle moved up one side, hung over that edge, then dropped down the opposite side, continuing its search and its probes.

Until, after only ten more minutes, it found the portal.

Kirk maneuvered the *Lowell* until it was poised over the center of the obelisk's portal. According to the shuttle's sensors, each side of the opening was just under one hundred meters.

"James," Tiberius cautioned, "this is only a shuttle. I can tell you how to move a starship between our two universes from inside the Badlands, or the Goldin Discontinuity, any region with plasma storms. My *Enterprise* is already outfitted with everything it needs. Let's go back and get a starship to blast this monster from space. We don't need to risk attack in this . . . this toy."

Kirk watched his sensor returns. Absolutely no signals reflected back from whatever lay inside the opening in the obelisk, as if the only thing inside was an infinite black hole.

"Maybe a starship would be too big a target," Kirk said.

"Maybe the fact we're in this toy is what's keeping this thing from noticing us at all."

"Don't go in there," Tiberius said.

"We have to."

"Why?"

Like a hologram resolving into focus, the answer came to Kirk, and he realized it had been there all along, just beneath the level of his consciousness, waiting until he needed it to surface.

"Because I think I've finally figured out what this thing is," he told Tiberius. "Why it's here. And what the Preservers are going to have it do."

Tiberius stared at Kirk with total bafflement. "What if you're wrong?"

"Only one way to find out."

Kirk pitched the shuttle down, and nose first, it dropped toward the obelisk, and the darkness within.

"Five years ago," Commander T'Rell explained pedantically, "the Halkan Council signed an education exchange agreement with the Ferenginar Trade Academy of Minerals and Resources."

In his chair in Captain MacDonald's ready room, Picard forced himself to listen quietly, resisting the strong urge to ask any number of vital questions. Exactly how, he wanted to know, had that agreement been negotiated? Precisely when had the negotiations begun? And what type of payment could have possibly been exchanged?

He was well aware that both Counselor Troi and Lieutenant Darno sensed his impatience, but there was nothing he could do about it. MacDonald had instructed her science officer to recite the facts as she saw fit.

Picard gritted his teeth as the Vulcan's imperturbable voice droned on. "The Halkans were to receive a new, optical planetary communications grid, constructed by a Ferengi consortium. In return, the Halkans allowed a second Ferengi consortium to use experimental techniques to map the planet's complete dilithium reserves."

Picard felt his shoulders sag. How naïve could the Halkans be? "The Ferengi are renowned for offering less-developed worlds inexpensive communications networks."

T'Rell knew why. "So they can install surveillance devices enabling them to surreptitiously monitor all communications transmitted through the grid for years to come, giving them an immense business advantage."

But there was more to the arrangement that troubled Picard. "And why bother to map the dilithium here if the Halkans will never permit it to be mined?"

T'Rell's explanation was prompt in coming. "That was precisely the argument the Ferengi Academy used, Captain. Since the Halkans would never permit any dilithium to be removed from their world, the testing of technology was benign. The Ferengi pointed out that if they tested their mapping techniques on other worlds, then any dilithium they found would be mined and could end up in warships. Therefore, by allowing the tests to take place on Halkan, the Halkans were contributing to galactic peace."

Picard put his elbow on the arm of the chair and rested his head against his hand. "And the Halkans believed the Ferengi?"

"Both sides kept the agreement, and all terms were successfully concluded two years ago," T'Rell concluded.

Picard sat up straight again. "Two years ago? Then how does the spacedock fit in? What about this Ferengi experiment you mentioned?"

"The spacedock was built to handle supply shipments during the construction of the communications network.

The Ferengi experiment that is to be conducted tomorrow arises from another agreement."

Darno gave MacDonald a look of warning. "He's becoming extremely agitated."

MacDonald leaned forward. "There's no reason to be. Look, Captain Picard, the Ferengi Academy tested all sorts of geological sensors. And they ended up leaving thousands of them behind as part of a long-term technology demonstration. Last year, the Nagal Academy on Frak III—"

"That's . . . a Ferengi colony world?" Picard interrupted.

MacDonald nodded. "A *very* religious Ferengi colony world whose central tenets are acceptable to Halkan ethics. They approached the Halkan Council and said that since the geosensors were already in place, could they use them for a geomagnetism study?"

Picard gave a sharp tug to smooth his jacket, to quell the frustration threatening to spill out of him. "Captain MacDonald, I recognize a Ferengi swindle when I hear one. There're too *many* layers. Too *many* complications. A religious colony studying geomagnetism on a sensor network conveniently left behind by another study group? Did you ever stop to ask why the Ferengi were being so generous? The tradertongue has fifty-three different words for 'profit.' To my knowledge, it has none for 'charity.' "

Picard heard Troi's respectful murmur. "Captain MacDonald is feeling very frustrated with you."

"How does it compare with my frustration?" Picard asked.

Troi and Darno looked at each other.

"We seem to have a tie," Troi said with a light shrug.

"What we *have* is a chain of coincidence," MacDonald insisted. "I see no ominous pattern in one Ferengi group finding an advantage in what another Ferengi group has done. It happens all the time. The Halkans are happy to receive the benefits of all this interest in their world. And the Federation is pleased to lend its assistance—meaning, this starship—to two independent governments who some-day might join us."

"The Ferengi aren't the ones who are interested in Halkan," Picard said pointedly. He turned to T'Rell. "What is this experiment in geomagnetism that's supposed to run tomorrow?"

MacDonald nodded to her science officer, giving her per-mission to answer.

"The planet Halkan is notable for its many ion storms which are disruptive to most forms of advanced communication. The experiment seeks to find out if their severity can be lessened by diverting some of their power through a large-scale dissipation system. In essence, a planetary lightning rod."

Picard tensed with alarm. "The Ferengi want to channel the energy of the ion storms *into* thousands of geosensors around the planet?"

"As I said," T'Rell confirmed.

"And those geosensors are in *direct contact* with the planet's dilithium reserves?" Picard was appalled.

MacDonald had had enough. "What *is* your concern, Captain?"

"Dilithium is unstable!"

"Certainly not under these conditions," T'Rell objected.

"But you don't have the slightest idea what the real con-ditions are!" Picard insisted. "You've all been blinded by some convoluted Ferengi scheme designed to make you think that what's going to happen here is innocuous."

"Captain Picard," MacDonald said sharply, "if this was an important event, or a dangerous one, then why did Starfleet send *me* to help with the experiment? I'm running a shakedown cruise, nothing more."

Picard wasn't certain he had heard her properly. "How are you supposed to 'help'?" he repeated.

T'Rell looked at him quizzically. "Tomorrow, we plan to induce ion storm formation by using our phasers to ionize specific portions of the Halkan atmosphere in conjunction with Daimon Baryon's ship."

Sudden understanding flooded through Picard. "They're using *you* to light the fuse. . . ."

MacDonald blinked at him, frowning, but Picard no longer had any interest in participating in the debate. The problem had finally been defined, which meant a solution must be found.

He got to his feet.

MacDonald followed suit.

Troi, Darno, and T'Rell stood, as well.

Darno's voice faltered. "Captain MacDonald . . . he's thinking of ways of stopping this ship . . . and stopping you. . . ."

MacDonald's voice became instantly formal. "This meeting is over, Captain. I suggest you take your concerns to Starfleet Command."

Picard stood his ground. "When is the experiment scheduled to start?" he demanded.

"In fourteen hours, local ship time."

"Then there's no time to get a decision from Command."

"Then there's nothing you can do," MacDonald replied.

But the competition wasn't over.

"Just watch me," Picard said.

TWENTY-NINE

☆ ---

Within the mirror universe, the *Lowell* shuddered as it passed through the obelisk's portal.

Tiberius was first to react. Negatively. "Was that a tractor beam?"

Kirk checked his board. "No readings. No energy output. The only thing physical is the far interior wall. And that's thirteen hundred meters away."

He looked up. Through the viewports, in the absence of light, there was nothing to be seen.

He switched on the navigation searchlights.

"That isn't physical?" Tiberius asked skeptically.

Now clearly illuminated, the interior of the obelisk revealed a docking chamber, slightly more than one hundred meters across. The silver-green walls of the chamber were textured here and there with triangular facets.

"Not according to our sensors," Kirk said. "It's not even holographic camouflage."

The *Lowell* continued on its course, heading for what appeared would be a slow collision with the near wall.

But the shuttle's proximity alarm didn't sound.

"Let's try something," Kirk said as Tiberius groaned.

He shut down the shuttle's engines and used maneuvering thrusters to come to a relative stop in the center of the docking chamber.

"Now what?" Tiberius complained.

Then the shuttle changed its orientation and began to move toward one of the walls, as if controlled by a tractor beam. Through the viewports, Kirk saw the portal they had entered through pass by.

Halkan wasn't visible through it. Only stars. The patterns were unfamiliar to him.

"We're not inside the obelisk," Kirk said suddenly.

"Where else would we be?" Tiberius asked.

Just then the shuttle thumped as it made contact with a solid surface which, according to its sensors, wasn't there.

At once Kirk ran an atmospheric analysis. It registered a vacuum outside the shuttle. As he had expected.

"Let's suit up," he said.

When the time came for the two counterparts to check the seal of each other's helmet, both paused, remembering the last time they had been in that same position, hands on each other's helmet locks, each trying to kill the other in the heart of the First Federation base.

Kirk knew he had seen fear in Tiberius's face then. He did not know—or care—what Tiberius had seen in his.

"You trust me to do this?" Tiberius asked over his helmet communicator.

Kirk was a realist when it came to his counterpart. Nothing had really changed in their pattern. They were still using each other. This time, so Kirk could look for answers, and Tiberius could look for escape. "Not really," Kirk said. "But you still need me. And I still need you." He made the test of the locks on Tiberius's seal. "Seal is good."

Tiberius did the same for him. "Seal is good."

As one, they moved their gloved hands away from each other's helmets. As one, they kept their eyes fixed on each other. It was as if their struggle in the asteroid had never ended, Kirk thought.

"Ready to decompress?" he asked.

Tiberius was.

Kirk punched the rear hatch control, felt the deck tremble as the hatch motors came to life, then saw the hatch fold down.

"That's odd," Kirk said.

"What? That we haven't killed each other yet?"

"No. That we didn't hear the atmosphere vent," Kirk said. "And we didn't see ice crystals."

Tiberius took the tricorder from his belt, pointed out the back of the shuttle. "Hard vacuum."

Kirk thought for a moment. "Use the tricorder on me."

Tiberius made an adjustment, pointed the device at Kirk. Grinned. "You'll be glad to know you have no life signs."

Kirk unlocked the air valve on his chestpiece, pressed the release tab.

Nothing. No hiss of venting air. No pressure alarm in his helmet.

Without giving a single thought to risk, he reached up for his helmet locks, unsealed them, twisted his helmet off. Breathed deeply while Tiberius stared at his incomprehensible action.

It was stale. It was metallic. But it was air with enough oxygen to support life.

Tiberius waited for a few seconds more before removing his own helmet. "Why don't our instruments confirm that any of this exists?" he muttered, suspicious as always.

"Maybe it doesn't," Kirk said. "Or maybe our instruments are blocked." He began to peel off his environmental suit.

"I think we should keep these on," Tiberius said warily.

"They could have killed us a hundred times over by now. Starting with you two years ago."

Tiberius looked out through the open hatch. "James, do you think they know we're here?"

"I think they know everything."

"You know, I think he'd actually fire on us," MacDonald said to her senior staff. "I honestly believe he would."

Listening to her captain as they all sat together in the *Pathfinder*'s mess hall, Andrea M'Benga wondered if she should prescribe a stress pill. Picard seemed to have punched all of Christine's buttons.

Darno agreed. "That *was* one of the options I caught him thinking about."

"But it makes no sense," MacDonald said.

"Captain Picard thought it did," the Betazoid countered. "The only thing keeping him from taking *immediate* action against us is that he knows nothing will happen for the next fourteen hours. He thinks that's enough time to talk you into stopping the experiment."

MacDonald took a quick swig and drained her tea. She put the fragile china cup carefully down in its saucer, then turned to her chief engineer. "Barcs, what do you think? *Could* we blow up the planet accidentally? Let alone destroy the universe?"

The bulky Tellarite shook his snout. "I tell you, Captain, there is no possible way this ship could put out the power required to detonate even a localized field of dilithium. Vaporize it, sure. But not set off any kind of reaction."

MacDonald turned to her science officer. "What about it, T'Rell? The *Pathfinder*'s phasers in combination with the planet's natural storm systems? Would that produce enough power to detonate a dilithium field?"

"No, sir. I do not see the reason for Picard's concern."

MacDonald consulted her last hope. "Bones? You saw part of what went on with Kirk and Picard on Qo'noS. Any insights?"

But M'Benga had already racked her memories and turned up nothing. "Whatever Picard's worried about, it has to be something involving Tiberius *and* Kirk *and* the Preservers. Even Kirk was convinced the Preservers were after Tiberius personally. I'd say those psychohistorians got to them."

"But there *is* no Preserver presence on Halkan." MacDonald sighed with frustration. "And *Starfleet* signed off on this mission."

M'Benga didn't see what was to be gained by debating the issues again. As far as she was concerned, there was another way out—the easy way. "Chris, why not postpone the experiment? Give yourself and Picard time to leave the system and talk to Command. Let *them* sort it out."

MacDonald looked pained. M'Benga couldn't read her mind, but Darno could.

"Sir—" The Betazoid's voice was compassionate. "It's not really giving up like you think. It's using command prerogative to determine the best course of action. That's completely acceptable and within the bounds of your orders."

"And it's certainly not as if we're under time constraints," M'Benga reminded her captain. "Remember, Picard's one of the best. If he has objections, no matter how strange, he's probably the one officer in the Fleet we should pay attention to."

"And mess up my first mission," MacDonald growled. But then she added, "No, you're right. Nothing to lose by passing it up the chain of command." She got to her feet. "I'll let Daimon Baryon know we'll be rescheduling." MacDonald grimaced. "Then I'll tell Picard."

"Nothing to lose," M'Benga said as brightly and as cheerfully as she could.

The captain didn't look convinced, but at least, M'Benga thought, Christine MacDonald had made the right decision.

Besides, Picard would never have fired on the *Pathfinder*.

"You want a plan of attack against the *Pathfinder?*" Riker asked in astonishment.

"I don't care who gave MacDonald her job," Picard said as he stepped from the turbolift onto the bridge with Troi and Riker at his side. "The Preservers or Grand Admiral Chekov himself—she's a starship captain. And that makes her self-centered, self-righteous, overconfident, and the stubbornest life-form in the galaxy."

"Present company excluded, of course," Riker said.

Picard ignored the gibe, sat down in his chair, his refuge. "Mr. Data, I want you to work with Geordi on determining exactly what conditions would be required for a ship of the *Pathfinder*'s capabilities to detonate Halkan's dilithium reserves. Be sure to include any variables that might be introduced by the planet's ion storms."

"Considering the power requirements necessary," Data said as he left his ops post, "I believe that to be impossible, sir. But I will work diligently to see if I am in error." The android left the bridge.

"And you're serious about attacking the *Pathfinder?*" Riker asked.

"I don't see what choice she leaves me, Will. *Something*'s going to happen here in the next fourteen hours. The psychohistorians say it's going to be the end of the universe. I don't see how that's possible, but . . . it would be irresponsible of us to rule it out. At the very least, I do believe we're looking at the potential destruction of Halkan, and I will not accept that.

"I don't know if we've accidentally stumbled onto some harebrained Ferengi scheme, a Preserver conspiracy, or just some one-in-a-billion accident waiting to happen. But it won't happen while *I'm* here.

"If MacDonald doesn't have the judgment to hold back and contact Starfleet Command so we can study this problem in depth, then I intend to *force* her to do so by disabling the *Pathfinder*."

"I'll be at tactical," Riker said. "Mr. Sloane, pull up all the schematics we have on Intrepid-class ships."

In the momentary pause of activity, Troi leaned forward from her chair. "Captain, for whatever it's worth, I did sense that Captain MacDonald believed she was right. I picked up nothing from her or from her science officer to indicate she was hiding anything from us. I also got no sense that she was being coerced, or . . . doing anything but what she considers it is her duty to do."

"I do not doubt her integrity, Counselor. Only her judgment."

"But if her judgment is suspect," Troi asked him, "then why did the Preservers choose her for this ship and this mission?"

At that, Picard turned to his counselor, speaking emphatically. "Deanna, we simply *must* keep our minds open on this. It could be possible that the psychohistorians' evidence of the Preservers' manipulating our history is exactly what it appears to be—a series of circumstantial coincidences. For the moment, I don't believe it *is* all circumstantial. But that is a possibility we must be willing to accept once—and *if*—we learn more."

"I just hope we have more time," Troi said, looking worried.

Before Picard could tell her he agreed with her, he was interrupted by an urgent shout from Zefram Sloane.

"Sir, two ships powering up in the spacedock."

Picard stared at the orbital structure on the screen. He wanted to call for battle stations, but the *Pathfinder*'s sensors would easily pick up his ship's heightened conflict condition. Instead, he touched his intraship comm button. "This is the captain. All hands, yellow alert."

A measured response; that is the best compromise, Picard reassured himself.

He saw a shape move within one of the spacedock's hatches. But the ship that emerged was not the one he had been expecting.

Instead of the *Pathfinder,* it was the orange, horseshoe-crab-shaped Ferengi starship, the *Leveraged Buyout.*

Picard's eyes narrowed. It appeared that Christine MacDonald had just thrown a new wager into the pot.

"Receiving a priority hail from the Ferengi vessel," Sloane said.

Picard sat up in his chair, preparing for the worst. "Onscreen."

A furious Ferengi in a pale-green headskirt appeared on the viewer. From his temple tattoos, Picard could see that he was a daimon.

Picard greeted him politely. "Daimon Baryon, I presume."

"Captain Picard," the Ferengi hissed through artfully twisted teeth. "Operating under the full authority of the Ferengi Alliance, I demand that you leave Halkan space at once. Your presence here serves no profitable purpose."

Picard didn't waste time checking with his counselor. Even Betazoid telepathy could not penetrate the Ferengi four-lobed brain. Fortunately, he had never—and suspected no one did—found the Ferengi all that difficult to read.

"I was not aware that the Ferengi Alliance had *any* authority in the sovereign space of another world. Unless, of course, you are intending to annex whatever is left of Halkan after your experiment has destroyed it, and who knows what else."

Baryon's tiny eyes seemed to grow to twice their size. "Captain MacDonald has just explained your dangerous delusions to me, *hew-mon*. It is my opinion—*with* the full authority of the Ferengi Alliance—that you are a danger to yourself, to this world, and to the ongoing good relations between the Federation and the Alliance."

"Sir," Sloane said in a low voice, "the Ferengi vessel has raised full shields."

Picard refrained from matching Baryon's provocative act. He knew from experience how difficult it was to convince a Ferengi to back down in a negotiation. The trick was to keep the opportunities for escalation under control.

"Daimon, if Captain MacDonald has indeed explained my concerns about the scheduled experiment, then you understand that I have no wish to stop it. Only to delay it until further study can be undertaken."

The Ferengi drew back in horror as if Picard had insulted his mother. "Further study! So the Federation can learn our trade secrets! Steal our advantage! I know how you lobeless creatures do business!" Baryon almost screeched. "Under the table! Behind the back! With big bulging eyes and disgusting white teeth, a glass of root beer in one hand and a plasma whip in the other!

"Well, not this time, *hew-mon*. You Federation types turned your back on Halkan a century ago. *We* developed relations with them. *We* invested in them. And now *we* will claim our rewards and not let *you* steal them.

"Captain Picard—you have five minutes to leave the system."

Then Baryon made a sharp gesture and his transmission ended.

The viewer showed the daimon's ship already in position by the spacedock. Now the *Pathfinder* was emerging.

"The Ferengi's putting weapons on standby," Sloane reported.

"What's the *Pathfinder*'s status?" Picard asked.

"We're being hailed, sir," Sloane answered.

At Picard's command, Captain MacDonald appeared on the main viewer.

"Captain," Picard said crossly, "this situation is getting out of hand."

"I know, sir. I followed that last exchange. That's why I think you should do what the daimon asks and leave the system."

Picard refused to allow his temper to get the best of him, though he was certain MacDonald's Betazoid would let her know how he actually felt. "The daimon has no authority here, not over my ship."

"Actually, Captain, he does."

Picard stared at MacDonald in shocked disbelief.

"You see, sir, I just finished talking to the daimon," MacDonald continued. "I asked him if we could delay the experiment, to give us all time to reexamine it, check with Command. As you suggested."

Picard checked with Troi. The counselor nodded, indicating that MacDonald was being truthful. Picard turned back, impressed. The young captain had listened to him, after all.

"But the fact is," MacDonald went on, "the Ferengi consortium behind this study has a great deal invested in the experiment proceeding as scheduled."

Picard cleared his throat. "Then let us open negotiations for an appropriate compensation. No Ferengi would be adverse to that."

"In this case, yes they would." To Picard, MacDonald

sounded apologetic. "I don't think any of us are aware of the bitterness that's been growing among the Ferengi, directed at the Federation. Did you know we're held responsible for the Dominion war continuing as long as it has—for not negotiating a peace settlement? Business has been disrupted in both quadrants. Profits are off. And, apparently, most Ferengi now tend to view us as meddlers who are only interested in our own well-being, and no one else's."

"Preposterous," Picard said. "That's completely untrue."

"I only ask that you see it from their point of view, Captain. Your presence in the Halkan system, attempting to . . . well, interfere in what is a very small Ferengi business venture, is exactly the flashpoint the Alliance has been fearing, *and* looking for. If you do make any attempt to intervene, Daimon Baryon *does* have authority to defend Ferengi assets."

Picard was almost speechless. Almost. "There are *two* of us here, Captain. The *Enterprise* and the *Pathfinder.* Not even Daimon Baryon would be foolish enough to engage us both."

MacDonald looked pained. "That's just it, Captain. The *Pathfinder* is present in this system under express Starfleet orders to aid our allies: the Ferengi and the Halkans. By your own admission, you're here to hinder them, and as far as I've been able to determine, *you* are not operating under any orders at all."

A hot flash of anger swept through Picard. He waved off Troi, who was looking concerned at the effect that Christine MacDonald was having on him. He felt himself actually begin to tremble, and didn't care if MacDonald saw it.

"Do you *dare* to suggest that you would stand with Daimon Baryon against me?"

MacDonald began speaking very quickly. "Captain

Picard, please, listen carefully. You have *no* authority here. The *Ferengi* do. If you act against them, there is an *extremely* good chance that the already-strained political climate on Ferenginar will swing against the Federation completely.

"I read the same casualty reports you do. We are strained to the limit. And between the Dominion and Cardassia and the Breen all fighting us, and the Romulans nipping at our heels, if the Ferengi Alliance declares war on us, too—or even if they just cut off our supply lines and remain neutral—it *will* be the end of the Federation.

"I am *not* willing to risk that happening, just so I can show respect to a starship captain I admire profoundly." MacDonald looked off to the side, at something on her bridge. "You now have one minute to leave the system, Captain. Please, don't start something that can only end in disaster. *Pathfinder* out."

Picard stared at the impossible image that replaced MacDonald on the viewer: both the *Pathfinder* and the *Leveraged Buyout* taking up attack positions.

"*Pathfinder* has raised her shields," Sloane called out from his station. "Both vessels are powering weapons."

Now Picard *was* speechless.

Riker stepped to his side. "What are your orders, Captain?"

Picard said nothing.

Because for one of the few times in his long career, he had absolutely no idea what he should do next.

THIRTY

☆

Kirk took his first step from the hatch ramp onto the surface of the docking chamber. In the reflected light from the shuttle's searchlights, the silver-green surface shimmered. It felt solid to Kirk, but his boots made no noise as they made contact.

Tiberius stepped off the ramp to stand beside him. "I know why you brought me here."

Kirk looked at him, waiting.

But Tiberius refused to continue. "You first. What's the purpose of the obelisk?"

Kirk saw a small opening in one of the silver-green walls, twenty meters away. He began walking toward it. Tiberius kept up beside him.

"It's a wedge," Kirk said. "We can let the two Spocks work out the details, but I think Halkan is the reason our two universes have remained connected, when all the other parallel dimensions remain separated." Kirk stopped talking, realizing for the first time that there was no echo here, as if whatever sounds he made never reached the hard walls and floor to be reflected back.

"I hear it, too," Tiberius said. "At least, I don't hear it. There's no echo. No reverberation. This whole chamber is acoustically dead."

As they got closer to the wall, Kirk saw that the opening he'd seen led into a curved corridor whose end was not visible.

"It was the ion storms," Kirk continued. "Maybe it had something to do with all the dilithium on the planet, too. But those storms weakened the field density between the two universes. Then, when you and I both used our transporters at the same instant, at the same power level, with the same landing party, we punched a hole from one side to another. Somehow, that made a permanent connection. Call it scar tissue. A wormhole tunnel. Something that's bound your universe and mine together, ever since."

They had reached the opening in the wall. It was narrow, barely enough room for the two of them to pass through shoulder to shoulder. But it was tall, at least four meters in height.

The walls of the corridor beyond seemed to be patterned with a random texture of small triangular facets. Kirk suspected the three-sided arrangement continued to the molecular level.

Tiberius held his hands up to the sides of his face, shielding his eyes from the dim light of the shuttle searchlights behind them. "There's another light source down there."

Kirk did the same, saw a pale glow.

He started forward, noticing that Tiberius did not object to him going first.

"So you think this giant obelisk is going to break that connection," Tiberius said.

But Kirk didn't reply. After a single step into the corridor, they'd instantly entered another chamber, this one twice as large as the docking chamber, and lit by shafts of light projected from triangular panels scattered across its walls, ceiling, and floor.

Kirk and Tiberius both turned to look behind them at the corridor they had somehow passed through. The opening was right where Kirk would expect to see it, still narrow and four meters tall. And again it seemed to curve off to the side.

"A transporter alcove?" Tiberius asked.

"Either that, or . . . the Preservers know something about topography we don't."

Kirk studied the new, more expansive chamber. In addition to being crisscrossed by beams of light, pillars of silver-green phase-transition compound angled out from the floor and stretched halfway to the distant ceiling. To Kirk, the arrangement looked like a skewed version of the Stonehenge monuments on Earth, Vulcan, and Andor. Except these stones were perfectly finished, not eroded, and much, much taller.

Kirk walked toward the nearest pillar. Its surface texture was different from the rest of the chamber's interior. As he drew closer, he saw why.

It was inscribed with row after row of Preserver letterforms, no taller than the width of his finger. He recognized them as the same symbols he had seen in the small chamber beneath the obelisk he had found on Miram III.

"An instruction manual?" Tiberius asked.

"Maybe it's a collection of the galaxy's funniest jokes," Kirk said lightly.

Tiberius snorted. "And I thought you had no sense of humor."

"And you do?"

"Cosmic," Tiberius answered.

"Then I guess I have one, too." Kirk looked again at the symbols. "It might even be a Welcome sign."

"Or a warning," Tiberius said. "That's always been your problem, James. You're always so naïvely hopeful. I've never made that mistake, so I'm never disappointed."

Kirk walked on to another pillar without responding, knowing silence was the most effective way to deflect his counterpart.

He was right.

"You were saying this was a wedge," Tiberius prompted. "To sever the universes?"

"I think so. Permanently."

As he examined the second pillar, Kirk glanced around, comparing the first two he'd seen close up with the others in the chamber, intently searching for any common feature among them, or a recurring pattern. Anything that might give a clue to their purpose.

Tiberius was still mulling over Kirk's last answer. "I don't know if I like the idea of a permanent separation."

"It's not as if we have a choice," Kirk said. He had just seen what looked like another opening at the far side of the chamber. "But, in a sense, separating our universes means the psychohistorians were right in a way—a universe will be cut off from us. Forever. I suppose that could be interpreted as a universe ending."

"Does that make sense to you, James? That it's something the Preservers would do?"

"I keep going back to the fact that for all their power, the Preservers didn't kill you."

"Maybe I'm not easy to kill."

Kirk hoped *his* ego never made him as predictable as his counterpart. "Look at the enormity of what's around you. They can predict where you'll be *and* when. You don't think they could have planted a fusion bomb in the First Federation base and set it to detonate when you turned up?"

"So they're giving me solitary confinement instead of death," Tiberius said.

Kirk shook his head. "Nothing like that. You'll have an entire universe. Your destiny will be your own. But as far as the Preservers are concerned, you—or anyone from your universe—will never again be able to transfer over to our universe and—"

"And interfere with their plans for you."

Kirk saw the measuring look that Tiberius gave him.

"Are you happy with that, James? Are you sure you wouldn't rather stay in my universe and be independent?"

"I'm just thinking out loud," Kirk said. He began walking toward the new wall opening. "I could be wrong."

Tiberius followed, without even questioning where they were going. "My turn. This is why I think you brought me: I'm your price of admission."

For all their differences, it was true, Kirk thought, their minds did work the same way. "I couldn't be sure the Preservers would open their doors for me. But I'm certain they want you back where you belong."

"So when do you suppose they'll hammer the wedge through whatever's connecting us?"

Kirk started to think through the possibilities. "Soon, I think. It probably depends on . . ."

"On what?" Tiberius demanded.

"Behind you," Kirk whispered.

Tiberius turned slowly.

Something moved in the shadows between the pillars.

Coming closer.

The instant Picard disappeared from the main viewer on the *Pathfinder*'s bridge, M'Benga confronted her captain.

"What the hell was that all about?"

MacDonald was out of her chair and pacing. "You heard

what Daimon Baryon said. The Ferengi Alliance has run out of patience with the Federation. All it would take is—"

M'Benga interrupted her captain. She had to. "Chris! Have you ever heard that about the Alliance before? Received any Starfleet briefings? Has any admiral pulled you aside—*especially* for this mission—and told you to keep the Ferengi happy because they're ready to support the Dominion?"

MacDonald's tight lips confirmed M'Benga's worst fears.

"You can't threaten to fire on the *Enterprise,* Chris. Get Picard back onscreen. Find some other way."

"There *is* no other way," MacDonald insisted defiantly. "Don't you think I've been trying to find one?"

"Jim Kirk would find another way. He spent his whole career finding *another* way!"

MacDonald gestured angrily toward the viewer where the *Enterprise* hung in a matching orbit. "And right now Kirk is on that ship. I know he's behind this."

"Then all the more reason to take a step back!"

"Kirk is not part of Starfleet anymore!"

"The hell he isn't! He's got the uniform!"

"He was blackmailed into rejoining by Admiral Nechayev. He needed her help. She needed to be able to hold command authority over him to keep him in line. He has no loyalty to the Fleet anymore. Only to himself and to that new wife of his."

M'Benga stepped back in shock as the real meaning of MacDonald's words exploded within her. "You're . . . jealous?"

MacDonald's nostrils flared, her face turned bright red. "*Doctor* M'Benga, you are so far out of line I should throw you in the brig."

M'Benga knew all the other crew members on the bridge were straining to listen to this altercation while pretending to watch their boards. So she dropped her voice as low as she could. "I don't mean jealous about his *wife!* I mean about his *choices*. His *decision* to turn his back on his career. To move on and do something different. You told me yourself you asked him to stay on the *Tobias*. But he *chose* to go back to Chal."

M'Benga stared at her captain with new insight. "You know you always wanted to be like him, since your first day at the Academy. But because he moved on, you took it as some kind of insult."

Breathing hard, MacDonald responded hotly. "That's not true."

"Then prove it," M'Benga challenged. "Don't do this by the book. Do it the way *he'd* do it. There's no Starfleet Command to turn to. You're as good as on the frontier, just like the first captains. So *be* a starship captain. Control this situation. Be the person you meant to be that first day you walked into the Academy."

Christine MacDonald glared at her. "I will *not* be the starship captain who plunged the Federation into a war it can't win. You may leave the bridge, Doctor."

"Chris . . . don't fire on the *Enterprise*."

"You may *leave* the bridge."

M'Benga held back the last word she wanted to spit out, then marched to the turbolift, aware that every eye on the bridge was upon her. Aware that she'd failed to talk sense into her captain.

Then the doors to the turbolift slid open just as Commander T'Rell announced, "Captain, the *Enterprise* is hailing us."

M'Benga looked back at the main viewer, hoping that at least on that other bridge, there'd be one person who still had sense.

• • •

"I can only hope someone on her bridge has a gram of sense," Picard said as he studied the image of Christine MacDonald on his main viewer. He hadn't established the audio channel.

"Captain," Troi reported, "she is extremely upset. Full of self-doubt. I believe she's been in a heated argument."

Picard activated the full communications channel.

"Captain Picard," MacDonald stated stonily, "your time is now up."

"Captain MacDonald, I *am* willing to leave the Halkan system as you requested. However, I ask that you allow me to remain for another ninety minutes, in order to retrieve a shuttlecraft that is currently off the ship."

MacDonald looked offscreen and cut her audio link. When she reestablished it, she said, "My science officer informs me no shuttles have left the *Enterprise* while she's been in orbit."

Keeping in mind Lieutenant Darno's inevitable presence on the *Pathfinder* bridge, Picard was completely truthful. "We beamed the shuttlecraft into the mirror universe. It will take us some time to retrieve it."

"That surprised her," Troi whispered to him.

"What's in the mirror universe?" MacDonald asked sharply.

"That's what our shuttlecraft is there to find out. As a sign of our intentions, though, I am now ordering our shields down and putting our weapons offline. But I do hope that—"

And then, whatever else Picard had been about to say was lost in the flare of the first explosion as Daimon Baryon opened fire on the unprotected ship.

THIRTY-ONE

─────────── ☆ ───────────

The shadows came closer. Silent. Erratic. Flicking from place to place. Discontinuous planes of black and gray. Coils of smoke through shattered glass.

Kirk didn't move.

Tiberius jumped sideways, lifted his arms in fighting stance.

One shadow zigzagged toward the intersection of three shafts of light on the floor.

Kirk tracked that one, squinting, trying to focus on a detail—any detail—visible in the indistinct shape.

The shadow darted into, through the light.

But even in the light, it remained a shadow.

The significance was not lost on Tiberius. He put a hand on Kirk's arm. "We're leaving." He began moving backward, pulling Kirk with him.

But Kirk shook him off. "Not till we know."

"Know *what?*"

"If those are the Preservers." To Kirk, the possibility was obvious.

Tiberius leaned in close, whispering. "They're not anything, James. They're just shadows or reflections. Some kind of automatic security system—vortices of negative energy. But whatever they are, I guarantee you they're dangerous."

Suddenly two shadows unfolded from a grouping of others.

They're watching us, Kirk thought.

"If you really want to explore this thing," Tiberius hissed in Kirk's ear, "then let's at least do it with a fully armed squad of my samurai. Not to mention an armada of starships standing by to beam us to safety."

"I want to get closer," Kirk said. He started forward again. The two shadows were humanoid. He was sure of that. He almost thought he could catch a glimpse of pointed ears on one of them.

That would explain a lot of things, Kirk thought, *if the Preservers turned out to be Vulcans.*

Now the two shadows were only a few meters away, half-hidden behind a slanted pillar. Just past them, Kirk saw others gathered in front of the far opening.

Kirk held out his hands. If they knew so much about humans, they had to know it was a gesture of greeting.

"I'm James Kirk of the . . ." Kirk paused. He was speaking from habit. *Well, why not?* he thought. "James Kirk, of the *Starship Enterprise.*"

One of the shadows—one of the creatures—moved forward. In one way, it was as if a human wore a suit of broken glass, each reflective surface displaying a different angle of whatever was inside.

Kirk watched in fascination as the creature manifested arms and held out both hands to him.

"That's right," Kirk said. "This is how we greet each other. Hands empty. A symbol of trust."

As if a large gemstone were taking shape in a transporter beam, the creature's face began to coalesce in a pattern of crystal facets, some no more substantial than smoke, others throwing off glaring reflections from the shafts of light.

But others offered Kirk a glimpse of what actually lay within.

And seeing that, Kirk trembled.

"Spock . . . ?" he whispered.

Then suddenly a hand was on his shoulder and Kirk stumbled back, pulled by Tiberius.

"Let me go!" Kirk protested.

"We're going back!" Tiberius insisted. "I need you to take me back!"

Kirk jabbed his elbow into Tiberius's side and as his counterpart twisted to keep his balance, Kirk pulled free. He looked back at the shadows, but they were twisting strands of dark reflections now, not even humanoid.

"I was getting close," Kirk raged.

"Didn't you see what those things were?"

Kirk looked at his counterpart, saw recognition in his eyes, saw fear. "What did *you* see?"

"They're Cardassians!"

"What?"

"The one in front of you," Tiberius said wildly. "I don't know what kind of holographic camouflage they're wearing, but it was a Cardassian. And the other was a Klingon. I know it!"

"Tiberius," Kirk said, "I saw a Vulcan. Maybe they're . . . they're composites. Or we . . . we're some aspect of them. I don't know. But they're there. They're solid. We can make contact with—"

Tiberius's fist came out of nowhere and Kirk fell back to the floor in midword.

"I need you alive to use the callback signal," Tiberius panted. "I need you conscious. But I swear I'll leave pieces of you behind unless you come with me *now!*"

Kirk looked over his shoulder. The shadows hadn't moved from their last positions. He looked back at Tiberius, then spoke as if he'd reconsidered. "You're right. We need Spock over here. And La Forge and Scotty. A full science and engineering team." He pushed himself to his feet.

"I really don't know how you managed to survive this long," Tiberius said scornfully. "Let's—"

Kirk's fist drove upward, caught Tiberius on the jaw, and sent him sprawling to the floor.

"By keeping my mouth shut," Kirk said.

Tiberius sat up slowly, hand to his jaw, his hard eyes on Kirk.

"Now you listen," Kirk told him. "Those shadows, whatever we think they are, they're not interested in coming after you or me. They're only interested in keeping us from going through that other opening."

"Then here's a suggestion," Tiberius said. "Let's not go through that other opening."

"Tiberius, think for once. You saw Cardassians and Klingons. They're your *enemies*. I saw a Vulcan. That's a *friend*."

Tiberius was on his feet. "So what?"

"Maybe there's a lesson in that. I can go through, you can't."

"You sure it wasn't a Romulan?"

"Go back to the shuttle," Kirk said.

"I can't use the callback signal."

"Then you'll have to be patient, won't you?" And before Tiberius could reply, Kirk turned and ran toward the far opening.

"James! No!" Tiberius shouted after him.

Kirk looked back. "Go to the shuttle!" Then he stumbled to a halt. More shadows had appeared to either side of the chamber, swiftly flowing back and forth around the bases of the angled pillars. They were moving toward Tiberius.

"They're after you!" Kirk shouted. *"Run!"*

Tiberius spun around, and rushed back toward the first chamber.

The shadows joined forces, flowed after him, but Tiberius was faster.

Kirk turned back to the second opening, then gasped as he jumped back.

Three shadows were before him.

Kirk tried again, held out his hands in greeting.

One by one, the three shadows coalesced, transformed, and did the same. Then—

zhimmmm . . .

Not a sound, more like a thought.

zhimmmm . . .

Or sensation.

zhimmmm . . .

Or memory.

Kirk's heart pounded.

"Yes," he said. "That's my name. Jim."

. . . zhimjimjim . . .

A new sensation engulfed him: the warmth of familiarity.

Kirk moved one step forward. This close, the shadows' gleaming facets shimmered like oil on water, and then another fractured image began to take shape.

An eye . . . a mouth . . . the smile . . . all facets, fragments, of the whole of—

"Gary?"

His long-lost friend—Gary Mitchell.

But even as he strained to see if that truly was the face behind the illusion, Kirk felt a hand on his arm, looked down, saw floating fragments of fingers reflected in flat planes, like a jigsaw puzzle fighting to reassemble itself.

And the memory of love claimed him.

"Carol."

. . . jimjimjim . . .

Kirk held his arms out wide, embracing the shadows, and their formless bodies flowed around him. They were anything but solid, their touch closer to that of a breeze.

The pattern became clear for Kirk.

Thought . . . Spock. *Sensation* . . . Gary. *Memory* . . . Carol. Two friends he'd trusted with his life. One with his heart.

. . . jimjimjim . . .

Jim. Not James. Not Captain Kirk. But the name the friends he trusted called him. A message. One he would accept from these messengers.

Then the shadows parted, revealing the second opening.

Narrow. Four meters high. Curving to the side.

Kirk did not hesitate. He moved through it and a single footstep brought him to the other side.

He was in another cavern even larger than the last. Triangles, lights, the three shadows. Always at the edge of his vision. Never anything he could see more clearly than an image in a half-remembered dream.

The thought came to him then that human eyes had evolved to see in only three dimensions of space and one dimension of time. But there were other dimensions, and in those realms, what could a human eye ever hope to see except for shadows of an unknowable reality?

. . . jimjimjim . . .

There was something waiting for him in the center of the chamber. In the center of the lights. In the place where the shadows led him.

He recognized its shape from fifty meters away. Not quite the same as the one he had seen before, but close enough.

And though he had crossed into a new universe, into new dimensions, the fact that he now saw something he had seen before, did not surprise him.

In a way, he had almost expected it.

In a way, he almost felt as if he had come home.

"Shields!" Picard shouted as the bridge dipped sharply and filled with the whine of the structural integrity field generators.

A second blast shook the *Enterprise,* but the force of the impact was much diminished and Picard knew the protective forcefields had been reestablished in time.

He sat back in his chair. "Damage report, Mr. Sloane."

"Direct hit to the sensor dish. Massive sensor damage."

"Who fired?"

Riker looked up from the tactical screen he had swung out in front of his chair. "The Ferengi!"

Sloane called out from his station, "Shall I target that ship?"

Picard's jaw tightened. A battle now might prevent him from ever retrieving Kirk from the mirror universe. And there were still thirteen hours to go before the Ferengi experiment was due to begin. For the moment, time was still on his side. "No," he said. "Hail her. And put MacDonald back onscreen."

In seconds, each of Picard's adversaries appeared on opposite sides of the viewer.

"Daimon Baryon," Picard said. "That was uncalled for."

"I gave you five minutes," the daimon hissed. "You chose not to use them."

"Daimon," Captain MacDonald broke in, "you attacked while Captain Picard and I were talking. That is hardly the mark of an ally."

The Ferengi was indignant. "He said he had sent a ship into the mirror universe! That is a deliberately provocative act! It could come out anywhere—even within my shields!"

"It is a *shuttlecraft,* Daimon," Picard retorted. "It can

only return to a cargo transporter on our hangar deck. It represents no possible threat to you."

"No, of course not," the Ferengi said. His smile was belligerent. "That's what *you're* here for."

"Captain MacDonald," Picard said, "I believe I had requested a ninety-minute extension."

"Ninety minutes," MacDonald agreed. "But I'd keep your shields up."

"Thank you. I'll advise you as soon as we've recovered the shuttle. *Enterprise* out."

Picard leaned back in his chair, eyes on the cathedral-like arched ceiling of his bridge, and braced himself for the bad news. "Casualty report?" he asked.

"None, sir," Sloane reported. "Exterior damage only."

Picard glanced over at Riker. "Small mercies. Continue with the plans for an attack on the *Pathfinder*. And build in an initial attack on the *Buyout* while you're at it."

"I take it we're not leaving in ninety minutes," Riker said.

"Oh, we'll leave. But not before we've crippled those two ships so badly they'll have to cancel the experiment."

Troi looked uncomfortable. "Would you actually fire on another Starfleet vessel?"

"Counselor, if my choice is between doing that, or letting the universe end, I won't even hesitate. But I'd like to at least *try* to bring Kirk back, first."

"For what it's worth, sir, given a choice between firing on the *Enterprise* or starting a war with the Ferengi Alliance, I sense that Captain MacDonald won't hesitate either."

"She's a Starfleet officer," Picard said grimly. "I wouldn't expect her to hesitate. Which is why next time I plan to fire first."

THIRTY-TWO

jimjimjim . . .

The shadows melted from Kirk as he walked back into the lights of the second chamber, all that he had seen in that third and final chamber etched forever in his mind.

. . . jimjimjim . . .

It was a fleeting final thought . . . sensation . . . memory. A last departing message from the shadows cast from other dimensions, other realities. The first word in a conversation that one day would bridge realms of space and time even Spock could not conceive of.

Kirk walked past the slanted pillars with their endless lines of symbols. As he gazed at them, another thought came to him, this time of captains' logs.

The pillars were, he was certain, the records of the missions of this device he was in, so much more than a starship, set down for those who would follow after him.

Kirk wasn't sure if he had been the first of his kind to be invited here. But in time others would come, he knew. And eventually, some would come who would understand everything that they saw here.

But that was a mission for other times and other travelers.

On his journey, Kirk had found what it was he needed to find. His mission now was to return with the knowledge he had wrested from this place, and use it as it must be used.

He saw the first opening before him, narrow, tall, with an impossible curve to the side. He stepped into it and was in the docking chamber at once.

He saw the *Percival Lowell* in the center of the dark chamber, searchlights blazing.

Then he heard Tiberius screaming.

Kirk's mind accelerated instantly. The call to action revitalizing, exhilarating, as if until now, in the chambers within chambers of the obelisk, he had been immersed in the weight of different, slower time.

Without echoes to confuse a sound's direction, Tiberius was easy to locate.

Kirk ran toward the shuttlecraft, closing in on the screams. Then swung around to the shuttle's far side to find Tiberius caught by the shadows!

There were so many of them that as they passed before his struggling body, their facets and reflections made Tiberius appear to break up and re-form. To Kirk, it was as if he were seeing his black-clad counterpart through a broken lens, or himself in a shattered mirror.

For a moment, Kirk hesitated.

Tiberius had been right. When Kirk had set out on this journey, without knowing his destination or what he would find, he had brought his counterpart with him as a key, or as a bribe, or as bait. Kirk had been willing to use Tiberius in any way he could to attract the attention of the Preservers.

In the end, that had been unnecessary.

This enormous obelisk was not what Kirk thought it

might be. What had been waiting in the final chamber had been waiting just for Kirk.

Tiberius had not been needed.

Tiberius had served no purpose.

Tiberius had never been anything more than a random error which deserved to be deleted.

Kirk stood frozen, watching, as the shadows folded around his counterpart, pulling, pushing, dragging him to the opening of another curved corridor. Away from Kirk. Away from any chance of escape.

Action or inaction? Kirk thought in that moment. The choice was his. It would be so easy, Kirk knew, to simply surrender Tiberius, finally let him go.

Tiberius was a monster who had destroyed worlds and civilizations, visited terror on a universe that did not deserve it. How could any fate befall him that was worse than the fate he deserved?

But in that moment, another thought came to Kirk, another sensation, another memory from his past—

In the abandoned ice mines of Earth's moon, with Intendant Spock and Kate Janeway, hearing what had happened *after* the first crossover, *after* his final conversation with Spock's mirror duplicate.

"One man cannot summon the future," the mirror Spock had said.

"But one man can change the present," Kirk had insisted. *"What will it be? The past or the future? Tyranny or freedom? It's up to you."*

But those weren't questions only to be asked in one place, of one man, in one time. They were questions that must always be asked, and always be answered.

"In every revolution," Kirk had said, *"there is one man with a vision."*

The mirror Spock had said he would consider Kirk's challenge. And when Tiberius had been returned to his proper universe, his Spock had acted upon that challenge.

"And because I did what you had suggested," Intendant Spock had said, *"the Empire did fall, and was replaced by one even more abhorrent.*

"And these abominations and massacres and acts of depravity in my world—all this evil—exist because of you!"

It would be so simple to abandon Tiberius, Kirk knew. But to do so would be to abandon his own responsibility.

With that realization, the choice was taken from him.

Because of who he was and what he believed, there was only one thing James T. Kirk could do.

He ran to fight for Tiberius.

He charged with a wordless cry of attack, plunged through the surrounding shadows to be at Tiberius's side.

His counterpart stared at him as if for an instant he believed that Kirk was another of his attackers, now in a more solid, human form.

"It's time to go back!" Kirk shouted.

Then the shadows attacked him as well.

Shifting fragments of hands and fingers reached for Kirk, as if time skipped forward and backward in a malfunctioning sensor record.

But Kirk found one full hand and grabbed its wrist and with that grip made the shadow solid.

The facets and planes of its face coalesced, made real by Kirk's contact with it, and Kirk saw with horror that just as he had been visited by images from his past, so was Tiberius.

But the shadows surrounding Tiberius were not those of friends.

Pavel Chekov, face pale and eyes sunken, a living corpse who had crawled from the agony booth where Tiberius had left him a century ago, grasped and clawed at Kirk as if to drag him down into the pit.

Kirk lashed out, splintering the mirror Chekov's face into a cloud of spinning shards that began to re-form as another skeletal hand grabbed Kirk's throat and spun him around and—

Kirk stared into the bloodied face of Christopher Pike, the captain Tiberius had murdered to win the *Enterprise*, mad eyes blazing.

A cry of primal fear escaped from Kirk as he pummeled the corpse's shifting form.

Pike's chest exploded into ribbons of smoke and before they could re-form, Kirk grabbed Tiberius, pulling him free from the other shadows that claimed him.

Marlena Moreau, the captain's woman, clung to Tiberius's leg. A young Leonard McCoy, rope burns on his neck, tore at Tiberius's clothes. Carol Marcus, throat slit, struck at him with the stumps of her wrists.

"Now!" Kirk shouted. *"Run!"*

Tiberius scrambled up, then stumbled forward, tripping, falling headlong into shadow entrails spilling out of unraveling stitches holding together the reflections of a tiny form—Balok, whom Tiberius had stuffed and then placed on display.

Tiberius gibbered and cried and kicked and hit and Kirk pushed him away from the shadows, driving him toward the shuttlecraft.

Then Captain Garrovick attacked, body drained of blood. And Androvar Drake. And a leering Sulu with a deep bleeding scar that ran down his face.

Tiberius crawled across the deck and Kirk held his ground, fighting the demons of Tiberius, knowing deep in his soul how close they had come to being his demons, too.

Kirk flailed with a final flurry of punches, and Will Decker evaporated into wisps of sparkling reflections, Finnegan exploded into puffs of vapor, Christine Chapel melted into smoke.

Then Kirk heaved Tiberius into the shuttle's open hatch.

Took one last look over his shoulder. Saw the shadows regrouping.

He ran up the shuttle's ramp, punched the hatch controls, started the autolaunch sequence.

Kirk felt the *Percival Lowell* buck up on antigravs as the hatch began to grind shut. At the same time, he heard the sound of scratching on the shuttle's outer skin.

Kirk activated the impulse engines, vented plasma, a blast of superheated air roared through the narrowing gap in the closing hatchway.

But the hatch closed and sealed unimpeded.

Kirk leapt into the pilot's seat, placed trembling hands on the controls, swung the shuttle around.

The viewports began to cloud and darken in the sea of shadows that still pursued Tiberius.

But Kirk had located the opening that led to freedom and the stars and he blasted for it.

The *Lowell* shuddered, escaped the docking chamber, and then, suddenly, the stars jumped and became the ones Kirk remembered surrounding Halkan.

Kirk rolled the shuttle, saw the mirror duplicate of Halkan beneath, then hurtled away from the vast orbiting obelisk.

Only then did Kirk realize his entire body was shaking, not just his hands. His uniform was torn, his knuckles bloody.

Only then did he hear Tiberius. "Why did you save me?"

Kirk put his hand on the callback signal control, letting the isolinears read his quantum signature and his life signs. With his other hand, he punched in his authentication code.

"The day you can understand the answer," Kirk said, "is the day you won't have to ask the question."

With a deep-felt, rasping sigh, Tiberius let his head fall back against his chairback. "You're as bad as Spock."

Kirk took that as a compliment.

Someday Tiberius might understand that, too.

THIRTY-THREE

☆

"There was another Guardian," Kirk said.

Picard put his hand on Dr. Crusher's shoulder to have her stop scanning Kirk with her tricorder. The others who were gathered around the diagnostic bed in sickbay—Spock, Teilani, La Forge, and Data—remained silent.

"Do you mean," Picard asked slowly, "another Guardian of Forever?"

Kirk nodded, and Picard could see how exhausted he was. But that didn't stop everyone from speaking at once.

"Fascinating," Spock said.

"Was it identical to the first?" La Forge asked.

"Could you determine if the Guardian was Preserver technology?" Data added. "Or had they simply found a second one?"

But before Kirk responded to any of his questioners, Teilani interrupted. "I don't know what that is. The Guardian of Forever?"

"In effect," Spock said, "it is a time portal. Sentient. Capable of displaying images from the past, and of allowing travel to other times."

"Who built such a thing?" Teilani asked. She looked startled. Reminding Picard that those outside Starfleet led more sheltered existences.

"Not even the Guardian will answer that question," Picard said. "It's probably been subjected to more study than the Preserver obelisks, but . . . there's only one that we know of, it's at least five billion years old, and quite particular about who it interacts with."

Spock seemed to think of something, turned to Kirk. "Did the Guardian in the obelisk interact with you?" he asked.

"It didn't speak to me," Kirk said, "but . . . it did show me the past."

"Indeed."

"It was a stream of images," Kirk said. "All from the Halkan perspective. I saw our first visit here, Spock. Our negotiations with the Council, the crossover. Everything that happened on Tiberius's *Enterprise*. But then, when Intendant Spock sent me back with Bones and Scotty and Uhura, the Guardian kept showing me Halkan in the mirror universe."

"You're certain it *was* the mirror Halkan?" Picard asked.

"I saw the occupation by the Klingon-Cardassian Alliance," Kirk said. His eyes stared away, and Picard did not want to imagine the horrors he had witnessed.

"And then," Kirk continued, "I saw the giant obelisk appear in orbit of Halkan. I saw our shuttlecraft enter it. I saw . . . what the obelisk is meant to do."

"The Guardian showed you the future?" Picard asked.

"Jean-Luc, I saw Halkan destroyed. The obelisk . . . glowed and beams from it shot down to the surface and . . . I saw the entire planet shattered by a web of explosions all at once. And the explosion seemed to hesitate, just for a moment, and then it was as if blackness expanded in a sphere and the obelisk was gone and . . . the Guardian showed nothing more. As if time had ended."

Picard puzzled over the possible meaning of those images. "Jim, did you see any indication that the mirror Halkan had its own network of geosensors?"

"No, the Ferengi had nothing to do with that Halkan."

"Then I don't understand how a runaway dilithium reaction could be triggered on—"

"The obelisk," Spock interrupted.

"Exactly," Kirk said.

Spock reached out for the edge of the diagnostic bed, as if to steady himself. "It is . . . staggering."

"I agree," Kirk said.

"What's staggering?" Teilani asked. "You two and your cryptic conversations."

"I must admit I'm at a loss, as well," Picard said. "Perhaps you would be good enough to fill us both in, Spock."

Spock complied. "In our universe, the Ferengi plan to direct a massive energy discharge into Halkan's dilithium reserves. Damage will be minimal because the unique four-dimensional lattice structure of dilithium will allow it to divert some of that discharge into subspace. But if, at the same time, in the mirror universe, the obelisk creates a transporter-beam effect to . . . to open a doorway between the two universes as happened before, the dilithium reserves of our Halkan will cross over to occupy the same dimensional coordinates as the reserves left on the mirror Halkan."

"But . . ." Picard protested, "matter can't occupy the same space as other matter."

Then Data gasped as his emotion chip apparently processed the implications of Spock's theory. "That *is* staggering, and quite terrifying."

"*What* is?" Teilani demanded.

"In the simplest terms," Spock continued, "the dimensional overlap that will occur when the dilithium reserves of two universes are forced to share the same eleven-dimensional coordinates in one universe will create regions of infinite density."

"You mean a singularity?" Teilani asked. "Like a black hole?"

"No," Spock explained. "Nothing like a black hole. But exactly like the vacuum fluctuation from which the universe was born."

Picard's gasp was the equal of Data's.

"Will someone please tell me what you're all talking about?" Teilani said.

Kirk slipped off the edge of the diagnostic bed. He reached out to hold her hands. "Teilani, the mirror Halkan will become the site of a subspace explosion equal in intensity to the Big Bang. That's what the Guardian showed me. A new universe will be born, and in seconds will inflate to a size larger than Federation space."

"If it's a new universe," Teilani said, "what happens to the one that's already there?"

"Erased," Kirk said. "Earth, Vulcan, Qo'noS, all the worlds of the Klingon-Cardassian Alliance, cease to exist in seconds. Our galaxy, gone in minutes. Then things settle down and the new universe continues to expand at the speed of light in all directions, eventually destroying the entire mirror universe like . . . like a parasite from within."

"What happens to *our* universe?" Teilani asked.

"Nothing," Spock said. "The vacuum fluctuation will forever shut the doorway connecting us. There will not even be any harm done to the Halkan of our universe."

"Then the psychohistorians were right after all," Crusher said. "A universe *will* be destroyed."

"They just picked the wrong one," La Forge added.

Picard could see how troubled Teilani was by this revelation. "But James, I still don't understand. You said the Preservers were ethical. That's why they didn't kill Tiberius. But now they're going to . . . to wipe out an entire universe of living beings? Every world? Every galaxy?"

"I don't pretend to understand, either," Kirk told her. "Especially since I think the only reason they're doing it is so the mirror universe can no longer interact with ours."

"Well, we can't let that happen," Teilani said.

Kirk looked at Picard. "We won't let that happen."

"No," Picard promised. "We won't."

But Data was concerned. "Captain, though I understand the emotional nature of your reaction to this unprecedented act of destruction, I feel I must point out that the Preservers are a formidable enemy to engage."

"Fortunately, Data, we will not have to engage the Preservers. Only the *Pathfinder* and Daimon Baryon's ship."

"Why engage them at all?" Teilani asked. "How could the Ferengi even think of going ahead with their experiment after James explains the truth?"

"I fear it is not a Ferengi experiment," Picard said. "Ferengi organizations have been used to set the experiment in place. But if we had the time and resources to examine the trail of reports and recommendations that set their plans in motion, I am certain we would find the hand of the Preservers influencing critical decisions."

Teilani looked even more troubled. "But Christine will understand? Won't she? She'll support you."

Picard felt everyone's eyes upon him. "I really don't know."

Teilani looked bewildered.

"At this point, she is not inclined to trust me," Picard said to explain his apparent indecision. "So I believe that our best strategy is a sudden attack with overwhelming force,

because as long as she truly believes the future of the
Federation is at risk, I'm not certain if I can convince her to
stand down."

Teilani's eyes flashed and Picard saw in her the fire that
he knew had first drawn Kirk to her.

"Then I can," Teilani said.

Picard blinked. "I beg your pardon?"

"I'm a negotiator, Jean-Luc. I brought Chal into the
Federation when half the Council wasn't 'inclined' to trust
Klingons or Romulans, let alone a combination of the two."

Picard saw Kirk give Teilani's hand a squeeze. "She
talked me into going to Chal that first time."

Picard wasn't convinced. "Captain MacDonald is a starship captain, she—"

"She's also a woman," Teilani said bluntly. "I know her.
I've worked with her." She glanced at her husband. "And
we have a great many things in common."

Picard did not look forward to engaging another Starfleet
vessel. But he knew he must be prepared to do more than
just disable the *Pathfinder*—he must be able to destroy his
sister ship and take responsibility for the deaths of scores of
Starfleet personnel, if that's what it would take to stop what
the Preservers had planned.

He needed a third option. Desperately.

"Data, how much time is left on the extension MacDonald
gave us?"

"Fourteen minutes, thirty-seven seconds, though I am
certain their sensors have picked up our successful retrieval
of the shuttlecraft. Captain MacDonald could call on us to
leave the system at once."

Picard looked at Kirk. "Jim, the experiment is due to start
in a little over twelve hours. From what you saw, is that a
reliable time?"

But Kirk shook his head. "Everything's in place, Jean-

Luc. The Ferengi could trigger the detonation at any time."

Picard felt as if he was stepping into empty air. He was used to dealing with time limits and deadlines and countdowns. But all that was already passed and he was poised on the brink of disaster. One mistake, one miscalculation, and a universe could die in an instant.

"All right," Picard told Teilani. "I can make the case that you're a neutral observer. Our goal is simply to have MacDonald stop the experiment long enough to contact Starfleet Command for further orders. You're not trying to change her mind, only delay her decision."

"I can do that," Teilani said confidently.

"What about Daimon Baryon?" Data asked.

The Ferengi was the least of Picard's concerns. "In a one-to-one fight, his ship is no match for the *Enterprise*. Riker is prepared to attack as soon as we see any sign he's getting ready to begin ionization of the Halkan atmosphere."

"So if worse comes to worst," Teilani said, "and you and the Ferengi do engage, all I have to do is make sure MacDonald stays out of the fight."

Picard agreed. Put that way, it seemed so simple a task. "I'll arrange a communications link from the conference room, so you'll be able to—"

"No," Teilani interrupted. "As I said, I know her. I need to see her face-to-face. You said she had a full Betazoid officer? He'll need to be able to have complete access to what I'm thinking and feeling, too."

La Forge snapped his fingers. "Wait a minute, MacDonald also has a Vulcan science officer. Wouldn't a mind-meld be faster? More convincing?"

Everyone looked to Spock, but he offered no assurance. "The possible involvement of the Preservers clouds the issue, Mr. La Forge. Even a master of the *Kolinahr* would require lengthy preparation before risking a meld with what might be a powerful alien intellect. There is simply no time."

Kirk put his arm around Teilani's shoulders. "She can do it, Jean-Luc."

Picard wanted to be certain Kirk knew exactly what was at stake. "Jim, if Teilani does go to the *Pathfinder,* and is not successful, I *will* have to fire on that ship."

Picard saw a flicker of fear in Kirk's eyes, quickly hidden, but it had been there, nonetheless.

Teilani turned to her husband. "I will be successful, James. You know I will."

"I know," Kirk said in a way that told Picard he was missing something important that had just passed between husband and wife.

"I'll contact MacDonald," Picard said.

He had his third option.

He just didn't know if it was any better than the others.

"You're not convinced, are you?" Teilani said.

In the main transporter room of the *Enterprise,* Kirk smiled at her, ran a light finger over the subtle ridges of her forehead. "Are you half-Betazoid, too?"

"I don't have to read your mind, James. You're worried."

Kirk looked back at La Forge. The engineer was trying to pay attention to some minor detail on the transporter control console he stood behind.

Kirk moved closer to Teilani, whispered in her ear. "I always worry about you. It's my job."

Teilani smiled. "Then I look forward to keeping you busy for a long time." She took his hand, squeezed it.

Kirk squeezed back.

"You can feel that?" Teilani asked.

Kirk held up both hands for inspection. "I think everything's grown back."

Teilani innocently raised her eyebrows. "Full sensitivity?"

Kirk matched her playful expression. "I believe so."

She delicately kissed his fingers. "We'll have to run a full diagnostic tonight. Just to be sure."

Kirk hugged her then, a sudden impulse.

"I'll be fine," Teilani whispered. "Chris is a reasonable woman. She reminds me of you."

They stood apart.

"There's so much I want to say to you," Kirk told her.

"I know."

"But there's never enough time."

"There will be," Teilani said. "For the three of us."

Kirk understood. No recriminations. Their time away from Qo'noS had done them both good. The past would remain in the past. Their lives together would go forward from the present, with their child. Their Joseph. Somehow, Kirk promised himself, with Teilani's help he would learn to accept his child.

The doors to the transporter room slipped open and Data entered, a small padd in his hand.

"Excuse me for interrupting," the android said. "Commander Riker asked me to show you this." He gave the padd to Teilani.

Teilani frowned. "A code?"

"For the *Pathfinder*."

Kirk tensed. "To do what?"

The android seemed to understand why Kirk asked the question. "It is not a self-destruct code, sir. There are too many safeguards in place to prevent that. However, if it becomes necessary, Teilani will be able to use this code to set a new, nonrandom modulation pattern for the *Pathfinder*'s shields. That will enable Commander Riker to precisely match our phasers to the same predictable pattern, permitting us to use pinpoint phaser hits to disable the

Pathfinder's weapons systems without collateral damage."

Teilani gave the padd back to Data. "And you don't think the Betazoid is going to pluck that fact from my mind?"

"Counselor Troi assures me that Lieutenant Darno will concentrate on your immediate thoughts. If you do not think about remodulating the shields until the moment you decide such an action is necessary, it should escape his notice."

"Should?" Teilani said. "Not exactly reassuring."

"I know how your mind works," Kirk teased. "One track, laser-focused."

"Is that a compliment," Teilani asked, "or a complaint?"

Kirk tried to smile, relieved at least to know that in the event things went wrong, Teilani would not have to be the target of an all-out assault, after all. Then Picard's voice came over the comm system.

"Bridge to transporter room."

"La Forge here, Captain."

"With great reluctance, Captain MacDonald has agreed to the meeting. She'll give Teilani an hour."

"How does Daimon Baryon feel about that?" Kirk asked.

"Furious, as expected. That hour is all MacDonald could get him to agree to."

"An hour is all I'll need," Teilani said. She gave Kirk a brief but loving kiss. "Stay by a communicator in case I need technical details."

"I'll get Spock, too."

Teilani stepped up on the transporter pad. "Back in an hour."

"Energizing," La Forge said.

Teilani faded into the light.

Never enough time, Kirk thought. He felt proud and anxious at the same time. But she'd be back in an hour.

"I have confirmation," La Forge said. "She's there."

Kirk turned away from the empty transporter pad, stepped out into the corridor. It felt good to be back in action, if only in a small way.

He looked back at the engineer and the android.

"What are you waiting for, gentlemen? Let's go save a universe."

THIRTY-FOUR

THIRTY-FOUR

———— ☆ ————

"Andrea, I'm *so* glad to see you!"

In the *Pathfinder's* main transporter room, Teilani stepped lightly off the transporter pad, ignored M'Benga's outstretched hand, gave the doctor a quick hug instead.

M'Benga took a deep breath to steady her nerves. "Have you heard . . . anything from McCoy?" She felt awkward, even if Teilani didn't.

"He's still waiting for the Romulan specialists to arrive. But the baby will be fine." There was no doubt at all in Teilani's voice.

"I'm glad." But M'Benga once again wished for the child's parents' sake that optimism was all it took to change the odds. To change the topic, she pointed to the doors. "Chris is on the bridge."

Teilani gave M'Benga's arm a small squeeze. "Andrea, this is going to work out, too."

M'Benga nodded, realizing why Teilani was such a good match for Kirk. Both of them were selfless when others needed help. Even now, when they were facing the worst themselves.

But M'Benga was also a realist. Deserving a change of odds was no guarantee of getting it, either.

Kirk stood behind Picard's chair, looking at the viewer. Little was different. The *Leveraged Buyout* and the *Pathfinder* still orbited Halkan. The two ships were to either side of the Ferengi spacedock, bows facing the *Enterprise*. The only thing that changed in the viewer was the moving landscape of Halkan.

Picard twisted around to look up at Kirk.

Kirk knew why. His fingertapping. With a nod of apology, he removed his hand from the back of Picard's chair.

"It's only been five minutes," Picard said. "I doubt if the meeting has begun yet."

Kirk nodded again, looked around the bridge. Sloane was at his security station; Data at ops; the Trill, Lieutenant Maran, at navigation. Will Riker was in his exec's chair, his tactical display unfolded before him. Counselor Troi was to Picard's other side, standing by in case of additional conversations that required her unique powers of confirmation.

Someone else's bridge and crew, Kirk thought, restless. But then his gaze settled on a familiar figure at the auxiliary science station. *Spock.*

Kirk walked over to his friend.

But the Vulcan's first words were anything but reassuring. "The situation is worse than I anticipated."

"How much worse?"

"Initiation of the ionization event that will trigger the dilithium reaction in the mirror universe will only require the firepower of one ship. Either the *Buyout* or the *Pathfinder.*"

"So if anything happens, we'll have to stop both of them, not just one?"

"I have already informed Commander Riker."

Kirk looked back at Picard, didn't envy him. "What if this had been us, Spock?"

"Do you mean, how would you have handled this situation if it had arisen during your tenure on the *Enterprise?*"

"Why use two words when ten will do." Kirk smiled at the long-suffering look that kind of teasing always provoked in Spock.

"I believe that you would err on the side of caution."

"Me? Caution?" Kirk asked, only half serious.

But Spock did not play that game. "You are forgetting that in this situation, time is not critical. Whatever schedule is driving the Ferengi experiment was set by the Preservers, not the events themselves."

The Vulcan continued, very serious. "Time has always been your friend, Captain. You have always chosen negotiation over conflict, whenever that choice has been available."

"And if the choice isn't available?"

"Then I agree, 'caution' is not a word in your vocabulary."

Kirk looked up to the viewer's unchanging image. "So, if that's what I'd do—wait, negotiate, talk things through— why isn't that what Chris MacDonald's doing?"

Spock swung his chair around to look at the viewer. "As Captain MacDonald perceives the situation, she is fighting for the continued existence of the Federation. She cannot be faulted for that."

"But . . . we're fighting for the survival of an entire universe."

"I have observed," Spock said, "that occasionally Starfleet officers face a situation where they must choose between being a good Starfleet officer, or being a good person. You have always chosen the latter."

Kirk thought about that. He had always considered himself a loyal officer, supporting Starfleet and the Federation

to the utmost of his ability. But then again, he had never let
the Prime Directive or other regulations get in the way of
justice. Yet wasn't the foundation of justice found in the
adherence to the regulations that defined a civilization?

"But have I made the right choices?" Kirk asked. The
question was not rhetorical.

Spock answered with a question of his own. "Why did
you save Tiberius?" Kirk's counterpart was back in his own
quarters now, under guard, as were Intendant Spock and the
psychohistorians, all of them clamoring for information.

Kirk had no trouble answering the question. "I felt . . .
responsible."

"Given all that we know about the history of the mirror
universe, that is not logical."

"But it's what I *felt*, Spock."

"And is there any argument I can make to counter that
feeling?"

Kirk frowned. *Why is Spock being so contentious?* "Of
course not. Right or wrong, logic or not, you can't deny that
at the time, that's what my feelings were."

Spock persisted. "Captain MacDonald feels she is saving
the Federation."

"Is that why the Preservers manipulated Starfleet to
place her at this place, at this time?"

"In this case," Spock said, "it is entirely possible that the
Preservers have specifically chosen the *wrong* person to be
present at a critical event."

And with that, Kirk understood the point of Spock's reasoning. "Teilani isn't going to be able to convince
MacDonald to stand down, is she?"

"I believe the task to be impossible."

Kirk's stomach fell as if the gravity generators had just
reset—every instinct in him compelling him to respond by
taking action. *But what?* he thought.

"MacDonald believes she's right. *We* believe *we're* right. Neither one of us will back down. What happens then, Spock?"

"There is only one possible outcome," the Vulcan answered. "Tragedy."

On the bridge of the *Pathfinder*, M'Benga listened, unsurprised. She had known what her captain would say to Teilani.

"I'm sorry. You haven't convinced me."

Teilani looked at Lieutenant Darno, who sat to MacDonald's left. "Ask the lieutenant. He'll confirm I'm telling the truth."

"I don't doubt that you are," MacDonald said. "At least, as you believe it to be."

M'Benga bit her lip, anticipating how Teilani's Klingon heritage would make her respond to MacDonald's condescension.

"Christine," Teilani said emphatically, forcefully, her erect posture even more impressive than before. "What I have said is not just what I believe is true, it's what James told me."

MacDonald shifted in her chair, impatient. "*James* was gone for more than an hour, in the mirror universe, inside a giant alien artifact, exposed to who knows what kind of illusions, maybe even mind control."

Teilani was silent for a moment. But it was clear to all present that strong, conflicting emotions were at war within her. At least it was clear to M'Benga, who had seen enough of Teilani on Qo'noS to know her Klingon temper, her Romulan intensity, and her human propensity to find a balance. What M'Benga didn't know, however, was which part of Teilani would win control of her now.

"Would you at least *talk* to James?" Teilani asked.

MacDonald was blunt. "I just told you, no matter what he says, I can't believe him. Not with the Federation at—"

"The Federation is *not* at risk!" Teilani said angrily. "The Preservers have manipulated the Ferengi into—"

MacDonald slapped the arm of her chair in a display of temper of her own. "I don't want to hear another word about the Preservers! I don't care what anyone says, I *earned* this command. It wasn't given to me by some cabal of billion-year-old aliens and I resent anyone who says otherwise." She stood up, tugged down on her jacket. "We've had our talk. My mind hasn't changed."

Teilani remained calm. "You gave me an hour. I still have twenty-two minutes left. Talk to James."

MacDonald glared at Teilani for a long moment.

From her position behind the command chairs, M'Benga kept her own mouth firmly closed, knowing there was nothing she could do or say that would help Teilani in this exchange. Not that Teilani actually needed her help, of course. She could be as commanding a presence as her husband.

"Hail the *Enterprise,*" MacDonald finally said with profound annoyance.

Picard appeared on the viewer. "Captain. Have you reached a decision?"

"Put Kirk on."

M'Benga watched as the angle of the viewer changed and Kirk moved in front of Picard, Riker, and Troi.

"Captain MacDonald," Kirk said cautiously. "How are things going over there?"

"Captain Kirk," MacDonald replied formally. "I don't know what it is you're really after here, but I cannot allow you to have me act against my orders to the detriment of the Federation."

M'Benga saw Kirk's look of consternation as he turned his attention from MacDonald to Teilani.

"Teilani," Kirk said, "*is* that the captain's decision?"

But before Teilani could reply, Lieutenant Darno was on his feet and shouting—"Captain! I can see it in his thoughts—she knows how to disable our shields!"

Then to M'Benga, safe at the back of the bridge, everything happened at once.

Even as Commander T'Rell leapt from her chair with her hand held to deliver a nerve pinch and MacDonald ran for the phaser storage locker and ordered the ship's computer to block all console commands to the shields, Teilani dropped and flipped the Vulcan to the side with Klingon strength, shoved the navigator to the side with Romulan speed, and tapped in a code sequence and—

"Stand aside!" MacDonald shouted, phaser aimed at Teilani.

But she was too late.

The bridge alarms drowned her out just as the *Pathfinder* was engulfed by destruction.

"Stop firing!" Kirk pleaded as he spun to face Picard.

But Picard was on his feet, sharing Kirk's horror.

"That wasn't us!" Riker shouted.

"Captain!" Sloane cried from security. "It's the Ferengi!"

On the viewer, the channel to the *Pathfinder*'s bridge was gone. Now it showed the *Buyout* banking around the spacedock as it laid in a dense barrage of phaser fire that easily penetrated the *Pathfinder*'s predictable shields.

The sleek starship was already beginning to spin as her internal stabilizers went offline.

"Target the Ferengi!" Picard ordered. "And *fire!*"

Kirk stared at the viewer as if trapped in a nightmare as Riker commenced his preprogrammed attack.

The bridge of the *Enterprise* rang as quantum torpedoes streaked toward their target and phasers lanced through space to make the *Buyout*'s shields flare with incandescence.

"The *Pathfinder* is going to collide with the spacedock!" Data warned.

"Baryon was waiting for his moment," Picard said, appalled.

All Kirk could do was whisper Teilani's name.

In space, the battle raged without logic.

The crab-shaped Ferengi ship nosed up, streaked back behind the spacedock, let fly with two flights of torpedoes.

One flight for the *Enterprise,* to drain her shields.

The other struck the *Pathfinder*'s unprotected port nacelle and turned it into plasma.

The *Enterprise* jumped forward under Maran's sure control to strike the spiraling *Pathfinder* with a series of tractor-beam impacts, nudging it just enough to miss the spacedock.

But as the *Enterprise* continued on its course to bring the *Buyout* into sight, the Ferengi ship launched another barrage of phaser fire that dropped beneath the *Enterprise* and struck the spacedock instead.

The spacedock was not built for battle. Its meager shields could not withstand the assault.

As it erupted into a cloud of debris and disintegrating phased matter, the *Enterprise* and the *Pathfinder* both were swallowed by fire.

The Ferengi ship made its escape.

M'Benga was on her knees by Darno, quickly stopping the bleeding from the deep wound in his scalp, even while knowing the brain damage was too severe for him to live much longer.

Smoke filled the *Pathfinder*'s bridge. So did the deafening assault of alarms, the whimpers and screams of the wounded.

M'Benga stood up from Darno, looked for her next patient, saw Christine MacDonald standing in the ruins of her command, fists at her side, blood streaking her face.

"Get me phasers!" the captain shouted.

T'Rell's calm voice answered. "Phasers online. Shields remodulated."

The physician looked up at the viewer. In place of the spacedock was a fiery cloud of debris, slowly dispersing to reveal the *Enterprise* listing.

"Target that bastard's bridge!" MacDonald shouted. *"Fire!"*

Eyes wide with disbelief, M'Benga watched deadly beams shoot out, first to splash across the *Enterprise*'s shields, and then—

—one beam broke through and hit her hull in a blazing explosion.

"Quantum torpedoes!" MacDonald commanded.

The viewer shifted as the hazy image of Picard appeared, his bridge equally smoke-filled and clamorous. "Break off your attack! It was the *Buyout* that fired!"

"Your *spy* compromised our shields," MacDonald shouted accusingly. "And you *will* pay the price!" She jabbed her finger at the screen. "Fire torpedoes."

The induction launchers sang through the bridge.

Then Teilani rose from the smoke-covered deck. "Chris, no! Reprogramming the shields was a last resort! The *Enterprise* was only going to target your weapons!"

MacDonald turned on Teilani, grabbed her by her tunic. "They knew they were sending you to a ship with a Betazoid! They would have told you anything!"

The channel from the *Enterprise*'s bridge cut out and the new image showed the quantum torpedoes striking their targets. This time, two broke through the primary shields and reached the hull.

Teilani pushed MacDonald away. "You have to stop this!"

"Oh, I will," MacDonald promised.

On the viewer, the *Enterprise* began to pull away.

"She's following the *Buyout*," T'Rell confirmed for her captain.

MacDonald wiped blood from her face. "I will not let Picard destroy the Federation! Plot an intercept and stop that ship! Ram it if you have to!"

And then the ship's computer interrupted calmly, *"Warp-core breach in progress. Detonation in thirty seconds."*

Chaos was descending.

THIRTY-FIVE

"We'll intercept the *Buyout* in three minutes!" Lieutenant Maran confirmed from navigation.

The fire-fighting sprays hissed through layers of smoke as Kirk watched the battered *Pathfinder* slide from the viewer.

"What's the status of MacDonald's ship?" Kirk asked, his heart like ice.

"Scanning," Sloane said from his station. "She's lost her port nacelle . . . main power couplings are—*she's got a warp-core breach!*"

Kirk spun to Picard. "We have to go back!"

"Thirty seconds to failure!" Sloane reported. "They've lost all automatic safeties!"

"Jim, we can't," Picard said, coughing, waving the dense smoke from his face. "You heard Spock. All it will take is one ship to—"

"We have to save them."

Picard put his hands on Kirk's shoulders. "We have to stop the *Buyout* and we can't do both. We're only one ship!"

Kirk pushed Picard away. Sick at heart. Mind racing

frantically. Took a deep breath. Steadied. Did what he always did. Reached for a third answer, a third option—

He had it!

"Detach the primary hull!"

Kirk felt the instant connection crackle between him and Picard. Veteran to veteran. Captain to captain.

Even as he calculated the logistics, Picard did as Kirk would have—he put the plan in motion.

"Mr. Maran—maintain intercept course! Mr. Sloane—status of the *Pathfinder*'s breach!"

Kirk knew Picard *had* to ask that question first. He *had* to know if the *Pathfinder* would be there when her rescuers arrived.

"They have blown the core hatch," Sloane said breathlessly.

"Aft sensors onscreen," Picard ordered.

On the viewer, the *Pathfinder* spun, out of balance. Then—

Kirk saw the slender needle of the ship's warp core shoot out from its lower hull like a missile and—

—detonate like a dying star.

Spots of light floated in Kirk's vision from the sudden glare. He heard Sloane's shout.

"Too close!"

Kirk blinked past dark afterimages, stared at the viewer, saw the *Pathfinder* spinning even more rapidly on her longitudinal axis. A large section—half her starboard nacelle—detached and tumbled off on an orbit of its own.

"She's holding together," Sloane reported. "I have multiple life signs."

Picard raised his voice so all could hear. *"This is the captain! All hands brace for emergency hull separation!"*

Kirk was ready for the blaring sirens and the flashing warning screens. The computer warned all crew to evacuate separation corridors.

Picard's every word was decisive now. "Picard to transporter control. On my mark, emergency point-to-point transport from the bridge to the battle bridge. For Picard, Riker, Data, Troi. Confirm!"

The transporter chief replied at once. *"Point-to-point transport locked and engaged. Standing by."*

Kirk and Picard faced each other, reached out to take each other's hand.

"Maran and Sloane are two of my best," Picard said gravely, "but, Jim, this is your ship now." He stepped back. *"Bonne chance, mon ami."*

Then the bridge trembled as the computer announced hull separation had commenced.

"Lieutenant Maran," Picard ordered, "as soon as the primary is free, you will set course for the *Pathfinder* at maximum speed. Captain Kirk has the conn."

"Aye, aye, sir!"

"Riker, Data, Troi—prepare for transport. Transporter control—*mark!"*

Instantly Picard and his three officers were swept away by the light, leaving Kirk with his own command staff of three: Spock, Sloane, and Maran.

The deck shook with a loud thud, then reverberation. Kirk didn't need the computer to tell him that the primary hull was clear.

"Coming about," Maran warned. "Maximum speed!"

Kirk stood in the center of the bridge, his bridge now, no one else's.

One more time, he prepared to cheat death.

No other outcome was possible.

In orbital space over Halkan, where there had been one starship, now there were two.

One was a weapon, its single hull and double nacelles

sleek like daggers, low in profile, overpowered for its mass, designed for war. The other was an artist's blade, stretched for speed, contained within a single hull, designed for safety.

The weapon sped on, slicing through space. The blade pulled up and angled off like a breaking wave.

One raced to save a universe.

One raced to save a dream.

But both raced time.

M'Benga slapped her spray hypo against her captain's neck.

Hunched over the *Pathfinder*'s navigation console, MacDonald coughed and wheezed, then pushed her physician away.

The bridge bucked wildly. The viewer flashed from black to red as the ship spun from the stars to Halkan's crimson disk, again and again.

"We have to abandon ship," M'Benga urged. She looked around. There was no one else conscious on the bridge. T'Rell and Teilani and Pini were down. Darno had died as she'd feared. "Give the order, Captain!"

MacDonald glared at her, eyes full of shock, and pain, and rage. "All safeties are off! We can't launch the pods!"

Heart racing, M'Benga looked up at the viewer. Halkan was filling more and more of the screen as the *Pathfinder* fell. "What *can* we—"

But MacDonald's hands were already flying over the console.

"We can land!"

"Intercept in thirty seconds," Data said.

Picard stood in the middle of the battle bridge of the *Enterprise,* behind Data at navigation, Riker at weapons.

Cramped, intense, not a single console or sensor station designed for exploration, the battle bridge existed for one purpose and one purpose only—to destroy the enemy.

Picard's eyes were fixed on the small battle viewer on whose lower half Halkan rushed past. And on whose upper half the orange crescent of the Ferengi ship hove into view.

"He is powering his phasers," Riker announced.

Picard smiled with grim satisfaction. As long as Baryon was firing at the *Enterprise,* he couldn't initiate atmospheric ionization. So Picard decided to give the Ferengi some motivation to keep his phasers pointed in the right direction.

"Return fire," he ordered.

Above Halkan, the *Buyout* changed orbits, shifted aim.

Phasers blazing, interlocking beams stabbing past each other, the two ships closed on a direct collision heading that neither could survive.

"The *Pathfinder* is dropping into the atmosphere," Spock said in surprise.

"Out of control?" Kirk asked.

"Controlled flight. Whoever is at the helm is attempting to land."

"Can it do that?" Kirk asked.

"Intact, yes it can," Spock answered. "But with the damage that ship has taken, it will not survive reentry."

Kirk turned to Sloane. "Do whatever you can—we have to make contact with whoever's flying that ship."

"Channel opening," Sloane said promptly. "Onscreen."

The image on the viewer was broken by static from damaged equipment. But Kirk could see MacDonald at the helm. M'Benga beside her. No one else. Just smoke and flashing screens.

Kirk stood before the viewer. "Captain MacDonald—"

"Go to hell, Kirk!"

Kirk heard the senseless paranoia consuming her, knew nothing he could say would convince her to listen. But had to try anyway. *Had to.* "Your ship won't survive reentry. Pull up and we'll beam off your crew."

"I'll survive—and I'll see you in prison for treason!"

Then she cut off transmission.

"Transport control," Kirk said urgently. "Can you punch through the *Pathfinder*'s shields?"

"There're a couple of gaps we might get through," the transporter chief answered.

"Begin transport at will," Kirk said. "Any life sign you can lock on to."

Then Spock was beside him. "It would not be wise to transport the captain while she is flying the ship."

Kirk knew that, immediately added a qualification. "Leave the bridge crew where they are for now."

"Acknowledged," the transporter chief replied. *"Energizing."*

Kirk looked at Spock. "How long can MacDonald hold that ship together?"

"Until she reaches the upper atmosphere. *Pathfinder* has lost too much structural integrity to survive the increased density past that point. No more than five minutes."

"How long to beam out the crew?"

"Standard complement for that class is one hundred forty-one. There will have been some casualties, of course, and we are operating with only half our—"

"Spock! How long, dammit!"

"Ten minutes. Perhaps a bit more."

"No," Kirk said. "I haven't come this far to lose by *five* minutes!" He pointed to Spock's science station. "Do what you can to help transport get through their shields." He turned abruptly to the Trill helmsman. "Mr. Maran, you will rig for atmospheric entry. We're going to match *Pathfinder*'s descent until we can get our shields around her."

"Jim, we're only half a ship," Spock said in true alarm. "We cannot take that strain."

"Thank you, Scotty," Kirk said grimly. "For five minutes, I'm betting we can."

Fire streamed from the edges of the *Pathfinder* as the ravaged ship dropped lower into the atmosphere of Halkan.

A thousand kilometers away, a second trail of fire appeared, arced in on an intercept course, gained speed: Kirk's *Enterprise*.

The hulls of both ships began to shudder, buffeted by air rapidly thickening around them.

Kirk knew that if he held this speed and angle too long, it would mean neither ship would survive.

But if his gamble worked, only one of them would have to.

Hit after hit from the Ferengi ship flared on Picard's battle-bridge viewer as the *Buyout* closed on its collision course with Picard's *Enterprise*.

But Picard did not order a change in heading. It didn't matter how much firepower Baryon's *Buyout* had. Or how much Ferengi nerve the daimon thought he possessed. Daimon Baryon didn't have an android at the helm of his ship, and no matter how fast Baryon thought he was, Commander Data was a thousand times faster.

"Set your own course," Picard told his helmsman. "I want to see you peel the paint off his hull."

"Adjusting trajectory accordingly," Data said cheerfully.

Full of faith and confidence, Picard didn't even bother bracing for impact.

• • •

The bridge of MacDonald's *Pathfinder* leapt and groaned without letup. Display screens rolled with garbled readouts. M'Benga clutched at the railing, unable to do anything more for the wounded sprawled on the deck.

The bridge viewer streamed with static. The exterior optical sensors no longer functioned. Christine MacDonald was flying by instruments alone.

But even M'Benga could feel the ship breaking up all around them.

"What's happening?"

Startled, M'Benga wheeled about to see Teilani pull herself up from the deck, green blood streaming from a wound on her face. It was her virogen scar, scraped raw.

"Teilani—Chris is trying to land us! But we're breaking up!"

Before M'Benga could even offer her assistance, Teilani was at MacDonald's side in an auxiliary chair, reaching for the tactical controls.

"Get away from those!"

"I can help."

"The hell you can."

"You're losing control," Teilani said firmly, shaking her head to keep her blood from obscuring her vision. "Can't you feel the ship fighting you? There's too much damage for aerodynamic flight."

"So what can you do about it?"

Teilani's hands moved swiftly over the adjoining console. "I'm going to reshape what's left of these shields for aerodynamic lift. Just like orbital skydiving."

"That's a stupid sport," MacDonald snapped.

"You should try it," Teilani suggested as she worked the controls. "Add some excitement to your life."

Christine MacDonald started to laugh. Teilani joined

her. And so did M'Benga. Until the sound of laughter on the *Pathfinder*'s dying bridge drowned out the alarms.

It's like having Kirk on board! M'Benga thought when she finally caught her breath. And that thought gave her hope they might actually get out of this.

"Captain Kirk," Maran called out. "The *Pathfinder*'s altering her trajectory."

Kirk tensed. "Is that good or bad?"

"Good, sir. She's leveling out. Holding steady."

"She's adjusted her shields for lift," Sloane added.

"Shields for lift?" Kirk repeated. Then he knew. "Teilani!"

He turned to Spock. "How are we going to do this, Spock? If we put our shields around her while her own shields are generating lift, she'll drop like a rock."

The Vulcan studied a flight graph on his screen. "There is a chance she will now stay aloft long enough for us to beam everyone off." He checked another screen. "We already have sixty-three crew members aboard. Four more minutes is all we'll need."

Hope soaring, Kirk called to Sloane. "Hail the *Pathfinder* again."

The *Enterprise* roared past the *Buyout* in a final flash of light.

The hull squealed.

"Aft sensors!" Picard ordered.

The *Buyout* spun like a top on the battle viewer.

"Our close approach overloaded his inertial controls," Riker said. "He's lost all stabilization! And I think we might have scraped his paint a little, too."

Picard grinned as he pictured Daimon Baryon and his crew pinned against the bulkheads, their sensitive Ferengi ears being spun into a maelstrom of nausea.

"Maybe we should leave them in there for a few hours. Or days," Picard suggested.

But then a whiplike phaser beam shot out from the spinning Ferengi ship. Then another, cutting through space in every direction.

"Random fire, sir," Data said. "But all he needs is one to hit the atmosphere long enough to cause ionization and he will trigger the discharge."

Picard took no pleasure in his next command.

But with a universe at stake, it was the only one left to him.

"Destroy that ship *now*."

A phaser beam sliced down through the atmosphere of Halkan, creating a fine tunnel of ionized gas that flashed lightning-like tendrils of energy to other regions in the sky already charged with natural ionization.

Then the energy distortions created by those connections rippled through subspace until they found other regions already primed to the point of instability.

Spreading more subspace ripples.

Combining more regions.

Intensifying more charges.

All seeking a site to drain the growing energy imbalance.

Then the first fine tendrils of energy reached a global network of geosensors. Sensors, in an apparent accident of design, arranged to work as amplifiers. Sensors focused on the greatest concentration of dilithium in the galaxy.

Only one second separated the universe that would die from the one that would survive.

Then one half-second.

Then—

The *Starship Enterprise* blew the *Leveraged Buyout* into atoms and the phaser beam stopped.

A new star blazed in the skies of Halkan.

The regions of ionization lost their charges slowly in the air.

The dilithium remained undisturbed.

A universe had been saved.

But elsewhere over Halkan, one last race against time remained to be run.

THIRTY-SIX

☆

"Kirk to Pathfinder! *Come in,* Pathfinder!*"*

On her ship's ruined bridge, M'Benga knew neither MacDonald nor Teilani could spare a second from their controls to respond. She went to Pini's communications panel, hit ACCEPT.

"This is M'Benga."

"Doctor, we're tracking you from five kilometers overhead. Spock says you have less than two minutes before atmospheric stresses tear you apart."

MacDonald didn't look up from her controls, but that didn't stop her from responding after all. "I told you to go to hell, Kirk!"

"James, I apologize for my copilot."

"Teilani!" The joy in Kirk's voice overcame even the static-filled, imperfect channel. *"I see you're giving your copilot a lesson in orbital skydiving."*

"Not for much longer. These shields are running off batteries. They won't last to get us down."

"They don't have to," Kirk said. *"We've beamed off one*

379

hundred eleven crew. The last five life signs we can read on the ship are all on the bridge."

Rapidly, M'Benga did the math. *A crew of one hundred and forty-one. One hundred eleven rescued already. Only five more to go.*

"Twenty-five dead," she whispered.

Teilani heard her. "But a universe will live," she said.

MacDonald vented her anger in a string of Tellarite invective. But Kirk cut her off.

"Teilani, listen carefully. The strongest shields are around the bridge. We need to be able to get a transporter beam through them."

"If I drop the shields, we lose lift *and* structural integrity," Teilani said.

"Teilani, Spock here. If you open up a shield fluctuation at the medial overlap perimeter, we will be able to beam off the rest of you."

"Not to cause trouble, Spock, but what keeps the ship up while you're doing all that?"

"Open the shields for three seconds with each fluctuation."

With that, even M'Benga understood what the plan was.

So did Teilani. "You're going to beam us off one at a time."

"And we must begin at once," Spock said.

M'Benga also saw the flaw in the plan, and from the quick look Teilani and MacDonald exchanged, she knew they saw it, too.

"Bones," MacDonald ordered, "get the injured off first."

"I'll open the first fluctuation in five seconds," Teilani said.

M'Benga scrambled to Commander T'Rell's unconscious form. She tapped the Vulcan's combadge, then shouted, "Here's the first lock signal."

"Opening the shields," Teilani said.

With the momentary loss of the shields that protected her and held her aloft, the *Pathfinder* became nothing more than a jagged piece of debris, unbalanced, irregular, hurtling through thickening air. To M'Benga, the whole bridge seemed to drop ten meters as the scream of the outside atmosphere rose to a shriek.

M'Benga fell back as T'Rell disappeared in the transport beam. It seemed to take a long time.

"First transport confirmed," Spock transmitted. *"Standing by for next opening."*

"Got to get it back in trim," MacDonald said grimly.

"Hold on, Spock," Teilani said. "We have to get the shields aligned again."

The bridge lurched suddenly to the port and M'Benga realized that the inertial dampeners were offline. Probably gravity as well.

"You're losing hull plates from the nacelle openings," Kirk explained. *"You've got to move fast."*

M'Benga made her way to Pini. The communications officer was on the deck, also unconscious, with bandages over her eyes and a splint on one arm. The doctor tapped her combadge. "Second signal!"

"Stand by for opening," Teilani said.

M'Benga could hear the tension growing in her.

"Now, Spock!" Teilani called out.

M'Benga flinched as a series of jarring bangs rang from the bulkheads and the bridge vibrated so strongly ceiling panels popped loose and two chairs snapped from their mounts. But beside her, the body of the communications officer sparkled, then vanished.

"Second transport confirmed," Spock said. But his voice was breaking up badly. M'Benga expected the circuits to fail any moment.

This time, it took even longer for the bridge to stop shaking and when it had finally leveled out, MacDonald said, "You're next, Bones."

M'Benga went to the two women at the navigation and ops console, knew they couldn't take even a second to look up from the controls they struggled with.

"I'll see you on the *Enterprise*," MacDonald said.

"I'll see you both there," M'Benga vowed. She reached out a hand to each woman, to touch their shoulders, but not to say good-bye.

"Stand by for the next fluctuation," Teilani advised Spock.

M'Benga stepped back, tapped her combadge. "Here's the signal."

At once the deck dropped out from beneath her as the ship screamed and Spock's voice said, *"Energizing,"* and everything turned to light.

Andrea M'Benga never saw the *Pathfinder* again.

"We've got the third one," the transporter chief announced.

Kirk's eyes were locked on the viewer. On it, the *Pathfinder* was a charred hulk trailing an incandescent streamer of fire and smoke and the occasional shattered hull plate.

Spock gave the countdown. "Thirty seconds to loss of structural integrity."

"They're both flying that ship," Kirk said tightly. "We're going to have to pull them both off at the same time." *So close.*

"Jim," Spock said, "we cannot. They would have to drop all shields and the ship would not last long enough for us to lock on to either of them."

Kirk felt his chest tightening. They were so close. There had to be a way. "Chris is flying it. Teilani's operating the shields. Who do we pull out first, Spock?" He couldn't make that decision.

But logic could. "Teilani," Spock said firmly. "Left on her own, she cannot fly the ship, but Captain MacDonald might be able to reestablish the shields long enough to keep the ship together for a second beam-out attempt."

Kirk exhaled in gratitude. It wasn't his decision. "Teilani, Chris—Spock says we have to pull Teilani out first. Chris, you have to reestablish the shields as soon as she's away."

No transmission came back.

"Reaching critical atmospheric density," Sloane warned.

"Chris—Teilani—acknowledge!" Kirk ordered.

"Acknowledged," Teilani transmitted. *"James . . . here's the signal . . . stand by for the opening. . . ."*

"Shields are open!" Spock said.

Kirk held his breath. The moment endless.

On the viewer, without shields, the hulk of the *Pathfinder* began to yaw, only a few degrees from breaking up entirely.

"We've got the fourth one," the transporter chief announced.

Kirk breathed again.

"She's out of control!" Sloane shouted.

"Tractor beams!" Kirk ordered.

"No!" Spock said. "They'll only tear the ship apart."

On the viewer, Kirk saw the *Pathfinder* begin to roll.

"Chris!" Kirk shouted. "Use the shields to bring the nose up, then drop them! We can still get you! Chris!"

"You've already got her," Teilani transmitted.

Kirk's heart stopped. "No . . . You were supposed to beam out!"

"Chris could never handle the shields, James. She's an amateur in orbital skydiving. She's never played like we have."

Desperate, Kirk called out to Spock. "Lock on to her!"

"She must drop the shields!"

"Captain!" Sloane shouted. *"Pathfinder* is breaking up!"

But Kirk could already see that.

On the viewer, huge gouts of friction-fueled flame shot off the violently-rolling ship as it lost all its aerodynamic stability.

"Teilani!" he cried. *"Drop the shields!"*

"They're the only thing holding it together!" Sloane warned.

"We have a lock!" Spock confirmed

"Dropping shields, James. Here's the signal. Tell Chris I'm sorry I slugged her and I'll see you—"

Then the skies of Halkan consumed the dying starship in a final explosive wall of fire.

On the viewer, the *Pathfinder* burst like a comet's tail, a thousand burning sparks spreading in a graceful, glittering cascade of light.

Kirk felt the bridge of the *Enterprise* spin around him, but knew it was an illusion.

Because nothing could move in this entire universe until he heard the transporter chief's report.

He willed that voice to come over the speakers.

He held up his hands as if to grasp those words from the air.

There was nothing in his world, in his existence, but that one long moment of waiting. . . .

Then he heard the almost subliminal click of the bridge speakers.

Yes, he thought.

"This is the chief. . . ."

Teilani, he thought.

"We . . . we do not confirm the lock."

Kirk stared at the beauty of the pyre on the viewer. But it wasn't real. It couldn't be.

"We . . . we do not confirm transport."

Kirk closed his eyes, but the dying comet burned against his vision, still there.

"I'm sorry, bridge . . . we lost her. . . ."

A thousand trailing sparks, stars fading.

Kirk couldn't speak. Couldn't stand. Stumbled back, knees buckling.

Spock caught him.

Kirk looked up at his friend, searching for one last chance, one last victory against the death that stalked him.

But he knew the truth when he saw tears in Vulcan eyes.

James T. Kirk had saved a universe.

But he had not been able to save his wife.

THIRTY-SEVEN

☆

Dawn came again to Halkan, to the blood-red plain where Teilani's journey had ended. But its light meant nothing to Kirk.

The remains of his life were in the scattered debris, the small fires that still burned in a random pattern out to the horizon. Pieces that could never again be reassembled, put right.

Somewhere inside, he was aware of the overhead hum of the hovering shuttlecraft, the beams of searchlights fading in the light of the rising sun, the charred scent of what was left of a ship that had plied the stars. Somewhere inside, he knew he stored the thoughts and sensations and memories of a day he could not bear to remember, or to forget.

There were tears in him somewhere, he knew. There was a pain he had never believed would be his again.

Never enough time, he thought. But in truth he had known that from the beginning, from the first moment he had seen her, another lifetime ago.

Ahead, in a deep furrow near the horizon, the blackened husk of the primary hull was all that had retained even a semblance of the *Pathfinder*'s shape.

It was, to Kirk, his heart.

"Jim," Spock said, "there is nothing more we can do here."

"I know, but . . ." He couldn't finish. *I'll never hear her voice again.*

He felt as if he were still on the bridge of the *Enterprise,* holding his breath, waiting for the transporter chief to speak, to hear Teilani one more time. His life continuing with hers.

"The *Sovereign* will be here soon," Spock said. "We will have to speak with the admiral."

Kirk understood he would have to prepare for that. Spock had already explained to Starfleet that the geosensor system must be disassembled at once. A permanent Starfleet installation must be put in place on Halkan. So this could not happen again.

Kirk thought about all the times he himself had cheated death. Each time knowing that someday, he would lose. Now he wondered if he had ever truly believed it could happen.

"It is a tragedy," a voice suddenly said behind him. "Tragedy, indeed, yes."

Kirk and Spock turned together to see T'Serl and Lept approaching. The young Vulcan held her short colleague's arm, helping him over the rough ground.

When she reached Kirk, T'Serl raised her hand in the salute that had so many meanings to her people, all of which conveyed respect. "I grieve with thee," she said in the archaic form, the closest she could come to showing him the depth of her emotions.

"A tragedy," Lept repeated, then coughed and wheezed, as if the smoke that clung to this desolate plain burned at his ancient lungs.

Kirk didn't know what to say, so said nothing.

Spock spoke for him. "I was not aware that Captain Picard had given permission for you to leave the ship."

Lept looked about himself with undisguised interest. "Things change, my friend. Captain Picard has better things to do than baby-sit a bunch of crackling historians who think alien obelisks are going to fall from the sky, I'll tell you." The old Ferengi clutched his chest as he half-laughed, snorting noisily.

Kirk responded to the disruptive intrusion by looking into the distance.

But undeterred, Lept babbled on. "A billion years the Preservers have been here, they think, and now one of their experimental subjects has raised a hand against them? Ha! My colleagues are all looking for a place to hide."

T'Serl, at least, made an attempt to distance herself from her partner. Almost apologetically, she turned to Spock. "We have learned that Admiral Nechayev wishes to hold hearings on the state of psychohistory and our knowledge of the Preservers. She has heard that our earlier reports to Starfleet authorities have not been forwarded through the correct channels."

"Given the circumstances of what *we* have learned, I am not surprised," Spock said.

Kirk looked up into the brightening lavender sky, trying to accept that the business of the galaxy must and would continue, even when a life had ended. How many times had he said to others, We must carry on? How meaningless those words were now.

Lept followed his gaze. Scratched his ear vigorously. "They're coming, Captain. More ships every hour. Even those strange ones from Project Sign, they say."

Spock moved imperceptibly between Kirk and Lept. "Has security contacted the Ferengi on Halkan who were part of the FCA?" he asked. "They would be a valuable source of information."

"I'm your last Ferengi on the planet. All the other ones— poof! Not a trace of 'em."

In the silence that followed, Kirk slowly realized that Lept and Spock didn't break eye contact. They looked at each other, almost as if a challenge were being made.

"If I were a Preserver," Spock suddenly said, "capable of taking on the aspect of any species, and wanted to infiltrate the Federation, I can think of no better form to take than that of a Ferengi—one of the few species whose brains are resistant to Betazoids and other telepaths."

Kirk forced himself from his mental lethargy in an effort to understand what it was Spock was really saying.

Lept threw back his head and whooped with delight until another coughing paroxysm bent him over and T'Serl handed him a handkerchief from her robes. But her eyes remained fixed on Spock. And Kirk realized that she was also puzzling over hidden meanings in Spock's observation.

"Oh, Spock . . . oh, Spock," Lept wheezed. "You Vulcans and your sense of humor." He shook a black-nailed, twisted finger at the Vulcan. "And don't you deny it because I know it's there."

The old Ferengi spit into his handkerchief, rubbed at his nose, then squinted up at Kirk.

"You know what I say, young man?" And at once, all artifice left the seasoned scholar's face and voice. "If I *were* a Preserver, given the task of educating an entire galactic Federation to prepare for its future among a universe of other federations, I could think of no more noble task than to teach the arrogance of the Prime Directive."

The diminutive Ferengi shook his great-eared head as if, somehow, deep within him, he lived with a burden the equal of Kirk's. "To have the power to preserve life and improve the conditions in which it can flourish, and yet *deliberately* choose not to accept your responsibility to *exercise* that power . . . Captain Kirk, I submit that despite what you see around you, there is no greater tragedy than *that*."

For long moments on the red plain of destruction, Kirk and Lept held each other's gaze.

To Kirk, all that happened had been the result of too many secrets, too little trust.

If Starfleet had admitted the mysteries it had uncovered, shared what it had learned, embraced the challenge of the unknown instead of refusing to accept its existence, he knew that none of this would have come to pass.

He remembered his conversation with Spock on the bridge of the *Enterprise*. How Spock, his friend and often his teacher, had answered his question with a question of his own.

It was an honored tradition, Kirk knew. Far better to have the student struggle to find the answer himself, than receive it as an effortless gift that might have no meaning.

He looked around the ruins of the starship, the ruins of his life.

Had it been a test? he asked himself. Was there a lesson to be found even in this sorrow?

Kirk stared into the small, hard, ageless eyes of the ancient Ferengi.

"I've never liked the Prime Directive," he said.

"Then perhaps, young man, that is why you were chosen."

The flesh on Kirk's arms crawled.

"And Teilani," Lept said. "And . . . your child."

Kirk stared, unable to speak, unable even to think that what he suspected might be true.

Lept bowed his head in farewell, then dissolved into light, and was gone.

T'Serl stared in unVulcanlike shock at the empty space where her colleague had stood, and at the empty footprints he had left in the rough ground. Only then did Kirk realize the Ferengi had made no request to beam up.

"I . . . I don't understand . . ." T'Serl said.

But Kirk did.

And with that terrible and final understanding, he sank to his knees in the red earth of Halkan and at last wept for all he had lost.

THIRTY-EIGHT

☆

"Come *with* me," Tiberius said.

Kirk looked up, dislodged abruptly from his reverie, angered.

Tiberius shrugged, as if sensing the futility of repeating his request, and stepped away, his footsteps crunching the thick layer of dried pine needles that carpeted the ground here at the edge of the forest.

"You seemed surprised by his offer," Captain Radisson said.

Kirk stared at her, at this latest version of the captain of Project Sign. Her skin was black, now, like Sloane from the *Enterprise*. And she was taller than Kirk, thinner even than Teilani had been, as if she had been born and raised on Mars.

"Is there no justice for him?" Kirk asked resentfully.

Radisson looked away from Kirk, down the low rise to the small village in the clearing below.

It was night, and Kirk could smell they were in a pine forest. The air was bracing, cold and clean. It might have been a dozen different worlds, but he recognized the bright full moon.

Radisson had made her ready room into a simulation of someplace on Earth. And because Kirk could see no sign of Lake Armstrong on the moon above, he knew this reconstruction was set sometime in the past.

But why—that he did not know. Any more than he knew which particular disaster was about to strike. Any more than he knew why Starfleet had inexplicably freed Tiberius to return to his own universe.

"Define justice," Radisson said pleasantly. "Is it punishment?"

Kirk looked over to his counterpart, standing away from them in the light of the moon. Although the arrogance that had been such a part of Tiberius was now greatly diminished, Kirk could still sense it. Only now, it was beneath the surface. Whether its absence signified change or deception was unclear.

"He's destroyed worlds," Kirk said. "His legacy is the enslavement of humans and Vulcans in his universe."

"And if we kept him here," Radisson said, "in this universe, in shackles in New Zealand or on a prison asteroid, would those slaves be freed? Would those worlds be restored?"

"Of course not," Kirk said. He stared down into the village, saw people walking through the makeshift buildings. The structures seemed to be cobbled together from scrap, and he could hear the generator that provided the electric lights that glowed through a handful of windows. Strange, discordant music played.

"Then what purpose does punishment serve?" Radisson asked.

Kirk was about to snap out something about vengeance, but Tiberius spoke first.

"I'm going to change things," he told Kirk.

Kirk wanted to laugh, but laughter had fled when Teilani

had died, ten long days ago. "How can anyone believe you?" he asked instead.

"We're not sending him back by himself," Radisson explained. She gazed up at the sky, the river of stars that flowed through the night, as if expecting one of them to fall at any time. "You knew Starfleet had committed to supporting the Vulcan Resistance."

"It's about time," Kirk said.

"The war with the Dominion will be ending soon. And we will be victorious," Radisson assured him. "But resources are thin, as I'm sure you've heard."

"Aren't they always."

"But there's a Sovereign-class starship at Starbase 25-Alpha, just doing nothing. The NX-1701. And there's an experienced crew in custody who would like nothing better than be back in space."

Kirk didn't believe what he had heard. "Intendant Picard's crew? You're sending them *all* back?"

"Under the command of Intendant Spock," Radisson said.

Tiberius strolled back to stand beside Kirk. "Isn't that what you wanted from the very beginning, James? Spock in command of the *I.S.S. Enterprise?* A man with a vision? Leading the revolution?"

"And *you* would serve him?" Kirk asked in disbelief.

"Like you, James, I will do what I must do to . . . to make up for the past. Just as you did. First for T'Val and Janeway. And then for me, in the obelisk."

Kirk remained silent. Tiberius drew the right conclusion.

"You'll see," Tiberius said defensively. "And someday, maybe we'll meet again and . . . compare our new missions."

Kirk appealed to Radisson. "You can't believe him. You can't send him back to that universe."

"You were the one who saved his life," Radisson said.

"Because I felt responsible for what he had become."

"Then accept that responsibility again."

"You don't understand. The first thing he'll do is run away. Raise an army. Look out only for himself."

But Tiberius took Kirk's arm to claim his attention. "Do you really want to know what the first thing I'm going to do will be?"

Kirk waited.

"I'm going to the Chal of my universe, James. I'm going to see if against all odds there's a Teilani there for me."

"What could you know about love?" Kirk asked bitterly.

"Everything you do," Tiberius told him. "Now."

"In the end, Captain Kirk," Radisson said, "it's not your decision to make."

"Whose then?" Kirk demanded. "Yours?"

Radisson's eyes flicked up to the sky again, then back to her guests. "That's why Project Sign exists. The Preservers. The mirror universe. Parasites of unspeakable powers that have three times tried to infiltrate Starfleet Command. Picard can tell you of the attempt he knows about.

"There are terrors out there you can't imagine. But we can. And we do. And the reason we keep our secrets is so all the rest of you can sleep at night, and believe there will be a better world to wake up to tomorrow."

"Who are you really?" Kirk asked suddenly, tired of mysteries and duplicity and deceit. He longed for the home he and Teilani would never again share. The life free of agendas and conspiracies and obsessions. "An old woman? A strong woman? The young horseback rider on Mars? The person you are now?"

Radisson smiled enigmatically. "I see you've all been talking again, sharing your stories. But you haven't been paying attention." She stepped closer. Kirk could feel the heat of her presence as he looked up into her wise, dark eyes. "You've all seen me as I really am. Not all of us were put here by Galen's ancestral species, Captain. And not all life is as you know it."

"Here they come," Tiberius said. He was pointing to the stars and Kirk looked up.

He saw a flash of blue. Then a point of light. It was moving to the zenith, rising overhead.

"Who's coming?" Kirk asked. "And where is this place?"

"A missile complex in Montana," Radisson said.

Now more streaks of light blazed down from the single moving point overhead. They grew in size, coming closer. Kirk heard a whistle in the air above. *Weapons?* he thought, instinctively recognizing the sound of an energy packet. *But in Montana? In the past? This never happened. This—*

The first light struck on the far side of the village and an enormous explosion slammed through the air.

Then screams, more explosions. More lights descending.

One directly above him, growing, growing, until it filled—

"End program," Radisson said.

And then Montana became the elegantly curved and sculpted ready room on the flagship of the Project Sign task force, the *U.S.S. Heisenberg.*

Kirk looked around the familiar room, with its desk flowing up from the deck, and the tall green plant and copper watering can.

For a moment, he stared more closely at the plant. But then he put the thought from his mind. It just wasn't possible.

He caught Radisson smiling at him, as if she knew what he was thinking.

"Why disasters?" Tiberius asked. "You showed Picard a sinking submarine. James a tsunami. Riker a terrorist attack. And me, first contact."

First contact? Kirk thought. Had that been Zefram Cochrane's Montana base in the simulation? But the Vulcans hadn't attacked the base.

"Perhaps Captain Kirk can answer that," Radisson said. "He believes he knows everything."

Kirk was confused, wasn't sure what was going on.

"Tell him what you believe, Captain. About why I make my visitors face death in this ready room. About why you can lose your wife, and still dream of the future. Why all of us can continue on in a universe that has no interest in us, no pity, and no comfort."

A lesson being taught, Kirk thought. Was *it all a test?*

He turned to Tiberius to say what he felt, but had never thought to put into words. "I believe that the closer we get to dying . . . the closer that demarcation line comes . . . the more we try to hang on, to fulfill every moment, to just taste whatever there is in the universe that we can, as quickly and as fully as we can, because . . ."

"Because there is never enough time," Tiberius said.

"Never," Kirk said. And he thought of Teilani.

Tiberius held out his hand.

In a universe where existence was so precious, love so fragile, how could there be time to waste on hate?

Kirk took his counterpart's hand. "You have a child waiting for you," Tiberius said.

"And you have a universe," Kirk said.

A child.

The stars.

Two ends of the same path joined by a journey.

No difference now between a man and his reflection.

"I'll let Picard know you're both ready to move on," Radisson said.

And they were.

But for all that Kirk was able to accept that he and

Tiberius had at last forged a peace between themselves—
and that each of them, in his own way and in his own universe, followed the same hopeful path to the future—he still
couldn't help wondering how it was their paths had
diverged to begin with.

But the answer to that question lay in the unknowable
past.

Kirk accepted that.

It was always his way to look to the future.

But still, he wondered . . .

THIRTY-NINE

————————— ☆ —————————

For the first time since World War III, Zefram Cochrane woke without a hangover.

The sensation was so odd, for a few moments he wondered if he were dead.

Then he heard Lily banging away in the kitchen alcove of his little shack, smelled what passed for coffee in postwar Montana, circa 2063, and decided things were much the same as they always had been.

And then he remembered.

Cochrane crashed across the cluttered floor, knocked over a stack of old *Physics C* journals, snagged a foot on a wadded-up something or other—sheet or shirt, he couldn't be sure—then yanked back the tattered curtain that covered the shack's single, makeshift window.

Truth be told, the window was part of a door panel from a '51 Boeing Majestic—one of the last great jumpcars to come out of Detroit—but ten years after the War to End Everything, there was little choice but to make do as best as one could. Door panel one day, bedroom wall the next.

Cochrane wasn't thinking about classic cars, though, or

about the morning chill of the wooden floorboards that penetrated the ragged holes in his thin, wool socks. Nor did he notice the cloud of dust that exploded from the seldom-moved curtain, or the unfamiliar bright morning sunlight that stabbed at his eyes.

Instead, the entire world rushed away from him except for what he saw in the town square.

Purple hull plates glinted in the sun. Dry soil bunched up around landing pads. Propulsion units—at least, what Cochrane assumed were propulsion units—poised in the air like the claws of a giant alien crab from one of those ridiculous mutant-monster threedies from the twenties.

That last thought gave him the word he'd been searching for.

"... *alien* ..." he whispered, remembering everything, and it was no different from remembering a dream. Except Lily Sloane was there to confirm it.

"You got that right," she said. She was standing beside him, two cups of pseudocaff steaming in her hands, heavy on the chicory.

"We did it," Cochrane said.

"*You* did it," Lily corrected.

The back-and-forth was so ingrained in their working relationship that he and Lily might as well have been married for a century or two. But today, more than any other, their sparring seemed charged to Cochrane. "Fine, I'll take back your fifty percent."

"Have it your way. *We* did it."

Cochrane reached out for his cup. He didn't take his eyes from the alien ship. *No, not alien. What was it they called themselves?* "... Volcanians."

"Volkanisians, I think," Lily said. "The woman said their planet was called Volcanis. At least, I think it was Volcanis." She used her free hand to scratch the side of her neck. "I think it was a woman. They're really not all that different from us, are they? Once you get past the ears."

"Sure not like the Borg," Cochrane said. He took a sip of his fake coffee and stared at the craft. The tall hatch above the entry stairs was closed. But it would open again, the leader had told him. In the morning. After a rest period.

Cochrane snorted. "Rest, my foot. They might have a better time-warp drive where they come from, Lily, but they sure as hell don't know how to party."

He threw back his head and laughed out loud remembering last night in the bar. He had given a good old-fashioned Montana welcome to his new, pointy-eared friends. Tequila. Beer. Twentieth-century rock and roll—those long-forgotten, predigital classics that only historians and eccentrics listened to these days. For all the good it had done to melt the ice. What did it take to get a smile out of those guys, anyway? He shot a sideways glance at Lily, expecting to see her smile, at least. But the woman was frowning.

"C'mon, Lily. We did it! We even . . . we even joined some kind of club, it looks like. Travel faster than light— join the galactic brotherhood. We just bought us a ticket to the big show, and we are going to be *sooo* rich."

Lily's frown deepened.

Cochrane turned away from the window with a sigh. "So what's your problem?"

"Who the hell are the Borg?"

Cochrane felt his jaw drop. "Excuse me?"

Lily was staring at him, as if waiting for an explanation, her hand rubbing at her neck. As if she had never heard of the Borg. Had never been aboard the starship from the future. Had never browbeat that fancy-pants Captain Jean-Luc Picard into fighting back and . . .

"What's wrong with your neck?"

"Something bit me."

"Let me see." Good engineers were hard to come by these days. Especially since the Kansas Inquisition established mass hangings as the proper career path for postdocs.

Lily only came up to his shoulders. Her neck was easy to see. Cochrane made a little noise of indeterminate meaning.

"What?" Lily said nervously. She wasn't as old as Cochrane, but she remembered the plague years.

Cochrane shrugged. "That's no bite." Looked more like a little scrape, actually. A touch of reddened irritation standing up just a fraction from Lily's dark skin. Might have been a dozen different things, but . . .

"And?" Lily asked. She had sensed his hesitation.

Cochrane scratched at his bristly, unshaved cheek. Not that scratching did much good with all his fingernails broken from years of hands-on spaceship building. "It's a perfect circle."

Lily's fingers touched the side of her neck, just below the ear. "Green's syndrome." Her voice was flat.

Cochrane shook his head emphatically, moved his blunted fingers from his cheek to his own neck. "If you had picked up a little leftover from Colonel Green and his boys, your blood would already be . . . damn."

Cochrane twisted his head to the side, leaned down to show his neck to Lily.

"Perfect circle," she said. "Half a centimeter." She looked out the window at the alien landing craft. "Think we caught something new from them?"

Cochrane thought quickly as he lightly traced the raised circle on his own neck, then straightened up in relief as he remembered even more. "Nah. It was Beverly."

Lily regarded him skeptically. "Some old girlfriend might have been chewing on your neck last night, but she sure wasn't chewing on mine."

Cochrane shook his head. Lily might know the difference between a flux capacitor and an overthruster, but she could be as dense as a transuranic element sometimes. *"Doctor* Beverly. Crusher. The blonde."

But those words clearly meant nothing to Lily. Cochrane suddenly felt a familiar flash of intuition. And he didn't like where it was pointing.

He tried again. "Dr. Beverly Crusher? The starship *Enterprise?* Came back in time from the twenty-fourth century when the Borg attacked?"

Lily stuck her tongue in her cheek, grabbed his coffee cup and sniffed its contents, suspicious.

"You made that coffee," Cochrane reminded her.

"Like that's stopped you before."

Cochrane felt unexpectedly indignant. "I haven't touched a drop of anything stronger than . . . Lily, listen carefully. The Borg tried to stop the *Phoenix* from making her flight yesterday. Afterward, everything worked out like the history books said. Beverly Crusher gave us both physicals and then she and Picard and everyone else went back to . . . wherever they came from just when our new friends set down."

Cochrane paused suddenly, thinking not only hadn't he had a drink this morning, he didn't *feel* like having a drink. In fact, last night when he had knocked back a tequila shooter with Spork or Sport or whatever the tall alien leader's name had been, he hadn't even enjoyed it. And he really hadn't had anything more after that first drink.

Cochrane rubbed his neck again.

"Are you all right?" Lily asked.

"She gave us shots," Cochrane said slowly.

Lily dipped a finger into his pseudocaff and licked it. "Shots of tequila?"

Cochrane shook his head, not rising to the bait. "No. Like

a doctor's needle. Only there wasn't any needle. It was a little pressure hypo, like the military uses. Only . . . it didn't have air tanks." He stopped again. How *had* Beverly's pressure hypo worked without a supply of compressed air to force the drugs through the skin?

"Drugs," Cochrane said. His intuition was taking him on a wilder ride than the *Phoenix* this morning.

"Now you're starting to make sense," Lily said. She handed him back his coffee cup, but Cochrane waved it aside.

"No. Beverly said she was giving us vitamins. That we were healthy, but could use some extra nutrients."

"What *are* you talking about?"

The tight look on Lily's face told Cochrane that while his fake coffee might have proved clean, his story was still not connecting with her. "You don't remember a thing, do you?" he said.

"About what?!"

"Captain Picard. The robot fellow, Data."

Cochrane recognized on Lily's face the same expression of concern for his sanity as when he had first tried to explain to her how he planned to travel through space faster than light by decreasing the volume of space-time in front of his spaceship while expanding it behind him. No Einsteinian time-dilation effects to contend with, hence the Cochrane All-Weather Time-Warping Space Drive, registered trademark and patents pending.

"Beverly didn't want us to remember," Cochrane said. It no longer mattered to him if Lily understood him or not, because it was making sense to him. He put his coffee cup down on a badly angled bookshelf. "I mean, they told us all about the future. Told me where the statue was going to be built. Even quoted things I'm not going to say for years."

"Maybe you should lie down."

"But why tell me all that? Because, if I know what's going to happen, then . . . then maybe I'll change things. You know, maybe take a chance on a new reactor design because Riker told me what I'd be doing when I'm fifty, so I'll think I'm going to be okay, but the reactor explodes and kills me, and I never would have tried it out if Riker hadn't . . . Lily, they *had* to make us forget."

"Zee, you're scaring me."

"So whatever Beverly shot us up with, it worked on you—you don't remember anything. But it didn't work on me," Cochrane said. "I wonder why?"

He had never meant to be a hero. He had never intended to be the kind of person who had statues dedicated to him or schools named after him.

He only wanted to be rich. And what better way to be rich than by creating something that could give people a way off this tired old world?

According to Riker and his pals from the future, he had done that and more. But by telling Cochrane what he had done, how could they be sure he'd still do it?

Cochrane looked back out the window. Some of the kids from town were gathered by one of the landing legs, apparently daring each other to touch it.

Lily placed a hand on his arm, to turn him toward her. "Zee, I'm thinking there might be side effects to what you did to yourself up there. The time-warp scrambled your brains or something. As if you have any."

"It has to have been a mistake," Cochrane said.

Lily's grip on his arm tightened. "The *Phoenix?!*"

"No. Beverly's amnesia drugs not working on me. It has to be a mistake. She didn't calculate the dosage right. Or I'm immune, or . . . I don't know."

"Zee, if you're really convinced that the people from the future didn't want you talking about what they told you, then maybe you should just stop talking about them right now. Put them out of your mind. Forget the whole thing ever happened."

Outside, a confusion of shouts filled the air.

Cochrane brushed Lily's hand aside. "Thank you, but I've been humored by experts."

The children were tearing away from the alien lander, leaving Montana dust in the air.

Because the entry hatch was opening.

Round two.

Cochrane straightened the vest he had slept in, looked around for his lucky cap.

"Are you going to tell *them* about being visited by time travelers?" Lily asked. Her sharp tone made it sound as if she'd break off their partnership, among other things, if he did.

Cochrane kept searching for his cap, considering for a moment Lily's question. He wondered why he hadn't told them last night in the bar. To tell the truth, he hadn't even thought of Picard and the others. As if Beverly's drugs had worked after all, but only for one night.

"Are you?" Lily repeated. She held out his cap. She always knew where everything was.

Cochrane planted his cap on his head, spun it around backward, then tugged it down tight. "They might not think it's all that crazy," he said. "I mean, get a load of their ship. And that's just the atmospheric lander. Spurt or whatever told me they have an orbiter up there. Fifty times the volume. They've got to know a lot more about time-warp drive than we do, Lily. Maybe they travel through time all the . . . time." He laughed. "I'm starting to sound like Deanna."

Lily's eyes were clear and all-seeing. "Maybe, just for the time being, we should let them cling to the illusion that they've landed on a planet with intelligent life."

Beyond the shack's window, Cochrane saw three robed figures appear in the entry hatch.

He knew Lily was right. She usually was. What could be gained by confusing this momentous event by informing the visitors that they had just missed time travelers from the twenty-fourth century?

Time travelers who seemed to have included a whole lot of humans, and not too many Volcanites or whatever.

"Please, Zefram," Lily said. "Don't tell them about Dr. Beverly and her friends."

But Cochrane had already pretty much made up his mind to keep that particular story to himself. At least for now.

"Don't worry," he assured his long-suffering partner. "If I told them, then everything from this moment on would change and Picard and his crew would probably never even be born. There'd be a whole new . . . future history."

Lily nodded, though Cochrane could see she still couldn't believe him or his story.

"C'mon," he said, holding out his hand to her, willing her to go along with him, just one more time. "Let's go talk to the Martians."

They left his little shack together, to make their way down to the square where two of the braver children were showing the aliens a baseball bat and glove.

As he and Lily walked down the sloping, dirt path, Cochrane dug into his pocket and pulled out his lucky coin. A genuine United States of America ten-dollar piece, dated 2026, with Lady Liberty on the front, and one of the first crewed Mars landers, *Aries IV,* on the back.

Cochrane saw Lily grimace as she saw what he held.

"Zee, you're not going to decide with a coin flip, are you?"

Cochrane held up the coin, admiring the way it caught the sunlight with a silvery gleam. "When we only had the money to crystallize either lithium or rubidium for the focus core, remember how we made that decision."

"We were desperate. You were drunk."

"The coin was right. Lithium worked."

"Zefram, I'm serious, don't tell them about your imaginary time travelers!"

Cochrane looked over her head to see the aliens raise their hands in that strange V for Victory salute they had.

"I'm not going to tell them about *our* time travelers," Cochrane said.

"Thank you for small mercies," Lily sighed.

Cochrane flicked his thumb under the shining silver coin, then sent it spinning into the crisp Montana air. He smiled as he saw all three aliens snap their heads up to follow the coin's flight, as if they expected it to change into a bird and fly away.

Maybe where they came from, that's what coins did.

Then he snatched the coin from the air and slapped it down unseen on the back of his hand just as he stopped at the aliens' side.

He grinned at the three visitors. They didn't grin back. He decided he'd have to get used to that. However smart they were, they seemed a touch stuffy. And they sure couldn't dance a lick.

"If you're not going to tell them about Beverly," Lily said in a low voice through her own tentative smile of greeting, "then what the hell is the coin for?"

Cochrane didn't answer. He kept the grin on his face as his eyes met those of the alien leader and neither he nor the alien looked away. The moment was unusual for one who had lived through the postatomic horror because Cochrane could sense no hint of challenge. Only open assessment and curiosity.

He wondered how long that openness might last if the

coin turned out to be heads and he told the three aliens about what was waiting out among the stars for them.

Not Picard and his starship.

But the cybernetic monsters so intent on enslaving the universe that they dared travel back in time to forever alter history.

An old thought experiment from Einstein's day slipped into Cochrane's mind. Schrödinger's cat. Locked in a box with a poison-gas capsule. The capsule either broken or unbroken, either result caused by the random behavior of a decaying radiation source.

According to some views of quantum physics, Schrödinger's cat was neither dead nor alive—its fate unknown—until the moment the box was opened and an observer actually saw the little prisoner. Only then did the probability waves collapse and one state or the other—life or death—become real.

Then again, Cochrane knew, according to other views of quantum physics, whenever the universe reached a decision point in which two outcomes were equally probable, the universe itself split, so that both outcomes had equal existence. In one universe, the cat continued to live. In the other, it died.

Cochrane looked down at his hands and felt the coin he hid between them. "Heads or tails," he said aloud. The order of history as it had gone before, or the chaos of something new and unpredictable?

It was time to let the cat out of the bag, or the box, as it were.

He lifted his hand.

The rest was history.

EPILOGUE

☆

In his quarters on the *Enterprise,* Kirk stood alone by the viewport, gazing at the stars above Qo'noS.

So many stars they took his breath away.

He knew he had been privileged in his life to touch a handful of them. Perhaps it was his destiny to touch a final few. He didn't know. No man did.

But he wondered how he could ever dream now to touch them alone.

His door announcer chimed.

"Come in," Kirk said.

It was Spock and McCoy. The constants in his life.

But in McCoy's arms, wrapped in swaddling, someone new, whose alert dark eyes were familiar, seeking his.

"Joseph," Kirk said. The name escaped from him, even as it touched him with apprehension. "He's . . . grown." He was unsure of what else to say despite how many times he had thought of this moment on the voyage from Halkan. Despite how many times he had dreaded it.

"Growing like a weed," McCoy said, almost with pride.

"But I thought . . . in stasis . . . he couldn't."

411

"Medical stasis had no effect on him, Jim. Just like his mother."

"But, Bones . . . he was asleep, in a stasis coma. Wasn't he?"

"That's what we thought, at first," McCoy said. "But if I had to guess—and I do—I'd say it was his own natural response to stress."

Kirk asked his question with his eyes.

"Jim, after every test, every study, every conclusion of more than fifty of my friends and colleagues from Earth, from Qo'noS, even from Romulus, we could only find one thing that we can definitely say is wrong with your child: He was born six weeks premature because of the attack on Teilani. Other than that . . . we just don't know how much of what he is, is what he's supposed to be, and how much is . . . well . . . something else."

"So my child could be . . . a monster?" Kirk asked, and immediately hated himself for using that foul word. What if Teilani had heard him say . . . He froze as he remembered his loss. As he always remembered she was gone—with the same sudden, unexpected intensity of that first awful moment on the bridge.

"I won't lie to you, Jim," McCoy said quietly. "Maybe . . . maybe Joseph is something that was never meant to be. But for all we know, which is so damn little, maybe . . . well, maybe, for him, he's perfect."

"Perfect?" Kirk said. "But . . . the way he looks . . . his face . . ."

Joseph had Teilani's eyes. But his skin was dusky rose; his skull ridged like a Klingon's but all the way across his scalp to the back of his neck; his ears pointed like a Romulan's, but with multiple canals; his fingers long and delicate, each with an extra joint.

The lines of the baby's ribs, the angle of his shoulders and hips, all were functional, but so different from anything human, or Klingon, or Romulan, or any other species Kirk had seen.

"Perfect," Kirk said again, struggling to find some essence of truth in that word. This baby was part of him, part of her, intermingled in perfect love. Shouldn't he be able to find that perfection in this child? If only for Teilani's sake?

"And is he . . . a *he?*" Kirk said, knowing as he asked the question, as he looked down at those hauntingly familiar eyes, that to Teilani the answer would not have mattered.

McCoy sighed. "Jim . . . he's not exactly standard issue. Inside, he has everything he needs to be male. And everything he needs to be female. And . . . well, there're even a few extras I've never seen before.

"But what I can say for sure is that this child has a lot of growing to do. Hell, for all I know, maybe when he's old enough, he'll have to choose which he wants to be. Maybe . . . maybe even choose to be something new."

Kirk repeated the only important words in all of that. "A lot of growing to do."

The baby burbled up at him.

"Look at that," McCoy said. "He just smiled at you!"

"Doctor, at that age," Spock observed gravely, "it is most likely gas."

McCoy frowned. "Spock, ask me if I knew you were going to say that."

"Very well, did you—"

"Spock, never mind."

Kirk looked down at the child, willing himself to see past its features, to see into those eyes and find the . . . the *soul* within. For wasn't it Teilani's soul he had seen, past her scar? Wasn't it her soul he had loved above all else? And couldn't it—*shouldn't* it be the same with his child? *Their* child?

"But for now, Bones," Kirk asked uncertainly, "just for now, is he healthy? Like this?"

McCoy's frown returned. "You have to remember, there's never been a child like him. Klingon, Romulan, human . . . But I have to tell you that a few doctors on the team, they thought that . . . that maybe this is how all those genes are *supposed* to go together. That it was wrong for them ever to be apart in the first place."

"That *is* most illogical, Doctor," Spock said. But then he reached out to lightly move a corner of the blanket from the child's face, and a tiny rosy hand grasped his finger and would not let go. "Though I have learned in my travels with you both that sometimes truth can be found in places other than logic."

Kirk studied that small hand, so fragile, so delicate. "If he's part Romulan, Spock, that means he's part Vulcan, too, doesn't it?"

"Indeed," Spock said as he and the child gently finger-wrestled. "He certainly has the grip of a Vulcan. It will not be difficult to teach him the *katra* disciplines."

"Hear that, Joseph?" McCoy said. "Uncle Spock's going to teach you the nerve pinch."

Spock shifted his eyes sideways at the doctor. "And no doubt Uncle Bones will teach you how to roast marsh melons, among other equally illogical endeavors."

Joseph gurgled as if in happy anticipation of that day.

"I think . . . I think maybe he really is smiling," Kirk said. And even he could hear the edge of growing wonder in his voice.

"A smile like his mother's," Spock and McCoy said together. And though the impossible had happened and the two were at last in agreement on something, the universe didn't come to an end.

For long moments as he stared at his child, Kirk didn't

know what was happening to him. He was racked by bitter
sorrow that Teilani had left him, never to know this
moment. But somewhere at his core, he also felt the first
stirrings of joy that he himself was here in this moment, to
see their child. In a storm of confusion as powerful as any
of nature he had seen on Qo'noS, it seemed every emotion
he had ever felt was drawing together in him all at once—
the full experience of life in all its contradictions.

To his astonishment, that unsettling sense of anticipation
made him feel alive.

It made him feel young.

"Jim . . . ?" McCoy said at last.

Kirk looked up, blinked to clear his eyes, realized that
McCoy held the child in outstretched arms.

"Oh, yes," Kirk said, for one of the rare times in his life
completely flustered and unprepared. "I . . . yes . . ."

Gently he reached out with fear and hope, sorrow and
joy, and for the first time took his child in his arms.

Kirk held Joseph close to him, gazing down at his child's
small, ridged forehead and pointed ears while impossibly
tiny fingers pulled at his collar and at his nose.

"Doctor," Spock said, "I believe young Joseph is as
happy as a catfish at a rodeo."

As Joseph tugged at his father's bottom lip, Kirk stared
blankly at Spock's impassive expression.

"I'll explain later," McCoy said. "C'mon, Spock. We
should let these two get acquainted. It's a long trip back to
Chal."

"*Is* that where we should inform Captain Picard you
wish to go?" Spock asked.

"Chal," Kirk said. Whatever else he felt, he knew he
needed to take Joseph to the house he had built. To show
him the clearing and the place where his parents were married. "Joseph and I are going home. For now."

"And later?" McCoy asked.

Kirk didn't have an answer. "So many stars," he said. He cradled Joseph carefully, tentatively, as they went to the viewport.

"So many dreams," McCoy said softly. His gift to the child.

"So many possibilities," Spock added. His gift, as well.

Kirk heard the doors open and close. He knew Spock and McCoy had gone. But they had not gone far and never would.

Kirk and Joseph were still at the viewport a few minutes later as the *Enterprise* went to warp.

"Here we go," Kirk whispered to his child, not knowing where this journey would take him. Knowing only, at last, that they would take it together.

The stars streamed by in all their colors, and safe in his father's arms, Joseph's perfect hands reached out to them, as if he meant to touch them all.

And knew someday he would.

THE ASHES OF EDEN

---------------- ☆ ----------------

AUGUST 9, 2400 C.E.

That night, like the others of Chal, Memlon walks silently through the woods. He holds a palm torch in one hand; in the other, the small, trusting hand of his daughter.

When they reach the clearing, they spread out with the others along the edges. Memlon recognizes most from the nearby farms, a few from City. On the clearing's far side, lit only by the faintest reflections from the small handlights that the visitors carry, he is sure he catches a glimpse of uniforms, Starfleet or Klingon, or maybe both.

Then, as the visitors and those of Chal settle in their places, one by one they switch off their lights, so in time, only the soft moonlight of Chal and its sparkling stars shine in the clearing.

Within that light, as in a dream, Memlon sees the old house in the clearing's center, never finished, but perfectly maintained through all the years and all the seasons by those who owe so much to the two who built it.

And by the path that leads up to the house, Memlon sees the gnarled stump that still remains. The last one in the clearing. He remembers how his mother loaned her phaser on the day of the wedding, so a promise could be kept.

A promise, in the end, unfulfilled.

And Memlon remembers that wedding. The floating lights. The songs, the dancing, how beautiful she had looked, how joyful he had been.

And there, where they had stood together to exchange their rings and their hearts, now a simple grave, marked only with a polished square of stone, her name engraved above a battered metal plaque from a starship he had once flown among the stars.

Memlon feels his daughter tug on his hand, hears her soft whisper. "What are we doing now, Papa?"

He lifts his daughter, holds her close. It is her first time coming to the clearing on this night, and Memlon thinks back to all the years of his childhood, to the nights he has come here with his mother. Now it is his daughter's turn.

"Waiting," he whispers back.

"For the man to come?"

Memlon nods.

"'Cause he always comes?"

"Always."

"And you saw him?"

"A long, long time ago," Memlon says. "When I was just a little boy your age."

And Memlon remembers that day so clearly. Remembers every word the man said . . .

Memlon, someday, when you're grown, you're going to pass by this field. And there will be a house built right where we are now. And you'll see the crops, and the trees, and you'll be able to say to your children, Jim Kirk made that field the way it is. He planted every tree, took out every rock and stump, hammered every nail into every board of that house. That's Jim Kirk's field.

The gentle night breeze brings a whisper from another part of the clearing. Then another.

"Papa . . . ?" the little girl says, unsure.

"Shhh," Memlon soothes. He points to the sky, to the stars. "Look," he says. "Look."

A star moves.

A single point of light in graceful orbit.

Moving until it is directly overhead . . .

"Now," Memlon whispers. "Look there." And he points to the polished stone.

There are stars there, too.

Joined by one pure musical tone.

Memlon watches the light of the transporter effect as it dances across his daughter's face, putting stars in those wide-with-wonder eyes, just as Jim Kirk and the stories of his adventures had put stars in Memlon's eyes so long ago.

And then the light fades from the gravestone.

His daughter claps her hands in delight.

For where there had been stars, there now are flowers. Just as there have been every year on this night since Memlon was a child his daughter's age. The flowers always the same: pure white, overlaid with shimmering gold, the leaves narrow, glossy, and evergreen.

Memlon remembers those flowers. The flowers she had carried to her wedding, worn in her hair as she had danced in the company of their friends and family.

"Papa," the girl says in wonder, "the man came."

"Now look again, look," Memlon whispers.

He points again to the moving star.

And the star becomes a rainbow.

A starship at warp.

Continuing the journey.

"Is it really him?" his daughter asks.

Memlon watches the rainbow vanish among the stars, becoming one with them.

Is it even possible? *he wonders. So many years after it all happened, could even* he *still survive? Or is it their child now? Or their child's child or the friends who had promised never to forget and who never will?*

"Is it, Papa? Is it really?"

No, *Memlon thinks.* Of course not. After all this time, it couldn't be.

But he looks back at the clearing, at the simple grave, at the last stubborn stump that still remains.

And at the flowers. Evergreen.

"Yes, it is really him," *Memlon tells his child, because he wants it to be true that some things will never be forgotten.*

And that some journeys are never meant to end . . .

James T. Kirk will return

For further information about William Shatner,
science fiction, new technologies,
and upcoming William Shatner books, log on to:

www.williamshatner.com

Look for STAR TREK fiction from Pocket Books

Star Trek®: The Original Series

Novelizations

Star Trek books by William Shatner with Judith and Garfield Reeves-Stevens

Novelizations

Star Trek: Deep Space Nine®

Warped • K.W. Jeter
Legends of the Ferengi • Ira Steven Behr & Robert Hewitt Wolfe
The Lives of Dax • Marco Palmieri, ed.
Millennium • Judith and Garfield Reeves-Stevens
   #1 • *The Fall of Terok Nor*
   #2 • *The War of the Prophets*
   #3 • *Inferno*

Novelizations

Emissary • J.M. Dillard
The Search • Diane Carey
The Way of the Warrior • Diane Carey
Star Trek: Klingon • Dean Wesley Smith & Kristine Kathryn Rusch
Trials and Tribble-ations • Diane Carey
Far Beyond the Stars • Steve Barnes
What You Leave Behind • Diane Carey

  #1 • *Emissary* • J.M. Dillard
  #2 • *The Siege* • Peter David
  #3 • *Bloodletter* • K.W. Jeter
  #4 • *The Big Game* • Sandy Schofield
  #5 • *Fallen Heroes* • Dafydd ab Hugh
  #6 • *Betrayal* • Lois Tilton
  #7 • *Warchild* • Esther Friesner
  #8 • *Antimatter* • John Vornholt
  #9 • *Proud Helios* • Melissa Scott
 #10 • *Valhalla* • Nathan Archer
 #11 • *Devil in the Sky* • Greg Cox & John Gregory Betancourt
 #12 • *The Laertian Gamble* • Robert Sheckley
 #13 • *Station Rage* • Diane Carey
 #14 • *The Long Night* • Dean Wesley Smith & Kristine Kathryn Rusch
 #15 • *Objective: Bajor* • John Peel
 #16 • *Invasion! #3: Time's Enemy* • L.A. Graf
 #17 • *The Heart of the Warrior* • John Gregory Betancourt
 #18 • *Saratoga* • Michael Jan Friedman
 #19 • *The Tempest* • Susan Wright
 #20 • *Wrath of the Prophets* • David, Friedman & Greenberger
 #21 • *Trial by Error* • Mark Garland
 #22 • *Vengeance* • Dafydd ab Hugh

Star Trek®: New Frontier

New Frontier #1-4 Collector's Edition • Peter David

#1 • *House of Cards*

#2 • *Into the Void*

#3 • *The Two-Front War*

#4 • *End Game*

#5 • *Martyr* • Peter David

#6 • *Fire on High* • Peter David

The Captain's Table #5 • *Once Burned* • Peter David

Double Helix #5 • *Double or Nothing* • Peter David

#7 • *The Quiet Place* • Peter David

#8 • *Dark Allies* • Peter David

#9-11 • *Excalibur* • Peter David

#9 • *Requiem*

#10 • *Renaissance*

#11 • *Restoration*

Star Trek®: Invasion!

#1 • *First Strike* • Diane Carey

#2 • *The Soldiers of Fear* • Dean Wesley Smith & Kristine Kathryn Rusch

#3 • *Time's Enemy* • L.A. Graf

#4 • *The Final Fury* • Dafydd ab Hugh

Invasion! Omnibus • various

Star Trek®: Day of Honor

#1 • *Ancient Blood* • Diane Carey

#2 • *Armageddon Sky* • L.A. Graf

#3 • *Her Klingon Soul* • Michael Jan Friedman

#4 • *Treaty's Law* • Dean Wesley Smith & Kristine Kathryn Rusch

The Television Episode • Michael Jan Friedman

Day of Honor Omnibus • various

Star Trek®: The Captain's Table

#1 • *War Dragons* • L.A. Graf

#2 • *Dujonian's Hoard* • Michael Jan Friedman

#3 • *The Mist* • Dean Wesley Smith & Kristine Kathryn Rusch

#4 • *Fire Ship* • Diane Carey

From John Vornholt
author of *Gemworld*

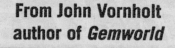

Book Two of Two

Based on the long-hidden scientific secrets of Dr. Carol Marcus, who has mysteriously disappeared, the dreaded Genesis Wave is sweeping across the Alpha Quadrant, transforming entire planets on a molecular level and threatening entire civilizations with extinction.

The finest engineers of three civilizations, including Geordi La Forge and his long-lost love, Dr. Leah Brahms, must race against time to devise some way of halting the deadly wave before yet another world can be transformed into something entirely alien and unrecognizable.

But even if the Genesis Wave can be defeated, Picard must still confront the greater mystery of what unknown intelligence dared to launch the wave against an unsuspecting galaxy—and for what malevolent purpose....

Coming in hardcover from

Pocket Books
A VIACOM COMPANY

STAR TREK
THE NEXT GENERATION®

TOOTH AND CLAW
Doranna Durgin

While Captain Picard attempts to negotiate a bargain that will save the refugees of a dying planet, Commander Will Riker accompanies a young dignitary to an exclusive hunting preserve. There, technology-damping fields and some of the galaxy's deadliest predators are supposed to test the untried noble's ability in the *kaphoora*—the hunt. But the shuttlecraft doesn't land on Fandre; it crashes. Riker and the hunting party must fight for their lives with the only weapons they can muster—spears and bat'leth, tooth and claw.

DIPLOMATIC IMPLAUSIBILITY
Keith R.A. DeCandido

During the Dominion War, on a conquered world, depleted Klingon forces were overthrown in a small coup d'ètat. The victorious rebels took advantage of the disruption to appeal for recognition from the Federation. Now Klingons have returned to taD and re-established their control of the frozen planet, but the stubborn rebels insist on Federation recognition. A solution to the diplomatic impasse must be found, a task that falls to the Federation's new ambassador to Klingon—Worf.

AVAILABLE NOW
FROM POCKET BOOKS

DITC.01